Myth

Dark World III

Danielle Q. Lee

Myth

Edited by Metaxa Cunningham

Cover design by Silviya Yordanova
https://www.facebook.com/MyBeautifulDarkness
http://morteque.deviantart.com/

ISBN 978-0-9865680-6-0

For Shelby

Acknowledgments

I'd like to thank Metaxa Cunningham, my editor extraordinaire; my readers and cheerleaders: Halston Blake, Jo 'Panda' Richardson, Melanie Kuehl, Lea Hebb, Jaclynn Quinlan, Pat Quinlan, and, last but not least, my husband and best friend, Chris. Without all of you, Dark World would not exist.

Crawl on me
Sink into me
Die for me
Living Dead Girl

Rob Zombie

The monster wandered the shadowy realm, his new home whether he liked it or not. Thick, hot, oppressive air held his lungs captive as blistering crimson sands branded the soles of his naked feet. Subterranean springs intermittently discharged scorching waters into the atmosphere whilst angry volcanoes raged endlessly in the distance, their garnet tributaries bleeding from earthly wounds that seemingly never healed.

This world, this dark land, seemed to embrace all things malignant, all things evil. What trace of humanity he had left lingering inside recoiled in fear and confusion, terrified of what might be waiting for him around every shadow-cloaked corner, but the dark passenger that now occupied the greater part his soul was elated, grinning, and pleased to be home again. This new malevolence twisted and crawled through the blackened web-like veins spreading all over his body, owning him as though he was possessed. Relentless hunger pulled at his innards; thirst for blood clawed at his throat. Despite his fatigue, every creature he'd happened upon inevitably lost the battle, becoming his next meal. This thing inside of him, this beast, could lash out and summon any strengths needed when the time arose. In those moments, he'd become powerful, godlike — indestructible. He'd torn at their flesh with his teeth, greedily, uncontrollably, but he was never rewarded satiation or reprieve from his inhuman suffering. The hunger always remained, always tormenting him, always controlling him.

Nevertheless, there was something else lurking amid the dark corners of his newfound hell. It was something stronger than the blood lust, something that diluted the poison inside: revenge.

He vowed to find his way back from this dark world. He would make them pay for this. He would find the ones responsible for his damnation and show them true pain.

But right now, he had to find food, and feed this unappeasable monster within; he had to silence the demons screaming inside. Then he would search for the one he sensed nearby.

The one he'd hurt first.

The one he'd sent to Dark World.

Scarlet.

Part I

The Quickening

Fate

Amidst the dark, red clouds roiling through the valley and thunder growling overhead, Fate's infrared gaze beheld a distant stream of light penetrating the forever night sky. Dark World was eclipsed by an assortment of light sources, though usually it was nothing more than the burn of a lava river meandering down the side of a volcano, or the far-off sapphire glow from a field of bioluminescent mushrooms. But this light was different, reaching and dominant it pierced through the thick shadows as though its power was no match for the darkness. It was as if it was the nemesis of the dark, the opposite of evil. It was almost — heavenly.

"That must be the Guf," Fate whispered, awestruck. Not once since she'd been banished to this world had she observed such beauty or — purity. She remembered it though; the very essence was burned into her memory. "The sun..." she uttered, breathless before the dawning inside Hell.

She looked down upon the yawning valley that stretched for miles in every direction. Before her lay an unwelcoming labyrinth of countless stalagmites, like pointed, rocky teeth matching the maw of covered sky overhead. How was she to navigate this? She could see no clear path to the Guf.

Then she recalled the potion in her satchel. The potion Kraton had given her.

"Drink this," the necromancer witchdoctor had instructed, handing her the vial. "This potion contains the memories of our ancestors. The memories will become yours, and they will guide you."

Fate eyed the little bottle filled with thick, silver liquid with hesitation. The last potion she'd taken had been tainted with dark magic that had turned her into far worse a monster than she'd been previously. Before, she'd been a shade, barely staving off the need to consume the souls of others; but now, she was something else—something horrible.

Black, lamian blood coursed through her veins, the blood of Legend. She'd been introduced to him as the Night Mare, a hauntingly beautiful black horse with flaming mane, tail, and hooves, imprisoned within the walls of the demon city, Legion. There was more to him than met the eye. He'd been born of a curse—and pure black magic.

Shaman Goretus, a kindly, blind demon inside Legion, had concocted the potion for Fate with the intention of curing her ravenous shade hunger, but had he intentionally poisoned her, altering her once again? Or did he have a little help in the matter? It seemed impossible to believe that such a gentle demon would harm her deliberately, but alternatively, it was quite possible that several others in the subterranean kingdom would gladly see her suffer. Who it had been, she might never discover—but she had her suspicions. Deme, Kane's lead tracker, was definitely on her list; although, the bossy demon didn't appear to be the type to beat around the bush when it came to her feelings about Fate, the first shade to cross the palace threshold as a guest. It didn't seem likely that she would do something so underhanded; she appeared the type that would rather provoke a fight face to face, a battle won fair and square.

Syphon, on the other hand, seemed more apt to do something devious. From what Fate had heard from Kane, Syphon appeared willing to do anything to win the rule of Dark World. Once, he'd even challenged Kane to a duel to the death, the victor winning the reign. But Kane declined, not because he feared losing, but because he felt an obligation to his father, Lucifer. An obligation to fulfill his destiny in becoming King of Dark World — the Devil.

She would likely never discover who aided in her current grief, but it certainly awakened Fate to the notion of just how much someone in Dark World despised her simply because she was a shade, which saddened her greatly.

She sighed, wrapping her arms around herself, trying not to pay notice to the network of ebony veins in her arms and hands, knowing there was so much more to see if she were to lift her shirt and expose her torso. Black blood scored every inch of her body except her face, gathering into a web-like array over her heart. Darkness writhed there, waiting for her to drop her guard. Before this, she couldn't imagine anything stronger than the possession of the shade over her, but the lamia was far more evil. Far more powerful, and unlike the impatient and untamed shade, it bided its time wisely. The monster contemplated, schemed — and waited.

Apparently the poison she'd taken wasn't the only way to become a lamia. Fate's thoughts drifted back to the savage little girl imprisoned in a near-forgotten pit beneath Necrosia. Born against the rules of Dark World's nature, born wrong, the little girl had left the Surface a human, but was reborn a cannibalistic abomination, destined to be destroyed.

Fate shuddered, knowing that was likely her destiny if she were to fail. According to Kraton, she had to find her soul in the Guf and lure it back into her ailing body. If not, she would face this dark world as yet another beast—but one that would need to be exterminated. She would lose the last of herself, her soul, and her love.

"Kane," his name danced upon her black lips, coaxing them into a soft smile. He was the only thing that kept her on her path, and from succumbing to her ever-darkening soulless side. She glanced at her left hand, fourth finger adorned with his last gift: a ring bejewelled with a Soul Crystal. He'd given it to her on one of their last evenings together in Necrosia. Kane had explained that it held but a tiny fragment of a powerful soul, the Light Being that created Dark World, and that the being, in the beginning, was very much alone. She'd conjured, from her own magical essence, another who was to be her mate. Only, she didn't realize that using her 'good' magic in a dark realm would manifest a curse against her. Her soul mate, upon his birth, was stolen from her and hidden away.

So, as the lore went, the Light being sent out tiny pieces of her soul, her love, in the form of an enchanted crystal: the Soul Crystal. Over the centuries, it became a tradition for lovers to gift the gem to those they deemed their soul mate, hence everyone that wore the gemstone would be helping the Light Being search for her one true mate. According to the myth, the Soul Crystal would react when it neared her true love. So far, though, no one had located him.

Fate gazed off into the horizon, wondering where Kane was, wondering what lands he wandered at that very moment—and if he was safe. Dark World was an unforgiving realm, harsh and bitter, and as dangerous as it was mysterious. Those on the Surface that first spun the lore of Hell must have indeed traversed the malevolent realm in person, considering the apt description over the centuries. How they'd come to visit Hell and then returned to the Surface again was a complete mystery though, given the underworld's harsh and unforgiving reputation. Not to mention, ever since King Lucifer's actions centuries ago, the crevasse leading to the world overhead was closed off, so if you were damned here—you were stuck here.

Fate turned her eyes upward, recalling the Surface with its lush environments, moody temperatures, and diverse seasons. She missed the wind running its invisible fingers through her hair, the scent of wild-flowers and pine lingering upon its touch. She longed for the open sky, the forever sea of blue overhead. What she wouldn't give to take a long, deep breath of fresh air, to play amongst the long grasses and rolling meadows or to feel the smatter of cool, clear rain upon her face as she strolled beneath a sullen, cloud-filled sky.

But it was the sun she ached for most. She missed the heavenly heat kissing her forehead and cheeks as she lounged beside a crystalline lake, the gentle caress of an amber ray warming every inch of her body. It was like it had worshipped her as it bathed her with unconditional love, hung suspended in the heavens like a glittering gold pendant. It was loyal, rising every morning to awaken her, as if it existed to greet her and only her. Even in the winter, when it pulled away from the world, it still sent its rays to sparkle brightly amongst the tiny snowflakes spread thick over the Canadian prairies.

And the stars, she mused with a longing shudder. Nothing but the luminosity of the sun could compare to the deep fathoms of the cosmos spattered with tiny dots of lustrous light. Endless reaching wonder lived up there, space beyond all comprehension, yet so open and free, just begging to be explored. She yearned to see again the blaze of the sun, the face of the moon, and to lie beneath the starry blanket of the universe.

The world above was in stark contrast to the one that glared at her now. A hellish, red tinge stained the air, filled with acrid smoke and choking ash. Steaming clouds rolled with anger in every direction, billows of black poured from ever furious volcanoes. It was as though Dark World were the Devil itself.

But Fate had already met the Devil—and she was worse.

Thank goodness she's dead and gone, Fate thought, though she felt as if she were lying to herself. The seeds of darkness had been sown; in her, in Ever, in Kane, in everyone that Malus had come in contact with. Would they ever truly be free of her memory? Her wrath?

Fate pulled in a deep breath, wincing at the burning sensation it built within her undead lungs. Guilt and worry coalesced inside as thoughts of Ever surfaced. She'd left Kane's daughter in the hands of the necromancers, with Vrill and Kraton and Aura. Had she done the right thing? Was the demon princess safe with them?

Aura could be trusted, Fate was certain of that. But Vrill? Or the witchdoctor? Unease settled on her soul, leaving her wanting to spin about and head straight back to Necrosia.

Kane had entrusted Ever's safety to her, and she felt as though she'd failed him.

Her hand fell to her pocket, the outline of Ever's letter felt as though it was burning a hole through the material. Tears found their way to Fate's glowing white eyes. Ever had asked that this letter be given to Kane, like a last request. Did she know something Fate did not?

For the thousandth time since she'd departed Necrosia, Fate was tempted to read the letter. Was it a goodbye? Did it contain a warning of some kind? Was Ever confessing a long-known secret to her father?

It killed her not to know, but she'd uphold her promise. This letter would get to Kane. She eyed Spark, her now teenaged phoenix, as he dove and played amongst the cloudy atmosphere overhead, leaving trails of fire in his wake. As much as she hated the idea of it, she knew she'd have to ask him to go; he had to deliver this note to Kane—if Spark could find him.

Fate felt a tug and nuzzle on her calf, drawing her from her thoughts. "Ick?" the little gargoyle inquired in his gruff, garbled voice, eyes shining like emerald orbs. Unlike Spark, Ick hardly seemed to have grown at all since she'd found him amongst the pillars of quartz inside the Crystalline Forest. It made Fate wonder if he was simply to stay that small, if his kind didn't evolve into larger creatures. He tilted his head inquisitively, his new furry family peering at Fate from behind him, contemplating her, trying to decipher whether she was friend or foe.

"Hey buddy, don't worry, I'm okay," Fate answered with a smile, patting the down-soft fur atop his head while sending an inviting smile to the other baby gargoyles. "I'm just trying to figure out what to do next."

His line of sight shifted from her to the ever-bright beam of light in the distance, indicating to her that it was the right way to go. She knew she had to see this journey through to the end; she had to retrieve her soul and cure herself, whatever the cost.

With a heavy sigh, she forced her feet forward, trudging towards an uncertain future—or certain death; she wasn't entirely sure.

Aura

Aura's throat was constricted with grief, her starry eyes watering like a seemingly endless stream of silvery-blue tears. Vrill's death, his brutal murder, had reverberated within her very core. In his last moments, she'd felt his pain, his horror, and worse, his confusion. Vrill's trust in others and his inherent goodness had led to betrayal, and finally to his untimely demise. Granted, he'd wandered into dark territory when he insisted that Ever held the remnants of Queen Malus, believing wholeheartedly that Kane's daughter was riddled with evil when, all along, it was Sybil, Vale's sister, who'd cradled the seed of the beast within. Aura suspected that Vrill's mind and soul had not been whole enough to discern the harm of his accusations. The entirety of the necromancer population was suffering a fever alongside an ailing world. Memories from her ancestors flooded her thoughts: the upheaval amidst the aftermath of the Crystal Pyramid's extinguishment and the slow severing of the telepathic bonds her race had always held so dear. The world as they'd known it for so long was no more.

Her troubled eyes searched the room with purpose, hopeful for even the smallest clue left behind or some shred of evidence that could guide them to the whereabouts of Vrill's killer.

Myth

Killer, her thoughts whispered, extending to the community of necromancers still weakly linked to her mind. Aura trembled at the word, knowing full well the name of the perpetrator—*Sybil*. She shuddered, recalling her first meeting with the oracle shade. Far from a murderer at the time, the oracle had staggered forward amid a storm of dust and debris during Aura's inauguration party, Sybil's true identity veiled by means of a powerful enchantment. Cloaked as an old woman, a seer, she'd eluded the queen's grasp for nearly a century. A single-born shade (a Surface human damned to Dark World using only one of the required three sacrifices), Sybil had wandered the lands aimlessly for the sole intent of staying one step ahead of the queen and her army of loyal shades.

Then, in the midst of the building war, Sybil had been kidnapped by the queen. Tortured and interrogated by Malus's shade army, clandestine information had been extracted from her. The location of Necrosia was obviously one of them as the queen and her army tore down the walls of the castle, finding not only the shade she'd been searching for, Fate, but a secret demon heir as well—*Ever*.

Prince Kane's greatest deception had been unveiled: his daughter's existence. For over a century he'd kept Ever hidden from his mother by having her believe he was dead, knowing the dire consequences should Queen Malus discover her granddaughter. Power beyond all comprehension resided within one, kind-hearted young princess.

And now the queen had her. She had the one person she needed to fulfill the most evil of destinies. For Malus herself had but minimal powers, despite having assumed the throne of the Devil. She'd merely taken what never belonged to her. By having King Lucifer killed, she'd only stolen what no one else would fight for. With thousands of shades fervently guarding her, no one could come within a few hundred feet of her and live to tell of it.

But then, in her haste for more power, Malus had made a crucial error. By exposing herself and rendering herself vulnerable, she'd made a rare appearance in Necrosia, leaving herself wide open for an attack. Though Malus was still very powerful, Vale had used his innate ability to wisp beside her and drive a sword through her heart—but not before the queen had publicly marked Ever, and secretly Sybil, with her evil brand.

With all suspicion then cast on the unconscious princess, the queen quietly resided like a parasite within the oracle shade. Waiting for the right moment. Biding her time to strike. A coiled viper cloaked amidst the shadows of doubt. For if anyone had truly suspected Sybil, Aura was certain the clues would have been apparent.

Aura shuddered, her heart filling with fear. What was to become of Dark World now? What would happen to her people? How would Necrosia survive without their beloved leader? Questions bombarded her mind, from both her own thoughts and the collective of necromancers.

Had Sybil known she was infected with evil the entire time she stayed in Necrosia? Or was she herself a victim of Malus's treachery? With both Ever and Sybil now missing, they might never uncover the answers. Common sense dictated that Malus would retreat to the protection of the Blood Palace, her home and an impenetrable fortress.

Most importantly, how was Aura to tell Fate and Kane she'd failed to protect Ever?

Aura folded her steel blue arms around herself, irrecoverably chilled by the scene that lay before her. A procession of necromancers and shades gathered into the room that once held the demon princess, and previous to her, the Soul Nexus, the perfect sapphire sphere that beheld the shared soul of the necromancers; the essence of Myth. Now, instead of Ever or the nexus as the centerpiece, death occupied the room. A large pool of pewter blood lay like a misshapen mirror upon the floor, Vrill's slaughtered body sprawled in the midst of it. He was so lifeless and still. Without the healing powers of the nexus, Vrill could not be reincarnated. He was gone. Truly gone.

Aura searched the memories of her kind, scouring the lineage to which she was privy by race. Was there any way to bring him back? What if they brought him to Myth, would their almighty goddess be able to revive him?

The answer was never clearer: No.

Myth was inexplicably ill, unable to give anymore of herself or her powers to her beloved necromancers. Without the light of the Crystal Pyramid to draw upon, she'd been rendered weak and near death.

Unwilling to admit it, all of the necromancers knew her time was near. Aura could feel the goddess's weakness circulating within her silver blood. Myth was dying, and in turn, so were the necromancers.

Even more disturbing were the images drifting in and out of Aura's thoughts. Scenes from which she could not identify the source, but she suspected she knew their purpose. As this magical body was dying, the memories of her previous life, her *human* life, were coming into focus.

She was starting to remember who she really was.

"We must...lay him to rest," Kraton stated, his voice hollow and uncertain. This sort of ceremony, one of such permanence, was new to the community of immortals. Whenever a necromancer's body had succumbed to old age or irreparable damage, they would simply transfer their essence to another vessel, living on as if nothing had changed.

However Vrill's condition was fatal, absolute. There would be no rejuvenation party, no celebration for the continuance of his life. This was untraveled territory. An unmarked road for a race that never died.

At least, not until now.

Aura nodded at Kraton, resting a hand on his shoulder as he knelt before Vrill's body. How she wished Vale were there, he might know what to do — but then, perhaps he would be too grief-stricken that his only sister had been the murderer? Would he, too, be preoccupied with the thoughts and questions that plagued everyone else in the room?

"How?" Kraton echoed her private sentiments. "How could we not have known? How could she have been amongst us for all that time — and we did not know? Why did I not sense her evil spirit?"

The witchdoctor lowered his head in shame as Aura helplessly watched on, unable to offer him the solace he needed, as she too, had no answers.

Myth

How did Malus reside within Sybil, the great prophetess, the oracle; for weeks without anyone noticing something was amiss? How did she live amongst them without giving herself away?

Most of all, Aura wondered if Vale had suspected his sister's treachery.

If he did—would he have told Aura the truth?

Pillars of hot mist rose from within sporadic fissures littering the face of the Crimson Desert. Deep, subterranean pools set free their captive vapours, every foggy release like an army of ghosts awakening from an ancient slumber, arising from their graves, stretching and writhing as they break free of their stifling tomb.

A shimmering cloud of giant, bioluminescent dragonflies droned high overhead, dipping and zigzagging as they rode the arid, impulsive breezes. Kane would have thought it too hot up there, midway to the canopy, but he surmised the large bugs were probably avoiding a fatal singe from the overzealous geysers below. On the ground, rat-like creatures with glowing eyes cautiously sniffed the air as the band of strangers passed by their underground dens, skittering beneath boulders whenever their steps ventured too near.

Despite being miles from the haunted canyon where Seren resided with thousands of lost souls, Kane felt the glare of his failures upon his back. Walking away from Seren was the hardest thing he'd ever had to do. To abandon her to misery and torment. He'd had no choice. She is now a poltergeist, her mind and soul forever compromised by hatred and vengeance. To release her trapped spirit, he would have to kill Vale's sister, Sybil, for she was the one to steal Seren's soul in the first place. There was no other way. And despite his undying devotion to his wife, he couldn't imagine killing the oracle, or devastating Vale after he'd just recently found his long-lost sister.

Someday, if destiny would have it on its own terms, Seren would be freed from her ghostly prison. For now, though, he had no choice but to turn away from her and move on with his original quest.

Dark World was in terrible danger, its inhabitants threatened to extinction if he did not find the remaining scrolls and bring the various races together in unison to open the fissure to the Surface and relight the Crystal Pyramid.

He realized, of course, that obtaining the scrolls was to be a far easier task than joining the races together in peace. Myth had three of the six original pages of the Devil's Bible in her possession, Kane had the demons', and the reapers' still had theirs with them in the Nether Caves. The last, according to lore, had been hidden on the Surface, though no one seemed to know where. And how was he to retrieve it when the crevasse to the Surface had been sealed so long ago? He hoped Myth would be able to help him with that when he travelled to Exile Island to see her.

However, uniting the races might prove to be impossible, thanks to him. He had caused a new rift between the demons and wraiths when he defended Fate against an attack in their city only months before. The wraiths were unlikely to assist without great resistance.

The banshees were no problem, as long as he could keep the very last banshee alive long enough to complete the circle. With Princess Sorcia's entire race obliterated by an unseen force, he now had just one banshee left in the entire underworld.

He was certain the necromancers were on board with the plan, as well as the rogue shades—but the reapers were another matter altogether. Not only had no one seen a reaper in centuries, they were purported to be extremely elusive—and extremely violent when provoked. The problem was that entering their territory was considered provocation.

He roughly adjusted the sheathed black diamond sword upon his back, inadvertently bumping the pointed shackles adhered to his wings. He sucked in a pained breath, silently cursing his mother, Malus, for the affliction. Now that she was dead, these shackles would forever be a reminder of her existence and of her cruelty. Without her, the curse could never be lifted from himself nor the countless other demons that carried the burden of her spite. He and all the others would now wear her vengeance upon their backs and upon their wings, forever. For whoever delivers the enchantment must be the one to remove it.

To give the demons back their flight, he thought wistfully, *would be to give them back their dignity, their honour—and their power. We are nothing without our wings. I...am nothing without my wings.*

His ebony talons dug into the flesh of his palms as he fought back unwanted emotions, a mesh of anger and sadness moved through his soul like a darkening storm. Again he faced resentment and bitterness for his father. Why had he left them like this? Left them to face Malus alone, helpless—powerless. Without the

Crystal Pyramid, the demons had nothing. No magic, no future—nothing. The bloodstone was the only thing that had saved them. It provided them with enough magic to keep them barely alive, giving them limited immortality, but aging nonetheless.

Kane's black hooves stirred up miniature billows of red as he rushed over the crimson sands, sweat beading on his brow and chest, dampening the ends of his blue-black dreadlocks.

"What's the rush, boss?" Vale asked with an edge of annoyance in his voice as he appeared in a haze of black smoke next to the quick-paced demon, utilizing his unique shade talent of wisping to stay beside the agitated prince.

Kane halted and glanced back, realizing his posse was struggling to keep up. Sorcia, flanked by her two enamoured necromancers, Slater and Mezza, had fallen far behind, Her sad, tired eyes averted to the red sands of the Crimson Desert as she walked. He'd forgotten how hard this must be on her; she'd lost everyone, her father, her sisters—everyone and everything she'd ever known. Now she carried an even greater burden: to assist Kane in restoring Dark World.

Vale, usually cool and aloof, looked haggard and possibly in need of sustenance. It would be grave indeed to starve the shade as he likely wouldn't be able to control himself once the lust for souls set in. The bloodstone would appease his dark needs, at least for the time being.

"I apologize," Kane mumbled, stopping on the spot to allow the others to rest as he retrieved some bloodstone for Vale and himself from his pack.

"Finally!" Vale sprawled the length of his body out onto a large boulder, lacing his fingers behind his head and half-closing his gleaming white eyes. "Where to next?"

Kane took in a deep breath as he handed Vale a small sphere of the crimson and jade stone, then crushed one for himself and consumed it. This was the question he'd been dreading to answer. Where were they to go next? Where was he to lead them? There was just so much to do. They'd been travelling south for several hours, leaving many options open to them. They could go straight to the wraiths and, after a possible altercation, ask them to join their plight. They could head south-west and come upon Legion, where Kane could check on his people, rest, gather fresh resources, and recruit assistance.

The reapers lived in the distant north, which would be weeks of travel in the opposite direction, though not far from Exile Island where Myth was purported to dwell. It made sense to keep moving south, despite his reservations with facing the wraiths again. Hopefully the newfound power he'd summoned during his unpleasant reunion with Seren and her loyal poltergeist followers would be more reliable from now on, so he could put it to good use if anything were to happen.

"Well?" Vale demanded petulantly, spreading his arms wide as he eyed Kane.

Kane ground his pointed teeth together, fresh agitation crawling over him. This was going to be a long journey. "We should turn to the west and head towards Legion," he answered sharply.

Vale scowled. "Why are we going there?" he asked with a palpable hint of anxiety creeping into his tone.

Kane couldn't blame him for being a bit nervous; the bitter relationship between demons and shades was renowned throughout the land. Surely they wouldn't accept him any more than they'd accepted Fate during her stay, especially if they were to discover that Vale was the one that had infiltrated the underground palace and stolen their scroll only months before.

"To gather help, supplies, and more bloodstone. As well as to have a decent place to sleep and freshen up for a night or two," Kane said, forcing a hospitable smile.

Sorcia and the two necromancers, who'd finally caught up and sat themselves down on a few spare boulders, nodded eagerly in agreement. Everyone was undoubtedly exhausted and could benefit from a decent sleep and meal.

Kane took a seat as well, drained from thought and worry over the matters he'd yet to attend. Strangely, as he considered the impending visit to Legion, he was eager, excited even, to see his people again. To share his recent experiences with them about the necromancers and tell them of his adventures over the last couple of months. Despite the uncertainty as to how they might react upon his arrival, considering he'd left them in search of Fate, who at the time had run away, he hoped for a warm welcome upon his return.

Yet deep inside his intuition cringed, preparing him for the worst.

Fate contemplated her descent into the labyrinth of tall stalagmites, the only obvious way to get to the Guf shining in the distance. She eyed the potion Kraton had given her, tempted to drink it down right then and there in hopes that it would lead her all the way through the maze unscathed.

But first she had to get down there. To her right, the face of the obsidian-rich mountain was completely sheer, nowhere to place even the smallest of footings. To her left, there was a very narrow ledge that meandered downward into the valley, but would leave her and her furry entourage with their backs pressed against the wall the entire way — they'd be precariously perched hundreds of feet above solid ground for hours.

True, most of the bigger gargoyles could fly down to the bottom, except for the smallest, whom Fate had nicknamed Nibbles (for his constant nibbling at Fate's fingers and earlobes) he was far too small to navigate his way safely to the ground. Perhaps one of the bigger ones could carry him down, but she wasn't sure they should risk it considering the unpredictable gusts of wind that frequently ripped through the valley.

Fate gazed down at her furred posse, concern welling within. She hadn't eaten for awhile, and there was no telling when the lamia monster inside of her would lash out like a coiled snake, devouring any-thing in its path. At least with the shade it was a growing hunger, and a bit more predictable. Fate had no control over the lamia and no foresight whatsoever as to when she'd lose control of herself. An image of her tearing through the downy soft fur of the baby gargoyles sprang forth into her thoughts, sending a jolt of pain through her heart. She couldn't live with herself if she harmed any one of these creatures — especially her little Ick.

"Ick," Fate began carefully, gathering the white gargoyle into her arms, his velvety fur like silk against her skin. "Before we go any further, we need to have a serious talk."

He purred and nuzzled her face like a kitten, lick-ing and tickling her chin as he professed his undying love and affection. At her feet, Ick's entourage of young gargoyles hugged her ankles and bit her softly. Fate giggled, stating, "I'm serious you guys. I have something I need to say."

Ick stopped, sighed like a sulky toddler, and paused to look Fate in the eye, as if to say, "What is it *now*?" The other gargoyles stopped to listen in.

"See this?" Fate asked of him as she pulled up her sleeves, exposing the network of black lines on her arms. Ick cringed, frowning as he eyed the dark art. "I'm...sick," she admitted.

Ick tilted his head, his hairy brow creasing in ei-ther concern or confusion, Fate couldn't tell.

"Do you understand? I'm unwell. It may not be safe for you at times," she explained, hoping he understood what she was saying. "There could be moments," she continued, averting her eyes from his ashamedly, "where you might need to run away from me."

This time she knew he comprehended her words as an expression of fear and sadness spread over his cat-like face. "Ick?" he questioned in his gruff little voice, tracing a fur-covered talon along one of the ebony lines running lengthwise on her forearm.

She assumed he was asking 'why', so she replied, "There's a monster inside of me, a new monster, one I can't control." Fate felt tears building behind her glowing white eyes as she explained further. "It isn't like before, when I could eat the bloodstone and feel better, this one eats…" she paused, wondering if she should elaborate, then added, "…something else."

The little gargoyle seemed to mull over her words, frowning and tilting his head until he finally paused, brought his eyes up to hers and pointed a furry finger onto his chest.

Pain swelled around what remained of Fate's soul as she nodded and whispered, her voice thick with emotion, "Yes, I would try to eat…you."

His spherical eyes widened as he absorbed this information, then he turned his chin up defiantly and pointed to the ground. She put him down as request-ed. He then gathered his comrades close.

Hugging her torso, Fate paced as she anxiously listened to Ick communicate to his fellows gargoyles by means of growls and hand-gestures. All of them watched with horrified fascination, their eyes shifting warily back and forth from her to Ick, as he described to them what Fate had just told him.

Finally, after several moments of quiet terror, each of the baby gargoyles turned their faces up to Fate.

She half-expected them to turn fuzzy tail and run away screaming, but to her surprise, they nodded and bowed to her as if telling her they understood, and even sympathized, with her plight.

Humbled, Fate turned her gaze to Ick, asking, "So, they understand that if I tell them to get away from me, it's because I don't want to hurt them?"

Ick exposed his pearly, razor-sharp teeth in a grin, nodding.

Fate had to admit that he was as smart as he was cute. "All right then," she said, releasing a shaky breath as she turned to embark on the treacherous descent down the side of the obsidian mountain. "Let's do this."

Kane

As resolute as patriotic soldiers, two massive obsidian pillars haunted the horizon, silent markers of the lost world veiled beneath it, guardians of a humbled, even humiliated, society. Sometimes Kane felt as though the people of Legion had burrowed beneath the sands, hiding in cowardice, ashamed of their own race. A once proud and dominant nation, the demons fell from unimaginable heights.

They had once been the feared, the powerful, until Malus assumed the reign of Devil. However ill-intended, Kane longed for those times before his mother's evil tyranny. The periods when the demons were revered, living immortal and plentiful existences. He had seen King Lucifer do great things, conquering lands, possessing the underworld with an iron fist. The races thrived, bathing in riches, and sat propped upon thrones of gold.

Only now did Kane realize that for one to sit upon a throne there had to be someone to bow before it. One's power did not come without another's suffering. The humans lived at the base of his father's chair, under the glaring eye of superiority. They were seen as powerless, weak, and easily controlled. Barely more than thoughtless creatures that mined the treasures and served the meals.

Until the Uprising.

Myth

Kane was sure none were more surprised than the demons. All were staggered by the humans' tenacity; their near blood-thirst for freedom; their lust for power and pride. Had Malus seen this trait in them all along? Is that how she came to wield such influence over the humans?

Kane nodded, knowing the truth. His mother, for all her treachery, had intuited the desires of the underdogs, had seen their needs, their wants, their desperation—and acted upon it. An uneasy weight settled on Kane's shoulders. It was the guilt and shame for his father's actions over the course of hundreds of years. He'd allowed and promoted the way in which the humans were to be treated. King Lucifer believed them to be markedly inferior to the demons, barren of magic, the currency of Dark World. But how could he have known any better? This lesson the demons and all of Dark World had learned was one that could only have come from being forced to their knees, bowed and humbled before a new world order.

Rumors from the Surface had it that the humans feared damnation to the underworld more than anything else. They dreaded the destination of their souls, terrified of where their immortal selves would spend eternity. And for a great while, Dark World was that Hell in which they'd dwelt. But now everything was different. There was no order, no calm within the chaos. Dark World lingered as a lost realm, drifting amidst a nameless purgatory. Limbo.

If his father no longer owned the underworld, nor his mother, then who was to rule?

Who indeed, Kane pondered, knowing the answer full well. It was his birthright, his destiny — his fate. Fate, he thought with a smile. She'd changed everything. No longer did he label the shades as pure evil, born soulless and ravaging an already devastated world. She'd opened his eyes and made him see for the first time that no one thing is born without choices, without a say to their purpose. She'd chosen to hold tight to her goodness, her human side, denying the shade inside of her access to what remained of her soul. She'd chosen the light over the darkness.

"Sorcia?" Vale's concerned voice drew Kane from his thoughts. He turned about to assess the situation. Several feet behind him, Sorcia had fallen to her hands and knees, her long red hair draping her face and pooling like blood upon the crimson sands.

Kane immediately dropped his pack and ran to her side, Vale beating him there by way of wisping. "Princess, what is wrong?" Kane inquired, placing a hand upon her back. Her breath was jagged and forced, bronze skin paled and damp. "Sorcia," he pressed. "Please, tell me how to help you."

There was no response. She suddenly went limp, unconscious, falling onto the ground. Without wasting a single moment, Kane looked to Mezza and Slater, who were watching in horror from a few feet away, and ordered, "Mezza! Slater! Can you transform into a bird and carry her to the pillars! We must get her to Ozen!"

The burly necromancers hastily obeyed, merging their singular forms into one and creating a large, metallic eagle. Taking hold of the princess around her waist with their six-inch talons, they effortlessly lifted her into the sky and flew toward the monoliths.

Beneath them Kane and Vale were already on the run toward the secret entrance to Legion.

"She'll be fine." Kane tried to calm himself. "My people will help her." His gaze then shifted to Vale, wondering how he would be received by the demons.

I guess we'll find out. Kane cringed inwardly, hoping he was wrong.

Fate

"Spark!" Fate called to her faithful phoenix who was happily playing amidst the steamy layer of atmosphere overhead. Fate shrugged, she supposed it was perfectly balmy up there for a phoenix. *He's already on fire, after all, she thought. It must feel like nothing more than a warm bath for him.* "Spark!" she called again, creating a megaphone with her hands cupped round her mouth. Finally, he spun about, diving and descending with astonishing speed as he flew to her location.

"Hey buddy," Fate said, smiling at him as he landed and shook his fiery feathers into place. "I have a huge favor to ask of you." The bird tilted his head inquisitively, his beady black eyes locked onto her face with rapt intelligence. Fate dug into her pants pocket and produced Ever's letter. "Would you take this to Kane for me?" Fate bit her lip, knowing how important this letter was to Ever, praying Spark would be able to find the demon prince and give it to him.

The bird's body crackled with fresh ripples of fire, as though he was excited to be given this honor. During the time she'd spent with him, Fate had deciphered some of his moods and meaning according to the intensity of fire he'd expel. As far as she could tell, he'd said yes and was rather enthusiastic about the quest.

Myth

"Thank you so much, my friend," she said as she ran her finger gently across the soft feathers of his head, the fires parting in allowance. "It means a lot to me. If you don't find Kane, bring the letter back, and...be careful, okay?"

After taking the note between his beak, he shot up into the air leaving a jet stream of hot air in his wake, flying off into the horizon like a tiny setting sun.

"Well, that's that," Fate said aloud as she turned her attention to the seemingly impossible descent down the mountainside, sighing. "And now, the really hard one."

Carefully, calculating her every step, Fate clung to the wall of the mountain. She tried in vain to dig her sharp, black fingernails into the obsidian; despite her effort the rock nemesis would not yield to her need for safety. Teardrops of salty sweat dripped endlessly over her brow; she couldn't be sure if it was from the sheer terror of her situation or the sadistic inferno that blew haphazardly through the valley every few minutes. Razor-sharp shards of obsidian poked and sliced at her palms, drawing thin lines of blood that she was surprised to see was still red in color considering the blackness of her veins.

Before she'd embarked on her death-defying balancing act into the pointy pits of Hell, she'd debated long and hard as to whether or not she would want to face the gaping cavern of imminent demise as she descended or hug the face of the cliff with her back to the thousand foot drop of doom—because there was no room to turn back if she were to change her mind. It took longer than she'd thought to decide, but she finally settled on shuffling along the three inch ledge all the way down.

"This...is not fun," she said to Nibbles who was marching along the narrow shelf beside her, prattling nervously in his own language and twiddling his tiny, fuzzy fingers as he repeatedly peered over the edge into the dark fathoms below. Barely discernible were the points of the stalagmites, their shadowy trunks hidden amidst drifting clouds of black smoke and ash. The occasional curious belch of air from the surface would momentarily disturb the cohesiveness of the vaporous mass, blowing mushrooms of dark mist upwards like miniature atomic bombs; other than that, it was eerily quiet below. Too quiet. Fate forced her imaginative ponderings of what she thought might dwell beneath the veil of smoke, it did her no good to worry about it now. She'd face that unknown when she reached the bottom. Knowing Dark World, she'd best be prepared for the worst.

Abandoned by the other gargoyles from the beginning of the descent, who apparently had no intention of teetering upon the slim ledge when they could just fly down; it was just Fate and Nibbles who dared to make the perilous journey by foot. There was no other choice; there was no way Fate was going to let the baby gargoyles fly her down, even though they'd been strong enough to lift the weird three-headed dog that had attacked her shortly after she'd left Necrosia. They'd managed, quite precariously, to lift the hellish mutt several feet in the air and carry it away, to save Fate from literally becoming a dog's lunch. So, in all fairness, they would have been perfectly capable of carrying her, but the gale-force winds ripping unpredictably through the valley dissuaded her from that idea very quickly. For some reason, the winds appeared to be picking up over the last hour or so, convincing her further that this plan was the safer one.

As far as she could tell, Ick and his buddies had made it safely to the ground below. They'd soared quite effortlessly over the valley, circling and dropping altitude at a constant rate. There were a couple of times where Fate had to suppress a gasp or two when a brutal gust would disrupt their flight pattern, but then, before she knew it, they'd disappeared beneath the cloak of ash. She hoped they were wise enough to hide once they'd landed inside the maze, or better yet become invisible until she arrived.

What funny little creatures, Fate mused as she inched her way along the rock wall. *They're called animals, but are so like us. They have feelings and thoughts all their own, yet we treat them as though they are incapable of intelligence.*

Fate glanced down at Nibbles, who was doing justice to his name as he anxiously gnawed on his claw-like fingernails. "Hey buddy, you're doing great!" Fate told him, hoping to inspire some confidence in the young creature. He looked up at her with his huge, spherical blue eyes and frowned, as if to tell her he was less than impressed with the situation and nothing she could say or do was going to make him feel better.

Shrugging, Fate plodded on by inching her way down the side of the cliff. It was in that moment she realized the air had become very, very still. Airless almost, as though a sphere of heaviness had begun to form around her—something wasn't right.

"Do you feel that?" she asked of Nibbles who replied with a frightened nod. Nerves knotted inside her stomach as she scanned to her left, then to her right, now annoyed that she'd chosen to face the rock as it limited her ability to see the full panoramic view of the dark valley below. The pressure continued to build; her ears felt as though she were inside an airplane descending much too fast.

Then came the noise.

A deep, baritone hum swept through the gorge, shaking the very foundation beneath her feet as though the mountain itself were trembling with fear.

"What is that?" Fate shouted to Nibbles as she pressed her palms to her ears, but he too had covered his large, pointed ears. Wincing in pain he curled into a ball.

Fate groaned as the force and droning sound built, her innards twisting and her mind threatening to surrender to unconsciousness. She cried out just as she thought she could stand it no longer.

Then it stopped.

Taking her hands from her ears, she looked to both her left and right, peripherally searching for the cause of her grief, but there was nothing. Although, with Dark World, you just never knew what could happen.

Fate checked on Nibbles, who'd also released his aching ears from his hands and was left to whimper in confusion. "What the heck was that?" she asked aloud, hoping for some explanation though unsure that she really wanted to know. All she cared about was that it was over. "Let's...keep going," she said to Nibbles as her hearing gradually adjusted to the now eerie calm.

Whatever that was, she thought, *I hope it doesn't come back.*

However, her instincts told her she'd better get down the mountainside as fast as possible.

Aura

Aura slowly descended the stone steps, leaving the room of death behind her. Though, she knew, it would truly never leave her. The horror, the terror and the pain, were all engraved upon her communal soul. All the necromancers had felt it, owned it like a black tattoo engraved upon their skin. Vrill's murder had left a hole inside of them that could never be filled.

Energy cannot be created nor destroyed, Vrill's voice, his inherited knowledge, whispered sagely through her thoughts. He was still there, still lingering amidst the void, despite the fact his physical body was gone. Aura felt her telepathic community sigh with relief as they still had him in some form or another.

A ghost? Kraton's thoughts offered as he was in another room across the palace. Aura smiled, nodding in response.

Yes, a ghost, she replied in thought, the ache subsiding a little. She still wished Vale were there to hold her and comfort her through this time. Who would guide them now? Who would become leader of the necromancers?

Would there even be a need? With Myth on the verge of collapse, the necromancers would soon cease to exist. Their long occupation within the dark realm could well be over. If Myth were to expire, her powerful soul would be forced to leave this world, taking the spark of life from within every creature with her. Dark World would be no more. It would be empty, barren of its peoples, its animals.

Maybe that would be better, Aura surmised, considering the bitterness between the races. Dark World had seen many wars, much blood spilt upon its sands. And all for what? To what end?

Aura shook her head as images of her ancestors spun through her thoughts. Long ago, they'd stolen away to a far off place to escape the unrest, hidden themselves from the rest of the underworld. The other races were selfish, cruel, and unobservant to the laws of the mystical energies. Greed and power had been ruler — and tyranny. Her heart felt heavy as she saw, in her mind's eye, the way the humans had been mistreated. Slaves, beaten down and humiliated, those who had fallen from the Surface had lost all that was good in them.

Until Malus offered them exactly what they needed. Magic.

Images flickered over her galactic eyes as memories of the Uprising unfolded. Malus stood upon the threshold of her new empire, the Blood Palace, and called to those humans who wished for her evil blessing. In exchange for her *gift*, they had to surrender their eternal souls. But what Malus didn't know was that the souls were never hers to own. No one can own another's soul, so they simply returned to where they were born — the Guf. Regardless of her loss, the humans-turned-shades worshipped her, obeyed her, and worst of all, killed for her.

And where, Aura pondered, *is my human soul? Is it dwelling within the confines of the Guf? If so, will I ever get it back?*

A shiver crawled the length of her spine as she considered her future. Without Myth's soul inside of her, what would she become? Would she just fall to the ground, shatter into dust and return to the earth from which she was once buried? As the days passed, she recalled more and more of her former existence. Especially the brief time as a zombie when she had to fight to live once more. While it was a brutal and confusing time, she remembered feeling such passion to feel alive again, such will to survive. Would it be that way again? Would she be given another chance to exist?

Shadows flickered upon the walls around her as rows of skeletal hands protruded from the walls, holding torches as they lit her path. Again, Vale found his way into her thoughts and sadness overwhelmed her. He was sure to be devastated by his sister's betrayal. For many years he'd sought her in the underworld. He'd died for her and relinquished his Surface life in order to find her. And now this. Her soul was compromised by Malus. For all intents and purposes, Sybil was Malus now.

The queen was now reincarnated within the oracle shade. Everyone in Dark World knew what it was to be possessed by a demon—and it wasn't good. Though two souls resided inside the body, the demon soul was in charge. As far as Aura knew, there was no way back once the transformation was complete.

Ever, Aura's eyes watered with fresh tears. Now she, too, was a prisoner of Malus. It was not known if

Malus had possessed the princess yet, but Aura was sure it was only a matter of time. She wondered, then, what would happen to Sybil? Would she become herself again, or would she forever be tainted by evil, unable to escape an internal nightmare?

Aura shuddered, releasing a sigh. The castle walls seemingly closing in on her as she wandered down the hall. She had to get outside and clear her head.

Upon exiting the palace, Aura felt the need to fly. She often took to the air as a griffin when she could no longer stand the confines of the castle. As a griffin, she learned she could switch off her connection to the others, the hundreds of necromancers' thoughts and concerns. Not that she didn't love every one of her brothers and sisters, but telepathy could be very noisy on occasion.

The courtyard's skull cobblestone path was smooth and cool beneath her bare feet as she padded to the center of the garden. Blush-pink petals snowed down on her from beneath a row of flowering plums, their soft scent carried upon a delicate breeze. Effervescent lightning bees flitted amongst the sapphire roses and blue begonias, carrying pollen upon their backs as they busily gathered more. Rainbow-colored wrens twittered and sang amidst the blooms and leaves of a weeping willow, its emerald fronds draping over the path like long silken hair.

As Aura walked through the veil of leaves, her transformation had already started, her silver skin turned molten, smelting into the likes of liquid mercury as she evolved. The quickening took but seconds to complete as her humanoid form dissolved, reshaping itself into the long, lean body of a lion. Aura's sight sharpened as the eagle's head took form over her face, long delicate wings manifested from her back, shivering and shaking themselves free as though a butterfly emerging from a cocoon.

Parting her silvery beak, Aura sighed, free once again, her mind silent of the constant chatter and worry of the necromancer palace. She pushed off with little effort, flapping her mighty wings then ascending quickly into the airspace above the city. Hot, thick wind pressed down upon her from amid the canopy, but she just pretended she was soaring over a sparkling blue ocean that hugged the island shores of Aruba.

Aruba? She mulled over the word, played it about her thoughts. *Do I know what that is?* Scouring her awareness, she realized with a thrill that she did indeed know what that was, or rather, where. It had been a vacation. Blue skies opened up inside her memories, smattered with billows of white, the sun's hot, golden rays beating down from the center. Sapphire waters lapped bronzed beaches, licking the toes of a tiny girl who giggled and ran into her mother's expectant arms, where she picked up the child and spun her around. Smiling. So much love. Warmth curled around Aura's heart, heat spreading throughout her body, soothing her soul.

The child, Aura realized. *The child is me! And she,* Aura's eyes watered as she focused on the woman, *is my mother.*

Malus

The outside walls of the Blood Palace bled scarlet, seeping like thick, dark ink into the lava moats below, stirring the suffering of others into the infernal rivers. An endless, raging tempest churned overhead whilst sharp forks of white lightning snarled and crackled every few moments, pausing only to hear the angry roar of thunder. Hundreds of shade soldiers, adorned in enchanted silver armor, guarded the walls and grounds below, their glowing white eyes glaring from beneath metallic helmets.

The Blood Palace, home to the Devil, sat nestled amidst the Walls of Agony. No one could enter. No could leave. There was only one way in or out—and Malus wasn't one for company unless she commanded it.

Screams echoed through her soul; pain, suffering. The wailing ghosts of thousands, millions, stormed her mind as penance for all the sins she'd committed over the centuries. For all the lives she'd stolen and rendered irreparable.

It was torture.

It was evil.

It was home.

Malus stretched inside her new body, the youth and vitality humming as though she were a newborn. In a sense, she was resurrected into a new existence and a new body. The body of her true heir—Ever.

Ever's gentle soul lingered, sleeping deep inside of the body. Malus could feel her granddaughter's essence sporadically gravitate toward consciousness, stirring every so often in feeble attempts to awaken. But the queen had total control over this vessel; it was hers now. She'd possessed but one other body than this: the oracle's, which was perceptibly inferior, limited and stunted magically by comparison. Once she'd slipped into Ever's body, she knew immediately it was her destiny, her fate to live eternally within. Of course she was still mortal, still vulnerable to harm and the effects of time, until she opened the crevasse and let the sun shine once more onto the Crystal Pyramid, then she'd never have to worry about death or decay; she'd be impervious to the limitations of life, able to heal any wound at whim and call upon the elementals with a whisper. But more importantly, she'd be the most powerful being in Dark World. Pure magic would course through her veins; she would be the embodiment of raw power. All would bow to her—or die horribly for their insubordination. Frankly, she looked forward to those moments; it pleased her to induce pain and torture upon those who would dare to defy her.

She turned towards the vanity, smiling wickedly at Ever's reflection in the mirror, eerily similar to her own, true appearance. The long, snow-white hair. The silk-soft ivory skin. All was so alike—save for the eyes. Where Ever's eyes bore the blue of a Surface sky, naïve and gentle and sweet, Malus's eyes were hard, cold, calculating, and especially, cruel. Though still shaded blue, a blood-red ring ran around her irises,

Myth

signifying the power in control, the soul that owned, possessed, the body.

This was her body now, her destiny. The gods of the underworld were truly in her favor. They must be, as it all had turned out even more perfectly than she'd intended.

Her plan had begun so very long ago, amidst her engagement to the then young Lord Lucifer. The realm required a King, and he being arrogant, powerful, and filled with lust for reign, was the perfect candidate for the job. Malus had seen great potential in him from the start—alongside great weakness. Lucifer had but one major flaw (he'd been an angel from the Light Realm, after all)—he could love. He was capable of a love so deep he could be blinded by it. Especially when Malus bore him a son, Kane.

Thankfully Malus had no inclination for such sentiments. She only longed for one thing—power over Dark World. When her scheme to assassinate Lucifer came to fruition, she was overjoyed as the shades bowed before her by the thousands, willingly, eagerly even. They'd waited so long to be free of their shackles; they had no reservations about relinquishing their souls into her waiting arms.

Only, their souls didn't surrender as she'd thought. Malus hadn't counted on the Guf taking back the yielded souls, leaving her far less powerful than she'd intended. In addition, Lucifer's little plot to deter her: closing the fissure to the Surface, rendered her totally mortal and without her beloved black magic.

It mattered not; it had all come around the way the gods had planned it. She should have known better

45

Danielle Q. Lee

than to doubt them; they'd been on her side all along. The gods that had created the demons; lent their seed to bear demonic fruits. They'd resented the Light One from the moment she entered the underworld, consuming it with her spark of spirit.

Myth, Malus seethed with the thought of the fifth elemental. Despite the fact that without Myth, none of beings of Dark World would exist, it infuriated the queen nonetheless. How dare a highborn, an angel, invade their world? It disgusted her that just a sliver of that altruist lie within herself. She had no business being here, in Malus's kingdom!

It was no wonder her own son allowed light and love into his heart. The four elementals were comprised of darkness and of the purest evil. They were her gods, her minions, her slaves to be bidden. But Myth contaminated their essence, brought light into the dark. If not for her, Dark World would not harbour life, true, but the life she bore, the light she shone into their souls gave them the one thing Malus despised: Free will. The choice to be virtuous or evil. The choice to follow or be followed. The choice to heed her — or not.

The queen's stare narrowed, glaring at her reflection in the mirror. Though it was Ever's body, it was now hers until the day she decided to possess another. No one could ever make her leave. No one.

A light knock at the door of her bedchamber pulled her from her thoughts. "Enter," she commanded, rising from her seat before the mirrored bureau. Dressed in a gown of crimson, fringed and elaborately detailed with gold thread, Malus noted again how her new, lithe body resonated with astounding power. It had been wise of her only son to keep this vessel of the gods hidden. Now Malus had no limits, no barrier to what she could do magically. Had she known she could harness this kind of power, she'd never have wasted her time on finding the single-born shades; those that would have made sufficient hosts should she have required a new body. Shades were not affected by the lightless Crystal Pyramid; their powers came from another source, a place even Malus herself didn't understand — within.

"Your Highness," Maxim bowed low, his long silver braid sliding over his shoulder with the movement.

The queen offered him a sincere smile, total obedience pleased her. "Maxim," she purred. "To what do I owe the pleasure?"

He rose, bringing his eyes to hers. "My queen, I wish to ask your intentions for the rogue shade."

"The oracle?" she asked, her eyes narrowing in suspicion. She hadn't given much thought to the shade since she transferred her soul into Ever. She had what she wanted; the shade was of no use to her now. "Why?"

Maxim hesitated. Malus scrutinized him, awaiting his answer. He finally responded, his expression wary, "The oracle, Sybil, speaks of the future, of things yet to pass."

"Yes?" Malus urged him to continue, now completely attentive.

The shade cleared his throat, then stated, "She speaks of your future, my queen...and of the prophecy."

Malus sighed, examining her nails with feigned disinterest. "Oh, and what does she say about that?"

Maxim averted his eyes a moment before he answered, "She claims to see your downfall, my lady. She sees your death."

Kane pounded on the ground with his hoof, a metallic noise resonating beneath them. He hammered again on the hidden doors to Legion and he waited, but no one came. No one opened the door.

"I don't understand," he admitted, dark brows wrinkling. "Why will no one answer?" His stomach churned with fear. Had something happened to his people in his absence? He knocked again, and waited.

"Perhaps they cannot hear," Vale offered, though his eyes betrayed him, showing doubt.

Sorcia moaned as she lay within Mezza's and Slater's arms, her body paling and her life force fading.

"We have to hurry," Kane stated. "Vale, can you wisp to the other side and open it?"

Vale nodded and vanished instantaneously, only a cloud of black vapour left behind. Despite the gratitude Kane felt for Vale's willingness to help, and his capability, he couldn't help but recall the last time Vale was here and how he'd stolen one of their most precious artifacts. So easily, so effortlessly. A twinge of displeasure ran through the demon's veins, so much of this could have been prevented if Vale had not been party to the theft. If only Vrill had not sought to steal the scrolls from the cities, despite his claim to be protecting them, things might have turned out differently.

With the merest thought of Vrill came the guilt of leaving Fate and Ever behind. How could he have left them? Were they okay?

His worries were pushed aside with the sound of metallic whining as the heavy iron doors were pushed open. Vale, looking pleased with a smug grin upon his black lips, stood casually to the side as he ushered them in.

"Well done," Kane forced himself to say, though it came out more as a growl.

"I know," Vale replied, blowing on his black nails and rubbing them against the lapel of his leather jacket.

They descended the stairs, closing the doors behind them, shrouding them in total darkness. Amidst the shadows, Kane's glowing, infrared stare narrowed. The torches weren't lit. Forever loyal, the eternal flames kept the sconces burning bright, leading the way to the underground palace.

"Wow," Vale's voice disturbed the eerie quiet. "It's pretty dark in here; you should have some lights installed or something."

Irritation clawed at Kane as he lifted his palms to the pitch blackness and summoned, "*Lucem ferre.*" His hands ignited with a bright, amber glow, causing creepy shadows to flicker along the jagged walls.

The dim orange light within Kane's palms illuminated only a few feet at time, slowing their progress greatly. A flutter of despair rose into Kane's heart. Why had his people not answered? Was something wrong? Waves of fresh guilt and remorse washed over him. He had left his people amid a dark time.

Myth

It was always his worry, ever since his father died, that he was not worthy of the position he'd been given. Why was it that the next in line for the crown had to be the heir? What if the heir was not adequate for such a task? Should not the successor be the person who best displays leadership and, gods forbid, actually desires the job?

He inhaled deeply, hoping to ease the ache building inside. His mother had desired the job, in fact, had murdered his father to get it. Kane supposed that the criteria for a position such as the Devil should require far more than one's desire, it should require the culmination of many minds, many souls, and many wishes; hence, the people should choose. Therefore, an heir to the throne was not what mattered, but the needs of the people adhering to that throne.

Kane could think of at least two others that would be far better suited for the job than he. Elder Ozen, of course, sprang to mind first. Despite his elderly age, the kind and tender demon would make a wonderful leader. Though soft-spoken, he was fair, considerate, and tolerant. Even Elder Syphon had governance qualities Kane did not possess, as much as he hated to admit it. Syphon was a born leader, though far more tyrannical in his approach. He demanded respect. He made swift, decisive orders. A true leader.

Kane had always wondered why the fates had chosen him to succeed his father. The drive and the aspiration to lead just wasn't there. He was always forced into that position because so few others would actually stand up and fight for the greater good.

A true king would surely be one who chose to lead, chose his own path. Sadly, there were many who'd offer themselves up as contenders only for the glory and power the position offered. They would not likely be 'good' kings, but merely reap the benefits of such a rank. Like his mother. She did not make for a great queen. She only cared for the power carried with the title. Her only desire was to have a world grovel at her feet and worship her, even if it is purely out of fear and not out of respect.

The entire situation made Kane tired, weary within. A king should want the job, hunger for it above all else; he should need to care for his people and love them. Kane didn't know what he felt about anything — except Ever and Fate. He was very clear on his love of them.

However, for Dark World left him with centuries of bitterness, consumed by racial upheavals, old wounds and a cold heart.

Kane shoved his dark thoughts aside, pressing forward through the tunnels, faster, leading his wayward group through the labyrinth of stone. Sorcia groaned occasionally. Every sound she made allowed Kane a spark of hope that she might survive whatever plagued her. Above all, he needed her. If they lost one of the races now, there was truly no hope to relight the pyramid.

Finally they came to the last stretch of cave before the heavy metal door that would guide them into the castle. Kane navigated quickly, anticipation squeezing his heart with every beat. Vale was close on his heels, wisely quiet during this moment of strain. The shade had some common sense, at the very least.

As they rounded the last corner, the light illuminated the gateway into the city. The thick, heavy, steel door that guarded the city from the outside world had been ripped from its hinges and left bent in half as though a raging monster had broken its way through.

Kane's heart was in his throat as smatterings of blood marked the entrance, trails of smears and scarlet fingerprints everywhere.

Then, as he stepped over the threshold, he saw nothing but dead bodies — everywhere.

Fate

Sharp obsidian edges tore at her clothing, slashing and slicing her pale skin. "We're almost there," Fate said to Nibbles between labored breaths, her eyes trained on the narrowing path at her feet, fingers fumbling for each and every concrete grip of stone. A silver bead of sweat meandered the slope of her pale forehead, dripping perilously close to her right eye. Fate grunted and groaned as she negotiated the wall of rock, losing her footing and slipping off the path every few paces. She could swear the ledge was tapering with every step. Stealing a peek over her shoulder at the cloud-covered ground below, she surmised they were still at least fifteen feet up. She considered taking hold of the little gargoyle and jumping down the last few feet, but there was no telling what they'd land on.

An uninvited shudder took hold of her shoulders. What was down there? What awaited her and her band of furry comrades beneath the visually impenetrable shroud of fog? She exhaled, nerves knotting inside her stomach. Dark World was so unpredictable, so wrought with unseen predators and instant enemies. Despite her true nature, so many still saw her as a shade. The plague of Dark World. So few had ever given her the chance to prove herself, to show that she wasn't the monster they believed her to be.

Myth

A warm smile slid over her black lips just then. *Kane,* she thought. *He gave me a chance.* Sure, it had been rough for the first while, before he realized she was different than the others. Since then, she'd met so many shades that had not succumbed to their damned nature. For instance, neither Vale nor Sybil had allowed the void to completely consume them. Both had retained a small sliver of their true selves, their human selves, enough to fend off the power of the curse.

The air around her had gone still again, too still. It was so quiet here, unnervingly so. It felt as though the gaze of a thousand eyes were upon her, watching her every move, her every step. The further down the mountain she got, the brighter the light emanating from the Guf got. What was this place? What secrets did it hold?

Part of her was excited, impatient even, to arrive at the mystical, mysterious place. The rest of her was skeptical and paranoid. But Dark World had made her that way. How could she not be wary of what awaited her around every corner. She'd been a prisoner in this place for many months now; she had seen many scary and inexplicable things.

Her thoughts fell back to the night she'd been damned to this world—the night that Rory Dean killed her. Uninvited tears found their way to her eyes with the memories, the pain, and the suffering she'd endured at his evil hands. Why would anyone do that to another? Why had he chosen her?

Despite her unwillingness to face the truth, she knew the answers. She'd been an easy target: weak and naïve. She'd practically walked into the lion's den at suppertime. She'd been a foolish little girl. Anger and shame coalesced within her, awash with disappointment.

My poor family, she thought as she closed her eyes. *And Shelby. This is truly all my fault.* But then she shook her head, knowing who else she should blame. Her black lips curled into a hateful snarl as she whispered, "*Rory.*"

She could almost feel the cool sharpness of the blade penetrating her chest with the recollection of that night. How he'd led his prey into the woods and used her infatuation with him against her. How he'd murdered her. Damned her.

Rage consumed her; the black lamian blood coursed violently through her veins. Hate rose up from the shadows of her severed soul, swirling within the pit of her stomach.

Then came the ache. The hunger. The overwhelming urge to devour anything in her path. Her pulse raced with the need for food, no, the need for *flesh.*

It was then that an overpowering, delicious scent wafted past her senses. An aroma so delectable, so powerful it made her mouth water. She looked down with her now-black eyes at the morsel beside her, the shivering baby gargoyle who stared up at her in sheer terror.

"Nibbles," she said seductively through shark-sharp teeth, reaching for him, for his neck. Saliva gathered inside her mouth, the image of ripping the fur from his body, of the meat torn from his bones consumed her mind. She licked her ebony lips, breathing in the aroma of his blood pumping through his veins.

Myth

Just one bite, whispered the lamia inside her.

Fate obeyed the voice, the soft, soothing tones seduced her, wrapping her in a cocoon of velvet comfort. She had no control, no will against the silken speech purring into her ears, into her mind and into her fractured soul.

The wall of rock forgotten, Fate turned her body towards the little gargoyle, her black talon-like nails reaching for him, for his neck, for his tiny, warm, blood-filled body.

Just a little closer, the voice cooed as Fate's fingertips grazed the downy-soft hairs atop Nibbles head. *He's almost yours.*

Nibbles watched her with his wide, blue, orb-like eyes; whimpering quietly and trembling every inch she came nearer.

"Just a little closer," Fate uttered, her one hand grasping the rock wall, the other reaching for his neck. Then, in one swift movement, she took hold of the baby creature, enfolding her long, pale fingers around his throat. She drew him to her face, her mouth already open and ready to shred him to pieces.

Nibbles struggled and cried out, his immature wings flapping frantically, his stubby arms and legs flailing. But Fate could not hear him. Only the lamia was there, the black blood of Legend owned her, controlled her.

Growling, Fate brought Nibbles to her open mouth, her razor-sharp teeth readying to bite down on him like a ripe, juicy apple. She felt the fur tickle her lips as she plunged her face into his soft underbelly, and quickly, greedily, snapped her jaw shut.

Except all she felt was pain as her teeth hit something impenetrable. She opened her eyes confused, realizing that the tiny, fuzzy gargoyle she held just moments before had transformed.

In her confusion, the lamia withdrew, taking the hunger and cloud of obedience with it. It was Fate again, shaking and trembling with fear and guilt.

She gazed at the little creature in her hand, no longer covered in soft fur, no longer breathing or warm and cuddly.

Like the sentinel gargoyles that sat silent upon the building tops of high rises on the Surface, Nibbles had turned to stone.

Aura

Aura's long silver wings carried her over high on-yx mountains splashed amber with lava waterfalls, and above crimson clouds churning amidst the drifts of silvery ash. Far below, her troubles seemed small and disconnected. Her griffin mind was in control, animal instincts sharp and aware, overtaking her necromancer side. Distantly, she wondered about Vale…wondered where he was, how he was. She sent her thoughts to her necromancer brothers, Mezza and Slater, hoping they were not too far away to receive the message. They must have been quite a distance as she could no longer sense them, or their thoughts and feelings. Before Myth's illness and the loss of the Soul Nexus, Aura was able to connect with all her brothers and sisters, no matter the distance. The telepathic bond was so close and so strong; it was as though they were all of one mind. But now, joining with them was as unlikely as picking up a radio station from the Surface.

Warm recollections embraced her along with the thoughts of the Surface. Memories and images of her family began coming into focus. A mother and a father, these things emerged like a dream, fuzzy and barely on the surface of her reminiscence, but there nonetheless. Who had she been? Who missed her? How had she died?

All these questions sifted through her thoughts as she soared far beyond the protective wall of Necrosia. The Crimson Desert stretched thousands of miles ahead of her. Its unyielding, unforgiving landscape scarred by blustering geysers and winding streams of inky, black rivers.

Pearlescent rocks gleamed up at her from the Opal Isle, a place of prayer and worship used by the necromancers during stressful times. They'd gather there to pray for guidance and assistance from Myth. There, it seemed, they were closer to her, as though their words were heard the moment they left their silvery lips. It was as though the echo of their longings were carried upon a swift wind that led directly to their deity.

Few had ever seen Myth in person, in fact, according to her inherited memories, Aura could recall only one who had seen the elusive goddess with necromancer eyes: Kraton, the witchdoctor.

The well-travelled medicine man journeyed from the safety of the city over a century ago, purely in effort to seek out the necromancers' creator. Whether it was for his own spiritual well-being that he pursued this venture, it is unknown, but through his eyes and memories, Aura could witness the splendour of the mysterious divinity known only as Myth.

The ancients say that all beings are made in the image of their creator. In this case, it couldn't be further from the truth. Myth was not a necromancer; she had neither metallic, lustrous skin, nor sapphire hair and star-spun eyes. No, she was something else entirely. Something not of this dark world.

Her wings aching a little, Aura regrettably decided to descend and take a rest. Not having flown in quite some time, her endurance appeared to have lessened. She scouted the ground below for a good place to land, spotting a small field of white rocks fashioned into a round hedge.

The hot wind pressed against the downy-soft feathers covering her face, caressing her as only a balmy breeze could. She landed gracefully amidst a sea of opal rocks, arranged in circular patterns. Some had fallen over, but most of the rocky arrangement remained intact. It appeared to be an older section of the Opal Isles, one that had been abandoned centuries ago.

Aura could still feel the power of the place singing around her, a hum of power resonating through her necromancer core. As she changed into her true form, she settled down upon one of the larger stones. Curious, she placed a silver hand atop one of the nearest rocks, and closed her eyes.

At first she felt nothing conspicuous, but then a sensation of electricity ran through her fingers, up her arm and into her chest. It wasn't entirely unpleasant, but it was enough to startle her that she stole her hand from the spot with a gasp.

"What was that?" she inquired aloud, inspecting the simple white rocks surrounding her. Frowning, she did it again, setting her palm upon the smooth stone. Again, the quiet hum of electricity ran through her, pulsing and peaceful.

Intrigued, Aura lay down on the bed of rocks, curiously warm and comforted. Quiet fatigue pulled at her, lulling her to sleep.

It was then that the quickening began.

Part II

Reflections

Rory's new body was a mixed blessing. On the one hand, he had insurmountable strength and profound endurance. He was a superhero. A god. On the down side, he craved flesh. A lot of it. Over the last few days, he had no idea how many creatures he'd consumed, over a dozen at least — and still he was famished. The empty, aching hunger in the pit of his stomach was barely tolerable, almost driving him to madness. He'd even been reduced to devouring any rodents or insects that crossed his path.

It was suffering at its best.

He wasn't surprised though, he was in Hell. What else would he presume but misery? After all, he had damned many a soul to this place, so how could he expect to escape his own doomed destiny. He'd known, even while murdering those hundreds of nameless victims, that he was going to wind up here himself one day. And he was fine with that. It had been worth it. To live as an immortal for over a hundred years, to taste even a drop of the power he'd been serving up to Malus, was worth every soul he'd delivered into damnation. Now he was here, amid the gods of the underworld, living a respectable undead life.

He would miss living topside though; it was a ride he'd never forget. The girls, the thrill of the hunt, and the satisfaction of the kill.

Myth

The sacrifices to Queen Malus.

Excited delight danced through his body just then as he realized that he could very well find and meet his deity, Malus. Was she as glorious as he'd imagined her?

He recalled the day he'd come across the scroll that had led him to her, hidden up in the hay loft of his father's barn. Tucked beneath a loose floorboard, Rory had discovered an antiquated chest decorated with exotic and unfamiliar markings. Within it, he'd found his future. The scroll sang to him, seduced him upon first glance. Not knowing what it really was and the power it held, he kept his discovery a secret for many months before he found the owner.

Late one night, beneath the silvery glow of a Harvest Moon, Rory followed his older brother, his cousin, and one of their friends out to the barn as they retrieved the scroll. Unseen by them, Rory watched as they dragged three young women, their eyes, hands and mouths bound to a secluded clearing behind their house. Fascinated, Rory watched with wide, greedy eyes as his brother and his minions staked the girls to the ground amidst three large pentagrams, donned long black cloaks and began the ceremony he himself would eventually come to know intimately.

He watched every move, savored every scream and whimper, learned every word and utterance. This, he knew as the cold blade plunged into the chest of each girl, was his destiny.

The real treat was learning that upon the sacrifices, Rory would gain certain supernatural powers: eternal youth and immortality.

Limited immortality, anyway. Rory hadn't counted on Shelby and her boyfriend having such tenacity, such drive for vengeance against him and the evil deeds he'd done to Scarlet. Left for dead inside his own pentagram, he supposed he had reaped what he'd sown. Not that he'd admit it to anyone, of course, but he wasn't wholly without scruples; he fully understood that what he had done were the endeavours of a monster.

This is where I belong, he thought as he gazed around his new, hot surroundings, smiling wistfully.

The searing winds had subsided a little, though the geysers exploded higher and higher into the air.

Evening, he surmised after observing the rhythms of the realm over the last few days. He knew from experience that the giant worms were on their way once the sprays of water had reached their peaks. His mouth watered with the thought of all that meat, but the big worms looked a little out of his league. They traveled in packs, and while he was certain he could tackle one of them, six was out of the question.

His feet throbbed with every step, miniscule crystals of smelted sand slashing and biting his exposed skin. He had to rest soon, and seek shelter for the night. Despite his god-like qualities, he'd found his limit.

Ahead, he spied an arrangement of rocks and quickened his pace to get there. He'd rest there as long as his starving stomach would allow. Perhaps, if he was lucky, there would even be water.

As he neared the formation, an evil, horrible grin pulled across his face. It appeared that the gods favored him more than he'd thought as they'd left him a tender morsel slumbering upon a bed of white stones.

His breath held in his lungs, he approached the sleeping beauty, her silver skin gleaming, short blue hair fluttering softly with the breeze.

She looks so beautiful, Rory thought. *And so delicious.*

Blood. Bodies. The rotting corpses of his demon family lay scattered and torn inside the Great Hall. Kane fell to his knees, his world warping around him. How could this have happened? How? Who?

It couldn't have been his mother; she'd been destroyed in Necrosia months ago. Who else would have done this? Who else could? His warriors were among the strongest, the bravest, and most highly skilled in the lands. They'd been trained endlessly, masters in the talent of combat, yet here they were, fallen and slaughtered; they'd been torn down like a tornado would rip through a house of cards.

Kane's sapphire eyes sparkled with unshed tears as he absorbed the scene. The ivory walls were spattered scarlet, so much so that it was difficult to distinguish what the original color had been. The steadfast marble statues of long-dead Atlanteans, those who had dwelt within the palace before it had succumbed to the greatest earthquakes of all time, stood as silent witnesses to an event too horrific for real eyes to see.

There are no dead foes, Kane noticed, disturbed. Had none of his soldiers been able to bring down their enemy? Not a single one?

His sight fell upon one after another, demons he'd known his entire life. Demons he'd sworn to protect. Were there none left alive in the whole palace? Once, long ago, Dark World had swarmed with demons, the population greater than that of any other race in the realm. But now, it was of the few thousand left following his mother's genocide, it looked as though the race was the nearest to extinction it had ever been. Who was he to lead now? How could he be king of an inexistent species? It occurred to Kane in that moment that it was pompous of him to think that the Devil of Dark World had to be a demon. Simply because his father, a demon, had been the first leader? What made him think it was an irrefutable fact that the demons had to be the leaders? What made any of them inside Legion believe that? The leader, the king — or queen — should simply be someone who loved the people, loved the land, and was willing to lay their life down for it. In that moment, the hulking black demon felt more humbled than he ever had. He'd realized the game he'd been playing, the rules he'd been following, was all an illusion. It was all a crazy farce they'd fallen for since the dawn of time. Did the people really need to be led?

Kane searched each face, each loved one, his heart weeping with every loss. What kind of monster had the strength to do this? The ability?

Why had he left them? He should have been here, should have stayed to protect his people. He would rather have died fighting alongside his fellow demon than happen upon this sight. His selfishness had done this. His foolishness in following Fate.

No, he thought vehemently, defending his own actions. *I had to go after her. I love her.*

His fists clenched as he cast his eyes over the faces of the dead, searching for Deme, his friend and best tracker. Face after face, he could not find her. He did, however, identify many of the Council of Elders. All but two—Syphon and Ozen.

"Kane?" Vale's voice was distant, barely a whisper to his ears. He couldn't focus. Couldn't think.

Behind him, the banshee moaned, rousing him back to a fragment of his senses. He stood, gathering himself as best he could. "Bring her," he said quietly, stepping over the dozens of mutilated bodies. "This way."

He led them down a darkened hall, trying not to look at any one corpse too long. There were so many, the wounds so deep. Kane had never seen gashes so pronounced, lacerations so clean that they went right to the bone. He glanced into every doorway, hoping to find someone, anyone—alive. There were plenty of dead to be found; no one appeared to be spared from the carnage.

His heart sank as he approached Elder Ozen's dwelling, the door slightly ajar. A chill rolled over his dark skin as he pushed it open fully, hoping he'd not see the sight he least desired: the dead body of his adopted father. The scent of herbs and various potpourris drifted past Kane, kindling memories of the tender-hearted old demon. He'd been the one to take Kane in when his father was killed and his mother went on her murderous rampage. Ozen had picked up where his father had left off by teaching him of the old ways of the demons, of alchemy and dark magic, and how it could be used for good. He'd trained Kane both physically and intellectually. Ozen taught Kane how to be a leader, how to be a king. And not just a king, a good king. Kane hoped that one day he would make the elder proud.

Myth

Even amid the dark years as a prisoner inside the bloodstone mines, Ozen rarely left the prince's side. Kane bowed his head, wishing he could turn back time, wishing he could have one last moment with his adopted father.

"Kane!" Vale shouted suddenly, startling the prince into the present. Vale's eyes were wide with alarm as he stood pointing at something on the other side of a counter full of broken vials and spilt pots of herbs.

Hope seeped into the cracks of Kane's broken heart as he surged forward; praying Ozen had lived through this.

Upon reaching the other side of the counter, his blue eyes settled on someone alive—but it was not who he was expecting.

A surprised gasp escaped Kane's lips. "Deme!" Drenched in blood, the demon tracker blinked rapidly as though to focus more clearly on Kane, as though she didn't believe her eyes.

"Kane?" she uttered, her voice barely a whisper. "Is that really you?" Her bleary, amber gaze traveled back and forth between the demon prince and Vale.

"Yes, it is me," he said, kneeling by her side and assisting her to sitting. "What the hell happened here?"

She held her head dazedly, replying, "We were attacked."

"Yes," Kane replied patiently. "But by what?"

She shook her head a little, still confused, a large gash oozing from her right shoulder. Kane noticed Vale search the room, then reach for something on his left. He then handed Kane a random piece of cloth and indicated with a glance to the wound that he should use the fabric to cover it. He nodded, taking the makeshift bandage and applying it to Deme's ruby shoulder, adding gentle pressure to stay the bleeding.

"Deme," Kane pressed her when she hadn't yet answered his query. "Who did this?"

She frowned in effort to think clearly, then responded weakly, "It came through the front door, broke it down."

It? Kane felt his stomach tighten. *Just one thing did all this?*

"It?" Vale interrupted, his faced tight.

She shrugged, tears of sorrow and fear rolling down her face. "We...couldn't see it, it just came in, like the wind. Tore them all down in...seconds." She buried her face in her hands. Kane was just as unnerved to see her cry as he was to learn of this unseen beast that killed most of his demon family.

"Deme," Kane asked with bated breath. "How long ago was this? When did it leave?"

She stopped dead, as if she'd awakened from a dream and landed in a nightmare. "Oh no, Kane!" Her eyes were wide and wild, searching the room as she whispered, *"It's still here!"*

Shock and surprise awakened Fate from her ravenous craze as she held the tiny, stone gargoyle in her hands. "Nibbles?" she uttered, almost a whisper. "You okay?"

Guilt sickened her to the core; despite the fact that she knew she had no control over the lamia's monstrous possession. When the shade's hunger overtook her, a large part of her still remained, as though she were simply herself but ridiculously hungry. When the lamia possessed her, however, it was as if she all but disappeared inside, vanished while the beast did its horrible deed. She still retained the memory of what she'd done, but was powerless in the moment.

"Nibbles," she repeated, her bottom lip trembling as she stared into his once bright and caring eyes. She cast her gaze downward as she considered the fate of Ick and the rest of the baby gargoyles. Why had she risked their lives? She knew better than to drag them along on this impossible trek. Was she really so lonely, so selfish, that she had to endanger the lives of these sweet, harmless creatures?

She considered her options, knowing that she had no choice but to go on—but it was obvious she couldn't carry him down with her. She'd either fall to her death trying to hang on to him and the wall simultaneously, or worse, she drop him and he'd shatter into a million pieces. She was left with no choice. Carefully, lovingly, she set the Nibbles statue upon the narrow ledge and backed away, wrapping her arms around herself. She didn't deserve friends. She didn't deserve to have such wonderful creatures be loyal to her. On top of dragging him down the side of a treacherous mountain, she'd tried to eat him! It was a wonder he'd tagged along with her this far.

Fate sighed, her fractured soul heavy with sorrow and regret. She looked long into the distance, toward the soft, heavenly light shining skyward. The light called to her, beckoning. Something about that light was so…perfect. She couldn't name what it was, really, other than it was familiar somehow. Maybe it was simply because her soul was there, she couldn't say, but it compelled her like a moth to a flame. She just knew she had to press forward no matter what. She had to get to that light.

It was her destiny.

With one last longing glance at Nibbles, she continued down the mountainside—alone. Never before had she longed so much for companionship. This journey seemed so hard without someone to keep her going. She just needed someone to tell her it was all going to be okay, that she was doing the right thing and she wouldn't regret it. Why was it so hard to tell herself these things?

Her thoughts moved to Kane. She'd give anything for him to be here. Even though they hadn't known each other very long, he completed a part of her that was missing, that had always been missing but she just hadn't known it. She had never been one to fully believe in the notion of soul mates, but once she'd met Kane, she sure felt differently on the matter. And how odd that she would meet him here, in this place and not on the Surface? How is it possible that her soul mate is a demon when she'd begun her life on the Surface?

As Scarlet, she had been convinced of the human dream: courtship (with another human, of course), marriage, kids; the works. Somehow her fate had become intertwined with a creature she'd thought was completely fictional until only months ago. So, either she was crazy, believing that there was some higher power that had paired her long ago with a mythological creature, or life was just chaos trying to match itself up with some random puzzle pieces, hoping to get it right.

It made her head ache as she tried to sort it out. Philosophy, she decided as she neared the base of the mountain, was best left to the sages.

The air became thinner and pleasantly cooler the nearer she got to the bottom of the mountain. Mist crawled and curled around her ankles like a nest of phantom snakes, sending a chill up her calves. She was almost upon the labyrinth of stalactites, their brown tips piercing the miasma. Only a few more steps and Fate would descend beyond the curtain of grey cloud that veiled what lay below. She couldn't help but worry about what horrors might await her beneath the haze. Nothing came easy in this world. She didn't fool herself for a second into believing she'd just breeze through this next obstacle. It was easier to believe it would be near impossible. She hated to be so pessimistic, but at least that would keep her on her toes rather than trusting the unknown and have something jump out from the shadows and tear her to pieces.

She inhaled, summoning the courage to enter the fog. One tenuous step at a time she dove deeper into the unfamiliar, the thick mist devouring her legs and torso, then swallowing her whole as she took the last step. In the back of her mind, she reminded herself that she'd once taken on a pack of sphinxes, considered one of the most deadly creatures in the Dark World. She wasn't just a shade, after all, she was almost a lamia. Her thoughts fell back to the little girl in the pit, her untethered rage and the sheer lust to quench her hunger. Even Fate had been frightened of her; she'd witnessed pure savagery behind the little girl's dark eyes. Vrill had made it sound as though the lamia were unstoppable, powerful beyond any being in the realm.

Right now, she hoped he hadn't been embellishing. She needed all the raw power she could summon if she was to face the mysteries inside the labyrinth.

With a final step, she ducked her head beneath the vaporous shield, icy cool tendrils licking her neck and face like hungry ghosts tasting her, sampling her as if she was their next meal. She quickened her steps, hoping to clear the layer of thick smog sooner than later. It was only seconds that she'd been inside it, but already it felt like hours, her anxiety clawing higher and higher.

For a paralyzing moment, she wondered if there was no underneath, that the fog was simply part of the labyrinth. That would certainly make finding her way through far more difficult! Her poor little gargoyles! They could be wandering within the miasma, trapped and all alone. Guilt overcame her, not just about Ick and his buddies, but about Nibbles. Again she relived the moment where she'd tried to eat him. Poor thing, he must have been mortified!

But he'd turned to stone, evading her attempt. How odd that he, and probably the other gargoyles, can transform into solid rock. These small beings were truly remarkable. They'd displayed such amazing talents. First, they could make themselves invisible upon command, and now, alter into a statue. It made Fate wonder what other tricks they had up their cute, furry little sleeves.

Finally, the mists started to clear. Her nerves were frayed by the time she emerged on the other side. She'd landed on solid ground, grateful to be finished with the narrow pathway but uncertain as to what was in store for her next. The dense layer of cloud hung only a few feet over her head so now, instead of not being able to see the ground, she could no longer see the sky. Rather than vertigo, she was now dizzy with claustrophobia. She wasn't sure which was worse at this point. The entirety of Dark World had a rocky roof over it, but at least it was more than two feet over her head.

Fate swallowed hard, forcing herself onward. Ahead, though dark and gloomy, she spied a large archway made of stone. Fat, dark-brown stalactite trunks loomed all around her like a forest of trees, naked of their branches and leaves. At her feet, a micaceous shale path led the way, though slightly unstable and ragged to walk upon. She guessed that not many had traveled this path as it appeared wild with a healthy growth of lime-green moss peeking out from every possible corner. The scent of must and mildew turned her stomach a little, reminding her of an old bathroom that never got cleaned.

Though it was the silence that bothered her most. Everywhere else in Dark World, there was always some form of life twittering and twitching about. Whether it was a swarm of giant droning bugs, a colony of skittering meegles, or simply the blows and blusters of the volcanic range in the distance, Dark World always made some kind of noise, something that made it constantly alive.

Her favorite place was the mystical garden inside the hidden city of Legion. It was where tiny, winged pixies darted amongst emerald fronds, giggling as they played and taunted would-be visitors; it was where Arcanum, the large copper and gold dragon, snored peacefully within his makeshift cave and where a dark horse with flaming mane and tail, the Night Mare, huffed grumpily and whinnied with attitude whenever anyone came near.

Even the Crystalline Forest where she'd found Ick literally hummed with energy, the crystal trees singing some harmonic song as they gleamed and glinted against the reddish hues inside Dark World.

Everywhere she'd been had life of some kind, had music or racket to enliven the silence. But not here. She felt as though she was in some kind of void: like a snow globe where she was trapped inside with dwindling air, hands pressed against the thick glass watching the world go on without her, banging but no one can hear.

She'd honestly never felt so alone. Even in her darkest hours, when Rory had murdered her or when she'd awakened within Dark World, she hadn't truly been alone. Without Kane or her friends, she felt the cold hands of solitude grip her and hold her captive.

But I'm not truly alone, she realized as she was reminded of her gargoyle posse wandering somewhere around the labyrinth without her. Where were they? Had they landed somewhere dangerous? Were they in need of her help?

Or had they seen what happened with Nibbles?

No. She shook her head. *They were already beneath the fog, they couldn't have seen what happened. What...I tried to do to him.*

Guilt trickled through her as she thought of poor, little Nibbles up there on the mountainside. She wished desperately that she could have carried him all the way down with her, but it was hard enough navigating the wall by herself. As soon as she could, she'd find Ick and send him up to retrieve Nibbles' statue, or whatever he was now. Pausing in thought, she wondered if he would turn back into the fluffy little guy he was before, or if he was doomed to remain in some kind of stony stasis forever. She really felt she knew so little of this world, anything was possible.

Soon she arrived at the labyrinth's entrance, dwarfed by an enormous stone archway strangled with thick arms of dark, jade-colored moss. Before her lay three definite paths, all identical, though only one seemed to lead in the right direction: straight towards the ethereal light in the distance. Something bothered her about that. It was too easy.

Perhaps now is the time to take the potion Kraton gave me, she considered, nerves crawling through her stomach. She hated potions now, not only because they always seemed to taste horrible, but because she'd learned the hard way that few people in this world could be trusted. What if this one turned her into something else? What if it caused her to lose her memory again? What if...it killed her?

Fate sighed as she pulled the potion from her hip pouch, gazing at the metallic liquid sloshing within. She had no choice, as usual. If she wanted help getting through the labyrinth unscathed, she'd have to trust Kraton and drink the stupid potion.

Releasing the cork with a soft *pop*, she brought the tiny bottle to her dark lips, hesitating for just a moment, and then tipped her head back—and swallowed.

Rory

He watched the silver girl breathe slowly and steadily, his mouth watering as he drank in the very sight of her. She was beautiful, that was obvious. It was pity he'd have to kill her, but the hunger would not relent. It would not show him mercy.

Rory crept forward, stalking despite her peaceful slumber. The beast inside of him watched with impatient interest, curious of the girl yet almost too hungry to care.

What is she? Rory wondered, gaping at her gleaming skin. It was as though she was made of metal; shiny, polished chrome. Her blue hair, cropped close to her head, was styled fashionably, framing her beautiful face, edging the gentle slope of her delicate cheekbones.

Curled up on her side, she slept upon a large pearly rock, the slightest hint of a smile dancing on her silver-blue lips. He found himself wondering what she was dreaming about, what images swam through her mind at that moment. Had she once been human like him? Did she dream of the Surface, of her former life?

He felt a pang of jealously surge through him. If she had once been human, once lived above this world, why had she been chosen to reincarnate as a beautiful creature when he was damned a monster? He examined the visible network of black racing

Danielle Q. Lee

through every vein in his body with a sense of disgust as the hunger raged within, churning his blood with longing and an unquenchable lust for flesh.

He knew the answer. He'd been a monster on the Surface, maybe he had not looked like one as he did now, but he'd certainly earned the title. An ironic realization struck him suddenly. Perhaps this place had a twisted sense of humor all its own. Maybe the afterlife was one big lesson in karma. If so, he knew he'd gotten what he deserved.

His dark eyes fell upon the silver beauty once more. She seemed to glow, to emit some source of light he could not name. Was she an angel? He shook his head.

Angels can't be in Hell, he thought. *Can they?*

Fascinated, Rory realized the hunger had subsided for the first time since his arrival. Clouds seemed to part within his ravaged mind; there was a sense of himself, of his old self, peering through the darkness.

Who was this creature? This girl who seemed to wear her soul upon the outside?

Suddenly she exhaled, sighing as she stirred. He watched raptly, examining every curve and contour of her naked body, realizing in that moment that he could not—would not—harm this remarkable being.

Not yet anyway.

Aura

The dream took her home, to her Surface home. It was so clear and so real, she could have sworn that Dark World was the place of imagination and she'd already woken up and left it far behind. Her mother was there with her long caramel hair swaying with a light breeze, wavy tendrils kissing her lightly freckled cheeks. Green eyes, sharp as jade, gazed at her with the fierce affection only a mother could give.

And her father. A big burly man, rounded in the belly by decades of gourmet meals and a love of cherry pie. He held her so tight, so much so she thought she might break in two from the sheer force of his love.

She was their only child, so all their love was reserved for her. They'd cherished her, and she'd felt it as wholly as any human could. Her life had been near perfect, a blissful journey for the entirety of her sixteen years.

But all good things, it seems, must come to an end.

Aura winced inside her dream, hot tears welling into the corners of her tightly drawn eyes as she recalled that night...the last night of her human life.

"*Prom*," she thought. "*It was the night of my prom.*"

"Sarah!" her mother called from downstairs, a melodic lilt in her voice. "Are you ready yet?"

"Almost!" she answered, turning to take in one last look of herself before the graduation supper. Her short blonde hair, recently trimmed, was coifed into an elegant faux-hawk while a delicate gold tiara dipped low onto her forehead, forming a point just between her brows. Her green eyes blazed behind long, fake lashes and emerald eye shadow. Her dress, her pride and joy, was made of pink satin and her shoes dyed to match. Ruffled and puffed out like a long tutu, she had made it with her own two hands. It had taken weeks and many a sleepless night. Sleeveless but for a thin strand of white lace draping her upper arm, the dress made her feel just like a statuesque ballerina on her way to perform Swan Lake.

Sarah grinned at herself in the mirror, anticipation rising within. Tonight was the night she'd been waiting for. To look like a princess for one perfect evening. Like Cinderella.

"Sarah! Hurry up!" her mother shouted again, though more urgently. "We'll be late for the supper!"

"Coming!" Sarah stole one last look at herself, spun once before the mirror and dashed out of her room.

She descended the staircase, her mother and father at the base of the stairs gazing up at her with tears glimmering in their eyes.

"You look amazing," her mother spoke with a hushed reverence, as though she might break some enchantment spell woven upon her only child.

Her father's mouth opened to speak but he closed his mouth quickly and turned away pretending to cough as a single tear dropped from his lashes.

"You like it?" Sarah reached the bottom of the stairs and whirled once for them, her skirt rising and falling like the blush petals of a Canterbury Bell.

"I love it, honey," her mother said, smiling as she took her daughter into her arms.

"Daddy? Do you like it?" She turned towards her father, knowing his answer but expectant nonetheless.

Her father faced her finally, staring at her face as if absorbing the moment. He reached out and touched her cheek, replying, "You are the most beautiful thing I've ever seen."

"Alright, let's get going!" her mother proclaimed excitedly. "Into the car!"

The late afternoon light painted the summer trees with a golden hue, a soft wind was swaying the boughs ripe with emerald fronds. From her vantage in the back seat of their blue sedan, Sarah watched the myriad of houses pass by in slow motion. She'd always dreamed of this day, this night. Why it was so important, she couldn't say. It was the culmination of twelve years of educational imprisonment, and she was finally being set free. Not that she hadn't enjoyed school, she was just so excited to start her life. Ever since she was small she'd wanted to grow up, get married, and have children. It was her dream, her only dream. To some, it might seem a simple desire, one that most people in the world could achieve, but to her, it was everything. She had no passion for a career or travel; it was children that lit up her soul and the prospect of growing old with her best friend, her future husband.

"Almost there," her father commented as they turned into the parking lot of the high school. Blue and white balloons hung in an arch over the gym doors, inviting the grads into the ceremony like the gateway into Heaven.

Girls dressed in a rainbow of frilly gowns and boys outfitted in freshly-pressed tuxedos filed through the doorway, their eyes gleaming with barely bridled anticipation and bliss.

Laughter and music embraced them as they entered the gym of the high school, followed by smiles and warm hugs.

"Sarah!" Jennifer, one of her best friends, ran over and taking Sarah into her arms, almost knocked her over. "Come sit by me!"

Sarah grinned, allowing herself to be ushered to a large round table decorated with blue flowers and streamers. Her parents sat to her right, while Jennifer chattered incessantly on her left about who was wearing what and who came with whom. Sarah nodded politely but couldn't help wishing someone had asked her to the prom. It was the only thing she'd hoped for that didn't happen. She shrugged inside, realizing there was no one in particular she hoped would ask her anyways, it just seemed like a romantic tradition.

The meal, the dance, the reminiscing; it was all perfect. A wonderful evening that was over too soon.

"Now Sarah," her mother began with a serious tone as she stood before her, picking at imaginary lint on her daughter's prom dress. "I'm trusting you tonight."

Sarah gave the obligatory roll of her eyes, grinning. "I'll be fine, I promise."

Her dad cleared his throat, adding, "We know, sweetie, it's just prom night is notorious for drinking and driving, parties, and..." He stopped short, cringing as he uncomfortably alluded to a father's least favorite word when conversing with his child: sex.

Sarah shook her head, hugging each of them in turn. "Please, you know me better than that. I'll be fine. And I'll be good."

"Sarah!" Jennifer called from the parking lot. "You comin' or what?" She turned to her parents, ignoring the looks of worry on their faces. "Gotta go."

They nodded, pulling her in for one last family hug.

"I think it's here, on the left," Jennifer directed her boyfriend, Austin, onto a dirt road.

"Weird place to have a party," Sarah said from the back seat as she fiddled with the hem of her pink dress, a peculiar wave of nerves bubbling up inside of her. She wasn't usually the kind to be shy, especially around her friends, but a pit party wasn't exactly what she was hoping for her prom night. A nice dance in the school gym or reception hall; but a booze fest in the woods?

She sighed, forcing herself to stay positive.

Maybe it will be fun. She shrugged, unconvinced.

"It's the only place we could find where the cops wouldn't bust us for drinking," Austin offered, giving Sarah a grin through the rear view mirror. "And it's private property, so they can't say shit about what we do."

Sarah nodded politely despite the fact she couldn't stand Austin. Jennifer adored him though, thought he was just the hottest guy ever and was ecstatic when he'd asked her out.

Sarah watched the last rays of the sun dip into the horizon, leaving the sky to blaze orange and dark pink. Before long, the silhouettes of a thousand trees reached for the remnants of the day before they were plunged into darkness, overtaken by the night. The only light she could see now was the flickering rage of the bonfire as they pulled up to the party.

Hundreds of kids stood near the fire, their bright, youthful faces transformed before the haunting illumination. For a moment, Sarah felt lonely and wished she were at home with her parents. Most of these kids were her friends, but right now the people she'd gone to school with for the last three years felt like strangers. Even though she'd spent day after day with them, passing them in bright hallways and chatting between classes (and sometimes during) she suddenly realized that she didn't really know them at all.

"Hey, there's Karli and Taylor!" Jennifer pointed to a group of girls across the fire, dragging Sarah by the elbow as she pushed her way through the crowd. Sarah apologized to a guy whose beer sloshed, spilling on his hand as Jennifer nudged her way through. He didn't seem to notice though; his glazed eyes indicated he was beyond comprehension at the present time.

Sarah's shoulders were freezing, and she wished then that she'd brought along a jacket. She hugged herself, rubbing her arms with her equally icy hands.

"Cold?" a deep voice asked from behind her.

Startled, she spun around. "Oh! Um, yes," she replied as she looked up into a pair of amazing blue eyes.

Before she could protest, the mystery guy had already removed his jacket and set it on her shoulders. Residual warmth and scent embraced her, and it was all she could do not to sigh.

"I'm Josh," he said with a smile that melted whatever was left of the cold.

"Sarah," she replied with what was probably a goofy grin, but she couldn't see herself, so she didn't care. "You...go to our school?" She frowned, examining him but knowing full well she'd never seen him before. She definitely would have remembered him.

He shook his head, a rogue curl from his wavy black hair falling onto his brow, which he immediately brushed away. "Nope, I'm just here with a friend."

Sarah felt her heart sink a little. Was he here with a girl?

Like he'd read her mind, he added, "Do you know Mark Jacobs?"

She grinned, nodding, thrilled that he hadn't been someone's date. "He's in my Chemistry class."

Josh smiled back, pushing his hands into his jeans' pockets. "So, Sarah, can I get you anything? There's beer in a cooler over there." He tilted his head, indicating a blue cooler on the ground behind him.

"No thanks," she said uncomfortably. "I don't drink."

His eyes lit up a little. "I don't either, just asking."

They stood there a moment, enduring the awkward silence before Jennifer bounced up to them, already riding a buzz from something. "Hey! There you are!" she slurred, then devoured Josh from top to bottom with her eyes, inquiring, "Who's your friend?"

"Um, Josh...I'm sorry," Sarah started, "I didn't catch your last name."

He held his hand out to Jennifer, grinning as he replied, "Dean. Josh Dean."

Deme rose to her feet with help from Kane and Vale, her eyes scouring the depths of Elder Ozen's room as though the beast might be lurking behind every shadow.

"Why were you in here? What happened?" Kane asked, his brow furrowing in concern as he continued to hold her elbow, keeping her stable.

"I was gathering some supplies to help the injured...that thing swept through the room...so fast." She held her head in her hands, trying to make sense.

"What is this thing?" Vale asked, his voice shaky as his luminescent eyes glanced uneasily about the room.

Suddenly, Deme's mind seemed to clear, her amber eyes narrowing at the shade. "What's he doing here?" Her voice was low and venomous as she turned to Kane. "You have a soft spot for all shades now?"

Kane inhaled, he knew Vale's presence might prove to be a problem. "He's a friend."

"Shades are the enemy, Kane. We learned that long ago...the hard way." She glowered in Vale's direction. Kane knew her pain and hatred, all too well. Until recently, until Fate, hatred for shades was all he'd known. But now things had changed—he just didn't know how to help Deme understand. "There's no time to explain, but I promise," he said, setting a comforting hand on her shoulder, "I will."

She shrugged away, putting space between herself and the group as she wandered towards the door under the guise of scanning the hall for the mysterious beast. Sorcia, who had been silent up until then, released a pained moan.

"What's wrong with her?" Deme inquired coldly, barely glancing back at the banshee.

"We're not sure, she fell ill along the journey," Kane explained. "We thought Elder Ozen might be here. That he might know how to help her." Kane paused, then asked, "Is Ozen...alive?" He held his breath, bracing himself for the answer.

Deme nodded and Kane exhaled sharply, relief swelling inside. "He's in the garden, barricaded with the others."

"Others?" Kane asked, excitement coalescing with his relief.

"Yes," she said, continuing to monitor the hallway. "Just over five hundred of us."

The dark prince closed his eyes. "Out of five thousand?" The words barely came out, disbelief crushing him.

She turned her gaze to him, nodding once. "If you hadn't left, you'd have known this," she said accusingly.

Kane bowed his head. "I know. I am sorry."

Despite his obvious regret, Deme continued her wrath. "How could you leave us? How could you have left us without a leader?" She left her post by the door and stormed up to him, poking him in the chest as she ranted. "This is your home! These are your people!" Her eyes raged alongside her accusations.

Kane exhaled, turning away from her, shame overwhelming him. He knew it was wrong to leave, even if it was to pursue Fate out of love. Deep down, he'd been relieved to abandon his post—and he knew it. He didn't know what to say to Deme as she stood there, awaiting his response, her red tail wavering behind her in agitation. He didn't know what to say, so he said nothing at all. A simple 'sorry' wasn't enough. He'd disgraced himself, his father, and his people.

What he had to do was make it up to them. But how? Now that so many had been butchered. So many slaughtered? He shook his head, even if he'd been here, he too could have been among the dead, and what would that have accomplished?

"Let's go to the gardens," he said finally. "Sorcia needs to see Ozen."

Deme snorted her disgust in his direction before she spun about and stormed across the room. Within seconds, she was in hunter and tracker mode, temporarily burying her anger at him. "It makes a noise before it attacks," she explained. "It's only a few seconds before, but it's enough to get out of its path."

"What is it?" Kane wondered aloud, knowing Deme had already said it had been too quick for her to see, like the wind.

"I don't know," she replied, "but we have to move fast if we want to make it to the garden. Ready?" She turned to the group, pulling a long curved blade from the sheath on her thigh. "Let's go."

"My death?" Malus repeated with a roll of her eyes and soft chuckle. "My dear Maxim, why did you even speak with her? Why even listen to her drivel?"

"Please forgive me, your majesty," Maxim lowered his fiery white gaze, "she conjures within her cell."

Malus paused, raising one her brows. "Conjures? Explain."

The shade appeared nervous suddenly, glancing around as though the walls were spies. "She...goes into trances and speaks of things she cannot know."

"Cannot know?" Malus was getting impatient, what could the oracle shade possibly know that would be of interest to her. Weary, she crossed the room, back to her vanity, and leaned back into the blood-red velvet armchair.

Maxim cleared his throat, offering, "I implore you to come see her for yourself, my lady, I believe it will be in your best interest."

"Fine," Malus snapped, tired of this foolishness. "I will see her in an hour; bring her to my sitting room. I'll not subject myself to the stench of the dungeon."

The shade looked relieved as he bowed and left.

Malus turned to admire her new reflection once more, examining her granddaughter's face, her new face.

Everything is so perfect, she thought, then scowled. *Except for that damned oracle!*

Myth

She seethed inside; she'd worked so hard for this, so hard for everything. Why couldn't everything just stay, just be, the way she wanted it? Why was there always a catch? Like when she killed Lucifer, earned the shades loyalty. It should have been flawless, but no, there always had to be a snag. She had no idea that when she summoned the souls from the enslaved humans that the Guf would reclaim them. She had no idea that Lucifer had sealed the fissure to the Surface, entombing her and extinguishing the Crystal Pyramid. She'd known why he did it, of course, turning off the Crystal Pyramid made her vulnerable, weak, and…mortal. Her blood boiled with the thought that he'd spite her even after his death. For over three hundred years she'd had to remain isolated in the castle, imprisoned to keep herself safe from outside harm, sending her minions out to do her evil deeds when she'd rather do it herself.

But now, she gazed into Ever's blue eyes in the mirror, she had the one thing her husband never counted on: her true heir. She could feel the power racing through her veins, the unlimited magic simmering just below the surface of her ivory, silk-soft skin. But she was still mortal, still aging, and still susceptible to death. She had to open the crevasse to the Surface, she needed the sun to shine on the pyramid once again, only then would she be immortal, only then would she be the most powerful being in Dark World's existence.

Except for Myth, a tiny, undesirable voice whispered from within. Yes, Myth would always be stronger than her. Always more powerful.

Malus smiled, evil alighting upon her grand-daughter's face. She knew a secret, a secret that would destroy Myth forever and render Malus the sole power of Dark World.

Fate

The silver liquescence slid down the back of her throat and unlike the last potion she drank, this one was cool and soothing rather than a slow and blistering burn. It slithered through her system. For a moment, it felt as if nothing had changed, that the liquid just settled into her stomach and sat benign. Then images began forming within her thoughts, dancing like daydreams before her eyes as the tonic stirred inside her. She saw memories stream by, her eyes spinning with stars and turning a metallic hue. She heard soft whispers tickle her ears, hushed voices pacifying her. Fate was inside the hive mind of the necromancers, she felt their feelings, knew their world, and lived their lives.

For the first time, she felt as though she wasn't alone, like she had a million people standing beside her, watching her, loving her, holding her up. It was exhilarating. Then the flashes started, glimpses of something so beautiful, so intangible, she could hardly wrap her mind around it. It was a being. A brilliant being so bright and filled with inconceivable and unconditional love. It encompassed her. Embraced her. Accepted her.

It was Myth. She knew it with all her heart and soul. This being, this ethereal creature, was unlike anything she'd ever encountered in Dark World or on the Surface. She realized how everything and everyone in Dark World was linked together. With transparent threads, each of them was tethered to one another's souls. Even the darkest beings, like Malus, bore the mark of Myth's eternal grace.

Fate stood there, before the entrance to the maze, with tears of happiness rolling down her face. What joy the necromancers must feel! What bliss to be a part of a soul community!

Soon the pictures in her mind settled on a single thought, a single image: the labyrinth. She knew exactly how to get through it. Every curve, every turn, everything she'd encounter along the way. Strangely though, she could not see what awaited her at the end. She could not peer beyond the last curtain in her mind. She could not see the Guf.

Shrugging, she walked under the stone threshold, head held high and confident for the next stretch of her journey. The three winding paths before her no longer leered like poisonous snakes, but rather welcomed her to move along, to choose one. All would take her to her destination, all would have trials. Her mind's eye, with its necromancer link, urged her to take the middle road, the one that appeared to lead straight to the gleaming, white light in the distance.

"It can't be that easy, can it?" she wondered aloud, a niggle of doubt crawling through her.

Yes, it is, a voice sounded inside her head, startling her and halting her in tracks.

"Hello?" Fate asked, bewildered. "Is anyone there?" She looked around, certain she'd see someone hiding amongst the thick copse of stalagmite trunks.

Nothing. Eerie silence surrounded her.

"Well, that was weird," she said, moving on with hopes that she wasn't losing her mind completely. It wasn't unlike the time she heard the voices in the dark hallway leading down to Vrill's training chamber. Ghostly voices had frightened her, whispering, "*Privus liberum*" as shadowy arms reached out from the walls and pulled at her. It had been quite terrifying. This new voice was far less menacing, but no less startling.

"Privus liberaum," she muttered to herself, wondering once again what the strange words might mean. They'd haunted her since that day so long ago. They'd felt quite important at the time, as they did now. It was as if the voices were desperate for her to know the words. If only she knew the significance of the phrase.

Fate shook her head, forcing her attention on her new task: the labyrinth. She would need all her energy focused on making it through and getting her soul back. As much as she wished didn't have to do this, she felt the cold shadow of the lamia closing in on her. The incident with Nibbles on the side of the mountain was proof enough that she had to hurry. Almost as if the creature inside of her had heard her, her stomach relinquished a growl. She wondered a moment if she should stop and find something to…eat. Wincing with the thought of tearing apart some poor animal, she remembered the jerky-like meat she'd put into her pack. She retrieved it and while it wasn't exactly what the monster inside of her wanted, it soothed the ache in her belly.

When she was done, she took her first tentative steps onto the middle path. At first, the labyrinth walls were made of the stalagmites, formed closely together, shoulder to shoulder. But the further she went; the pillars began to fuse together, entangling themselves together to form a net-like wall. Like lattice. Like a jail.

Nerves fluttered in her stomach, and for the first time since embarking on this journey she was truly afraid. Something about this place didn't feel right. Something was off, but what? The path was so clear inside her mind, like she'd already been there and back again. With the exception of the entrance to the Guf, she knew every turn, every stone, every...monster.

"Monsters," she whispered, realizing she'd have to fight each of the creatures to move forward. It was then she realized that only the path itself was easier, but not clear of dangers.

The first of the beasts manifested inside her thoughts, a great, massive spider, fangs dripping with venom, the cocooned bodies of hundreds strung about his den like Chinese lanterns. According to the necromancers' memories, he wasn't far from her location.

She sighed, wondering again if all of this was worth it. Did she really want her soul back that badly? Was it really worth all this trouble? She knew it was. She didn't want to end up like the little girl in the pit, a rabid shell of herself. She didn't want to kill for flesh any more than she'd wanted to kill for souls. A fleeting sense of regret and anger surged through her blackened blood.

This was all Rory's fault, and her own as well for trusting him. But he'd lured her, used her innocence against her, baited her with his charm—then murdered her. The murder part didn't piss her off as much as the whole damning part did. To kill her was one thing, but to send her to Hell was just plain rude.

Fate brushed off her anger and resentment; neither would help her through the maze. She set her sights long into the distance, focusing on the beam of heavenly light reaching for the heavens, and put one foot in front of the other.

The body count continued to pile up as they made their way to the garden. Hundreds of demons, slain and torn down in mid-stride, lay in their midst. Deme led the way, her jaw locked and eyes set forward, avoiding the mass of dead figures at her feet. Kane, however, could not ignore them. The multitude of young and old, friends and family; it was so much more than his heart could take.

What could have done this? Kane wondered, the black diamond sword in his hand giving him little confidence. *What monster could slaughter so many, so quickly?*

"So, this creature, what does it do—exactly?" Vale asked the prince in a low voice, his expression a combination of revulsion and anguish as he waded through the carnage.

Kane looked back, beyond Vale, to see how Sorcia and the necromancers were fairing before answering. He observed Mezza and Slater carrying the banshee princess carefully and without much trouble despite the multitude of obstacles. Physically, these two were impressive, their silver chests and arms a mecca of muscles, but it was the inexhaustibly tender expressions they wore that impressed Kane the most. Gratitude warmed his heart a moment, thinking how invaluable these two kind-hearted beings had been over the course of their journey. They'd been nothing but loyal, undeterred, and never uttered a single complaint. Kane had to hand it to the necromancers; they were a strong and benevolent race.

Vale repeated himself, "What signs are we looking for again?"

Kane answered Vale's query, "Deme says it makes a noise before it attacks, other than that, I do not know."

At this, Deme responded without pausing her forward march, "It's invisible, as far as I've seen, but begins as a pressure and then a loud...*humming.*"

Vale scowled. "Humming?"

Stopping in her tracks, Deme spun around, fangs exposed. "Yes, humming. A deep resonance." She glared at him before turning and continuing.

Kane suppressed a sigh. He understood Deme's frustration, there were times he wanted to take Vale by the neck too, but her rudeness was wearing thin on his patience.

Unfortunately, Vale was undeterred by her temperament, and kept pressing her for information, asking, "What happens after the, uh, humming, as you put it?"

Deme paused, not facing him as she said, "Death."

Vale swallowed, a flicker of fear shadowing his illuminated stare. Kane watched him a moment, wondering how a being such a him, a shade, an undead creature whose kind has had the upper hand in nearly every recent battle in Dark World's history, could be so afraid of the unknown. Was it his human side, the remnant memories of a life so fragile, so prone to illness and injury, that continued to dwell inside him?

This puzzled Kane, how Vale, after so many years in this underworld, an entire century, could still be held by the boundaries of his Surface life. Did he not know how powerful he was? How his kind had slaughtered so many? If he'd seen the massacre of the first wave, the initial attack Malus had ordered, perhaps the shade would not harbor such fears. Nothing could stop the white-haired humans; their eyes alight with vengeance and power. The Crimson Desert undulated with them as they ran across its back, swarmed like locusts devouring anything in their path—and all with their bare hands. They'd consumed hundreds, thousands, of inhabitants in a single day. The rest, the poor souls that lived through the first attack, were taken to the pits to mine blood-stone for Malus and her army of darkness.

So how was it that this should-be fearless creature be so consumed by dread? Did he have so little faith in himself, in his abilities?

Then Kane thought of Fate, her inherent kindness, her warmth, and capacity for love. The way she'd scooped Ick up into her arms like a baby and coddled him, never once a threat to him, denying the wicked shade alter-ego that begged her to tear open his chest and ravage his soul. She'd chosen to be noble, to side with good instead of evil. Until he met her, he was convinced that the hunger of the shade overshadowed the human side completely, leaving no trace of the being that had once dwelled on the Surface.

But he had been so wrong about her in the beginning, so terribly wrong.

His heart tore a little at the thought of her. How he missed her, her touch, her scent, her kiss. What he wouldn't give for all of this to be over with, to already have the scrolls in his possession, have the races gathered, and the Crystal Pyramid reignited. What would the world be like once he'd given Dark World back its light, its magic? Would they recognize their second chance? Would they begin their world anew? Forgiving old wounds and moving on to live a life with a fresher, kinder perspective?

He hoped so, with all his heart, he hoped so. His cerulean eyes gazed about the dead with a mixed sense of hope and dread. What if all this was for naught? What if no one learns from this? What if his descendants, his family, continued to ignore the sacrifices he and so many others made for them to live their lives free?

What if...?

His thoughts were suddenly shattered into a million pieces as a horrible noise; an overwhelming hum took over the hallway. He dropped his sword, pressing his hands to his ears. "What is that?" he hollered to Deme, who had dropped into a crouch, eyes scanning their perimeter wildly.

Kane could hardly stand the pain resonating inside his head, the pressure building and building, his head feeling as though it was about to split apart. Even Mezza and Slater had dropped their beloved princess, brought to their knees by the throbbing sound.

"Deme!" Kane shouted.

She only turned her eyes to him, wild with fear, as she screamed, "Run!" Her amber eyes blazed with fear and pure resolve. Kane could only manage one quick glance back to his small posse before facing forward and running. Mezza and Slater had shifted into two large silver panthers; Sorcia lay inert upon one of their backs. Kane couldn't tell one from the other, but in that moment he felt confident that they were doing everything they could to ensure both the princess's survival as well as their own.

The walls shook around them, the pictures flying off and striking them as the mysterious force took over the hallway. The floor quaked beneath them, making the bodies of the dead tremble and writhe as though coming back to life. Kane put his hands to his ears, wincing from the pain of the low frequency hum. It was like being in the center of a hurricane, a storm of unfathomable strength.

Kane fought against the powerful wind with all his might because simply trying to walk, to stay upright, was nearly impossible. Debris struck him hard in the face; he could barely open his eyes to see what it was around them. He so desperately wanted to turn around and see how the necromancers were fairing with the princess. Strangely, he was even quite concerned about Vale. Despite their animosity towards one another, he realized that there was a true camaraderie developing.

He considered the bodies beneath him, knowing they'd been subjected to the same unnameable monster, yet it seemed as though they'd been cut down in an instant. Kane wondered if they'd endured this same scenario. Something inside told him that the invisible beast had wasted no time killing his people. Something told him that this time—the monster was toying with them. Why? What could a nameless monster gain from playing with his prey?

He had to duck as a table flew by, smashing into a wall behind him. This thing was strong, so very strong. It could kill him and his friends with a single breath. What was it waiting for? What was its strategy?

Ahead, Kane could distinguish Deme forging through the whirlwind, her body at an awkward angle as she fought against the gale.

He looked past her, to a door. They were so close. The entrance to the garden was only a few feet away. Kane wondered what this thing was and why it had been unleashed upon him and his city? A dark thought crossed his mind; there was only one person vindictive enough—and powerful enough—to unleash a beast of this magnitude: Malus.

But no, he thought, *she's dead...isn't she?*

With his eyes closed but for a narrow slit, Kane recognized the door to the garden. *We're almost there! If we can just get...*

His thoughts were cut short as a horrific blast sounded around them, as loud as a thousand eagles shrieking all at once. Kane fell to his knees, his sanity threatened as the noise pierced his head.

Then, silence.

It was just gone.

And so was Vale.

While the mazes she'd come to know on the Surface were usually formed of leafy hedges, corn, or even sunflowers, this one consisted purely of stalagmites; sharp spikes of hardened limestone. But somehow they'd grown sideways as well as vertically, locking the would-be maze traveller within impenetrable walls of solidified minerals.

The rock labyrinth had an eerie, hollow quality to it. The air was so still, it was almost stifling. The ceiling of fog prevented any connection to the outside world. The familiar had become a memory, leaving Fate feeling as empty and alone as the day she'd fallen into the darkened world.

However, amid the solitude and silence, she sensed a presence within the darkness. It was a new, higher consciousness: the necromancers' unified soul. Their memories sat nestled inside her, like a treasure box she'd opened, flooding her mind with silver light. She realized then that Kraton had not conjured up a potion, a simple vial filled with various magical substances, but given her his own blood to drink. To anyone else, it might seem gross to digest the blood of another, but this was a gift like no other — one that Fate desperately hoped to keep forever. The silver liquid she'd drank had enhanced her somehow, enlightened her in a way she couldn't hope to achieve with a thousand years of study. The blood not only held power and wisdom, it contained all of the nec-romancers' combined experiences and memories.

The necromancers' memories, good or bad, were not judged, only observed by the beings. They did not believe in things, they knew of them. Their deity, Myth, had bestowed upon them the gift of divine knowledge and grace. They had no fear of death because they knew death did not exist, only transfor-mation. True, loss still saddened them, but they embraced change, knowing that it was the only way to grow. However, with Myth's accelerating ailment over the last few years, the necromancers had grown weaker in their faiths. The connection to their god-dess, and to one another, was failing.

Fate wondered how it would be to be tethered to their thoughts. An entire community chattering inside her mind. She could see how that would be tiring. The lack of privacy might get a little unnerving at times. How did Aura and Vale have any private time? Was there a switch to block out the rest of the necro-mancers? Fate frowned, making a mental note to ask Aura once she saw her again.

Ahead of Fate, the maze veered sharply to the right, but curved; strange considering that most labyrinths she'd ever seen were designed utilizing right angles; and she'd expected a choice of either left or right. Shrugging, she continued, assuming it was the correct path. Her necromancer memories didn't agree or disagree, which left her feeling a little disori-ented. Was it possible that the maze had been changed somehow?

"I guess I just have to trust it," she said under her breath, pressing forward. Again she wished she wasn't alone. It would have been nice to have someone else to confide in, to assist in making decisions. Ick and his buddies would be an especially welcome distraction from the smothering quiet. Dark World was rarely silent like this, so far as she'd observed.

From her inherited recall, she knew that the oversized spider should be near. Through the mind's eye of the necromancers, she could see that its weakness was in its legs, the joints specifically. Dreamlike images showed her a group of silver beings taking down the large beast by striking it at the point where the leg bent, specifically the gap in the joint. She nodded, knowing what to do though still nervous.

"He should be right about...here." She slowed her pace as she rounded another corner, expectant butterflies taking flight inside her belly. Her luminous, infrared eyes searched the area, seeing no movement or anything amiss. There was, however, an odd clearing, a perfect circle of emptiness amid the lattice of entangled stalagmites.

Nothing looked familiar, nothing at all. Again, she felt a sickening sensation go through her. The necromancer memories were not aligning with what she was seeing. She searched her new memories, hoping to find something that would explain this phenomenon. But all she could draw forth was a clear path to the Guf, littered with a few beasts to overcome. What lay before her was not in her thoughts, not part of the necromancers' vault of reminiscence.

She stood there, undecided as to what to do next, unsure as to whether she should retrace her steps. There didn't appear to be another exit from the strange circular enclosure, yet something compelled her forward. Something about this situation was now familiar, she realized as she took a few steps inside the circle.

The reddish sands crunched softly beneath her feet as she reached the center; there she gazed about, trying to place where she'd seen this scenario before. Suddenly there was an odd noise behind her, a groaning of sorts. Fate spun around just in time to witness the entrance seal shut with growing limbs of stalagmite.

"No!" she yelled, lunging for the only exit. But it was too late; she'd been entombed within the circle. "Dammit," she said quietly as nearly all hope escaped her. What had she done? Why was she even here?

Now she was trapped. No one would ever find her.

Why didn't I just stay in Necrosia? She thought as she pressed her back to the jail-like structure and slid to the ground, burying her face in her hands. *Maybe they could have found a cure? Maybe I could have fought the lamian blood in my veins? Maybe…*

She knew it was no good. The only way anyone knew to rid them of the curse was to get their soul back. Only now, she was stuck. Trapped inside walls of rock, her soul far away in the Guf. Panic raced through her body, threatening to consume her completely.

Dark World was riddled with nightmares that were all too real for comfort. Though many a wondrous thing had come of this place, specifically Kane, Ick, Aura, Vale, and countless other friends she'd met that she now considered family.

Family, she thought wistfully, her Surface family entering her mind. How she missed them. She'd been so lucky, and always knew it, that she had such loving parents. Even her brother, Greg, was tolerable at times. She laughed inside as she recalled all the bickering and torment they enjoyed with one another. And her sweet Shelby. True, Scarlet had only one friend up there, but sometimes one was all a person needed. One true friend.

Fate wondered how they would treat her if they knew her now. Now that she was an undead monster of sorts that had slain beasts many times larger than her. Would they still accept her? Would they treat her as before?

She sincerely doubted it. She knew that she was different now, inside and out. She'd learned of death first hand. She'd learned what it was to kill another living creature. No one was left unchanged after something like that.

Sighing, she leaned against a wall within the circle, scrutinizing her lack of options. How was she going to get out of this one? It was indeterminable just how high the walls were as they were literally cut off at the top by the thick fog. Even if she decided to climb them, she'd surely be lost trying to find any way out as the mists concealed the way in every direction.

Fate closed her eyes, searching through her new necromancer memories. Perhaps the answer lay with them. Maybe they'd experienced this, maybe...

Something growled. Low and menacing. Only a few feet before her. Glowing red eyes appeared between the dark slats in the latticed wall, hundreds of them. Like...spectators.

Myth

Suddenly she realized the purpose of this circle.
It was an arena.

Malus scrutinized the memories of the princess, the granddaughter whose body in which she'd stolen to bury her soul deep inside. Flickers of her existence streamed behind Malus's eyes. Ever's life had been so limited, so sheltered due to her underground captivity in Legion. She skipped over the girl's years of youth, determining that they were of little use to her. The queen paused on certain conversations the princess had exchanged with her father, and specific elements within the subterranean city. Particularly the garden. There was something of great interest to her there, or rather, someone.

She scanned the layout of Legion, learning for herself how to get to certain places. One day, when she felt it was safe, she would go inspect the dwelling for herself — and retrieve her prize from the garden.

The queen sneered as she considered her latest gift to the demon community, and she wondered how it had been received. Surely they could not have been prepared for such a creature, since it had not been released from its imprisonment for several centuries. She'd kept him, among the others, her own little secret. Imprisoned until such a time arose that they were needed — like now.

Knowledge was true power, she'd realized that eons ago when first planning her husband's execution. Had she not happened upon his bible, she wouldn't have been able to devise a way to turn the humans into shades, thereby stealing their souls and creating an army of undefeatable undead. True, her plan turned out to have flaws; such as the souls she'd planned on utilizing herself had instead returned to the Guf, but she was not deterred. They'd still followed her with unshakable loyalty.

The males, that is. The females were a bit more resistant. They had often needed a bit of persuasion to increase their loyalty. If the shades were three-born, they were usually fine; however, two-borns were unpredictable. A single-born, however, was exceedingly rare since the ritual on the Surface explicitly required three sacrifices.

During the Uprising, Malus had to be certain her silver-haired soldiers were completely loyal, so she had a test in place for every newborn brought to the Blood Palace. It was simple, those who passed the trial, lived. Those who didn't — were fed to her favorite pets.

A soft knock at the door stirred her from her reverie. "Enter," she responded, rising from her seat before a raging fireplace.

"My Lady." Maxim bowed before fully entering, dragging a chain behind him to which the oracle was attached by a thick, steel ring around her neck. Her long silver hair was a tangled mess, her face filthy with black dirt and dried blood from which Malus surmised the oracle had received plenty of beatings from the other prisoners. Her clothes were tattered and torn, hanging from her starved body. Malus gave her a wide grin, adjusting the gold straps of the gown hugging her new, youthful body.

"Oracle," she said, sashaying down the steps of her raised sitting room. "How nice to see you."

Sybil did not acknowledge Malus as she kept her head down, face hidden beneath the curtain of mussed silver hair. Maxim frowned at her insubordination, yanking hard on the shackles to elicit the appropriate response for the queen.

Malus ignored the shade's defiance. "Maxim here tells me you have some news for me," she ventured, though contemptuously. "Please, enlighten me as to your psychic revelations."

At first Sybil did not move or speak; then slowly she raised her head to Malus, hatred burning in her stare. "Why would I tell you anything?" she spat.

Malus chuckled, playing with a strand of Ever's long white hair. She took a few more steps towards her prisoner before answering sweetly, "Because I've heard you have seen things about me, and frankly, while I personally believe your predictions are completely ridiculous, Maxim here has expressed a deep concern for my destiny, the destiny you're spouting is doomed." With that, the queen quickly closed the distance between them and took a handful of the oracle's hair within her fist and yanked Sybil's head back to glare into her glowing white eyes, adding in a low demonic voice, "So if you have something to say, say it now!"

Fear now flickered behind the shade's eyes, her broken body weakened as she fell to her knees before Malus. "I saw your death," she spoke quietly.

Malus backed away, examining her manicured nails in feigned boredom. "And? How was I to die? Who was going to kill me?" she inquired with a mocking tone as she climbed the stairs to once again seat herself before the fire.

At this the oracle smiled. "I'll never tell."

Josh took Sarah by the hand, leading her away from the bonfire. His skin was warm and soft, sending shivers of excitement up Sarah's spine. She felt herself tremble a little, wondering where this was leading. She'd never had a boyfriend before, never even kissed a boy (other than her cousin, Edward, but that doesn't count).

"Where are we going?" she asked, not really caring but curious.

He turned his head to answer, not stopping his forward quest along the wooded path, "Just a little ways away from all the noise. To get some privacy."

She smiled in spite of herself, but something uneasy squirmed inside of her. She wasn't sure she liked the idea of being alone with some boy she'd just met. Even though he seemed really nice, and he was very cute, she knew better than to put herself into a bad situation.

Heeding her instinct, she spoke up, "Actually...I just want to go back. If that's okay."

He didn't stop, and his grip tightened on her hand as he continued to lead her into darkness. "It's not far now," Josh said, his voice a little firmer now.

Suddenly his jacket felt like a ton of weight on her shoulders, prickles of intuition stinging her body. "No thank you," Sarah replied a little louder, adding an edge of annoyance as she yanked her hand free from his. "I'm going back." She glanced behind her, the orange flicker of the bonfire was so far away now, nearly extinguished through the thick trees.

Sarah turned on her heel and started to head back towards the light and cacophony of partiers.

"Sarah, don't you want to hang out?" Josh called out to her as he turned to follow her, his voice a mesh of seduction and suppressed anger.

"Nope," she replied, cursing under her breath as finger-like branches scraped at her bare arms and nettles scratched her ankles.

Suddenly she heard his pace quicken behind her, his feet pounding the forest floor as he raced up behind her. Before she could even let out a scream, he'd grabbed her around the waist with one hand and covered her mouth with the other. "I think," he whispered into her ear, "you'd better just shut up and come with me."

Fear threatened to consume her, but rage won in the end. Sarah opened her mouth wide, clamping down on the soft part of his palm with her teeth, the taste of warm copper sliding past her tongue. At the same time, she bent her right leg and kicked it back with full force into his knee, hearing a loud crunching sound as her heel made impact. He screamed, setting her free as he doubled over in pain.

Sarah grinned in the dark as she stared at the shadow writhing on the ground before her. "When a lady says no, she means no," she said matter-of-fact as shrugged off his jacket and tossed it on his moaning form; then she turned about and head back to the fire.

Once she returned to the party, she was intent on finding Austin and Jennifer in the hopes of getting a ride home. She wasn't interested in staying now that she'd nearly been assaulted and, consequently, crushed some guy's kneecap.

Sarah scanned the drunken crowd for her friends but couldn't locate them anywhere. Everyone was already completely inebriated and incapable of driving. She shivered with the cold air, despite the raging inferno before her, wishing she hadn't come out here at all. Tears burned behind her eyes as she realized she might not be able to get home tonight. She didn't want to ride with anyone drunk and she sure as hell wasn't going to ask Josh for help.

She knew her parents would come get her if she called, but quite honestly she had no idea where to tell them she was.

If only I'd listened to my parents and taken Driver's Training last month, she thought with disdain. *Then none of this would be an issue.* Of course, then she would have been forced to steal one the vehicles before her; but at this point, she wouldn't have cared about the consequences. She considered the notion further, wondering if she should attempt it. She knew the basics of driving, but not enough to cruise home on a dark highway in the middle of the night. In the end, she decided it was far more dangerous for her (and everyone else on the road) to drive herself home.

She filled her lungs with the cool, fresh air, centering herself. *I'll just walk;* she decided as she marched through the crowd and started down the rustic country road that led to the highway. *Then, I'll find a road sign, call my parents, and they'll come get me.*

The farther she got from the party and the fire, the darker—and colder—the night became. If not for the moon, she'd be wandering in complete darkness. Her nerves frayed more and more with every step as bushes rustled around her and the wind whispered through the trees like a formless phantom. She hadn't realized just how alive the environment could be when left unpolluted by city noise.

She rubbed her shoulders with her icy hands, hoping the friction would create just a little warmth. Suddenly, she felt stupid for leaving the party without telling anyone; but who would remember anyways, they were all too drunk to stand up properly.

Sarah suppressed a frustrated growl. She hated this entire predicament. It was like those scenes in a cheesy B-movie where the stupid girl makes yet another stupid decision and gets herself killed by the werewolf hiding in the bushes. Why hadn't she spoken up when she had the chance? Why had she allowed herself to be driven out to the middle of nowhere by a guy she didn't really know? She knew Jennifer, of course, which was why she assumed she'd be safe, taken care of for the evening.

What a sad waste of a graduation night, she thought. It was supposed to be one of the best nights of her life. She cursed her romantic notions, her idealistic ideas of what should be. The dark truths of life always seemed to overshadow her hopes and dreams.

In a way it made her bitter, that reality felt obligated to smother the goodness that comes from being young and naïve.

The darkness closed in on her as a thick cloud drifted over the moon. She trembled a little, reaching for her phone in her tiny satchel. She had no choice but to call her parents now, knowing they'd be so worried for her. Sarah touched the screen, initiating the phone application. The phone's light illuminated her surroundings and for a moment she breathed a sigh of relief. Why hadn't she thought of this before? Her phone could be her flashlight.

She hit the call button, waiting for her mom or dad's loving voices to answer but was abruptly cut off by an automated operator. She had no signal out here. Nothing. No way to contact her parents or call for help.

Anxiety started to claw at her, and she thought she should turn back. Maybe she could still find Jennifer and Austin, maybe they were just making out in the car or something. Still, they'd definitely be too drunk too to drive.

Then, up ahead, a car went by, its stream of head-lights flashing past. She wasn't far from it at all! Nearly running, Sarah used her cell phone to guide her towards the highway. From there, she'd flag someone down and ask for a ride to the nearest gas station. She hated the idea of allowing herself to be picked up by a stranger, but she was becoming desperate and considering her present state of mind, the person giving her a lift might be the one in danger if they tried anything.

Elated with her new plan, she ran along the old dirt road towards salvation—unaware of the car coming up behind her.

Fate

So many red, glowering, judgmental eyes were staring at her through the slats of interlaced stalag-mites. Fate instinctively knew whose side they were on, who they wanted to win—and it sure wasn't her. If not her, then who? What new fiend was she about to meet? What novel beast would she attempt to slay?

With Dark World, you just never knew what you were going to get. She was going to have to fight her way out of this place—and something told her it wasn't going to be easy. For a moment she felt be-trayed by the necromancer memories. They'd im-planted a series of images inside her mind that she assumed would guide her safely through the labyrinth and into the Guf. Perhaps the maze had changed? She couldn't see the necromancers deliberately putting her in harm's way.

Or would they? She'd been double-crossed before, by the demons when they'd given her the lamia curse. Why should the necromancers be any different? Everyone in Dark World seemed to have their own agenda, their own devious plot for revenge or spite, so why wouldn't Kraton betray her?

She didn't have time to contemplate the answer to each of her questions as the ground had begun to quake beneath her feet. The earth before her split in two as something rose up from under the ground—something very, very big.

I can do this. I've taken on creatures that no one in Dark World could. I'm a supernatural being, forged by dark magic and…

Her internal pep talk was cut short as a huge beast was birthed from the soil. It was unlike anything she'd ever seen with her own eyes, but the necromancer memories whispered a name for the gargantuan fiend: Behemoth.

He roared as he pulled himself to standing, his deafening, guttural bellow sounding for miles. All Fate could do was stand there, gaping at the monster, mouth ajar. He appeared to be made of black roots, hundreds of thousands of strands of thick roots wound together to make one very big beast. He had no facial features to speak of, other than a mouth which displayed row after row of what resembled shark's teeth. His hands had no real fingers, just four long, razor-sharp claws. And he was so big! Fate was no taller than half the height of his shins. He was more than enormous — and he looked really pissed.

She seriously contemplated crying as surviving seemed completely and totally impossible. Maybe he'd let her surrender? Just say, "Uncle" and be done with it.

She sincerely doubted it.

Behemoth roared, the ground shaking violently beneath him, throwing Fate off balance. He was so large that his voice alone could knock her over. She was thoroughly anxious now, sure she was undead, but it didn't mean he couldn't squish her!

As though reading her thoughts, Behemoth raised one of his trunk-like legs and slammed it down, aiming for her. Fate quickly rolled out of the way as the ground behind her began rocking and splitting from the force of impact.

Well, that's one thing I've got over him, she considered with a thread of relief. *I'm quicker.*

She needed to formulate a plan; she needed to find his weakness. He was slower than her, but that wasn't a way to take him out. Everything had a weakness, a soft spot. She examined the brute towering above her, scrutinizing his form. He had knees, maybe she could find a weapon and...but there was nothing, absolutely nothing within the arena that could help her. It was just an empty circle with a sandy floor.

Before she could strategize further, he closed his fists and brought both down onto her location. She dove out of the way just in time, disrupted dirt spraying in all directions. Fate looked to where she had just been and saw that a large crater had taken her place. Cheers and giggles erupted from behind the walls where the owners of the red eyes so eagerly anticipated her demise.

Behemoth opened his maw and thundered an ear-splitting roar; spittle flying as he voiced his frustration, enraged that he'd missed her again. She knew she couldn't keep this up forever, just running from him, circling the arena like a mouse evading snake inside a cage. She'd have to try to bring him down, but how? She was so small, and he so big, there was no way she could defeat him.

She wanted to give up. The cackling crowd behind the wall wanted her to give up. Maybe it would be better this way; maybe she should just let go. There would be no shame in it; no one would even know. No one, including Kane, really knew her whereabouts.

Fate lowered her head, closed her eyes and waited. It wouldn't take much for the beast to end it all with just one mighty swing of his fist.

Suddenly, from the depths of her new necromancer-recall, a quiet voice whispered. A very loving and familiar voice said, *"You can do this! You are special. Different. You are not just made from magic...you are the magic."*

"Vrill," Fate replied, close to tears as she felt his presence within. She had to admit she really loved this necromancer blood.

Behemoth was winding up for another massive blow when Fate felt her power rising within.

"Get ready, big boy," she said with a wicked smile as she willed the magic forth, feeling her blood begin to boil as she summoned black energy from her core. In a split second, a crackling sphere of ebony emerged from her torso, hovering in the air as it awaited command.

But she wasn't ready just yet. Fate then beckoned the dormant powers of the shade, manifesting a shield of white light around her body.

Now she was ready.

"Go," she uttered through her black lips, flashing a snarl at the slobbering beast before her. Her conjured orb obeyed eagerly, racing towards Behemoth with a bloodlust. The instant before her spherical weapon struck his chest, Fate focused a surge of super nova in his direction utilizing the illuminated buffer surrounding her. It spread out wide, consuming the arena in a flash of brilliance. The black orb struck Behemoth in the chest, exploding like a bomb and shattering his rib cage made of roots. A few large chunks of him flew off, landing with wet splats and thuds upon the dirt—then the white wave of light hit him.

And Behemoth was no more.

The crowd of red eyes fell silent, then slowly disappeared into the darkness behind them. Fate watched as the prison walls seemed to melt before her eyes, leaving a doorway leading back to the labyrinth.

With a quick sigh of relief and a mop of her sweaty brow, she smiled as she walked proudly out of the arena.

She'd won—this time.

"Where's Vale?" Kane glanced around, panicked as he looked for the shade. Deme shot an expression over her shoulder that said, 'Who cares.' Disregarding her blasé attitude, he continued in his plight. There was no sign of Vale's body; the calling card of the beast was to emit its loud, strange noise and then leave behind a slaughter. Perhaps Vale had wisped to safety, but to where? Inside the garden? He certainly hoped so. Despite his initial distaste for the guy, the shade had grown on Kane—like a fungus, perhaps— he was fonder of him, nonetheless.

"Let's get in there," Deme stated wearily, her exhaustion obvious as she rapped three times on the door to the garden. "They have it barricaded," she explained.

Kane looked back to see if Mezza, Slater, and the princess had fared well. Now back in their necromancer form, they resumed fussing over their beloved, though still unconscious, banshee. For a moment, Kane was almost envious of her; she'd gone through the recent terror completely unaware. He wondered what could be wrong with her. Was she ill? Or was her condition caused by the stress of losing her entire family? It wouldn't surprise him; he'd endured just a taste of what she'd been through, what with more than half of his demon family slain and laying at his feet. He didn't blame the girl for wanting to be away from it all, because he'd choose the same thing if he didn't have a duty to fulfill.

He did, however, hope that he'd find help for her on the other side of the door, which thankfully, was just opening.

"Kane!" a familiar voice called out.

Kane smiled, relief washing through his system. "Elder Ozen, I am so pleased to see that you are well."

"And I, you!" The stout senior demon took the prince's hand and shook it enthusiastically, unshed tears glistening in his eyes.

Kane scoured the room for Vale, but could not locate him. Where had he gone? Was he safe from the invisible beast and from the demon clan as well? He hated to think of what might happen to the shade if any of his people found him before Kane could explain his presence in the palace.

Hundreds of demons stood about the garden, while many others lay wounded upon the floor. Their eyes fell upon Kane with mixed emotions. Some simply looked surprised to see him, others looked angry. Very angry. He understood their turmoil; he hadn't been there for them in their time of need. They likely felt abandoned, afraid, and alone without their leader.

Nevertheless, he was back. He'd returned to them—but for how long? He still had his quest to finish. There were scrolls to locate, races to gather and bring together to heal Dark World.

He couldn't allow his new duties to interfere with the old. Something had to be done for his people. They needed a new home; that would be the first priority once the Crystal Pyramid was renewed. Not only was it no longer safe inside the fortress, it apparently wasn't a secret to their enemies anymore.

They also needed a leader. One, albeit temporary, that would guide them until his return.

And he knew just who to ask.

"Pardon me a moment," Kane said as he marched across the room to greet a familiar, though not entirely friendly, face.

"Elder Syphon." Kane nodded in stiff greeting. "I'm glad you fared well."

Syphon glared at the prince with his one good eye, the other marked with an old, thick scar. "And I you, Prince Kane," the elder remarked coldly.

"I wonder if I might have a word with you," Kane said, taking the older demon by the elbow and leading him to a private corner of the room. Syphon looked oddly curious, yet suspicious. "As you may know, I'm in the midst of a quest to locate the scrolls, as well as acquiring a volunteer from each of the races to complete a vital ritual...I was wondering, perchance, if you'd do me the honor of leading these people in my absence?"

Syphon's good eye widened, his mouth hanging open, obviously at a loss for words. Their relationship had always been strained at best, what with Syphon's incessant badgering and protesting to nearly every word Kane had spoken. But the bottom line was that Syphon showed ardent care and concern for his fellow demons. Despite his methods, his motive rang true: he was loyal to his people—and Kane had to respect that.

Finally, after several moments and a couple of throat clearings, Syphon replied, "Why yes, I believe that I can assist you with that." The older demon puffed out his chest a little, his shoulders squaring.

"Great then, I will brief you shortly with the plan." Kane grinned, patting the elder on the shoulder as he walked away, rejoining Elder Ozen.

"Are you sure that's wise?" Ozen inquired when he heard of the news, a twinge of envy lurking behind his aged eyes.

Guilt twisted at Kane's insides, he knew that Ozen was going to be hurt by his decision to award Syphon the leadership, but it was for obvious reasons: Syphon was the more capable choice. Ozen was an amazing demon, kind, intelligent and loving; whereas, Syphon had always been the thorn in Kane's side, boisterous, aggressive, and defiant. Kane had considered handing the leadership to Ozen for the while that he was gone, but the demons needed a soldier to pull them through this situation with tough love. Ozen wouldn't be able to do that, he was guided by his heart, not his head. Syphon, for all his flaws, would guide the people with a firm hand, taking their lives into consideration more so than their feelings. At this point in time, with lives at stake, emotions were to be placed at the bottom of the list.

"I understand your concern," Kane began with a confident, yet sympathetic, tone. "I just feel that Syphon's military background will serve Legion best right now." He watched as Ozen's bright eyes looked to the ground. "Besides, I need you for something far more important."

"Oh?" The elder brightened, his gaze returning to Kane. "What's that?"

Kane smiled, a twinkle behind his cerulean eyes. "I need a favor."

The night was alive around her. Trees whispered with the wind's caress and twigs snapped beneath stealthy paws. Crickets chirped their odd, sweet melodies, serenading the darkness. Stars winked at her like the distant lanterns of a lighthouse, guiding her through veiling mists to an unexpected shore. If the situation hadn't been mildly upsetting, she'd actually be quite content to stroll amid the evening, breathe in the cool air, and enjoy the quiet songs of nature surrounding her. Most girls would likely be frightened of the predicament, wandering through the shroud of night down an unfamiliar dirt road.

Sarah, however, had never been afraid of the dark, which she thought was odd since most kids suffered some ill effects in the night. From the sounds of it, what with tales from fellow schoolmates and cousins, she was a bit of an anomaly when it came to childhood dreads. Most of them chattered about their fear of the dark, of spiders or bees, of boogeymen and ghosts and an invisible presence that chased you up the basement stairs whenever you'd dared to venture to the lowest level of the house. But not Sarah. She'd never been afraid of anything. Perhaps, she considered once, it's because she was an only child, ever content with all the love and attention her parents could offer. Sarah had never wanted for anything, especially shelter from whatever lurked in the dark corners of her imagination. Some would call her spoiled, and that was all well and good in her mind. She'd much rather be considered spoiled than live with lack of support and love from a mother and father, as she witnessed more often than not with her friends.

The difference was that she knew how lucky she was. She realized how rare it was to have parents that gave her their undivided attention. She smiled in the darkness, happy that she'd soon reach the highway, call her dad, and know that he'd be overjoyed to be her knight in shining armor, even if it was the middle of the night and down a dark road she probably shouldn't have gone.

Ahead of her a car passed, its headlights flashing by like a bolt of lightning. It wasn't far now, she'd only need to walk a few more minutes before she reached civilization where cell phones worked — she hoped.

Suddenly there was a sound behind her, a crunching noise like gravel snapping beneath tires. Sarah spun around in time to see a car, its headlights turned off, creeping up the dirt road. The moment she turned to face it, the driver hit the gas. She shrieked as she dove into the ditch, rolling into a thicket of prickly bushes. Her naked arms and legs stinging as long, fresh scratches began to weep scarlet.

"What the hell are you doing!" she hollered as the car shot past her. She hadn't seen who was driving but suspected they were probably from the party and likely drunk. *Great,* she thought as she stood and cleaned herself of leaves and debris. *Now they're going to drive on the highway and probably kill someone.*

Myth

Sarah staggered out of the ditch, still pulling twigs from her hair when she noticed that the car had stopped a few feet away. Enraged, she stormed towards the vehicle, intending on giving the driver a piece of her mind. The taillights blazed hot red, resembling a huge demon glaring at her in the darkness. She marched up to the back of the car, the quiet growl of the motor unnerving her. Who was this? Who was toying with her?

In an instant she knew, just *knew*, and her blood chilled in her veins.

It was Josh Dean.

The second she realized it, she turned running back towards the party. She had to find people to be around, drunk or not, it was safer that way. Her legs were battered and bleeding so Sarah began to half-hobble, half-jog down the darkened road. It couldn't be that far. She didn't think she'd walked that far already, but the bonfire was merely a blur of orange illumination in the distant sky. How long had she been walking?

Before she could think about it further, the car behind her clunked into reverse. Gravel spitting beneath the tires, the engine roaring to life.

Oh god! He's going to run me down!

Hot tears slid down her cheeks, and for the first time in her life, Sarah was truly frightened. Never before had she thought about death, never had she considered it a possibility before she was an old woman warm in her bed. But here it was: Death chasing her down an old, abandoned dirt road. She looked back, the car still in reverse was gaining on her.

She cried hard. She wept for herself. She wept for her parents. She wept for the life she would never live.

First there was the pain.

Then the darkness.

Silence.

Rory

Her eyes fluttered rapidly beneath their silver lids, blue tears escaping, caressing the curve of her cheek. Rory watched with rapt fascination as the metallic-skinned girl shook inside the grips of what appeared to be a terrible nightmare. He hoped she'd wake soon, he wished to meet her, to know her…

Flashes of his former life, his other existence on the Surface, consumed him. He'd been a true monster then. Compelled, obsessed with obtaining more power, more victims, and more magic. He'd sacrificed everything and everyone in his life to obtain immortality and have magic surge through his human veins. After a century of living, he couldn't even recall how many souls he'd damned to the Underworld. He'd given Queen Malus many more than even required. He had loved it. He had been a true serial killer; only unlike most cold-blooded murderers, he was given a supernatural gift each and every time.

He reminisced of the pact he and his brother and cousins had made; a sacred oath of the Dean clan. Of course, there were many others on the Surface that had learned of the spell, of the ritual to perform if one wanted unending life, but they'd had the scroll, the original parchment delivered to their ancestors by a real demon. Generations to come would follow in their footsteps, all the Dean boys were christened into the brotherhood, all willingly reborn as immortals. It became a trend, after a while, to rename oneself a 'Dean' once they'd sacrificed their first victim.

Rory had been proud then, eager to please his subterranean goddess, delivering unto her the youthful spoils of society.

But now he had other feelings, conflicting emotions. As he stared at the silver girl, he realized the error of his ways. Somehow, in her presence, he was changed...enlightened. All those teenagers he'd offered to Queen Malus, they weren't deserving of his wrath.

They didn't deserve...

A sudden pang curled within his abdomen, the foreign black blood screaming as it ran through his veins. The hunger had awakened. Had risen from a rare respite, ready to feed, ready to kill. Rory slammed his eyes shut, forming his hands into fists at his sides. He didn't want to kill this girl. This alien creature had so enraptured him, luring him to a side of himself he'd never known, and desperately wanted to know. His mouth watered inadvertently, stomach pulling, compelling him to take her, devour her...destroy her.

The dark creature dwelling within overshadowed his spirit, forcing compliance, willing him to do what he did not. Blackness possessed his soul like an evening storm eclipsing the diaphanous silver rays of the moon. Hunger reached out with his hands, forcing his mouth open, exposing the weapons within. The beast inside Rory lunged forward, maw clamping down on the silver girl's arm.

Only he was met with pain. Denied the privilege of sinking teeth into flesh. Rory opened his eyes, astonished by what he now saw.

Myth

She was gone, replaced by a beautiful ivory cocoon. Tentatively, he slid his hand the length of it; it was so very smooth, but hard as rock, like the opal stones surrounding them. Confounded, he sat back, watching the chrysalis shimmer pearlescent against the darkened illuminations of the underground world. Part of him was glad, relieved that she'd found a way to keep herself safe. The dark part of him was furious, raging with the power of a tempest.

Still hungry, he stood with the intent to leave to find anything he could to eat. With one last, longing look at the strange and beautiful girl now encased in pearl, Rory turned about and shuffled off through the red sands.

Ahead, shining like a beacon at midnight through stormy waters, was a light so bright it pierced Hell's black skin. A white light like Heaven's doors. Drawn to it like a bewitched moth to a deadly flame, Rory trudged ever forward.

To the Guf.

Upon exiting the arena, Fate found herself back within the confines of the labyrinth, and even better, she recognized the path again. The necromancers' memories flashed vividly inside her mind, cheering her on as she took each and every corner with speed and confidence. It was as though she'd traveled this winding path herself, only moments before.

Why then, she wondered as she strolled down the well-worn footpath, *was the arena and Behemoth a mystery to me? If all this is familiar, why would the beast be different? Not a spider like I'd seen in the memories?*

As if the necromancers were right beside her and heard her telepathic query, she was given a response inside her thoughts, *"The labyrinth offers you growth by forcing you to face your weaknesses,"* the voice whispered kindly. *"Every task will be different, but one. You need to prove yourself worthy of your soul."*

Fate shuddered with both awe and enlightenment. It all made sense now. The beasts she was going to face were a test of her worth, of whether or not she deserved to reacquire her soul.

This both thrilled and frightened her. It was a brilliant and almost exciting challenge — but one based on her greatest fears and faults. She'd have no choice but to come face to face with the evils that lurked in the dark corners of her mind. Over the last few months in

Dark World, she'd come to appreciate there was much more darkness inside her than she even realized.

She couldn't help but wonder what was next — and whether or not she really wanted to know.

As she turned sharply to the right, a long, gloomy trail loomed before her with the visually impenetrable roof of mist lingering, just out of reach. She was thankful she had the ability to see in the dark, her illuminated infrared eyes gleaming in the pitch of the maze. As she narrowed her eyes, looking long into the distance, she could see a bumpy mass of grey. Frowning, she thought it looked like a pile of rubble. Curious, yet cautious of her impending test, she approached the peculiar formation. The nearer she got, the more she could discern sharp angles and even hands, feet, and…wings!

"Ick!" Fate's heart plunged into her stomach, racing to reach his side. "No!" she cried as she fell to her knees next to the statues of Ick and his furry pals. All of them, transformed into stone, trapped as gargoyle figurines.

A tear glistened in her eyes, then glided down the curve of her pale cheek. What had happened? She looked at every one of their faces, all frozen in expressions of terror. Something had clearly attacked them, forcing them to defend themselves just as poor little Nibbles had to save himself from Fate's attempt to eat him.

Guilt overwhelmed her as she sat down beside them, placing her head in her hands. She shouldn't have asked them to come along. It was out of pure selfishness that she had. She didn't want to be alone, to face the wrath of the labyrinth by herself. They had no reason to follow her other than she'd requested it.

Fate lifted her head, forcing her sight upon her tiny friends. What had attacked them? What could have frightened them more than the three-headed dog they'd valiantly carried off in order to save her? She seen Ick fight before, he was good at it. Something felt wrong about all this. Something was off.

But what?

She stared at their little faces, trying to will the answer forth.

Suddenly she knew. Whatever had attacked them had surprised them. Caught them off-guard. Otherwise they would have taken to the sky, or become invisible to evade a predator. No, something else happened here, something out of the ordinary.

Something—or someone—had to have gotten close enough to...

"Hello, Fate," a chillingly familiar voice spoke from amid the darkness.

Fate jerked her head up, squinting as a lithe silhouette sauntered out from the shadows. She quickly stood up, readying herself for an attack. This was obviously her next challenge, she could feel it.

"I thought you'd never get here," it said, grinning as she came into focus.

Fate just stared, gaping speechlessly at the figure before her. Suddenly it made sense why the Ick and the other gargoyles had been taken by surprise, completely unaware they were in danger.

It was like looking in a mirror. A perfect twin.

It was—*herself.*

Kane

Much of the garden had been transformed into an infirmary for the wounded. Many lay covered in blankets made of oversized leaves or donated cloaks. Ozen led the medical team as he examined each and every one of the injured personally; prescribing the poultices and remedies that were accessible to him. Thankfully, the garden contained the greatest assortment of fresh herbs available inside Legion. In one corner, a makeshift homeopathic counter had been erected where several volunteers collected and, according to Elder Ozen's strict specifications, produced herbal therapies for each of the patients.

Mixed emotions consumed Kane as walked amongst the hurt and dying. Part of him was proud as he watched his people take care of one another with selfless compassion. The rest of him was wrought with guilt and regret. So many had died. He couldn't help but wonder if he was to blame. Would the outcome have been different if he had been here? The polarized feelings battled within him, tearing him up and leaving his soul in pieces. He had left for Fate. Left to find her, but he'd also gone in hopes to find the answers to save his dying world. If he didn't find all the scrolls, if he didn't adhere to the prophecy, the Crystal Pyramid could not be relit. If the pyramid did not shine on the realm soon, Myth would die — and everything along with her. She was their source, their spark of life. He'd learned many things from the necromancers, especially from Vrill, their devoted leader. Of these things he'd come to know, this was the most pressing, the most important of knowledge: if Myth dies, Dark World dies.

Kane scanned the garden sightlessly, his vision blurred by emotion. If he didn't hurry, there wouldn't be many of his people left to save. Of course, with his mother now gone, he was the leader of the entire the underworld; he had more to think of than just his own kind. He had all the races to consider. All the creatures—both the good and the bad.

The bad, he thought with a wave of bitterness rolling through him. Whatever beast had broken into Legion and murdered his people, whatever monster had ushered in the near extinction of the banshees…should he save them alongside the good people? Should he spare their lives despite their callous destruction?

Someday Kane would discover the power behind the forces that sought to destroy him and the world he protected—and then they will know true wrath, true justice.

In the far corner, the Night Mare whinnied, his voice carrying over the hushed voices of the many. His flaming tail, hooves, and mane blazed a little brighter as he huffed and snorted in Kane's direction, as though he sensed Kane's turbulent thoughts.

Kane observed the beast for a moment, mesmerized by his quiet power. Again, as he had so many times before, Kane wondered about the origins of the ebony stallion. Heads taller than even Kane himself, the mammoth horse towered over the stall in which they kept him. Though chained to wall for safety, Kane had often thought that the creature was surely strong enough to rid himself of his shackles and break free from his prison. Why did he stay? Why did he not fight back or choose to win his freedom?

Panning his gaze over the garden, over the mass of castaways stranded amid the garden, Kane understood. The Night Mare chose to stay, chose loyalty despite hardship. Not unlike the demons, he remained because he waited to be given the choice.

A shadow of wistfulness cast over Kane's heart as he realized just how honorable his people truly were. Through hardship, loss, and even abandonment, they had remained true to Legion. To Lucifer. And to Kane.

It was time he gave something back.

"What is this favor you ask of me?" Ozen asked of Kane once they found a private place in the garden to speak. The elder's ancient ochre eyes examined the prince with quiet question. Long vermillion fronds from an enchanted oak cascaded around them like a shawl, shielding them from prying eyes and ears.

Kane considered how to word his request as he swatted at a tiny blue-haired pixie buzzing about his face. "I require your assistance in a matter," Kane began.

"Of course," Ozen replied. "Anything."

"As you know," Kane started, "I need to travel to many lands to beseech the races for their support in reigniting the Crystal Pyramid."

The elderly demon nodded attentively.

Danielle Q. Lee

Kane continued. "I was wondering, perchance, if you would be so kind as to create an enchantment for me...a very unique enchantment?"

Ozen's eyes lit up, intrigued. "What kind of enchantment?"

"Do you remember the time Father went to war with the wraiths?" Kane asked with a twinkle of mischief in his eyes. "*That* enchantment."

The aged demon's eyes widened. "Are you certain? That will require much time...many ingredients!" Ozen exclaimed, flustered.

Kane smiled as he placed a confident hand upon his mentor's shoulder. "I have faith in you, old friend."

Ozen shook his head, confounded as he muttered, "Going to take a lot more than faith for me to complete that one in due time." He sighed, adding, "But for you, my prince, anything."

"Oh, and one more thing," Kane said, cringing as he knew he'd asked for too much already. "I require two enchanted boxes for carrying the scrolls in once I retrieve them."

Ozen huffed as though in preparation to dispute, but then after a settling breath, he replied calmly, "Of course, sire."

"Thank you." Kane then pushed through the veil of trailing leaves, exiting the isolated area. The moment he entered the open garden, he was approached by Elder Syphon. A ripple of the old resentments stirred inside Kane, and he had to suppress them quickly before they manifested in his expression.

"Greetings," Syphon began with a formal tone, his own ghosts of rivalry haunting his eyes. "I have the numbers you requested."

"Go ahead," Kane responded, a fresh flutter of nerves rising in his stomach. He hoped for the best, it's all he could really ask for.

"Twenty," Syphon replied in a confident voice, though his eyes betrayed him, showing that he, too, was disappointed.

Kane felt his heart sink. Twenty. How could his plan work with only twenty demon soldiers? "Is that all that volunteered?"

"Yes, your majesty." Syphon stood before him, hands folded behind his back, the silver armor covering his chest gleaming by the soft light of the garden's enchanted illumination.

Kane sighed. "Okay, thank you very much." He nodded as he moved past Syphon, now plunged deep into thought. He had to do something quickly to uplift his people, raise their spirits.

He paused, knowing what he had to do.

It was time to tell them.

Vale

For the first time in almost one hundred years, Vale awoke to complete darkness. Betrayed by his infrared vision, he raised his hands to feel his way. The ground beneath him felt solid enough, though not natural as would the Crimson Desert beneath his feet or the rocky floor of a cave. There was no noise at all, nothing to tell him anything about the room he was in. He reached into the empty air ahead and beside him, probing for clues; walls, furniture, anything to give him bearing as to where he'd arrived after wisping.

Nothing. There was nothing tangible there in the pitch darkness, where his supernatural senses appeared to have failed him for the first time since he became a shade over a century ago.

What was this place? This void? The last thing he remembered was running behind Kane and Deme, fleeing from the terrifying and mysterious noises that chased them down the corridors of the crumbling demon palace. All he recalled was the terror he felt as he navigated the hallway, floors littered with the massacred remains of Kane's people. The thunderous humming had grown louder and louder, the pressure in his ears unbearable as the sense of impending doom threatened to shatter what remained of his fragile soul. Vale could stand it no longer. His instincts possessed him, and in the last moment before they reached the garden doors, he had dematerialized with the intent to re-emerge on the other side and open the door for Kane and the others.

Only, apparently he'd wisped somewhere else entirely.

The air around him was cool and unmoving, as if inside a vacuum. Had he accidentally manifested into an enchanted room inside the citadel? Or between the walls of existence? Nothing like this had ever happened to him before whilst utilizing his talent, and he'd been wisping a very long time indeed.

It puzzled him, as he moved sightlessly about the blackness, that he could find no walls. What room could imprison such darkness, yet possess no barriers against the light?

A thread of panic wound through him as he stopped, wrapped his arms round his torso and sank to the floor—his only certainty at the given moment. While he was sure this was a place he'd never been before, it felt ominously familiar.

Trapped in the dark.

Alone.

Afraid.

Dying.

It happened over a century ago—but he remembered it like it was yesterday.

"Vincent!" Sybil called out, cupping her hands around her mouth to amplify her voice. "I know you're hiding in the barn!"

Vincent Kavanagh grinned as he watched his younger sister wade through the tall, golden wheat grasses, making her way to the outbuilding. A gentle breeze wove transparent fingers through her long, chestnut hair, tickling her forehead and cheeks with an affectionate touch. Every few seconds she swept the rogue strands from her face, smiling as she approached the barn.

From his vantage atop the loft, he watched as she stepped over the threshold and gazed upwards. "You always hide in the same place, you can't fool me!"

With a sigh, Vincent crawled out from between the cluster of small, square hay bales which had served to conceal him, stood, and bowed at his sister. "There you have it," he offered with a grin, shucking flecks of golden hay from his pants and shirt. "You've caught me once again, my lady."

"What are you reading now?" she asked as she took hold of her long skirts and began climbing the wooden rungs of the ladder. "You know father will have your hide for not doing your chores."

Vincent took her hand when she was high enough and eased her up onto the loft. "What he doesn't know won't hurt him," he said as he let her go and began pulling stray threads of straw from his unruly hair. "Besides, he went to Kinsella today to buy feed for the sheep. He won't be back until supper."

"So, what are you reading?" Sybil repeated, her green eyes turning to the book on his lap, glinting with curiosity. "Will you read it to me?"

He smiled warmly at his little sister, only two years his junior yet still a child in a woman's clothing. Vincent himself had only just turned seventeen but always felt he'd harbored an aged soul, trapped within the guise of a young man.

Myth

"This one's called...*Frankenstein,* it's about a monster that was created by a crazy doctor. His body was sewn together with parts from dead people!"

Her eyes widened, alight with a mixture of horror and anticipation. Sybil arranged herself into a comfortable sitting position as she waited for him to begin, her hands clasped excitedly in her lap. Ever since Vincent had revealed his newfound ability to read, she'd become infatuated with the stories he'd smuggled home from the town's humble library. He had every intention of teaching his sister to read, soon. But he had only recently learned it himself, thanks to his new friend, Blake.

Blake was a recent addition to the Fort Saskatchewan area. No one really knew where he'd come from, only that he had a foreign lilt and an exotic appearance that had the local girls swooning. Even Sybil, who'd sworn off the notion of marriage in favor of someday joining a convent, appeared smitten by the newcomer.

Vincent, on the other hand, was taken by Blake for his own, more selfish purposes: learning.

"What's the best place you've been?" Vincent quizzed the foreigner upon on of their first days working together at the resident mill while prepping timber for construction.

Blake chewed his lip, closing one eye as he pondered. "I'd have to say Italy."

Vincent tried not to look too surprised despite being flabbergasted that Blake had been to a land he had only heard about from old man Santucci who prattled on about his childhood in Naples. "You've...been there? In person?"

151

"Of course," Blake replied with a wide grin, coaxing two perfect dimples into formation on either side of his sun-kissed cheeks. There was little wonder why the newcomer had the ladies of the town enamoured. "I have a book at home all about it. If you want, you can read all about the area."

Dragging his arm across his sweaty brow, Vincent cast his gaze to the ground. "Nah, that's okay," he said, his voice turning lifeless and monotone as he moved to retrieve another piece of lumber for the saw.

Blake paused, examining Vincent before quietly asking, "Vince, can you read?"

Vincent remained quiet as he lowered his head, allowing his shaggy, untameable brown hair to drape over his eyes. He hated to confess such a thing, to admit he wasn't just an unworldly hick, but an illiterate one as well. It wasn't that he hadn't ever wanted to learn to read, it was just that his Pa didn't believe it was necessary. The old man figured he'd gotten along in all his years without requiring it, so it was only natural that his children shouldn't need to read either. Ma could read a little, Vincent had discovered this quite by chance when she'd received a wedding invitation by post, but even then she appeared to struggle as she sounded out the letters all jumbled together upon the modest ivory document.

The Kavanagh family had spent so much time moving from one town to another, looking for work, there was no time for or sense in attending school when the kids were needed at home. Then, once Vince was old enough, barely eight, he was put to work in the fields with his father. Now that they'd seemingly settled in Fort Saskatchewan, having purchased a farm and all, Vincent had hoped to attend the local school. He'd summoned the courage once, not long ago, asking his father if he and Sybil could take part in the educational system provided within the town. The answer came swiftly — and painfully — in the form of a swat upside the head.

"You don't need no special learnin' boy, everythin' you need to know is right here on the farm," he explained in that gruff, all-knowing tone Vincent had come to loathe. "I never went to school like all them fancy people in the city, but I put food on the table and a roof over my family's head. It's all that matters."

"Vincent?" Blake's brow furrowed, concern shadowing his stare. "Do you want me to teach you?"

With just those few words, Vincent felt his heart light afire. Learning to read was something he had only dared to dream. It opened up a whole new world of possibilities. His eyes met Blake's, heart pounding with excitement. "You...you'd teach me?"

"Of course," Blake said with a nonchalant shrug of his shoulders, as though it were the simplest of tasks. "Meet me by the old bridge after supper and we'll start."

And start they did. Within just a couple of weeks, Vincent was amazed at his own progress. While it was frustrating at times, what with all the rules to remember, he was surprised at just how easy it was when you knew the basics. He felt confident he could teach Sybil what Blake had taught him.

In that moment, up in the barn loft with his sister's delighted gaze cast upon him, Vincent felt a new sense of pride settle upon his shoulders. It was a fresh start to a life he'd once worried would begin and end with his father's oppression. Now, he felt an adventure stirring amid stagnant waters, all from a simple act: reading. Vincent cracked open the antiquated book on his lap, appreciating the feel of the paper as he slid his finger along each narrow page, turning them over slowly and carefully. Once reaching the beginning of the first chapter, he cleared his voice and began reading Sybil the tale of a man-made monster.

A tenacious September wind pressed against the outside walls of the humble Kavanagh abode, generating ghostly moans and whistles through the many cracks and crannies of the dilapidated boards. Heavy snowflakes fell noiselessly, twirling and pirouetting, dancing to a silent waltz as they blanketed the copper and gold carpets of autumn. The last rays of sunlight were sinking below the shoulders of the horizon, leaving a pink, purple, and grey marbled sky to usher in the shadow of night.

Vincent lay on the top bunk in the bedroom he shared with Sybil, his back facing the door as he dared to devour just a few more pages by candlelight. Even if his parents came in unannounced, he'd have more than enough time to stash *Frankenstein* under his pillow and snuff out the light. He wasn't all that concerned though, his mother was busy stitching up Pa's torn britches by the fireplace, and Pa, enjoying his post-supper nap, had a thunderous snore that infiltrated every room in the house.

Swaddled in the embrace of the words Mary Shelley had so eloquently trapped onto paper, Vincent allowed himself to be held captive by the story, the characters, and the music of the words. How they flowed, turned and twisted, never letting go until finally, a crescendo! An ending so powerful, it held him paralyzed but for a moment. He sat in disbelief that such a simple thing like writing and reading could be so powerful. How was it that words, simple markings made on parchment, could hold such...*magic?*

"Where are you going, young lady?" Vincent heard Ma ask of Sybil, wrenching him from his paperback adventure. He raised his eyes to a narrow gap between the boards of the wall, giving him a small, but clear, view of the sitting room. Through it, he saw Sybil just as she reached to put on her boots and coat. "It's just startin' to snow out there, and it's gettin' dark." Mother's brow pinched as she eyed her daughter with a tired and annoyed gaze.

Sybil turned around, securing her jacket around her and then freeing her long hair to cascade over her shoulders. "Um, I promised Carolyn I'd meet her on the bridge, she wants to borrow my red dress for the social tomorrow night."

Mother muttered, glancing in the direction of our slumbering father. "Well, hurry up then, you don't want to catch sick. I want you back within the hour, you hear me?"

"Yes, mama," Sybil replied, then turned and whisked out the door leaving a stream of snowflakes to steal into the room like a swarm of white butterflies.

Vincent frowned, wondering what his sister was truly up to. Ma hadn't noticed, but he did, that Sybil didn't have the red dress on her person, the one she'd apparently promised to Carolyn.

Carefully, quietly, Vincent descended from his perch on the bunk bed, stashed his precious book under the mattress, and quickly devised a plan to follow his sister.

A fountain of blood sat as the main centerpiece in the great hall, dribbling crimson over a marble statue of Malus, nude, armed with an obsidian sword raised as though to spear the heavens. The queen eyed her previous form with a strange sense of loss. Despite owning a new body, Ever's youthful and powerful body, she had to admit that she missed her true self just a little bit. She'd never been inside anyone else for any length of time, save for the oracle shade, and being inside her for even just a couple of months was positively dreadful. What a loathsome, whimpering creature she was; Sybil was nothing but a child, a mere human girl undeservedly gifted with magic blood. Malus would lie awake at night, her formless soul hidden deep inside the shade-girl, probing her thoughts, her memories, and her simple-minded hopes and dreams. It was a small wonder how the shade had eluded her and her army for so long. The girl thought of nothing else but going back to the Surface and finding her family (which, of course, were all very likely dead and gone, save for her meddling brother). The girl hated Dark World passionately, despite the amazing talents she'd acquired when damned to the realm. Several times, Malus had to bite her tongue to keep from screaming at the girl, of informing her of the privilege she'd been given, the rare and precious gift she obviously didn't appreciate.

But to do so would be to give herself away. The shade had no idea Malus was there, concealed amid the shadows of Sybil's withering soul. Although, she had learned so very much whilst veiled inside the shade. Malus had heard so many secrets, so many whisperings, while the shade dwelled inside the necromancer palace—especially when Sybil was around Kane.

He'd spoken of the attacks in passing one night at supper, particularly the strange behavior of the elemental, Ba'al. Kane had been pursued by Ba'al during his journey to find Fate, the tempest of his blood rains nearly consumed Kane. He'd expressed his worry over this matter, as to why the elemental would torment him when he was supposedly the true heir to the throne of Dark World.

Then Kane fell upon the truth without even knowing it.

"Prince Kane, Fate, thank you so much for joining us!" Vrill bowed, his silver hands folded in prayer as he greeted the twosome. "Please, sit, enjoy the feast." He offered seats on either side of himself to the fashionably late couple. Bashfully, Fate took the seat next to the necromancer leader while Kane sat on her other side.

Malus watched through Sybil's eyes, noting every movement, every glance. She was studying the enemy, learning everything she could about them. She'd not been long without her body, mere weeks at that point, so she was weak and unable to retain consciousness for long. But for this, she had to remain aware. Despite being weary, she needed to hear what they had to say. Possession was far more trying than she'd initially suspected, and her host was certainly not the match she'd anticipated. Malus had hunted for Sybil when she'd first heard of a single-born shade arriving in Dark World; it was what she'd been waiting for. Of course, she hadn't known at the time how desperately she'd need the unique shade once her own precious form had been brutally murdered, but there were other things she needed from the rare shade: Power.

Long before the prophecy of the single-born shade had come to light, Malus learned of a secret regarding the shades. A secret she didn't want anyone, especially her son, to know. That was when she herself spread the rumor of her magically aged and dying self across the land, allowing no one to see her in person, as to not spoil the ruse. She told her minions to let it be known that she had touched one of the enchanted scrolls (Lucifer's pathetic attempt at protecting the scrolls from her), aging herself one thousand years in the blink of an eye, and that she desperately needed the prophesied shade — the single-born female — in order to transfer her soul and continue her reign.

Although, that was not why she wanted the wretched girl, the oracle that had slipped through her fingers so many times over the course of a century. No, she had needed her for something far more sinister.

Something that would change everything.

"So, Prince Kane," Vrill began as he speared a small blue vegetable on his plate. "How have you enjoyed your time in Necrosia?"

The demon prince nodded his horned head, chewing slowly on a piece of medium-rare sphinx steak before answering, "Very much, thank you."

"And you, my darling Fate," the necromancer asked, turning his swirling silver eyes onto the shade.

Fate surrendered a shy smile. "I love it here."

Vrill grinned, his pleasure evident. "I'm so glad. Of course, you are welcome to stay as long as you like."

Kane cleared his throat, his expression turning serious. "Thank you, but we must be on our way soon." He paused, taking a sip of black cherry wine. "There is much to be done."

"Of course, of course," Vrill agreed. "Where will you travel to first?" he inquired with an impish smile.

The prince inhaled, frowning. "I'm not sure, but I'll certainly avoid the plains between the Crystalline Forest and Dread Mountain."

"Oh?" Vrill's gaze adopted a hint of sincere concern. "Why is that?"

Kane's ebony skin flushed, his shoulders rising and falling almost imperceptibly. "It was nothing really," he muttered.

"Nothing?" Ever piped up suddenly, her sapphire eyes alight with surprise. "I should say it was a bit more than nothing."

Everyone at the table seemed to hold their breath captive in their lungs, awaiting Kane's explanation. Even Sybil, Malus noted, set her fork down and ardently observed the scene as it unfolded.

Finally Kane surrendered a response; his dark cheeks bruised purple with embarrassment. "Ba'al," he revealed. "He chased me down in the Crimson

Desert with his damned Blood Rains." He poked at his supper, obviously perturbed. "But thankfully," he said as he then raised his head, smiling at Ever. "Ever and Arcanum came to my rescue, just in time."

"Oh thank the gods!" Vrill threw his hands up, visibly relieved at the conclusion of the story. "Of course," he then added, "why would Ba'al have been set upon you in the first place? You are, after all, a member of the royal family, Lucifer's heir. Curious."

Kane nodded in agreement. "Exactly my thoughts. The elementals have always been loyal to my father and our family. Why Ba'al attacked me is beyond my comprehension. Even my mother shouldn't have had the power to sway them. It makes me wonder if I've done something to provoke them."

Malus smiled inside the shade, careful to keep her emotions from spilling over as it might alert Sybil to her presence. Kane had hit the mark without even knowing it. While Lucifer had always maintained a peaceful existence with the elementals, they did indeed have their own agenda. Kane, as oblivious as he was, had been treading on dangerous territory without even knowing it.

And Malus knew why.

From head to toe, it was her. Long silver hair, glowing white eyes, identical clothes; even the length of her nails appeared the same. Fate stared at herself in awe, dissecting every inch, every curve.

Are my thighs really that big? Fate wondered, then admonished herself for the thought. This really wasn't the time for vanity.

"Do you like your little friends' new look?" the other Fate inquired, glancing callously in the baby gargoyles' direction, their cold, stone faces locked in expressions of terror.

"What did you do to them?" Fate questioned around a snarl, heat rising in her core. The Other Fate just laughed, tossing back her head, her long mane swaying behind her.

Once composed, the Other sneered in Fate's direction, answering, "It would be easier just to show you." She laughed again, a maniacal giggle, eyes alight with madness as she raised her hands above her and summoned a crackling sphere of black power. She grinned at Fate as she hurled the ball of dark energy at her. Fate dove out of the way just before it hit her; it then exploded behind her, obliterating an entire wall of the labyrinth.

"Shall I tell you how they cried? How they whimpered when they realized that their beloved Fate was going to kill them?" she jeered, taking a few steps closer to Fate with a feigned pout.

"Shut up!" Fate shouted as she scrambled to her feet, enraged. The labyrinth suddenly seemed to close in on her, the air felt thick and hot as she inhaled it into her undead lungs. Her head swam and skin prickled with anxious energy. If she were human, she would have prepared herself for fainting. But she wasn't human, and she knew this wasn't a natural response. This was something else, something dark. This was what she'd feared since the moments after she learned of the lamia writhing inside her. Fate sensed the black blood in her veins begin to boil, throbbing as it meandered through her system. The human part of her recoiled into the shadows, shuddering as the lamia forced its way to the surface. Anger replaced conscious thought, pure fury snaked around the remnants of Scarlet's essence.

She was losing herself. Her spirit, once teetering upon the edge of a bottomless abyss, fell headlong into a dark oblivion. Deep inside, Scarlet screamed but it only sounded as a whisper amidst the evil cacophony. Her fists balled at her sides, throat surrendering a growl she herself didn't utter. Parting her lips, Fate panted as an animalistic side took over. Possessed her.

The Other laughed, flashing a shark-like smile. "You're so easily angered," she purred. "I like it."

The lamian blood raced throughout her, pulsing from a dark source inside her solar plexus. Fate felt her fragmented soul crack a little from the pressure as the hexed ink in her veins pressed further into her face, reaching for her eyes, reaching for her thoughts, tainting them, destroying her. She raised her hands, the power too strong to reign in. Red sparks fired from her fingertips at the Other, knocking her to the ground. The Other continued her laughter, her prodding and her taunting; even as the skin began melting from her face, she never stopped.

Fate felt as though she was only an observer, trapped deep inside a supernatural body that was no longer her own. The world around her had a dream-like quality. She could barely focus as the lamia continued on its warpath. She could see herself doing the unimaginable, but could do nothing to stop it.

Suddenly, Fate heard the voice of a thousand of necromancers sounding inside her mind.

Stop! This is what it wants!

She ignored their pleas, continuing the onslaught of lightning, burning the flesh from the Other's bones. The black blood seeped further into Fate's face, shrouding her thoughts.

Fate, Vrill's patient and kind voice forced its way through the shadows. *This is what she wants, Fate. Don't give her what she wants. You are stronger than she. This is the test. If you fail, there's no turning back. You will become the monster. You will be no more.*

Fate paused, wrenching her glare from the cackling Other to that of her little Ick, his frightened face trapped in stone. How could she quit now? She had to avenge him and his little friends. They'd followed her here, helped her, she couldn't just quit and let the fiend with her face win.

Fresh wrath flooded her system, the darkness consuming nearly everything light that was left inside. Tendrils of crimson sparked from her fingertips as she stepped closer to the doppelganger, every ounce of power she had surrendered to anger.

This is how she wins, Vrill's weakening voice whispered to the last sliver of Fate's shattered soul.

This time Fate heard him—and understood.

Immediately she stopped, wrenching the dark power back into herself. Her body shrieked in pain, dark voices rose and swirled like a tempest throughout her entire body, overriding every cell, every corner of her essence. She closed her eyes, willing it away, attempting to tame the beast within.

The Other howled in anger, and resumed her vicious taunts. "Come on, you coward! You can do better than that!"

The lamia screamed with rage inside of Fate's thoughts, ordering her to continue, forcing her. But Fate fought back, fought against the fog clouding her mind, against the demon that sought to possess her.

Fate felt herself losing, the lamia rising once again to the surface. In the same moment, the Other had recovered and was now standing over her.

"You're pathetic," she stated, hands on hips, shaking her head with an expression of disgust. "No wonder Rory tricked you so easily. You deserved to die."

It was then that the Other's facial features changed, her hair transforming from silver to brown, white eyes melting like ice into a pool of blue. She was Scarlet now, standing there, her face filled with mocking fear. "Oh, boo hoo," she pretended to cry. "I'm a stupid little bitch." Then she scowled. "Why?" she asked of Fate, her voice blaming and cruel. "Why did you follow Rory into the woods? Why didn't you fight harder? Why, Scarlet, why?"

A teardrop fell from Fate's eyes, slid over her cheek, wetting her jawline. Emotions burned in her chest, anger and hatred, but mostly regret. While she loathed the words the Other was saying, deep down she knew they were true. She had followed Rory into the woods, willingly, eagerly. Despite every hint that something was wrong, she ignored her instincts, turned her back on her intuition. As a result, she'd lost her family, been damned to Hell, and now, risked losing what remained of Scarlet.

It was all her fault.

Fate groaned, her body still not her own as she fought the demons within. The Other laughed again, switching into Fate's shade form once again. "Get up!" she screamed. "Fight! Fight for your life!"

"Help me," Fate whispered through trembling lips, pleading for anyone, anything, to hear her. "Vrill? Necromancers? Please, help me."

"Help me," the Other mocked, kicking Fate in the stomach and then spitting on her. "Pathetic. I can't wait to finish you off—*and then take your place.*"

Fate froze. So that was the creature's plan. She imagined someone else in her skin, living her life, laughing with her friends, fighting her fights— *touching Kane.*

That did it. Fate shot up, bringing her fist up and smashing the Other under the chin. The Other stumbled back, blood leaking from her bottom lip as shock registered in her eyes.

"There's no way I'm letting you take over my life!" Fate yelled, taking another swing at the spitting image of herself. The Other whimpered, arms raised for protection as she cowered away from the raging shade.

"Please! Stop!" she uttered as Fate drove another shot to the side of the Other's head. "I'll go, you win!"

"I what?" Fate paused, feigning that she hadn't heard, cupping round her ear with her hand. "I didn't hear you."

"You win," the Other spat and suddenly morphed from Fate's figure to that of a sinewy green creature. Its glowing red eyes blazed, glaring at the shade that had bested it. Fate realized, upon recognizing the eyes, that this was the one of many beings that had been hidden behind the labyrinth's walls when she was fighting Behemoth.

"Get out of here," Fate ordered, pointing towards an opening in the maze.

The creature started to leave, then paused. "You're...letting me go?"

Fate nodded as she dusted herself off.

"Why?" the creature asked, its fish-like lips twisted downward, head tilted inquisitively.

"Because I'm not a killer, I'm just a teenage girl who wants her soul back," Fate replied triumphantly.

The creature frowned at this, pondering it, then pointed at the Guf's light in the distance. "You have one more test before the Guf's doors will open. Be warned: only one other before you has passed." With that the creature departed, leaving Fate to gaze at the light ahead, wondering if this was to be the end...or a new beginning.

Kane stood before the Night Mare, watching in return as the beast observed the demon prince with aged, untamed eyes. Tendrils of flame cascaded the length of his back resembling a waterfall of fire. His jet-black coat shone as though polished, reflecting hues of dark purple amid the blaze of his mane. Black-as-night hooves pawed at the hay-laden floor, indicating his restlessness, his desire to be free from captivity. This horse, this magnificent creature had been there nearly as long as Kane had. If only he knew it was for his own wellbeing, his own protection, rather than for the selfishness of the demon community. He was the only one of his kind, not unlike Arcanum or the nest of phoenix birds on the other side of the garden. The shades had devoured nearly all the mystical creatures in Dark World, their soulless phantoms wandering the face of the Crimson Desert forever. Kane had taken it upon himself to preserve these creatures, even if that meant eternal imprisonment. He believed it his duty to keep what remained of the endangered beasts from further harm.

His father was the one who began it all, long before the threat of the shades even came to light. Lucifer strongly believed in the preservation of a species, regardless of its purpose or uses. Even when they'd had an opportunity to wipe out a dangerous and hostile breed like the sphinxes, his father refused to act upon it, stating that it was the duty of the wiser to aid those unable to fend for themselves.

Kane thought of the banshees, or rather, the banshee. Sorcia was alone now, the last of her kind. Once she passed on, there would never be another like her. It saddened him to think of that day, when an entire race would fade into memory.

He sighed, weight accumulating on his shoulders. So many depended on him, so many lives were altered by the choices he would make.

The Night Mare whinnied then, bringing Kane back to the moment. He smiled wistfully, thinking of the first time he'd laid eyes on the magnificent beast before him. They'd discovered him quite by chance on a hunt one evening. Kane let his thoughts drift back, his memories forming behind his eyes as though it were merely yesterday.

"There's a pride just beyond this valley," Deme stated, pointing her spear westward.

"How many do you guess?" Kane inquired, concerned the meager hunting party might not be able to defeat more than one or two sphinxes.

"Six? Seven? Perhaps more," Deme replied nonchalantly, as if they could handle any number of the deadly beasts.

Kane stifled a cough. "Seven? Deme, there aren't enough of us..."

She cut him off, saying, "We have plenty. I have a plan."

"Oh?" He couldn't help but grin, her tenacity was something to be admired.

Ignoring him, she marched on, using her spear as a walking stick.

The prince shrugged, knowing it wouldn't do him much good to argue, she was determined to do it her way, and considering her track record, she had yet to fail, so he heeded.

The posse of ten scrambled up the side of a slope; on the other side was an open landscape, a field of sorts for the pride to graze upon. Kane peered over the side, counting quickly before squatting down once more. "Deme!" he whispered through a hiss. "There's at least eight!"

She grinned. "And?"

"And we only need one to restock the meat cellar." He shook his head. "There's no way this will work. They'll see us coming; they'll have the advantage."

The other demon hunters nodded in agreement with their leader, dread clouding their expressions.

"Trust me," was all she said as she turned and led them back down the slope. "This way."

They complied, though warily, following her around the base of the small rise. Finally, after another few minutes of walking she stopped, fell to her knees, and began to clear away brush and sand from the base of the mountain.

"What are you doing?" Kane asked, keeping his voice low as not to alert the sphinxes of their presence, being that they were just on the other side of the short divide and had remarkable hearing.

Deme continued her plight quickly and quietly, as though he wasn't even there. Just as Kane was about to demand an answer, she appeared to have found what she was looking for. Then she dug a little deeper to reveal a large round stone. "Help me," she ordered as she stood and began pushing the boulder away from the mountainside.

The others obliged, pushing with all their might. Finally the stone gave way, revealing a dark passage—a tunnel going under the mountain.

Pleasantly surprised, Kane smiled, convinced once more that he had the best tracker in the lands.

"This way," she said quietly. "We'll have to crawl for a ways, then the tunnels open up."

The opening was narrow, so narrow that Kane's shoulders grazed either side. Claustrophobia dangled like a dark, obsessive thought, taunting him, daring to hold him prisoner amidst the small, shadowed passage. A moist stench assaulted his nostrils the moment he entered, a pungent scent of mildew, sulphur, and aged things that likely hadn't seen the light in several centuries. It was so dark that even his infrared vision threatened to betray him. As he silently cursed Deme, Kane inched his way through the passage, wincing every time his shackled wings bumped the ceiling.

"Almost there," Deme voiced amid the pitch blackness from somewhere up ahead.

While he had full trust in Deme, he couldn't help but wonder if this would be the first time she messed up. There's always a first time.

Thankfully, just ahead, smatterings of light appeared, ushering them towards the opening. Deme's shadowy form exited ahead, leaving even more illumination to guide him forth. His pointed ears shifted with the sound of dripping water, hollow and echoing as though inside a cavern. Sure enough, reaching the end of the dreadful tunnel, he was greeted by slivered rays of brilliance. As refreshing as a light rain on his face, he felt the soft sprays of water droplets kiss his skin.

Freeing himself completely from the hellish hole, standing and arching his ancient back, he then took in a beautiful sight. The cavern, though not large, looked to be the innards of a mammoth geode. Crystalline shards colored aqua, turquoise, and pale lavender, grew outward from every corner of the cave like hundreds of sparkling spikes. In the center of the rounded room, a bubbling whirlpool tossed its hot waters about, spinning into the center of itself as froth and steam played atop the surface. It actually looked very inviting as a bath, had the situation not been so completely austere.

The one thing Kane did not see amidst this wonderland of gemstones was a way to get out.

"Okay, now what?" he inquired of Deme who was pulling a long rope from her pack, a hook affixed to one end.

"Up," was all she replied with an upward nod.

Kane turned his face up to find yet another small opening, just overtop the warming pool, that he didn't particularly want to squeeze through. "Where are we, exactly?"

"Inside a geyser," she said as she readjusted her pack and weapons, positioning them securely onto her back.

Kane felt his eyes widen. "A geyser! What happens if we're in here when it goes off?"

She smiled, her amber eyes gleaming mischievously, taking aim at the hole above with the grappling hook. "I don't recommend it."

He shook his head in mild annoyance, perturbed he'd allowed her to drag him along. "Alright, let's go."

"Okay," Deme explained. "Once we all get to the top, there's a large shrub that will keep us from being seen until we're all ready to jump out and ambush one or two of them."

Kane frowned. "What's to keep the rest of the pride from coming at us?"

She shrugged, replying, "Be quiet and that shouldn't be a problem. They like to keep their distance from one another while they graze. We only need one loner to pull this off. The rest won't even know we're there."

The prince had admit, it could work, if all the stars aligned. Problem was, until they popped their heads out, there was no telling what awaited them.

"Let's go, it'll be fun," Deme grinned.

"Famous last words." Kane feigned a grumpy look but was predictably impressed with his fearless tracker. She had a way, a natural ability, that far surpassed any of his male trackers, warriors included. Not that he was sexist in any way, thinking her less because she was female; quite the opposite — she often made the boys look bad.

Deme hoisted herself up using the rope; the hook adhered near the hole at the height of the dome. Once safely at the top, she eased herself through the impossibly small opening. Kane's skin crawled with apprehension, certain that he would not fit through the exit as easily as Deme did, considering she was far more petite than himself. After a few seconds, she tossed the rope down and then assisted each member of the hunting party until all had joined her on the surface.

Hidden, but only barely, by a large, oblong boulder, Kane was surprised to find that they were only a few feet from the nearest sphinx, the others grazing several dozen feet away.

Kane leaned close to Deme's ear, whispering, "How can we kill it without alerting the others?"

She pressed a ruby finger to her lips, winking at him. Crouched low, knees nearly touching the ground, she ambled towards the unaware beast. One and a half times taller than the largest of demons, a sphinx was surprisingly fast and harboured a quick intelligence.

His heart thudded in his chest as he watched her approach the beast from behind, silent as a calm preceding a storm. What was she doing? How did she think she was going to take the creature down alone when it usually requires at least six demons to kill just one?

The hunting party watched in breathless anticipation as Deme crawled right up behind the beast, only inches from his rear haunches. Kane wanted to close his eyes, not willing to watch his friend and confidant become a quick and savory meal for the huge cat-like predator. He had to trust her though. She'd lived this long, there had to be a reason—other than pure luck.

Carefully, she reached back into her hip pouch, retrieving something Kane could barely distinguish: a rope. Not just any rope, though; he could tell by its fluorescent pink gleam that it had been enchanted. Silently, ever so gently, she placed the end around the sphinx's back paw, not touching it, but leaving a loop in a circle on the ground surrounding it. Then, quickly, she formed a lasso-type knot.

The entire procedure had only taken a few minutes, but to Kane it felt like hours; he was certain he'd aged during the harrowing process. As silently as she'd come, Deme backed away, leaving a trail of rope behind her.

"You're crazy," Kane hissed upon her return. "You know that?"

"Yup." She grinned. "Now watch this. Oh, everyone, hang on to this really tight," she said, holding the rope out to each member.

Again, she reached into her hip pouch, this time pulling out a small ox horn, which was obviously enchanted as it shone with a preternatural glow. With a mischievous raise of her brows, Deme blew the horn as hard as she could three times fast, the enchantment raising the volume tenfold so that it thundered right up to the roof hanging over Dark World, rattling the teeth-like stalactites.

The reaction was instantaneous. The entire herd shot in the opposite direction, the rope the demons were holding was nearly yanked from their hands. "Hang on!" Deme yelled over the cacophony of thunderous paws racing over the Crimson Desert.

Pulled quite viciously from their hiding spot, all seven of the demons were dragged over the sands for well over fifty feet before the enchanted rope had time to sedate the disconcerted sphinx; for once the rope tightened and made contact with his foot, he was promptly lulled to sleep. Kane glanced around, noting that every other member of the pride had completely vanished, probably several miles from there by then.

"You know," Kane said between catching his breath and spitting sand out of his mouth. "You could have told us what you were planning."

"Yeah," Deme replied as she let go of the rope and rolled onto her back. "But that would have ruined the surprise."

Kane laughed in spite of himself. Upon standing and wiping the grit off himself, he noticed an odd formation in the distance. A large, black rock with wide, vertical striations running from the peak to the base, the inside of the cracks glowing dark orange. It seemed too small to be a volcano; there didn't appear to be a mouth in which lava escaped, nor was there smoke rising. It was unlike anything Kane had seen before.

"What is that?" Kane asked, narrowing his gaze at the anomaly.

Deme exhaled, hands on her hips. "I wondered that the last few times I came here, but I was alone so I thought better of it. Shall we explore?" she asked with a grin and a mischievous raise of her eyebrows.

The two left the hunting party to butcher the sphinx for easier transport home while they investigated the odd rock formation. The closer they got, the more perplexed they became. The amber shafts seemed to illuminate from within, not from lava as they'd first suspected.

"What could be powered from the inside like that?" Kane wondered as they reached the base of what he now recognized as an obsidian mount. Power, of an enchanted sort, emanated from the mass, leaving the hairs upon his arms to rise. Aside from the anxious thrumming inside his own chest, Kane could hear—and feel—a low frequency drumming, like a heartbeat originating from inside the stone.

"It looks to be..." Deme's voice trailed off as she reached out to touch the odd rock, "a shell or cocoon of some kind. It's warm," she added, pressing her palm against the outside wall.

Kane agreed, speechless as he walked around the base, fully inspecting it from all angles. "There doesn't appear to be a way in," he said quietly.

"Or out." Deme met Kane's gaze, curiosity mixed with unease surfaced behind her ocher stare.

"I wonder," Kane uttered, an idea springing into his thoughts.

Deme eyed him. "Wonder what?"

He set his palm upon the heated obsidian, his heartbeat adopting the pattern thrumming within. Without knowing why, he whispered, "Expositus." The magical Attra word for open.

The moment the disenchantment left his ebony lips, the pod began to shudder. Both demons backed away, unnerved by what this oddity might birth. Amid the illuminated amber striations, cracks formed—and began to open. Like a black lotus, the stone flower blossomed. Smoke rolled out and upward as the rock formation split apart and fell to the red sands of the desert.

Kane and Deme stood in silent shock, gaping at the beast revealed. There, standing amid the debris, was an enormous black horse, nearly twice the height of Kane himself. Ripples of orange fire roiled from his mane, tail, and hooves, his black eyes wild as he appeared to take in his environment.

"Deme?" Kane whispered suddenly, gathering his senses. "Do you have another of those enchanted ropes with you?"

He sensed her nod, and she reached slowly into her pouch.

After several attempts—and being burned by his mane—Kane and Deme were able to lasso the beast and bring him to Legion's garden, where he had resided ever since.

Kane eyed the majestic horse like he'd regard an old friend, just as he would Arcanum. These creatures seemed to harbor far more intelligence than they were credited. He wished, even for a moment, to be able to speak with the beast, to hear his thoughts and know his secrets.

Kane did not know the Night Mare's purpose, or reason for its mysterious creation, but he hoped one day, he'd find out.

Vale

The forest was awash with silver moonlight, beautiful if not for the eerie quietude. The branches of tall, leafless trees, like arms outstretched, were dressed white with layers of lacy snowflakes, like statuesque brides readied for their wedding. It was colder than he thought it would be, the chilled air burned his lungs with every inward breath as frost stung his nose and cheeks. He pressed on through the woods, tracking his sister's footsteps in the fresh-fallen snow.

She couldn't have gone far, he thought, narrowing his gaze through the rain of flakes. He wondered what would possess her so fiercely that she'd brave an evolving blizzard in order to achieve it. Maybe she truly was meeting her friend? Perhaps he'd simply heard wrong about the dress she'd intended to lend to Carolyn, maybe it was the other way around?

No, he knew what he'd heard. And he saw that she'd no item in her hands.

He was almost upon the bridge when he heard voices — and one was most certainly male.

Ah! Vincent pondered with a roll of his eyes. *That makes sense now. She's meeting with a boy!*

But it didn't make total sense as Vincent considered Sybil's long interest in joining the church. Ever since she was a small child, all she'd ever talked about was becoming a nun. When she was little, Vincent attributed it to his sister's love of long dresses and singing, rather than a desire to serve the Almighty. However, as the years passed, he witnessed Sybil's devotion to the church; and with his own newly attained ability to read, she longed to learn to read the bible.

So this, meeting up with a boy, was an interesting development, one that Vincent wasn't too sure he was keen on.

With measured steps and stealth, he moved closer to the couple as they chatted and giggled, his warm breath escaped his lips to meet the ice-cold air, creating ghost-like puffs amid the snowstorm. He shivered beneath his wool sweater, wishing he could have grabbed his heavy jacket before he left the warmth of the shack, but to have done so, he would have had to pass by mama stitching by the fire and answer to why he, too, was leaving during a blizzard.

A veil of clouds moved over the face of the moon, throwing a dark blanket over the forest. Hardly able to see what was before him, Vincent waited until the shroud had passed before he continued. One false step and he'd alert Sybil and her suitor to his presence. Shortly, the midnight sun shone brightly, and he drew closer again.

A thin layer of ice lay like glass over the slowing river, Vincent was careful not to shatter it as he gained footing beneath the arch of the stone bridge. He still couldn't hear exactly what they were saying, their voices hushed, clandestine. Every so often, his sister would laugh flirtatiously, fueling Vincent's need to know who she was with.

"I should go," Sybil said, loud enough for Vincent to hear.

"No, stay," cooed the mysterious voice.

Vincent took a chance then, peering round the corner and up towards the voices. He narrowed his gaze, an army of snowflakes bombarding his face. Straining, he wished in that moment he had some kind of special ability to see in the dark. After a few moments, he realized it was simply too dark for him to make out the perpetrator's face. Frustrated, he squatted and decided to wait it out, perhaps an opportunity would arise.

"No," he heard Sybil say a little louder. "I have to go, I told my mother I'd only be a few minutes."

The response was muffled, but Vincent was sure it ended with a kiss. Annoyance, and some other unidentified emotion that seemed like anger, rose up inside him. He hadn't ever been in this predicament before, having to protect his little sister. Why did he care if his sister had a beau? What did it matter? Why was it even his business?

Unless she got hurt. Then it was his business.

Cold and bored, Vincent sighed a bit louder than he intended.

"Did you hear that?" the male asked. Vincent froze, holding in his breath.

"What?" Sybil asked.

"I heard something."

"It was probably an animal or the wind," she offered. "I have to go now, okay?"

"No." The voice darkened, bringing Vincent to standing, readying for a fight. Nobody hurt his sister. Nobody.

"Blake," Sybil said with a nervous laugh. She'd said something else too, but Vincent didn't hear it. All he heard, over and over inside his head, was the name, *Blake*.

How could Blake keep a secret like this from him? How did Blake and Sybil meet? When?

"Meet me again, then," Blake said suddenly. "Tomorrow."

He strained his hearing, awaiting his sister's reply. "Okay, I'll be here."

Vincent gritted his teeth. *And so will I.*

Kane

Kane pushed through a veil of lavender fronds, draped long and thick, hiding the contents of the makeshift intensive care ward. This is where the demons brought those in critical condition; those they believed might not survive.

Swallowing hard before he entered, Kane worried he would be disturbing those that needed rest. He didn't know how many souls resided here, in the back of the garden, but he hoped that one in particular had not succumbed to their puzzling ailment.

"Prince Kane," Elder Ozen greeted him as he stood at the threshold of the infirmary, his arms folded across his rounded belly, hands tucked inside the long sleeves of his cloak. "Please, come in."

Kane took a few tentative steps in, his eyes wandering the room, searching. "Where is she?"

"Princess Sorcia?" Ozen replied. "She's just over here." He led Kane to left, then back behind a large coniferous fern.

Several female demons surrounded the ailing banshee, nursing her with what little their medical team had to offer. With the mysterious beast still potentially wandering the halls of Legion, the dwindling citizens had to make do with what they had in the garden.

"How...is she doing?" Kane inquired, not sure he wanted the answer as he took in the scene. The banshee's face, once youthful and full of spirit, was now pale and damp, wet with fever. Her buoyant, curly red hair lay as a lifeless fringe upon her pillow. But the most alarming of symptoms was her skin; it appeared cracked, fractured like the arid desert floor after a year without water to grace its sands.

"Do you know what is wrong with her?" Kane asked, almost afraid to breathe in the princess's presence, fearful that the slightest disturbance might break her apart like parched leaves.

Ozen shook his head. "We know so little of the banshee race. They hid themselves away so many centuries ago; we have very little literature on them and their species."

Kane turned to his mentor. "What literature do you have on them?"

Ozen shrugged. "I have no access to it now; it's in the library."

The prince sighed with frustration. The library was on the other side of the palace. They'd have to leave the safety of the garden and venture out into danger-ous territory. He wished, now more than ever, that Vale was with them. His ability to wisp would be more than helpful with this task. Kane's heart sank a little with his thoughts on the missing shade. It wasn't likely that he'd survived; he would have surfaced by now.

Kane pushed the thoughts aside, there were more important matters to attend to: like how he was going to save the last banshee. Without her, the ritual could not be completed and the Crystal Pyramid could not be relit. Exhaling, Kane made a decision.

"Tell me what you need from the library."

Ozen turned a surprised eye to the prince. "No, it's too dangerous. You can't go out there!"

"I have to," he said, turning his gaze onto Sorcia. "We need her."

"We'll help you," two voices said in unison behind Kane.

He turned to see Mezza and Slater, who'd been silently watching over Sorcia from the corner of the room, their faces locked into an expression of fierce determination.

"Okay then," Kane said with a wary grin. "Let's do this."

"Remember, the book has gold binding, and it's called *Encyclopedia of the Races*," Ozen informed Kane as he and the necromancers readied themselves to exit the safety of the garden. "It will hopefully give us some insight on how to help the poor girl." Elder Ozen twiddled his thumbs nervously, watching Kane with evident concern.

"I understand," Kane replied, arming himself with his obsidian sword, not that it would do much good against an invisible enemy that moves like a tornado, but it made him feel better to carry it, nonetheless.

"Be careful," Ozen uttered with concern.

Kane bowed his head slightly, giving the elder a heartfelt smile. Then he turned to face the door. "Ready?" he asked of Mezza and Slater, who had already transformed into formidable cats of prey. They nodded.

The demon guards moved the large boulders barricading the doors aside, leaving just enough room for the three to fit through. Kane drew a steadying breath, summoning courage where fear was leaving its uncertain footprints. He and the necromancers stepped through the narrow passage, and the garden doors were swiftly sealed behind them. Once out in the hall, Kane noticed the quiet first, the piercing silence that seem to own the air. He couldn't help but feel paranoid, like they were being watched as they took tentative steps down the hallway. They had a long way to go to reach the library.

Kane willed himself to focus on the task at hand, ignoring the flood of nervousness in his stomach and the sound of pumping blood whooshing inside his head. Carefully, he navigated the hallway, avoiding the plethora of rotting bodies. The scent of decay hung thick in the air, burning his nostrils the further he moved through the halls. Something would have to be done, a mass burial of some sort.

He couldn't think of it now, because right now it was time to concentrate on getting that book. Hopefully it would have a cure for Sorcia, or at least an explanation for her condition.

"This way," Kane whispered, the two necromancers — one a silver panther, the other a tiger — complied. Their paws padded silently along the carpeted hall, swirling, star-like eyes scrutinizing every shadow-cloaked corner. Less than half of the enchanted torches remained lit; the rest had been ripped from the wall and left to die alongside the sea of dead demons.

Everything was quiet, too quiet. Kane wondered if the beast had left, satisfied with the death and destruction it left in its wake. A glimmer of optimism kindled inside his chest, hoping he was right and the invisible monster had left them alone. While he didn't want to let his guard down just yet, he had faith that at least part of this nightmare might be over.

"It's just ahead," Kane told his comrades, leading the way with growing confidence.

Ahead, Kane could see that the library doors had been torn from their hinges and left mangled in hallway. He stepped over the debris and into the room of books. "Guard the doors," he ordered the silver cats as he located one of the many broken torches within the room, relighting it. A mess of books lay before him, none in their rightful place upon the shelves. He sighed; it was going take some time to sort through them, to find the one Ozen needed.

Further and further he pressed through the havoc of the room. He could no longer see the front entrance as he navigated fallen bookshelves and toppled statues. The light from the torch glowed orange, giving the dark room an eerie hue. Shadowy corners seemed to twitch from the flicker of the flame, growing and shrinking, reaching for him. Kane did his best to ignore his growing paranoia, picking up every book and examining it.

"It has to be here," he said aloud, his voice echoing off the empty walls. Upon examining book after book, he began to worry he'd never find it and the last banshee would die before he got the chance to save her.

He spun about, the light of his torch reaching all corners of the room. In one dark corner, something gleamed gold, almost as though it had heard his call and responded. Excited, Kane stumbled over the mess of books and located it. Upon picking it up, he grinned. Gilded words, The Encyclopedia of the Races, danced before his eyes.

Kane hurried back to the doorway, anxious to get back to the garden. "I found it," he said, realizing in that moment that his loyal necromancers were not at their post. "Mezza? Slater?" he said, lowering his voice. They'd probably gone to investigate a sound or something. After a few minutes of awaiting their return, Kane began to worry. He glanced up and down the hall, neither direction providing a clue as to their whereabouts.

Where would they go without telling me? Kane worried. *Perhaps I should head back by myself.*

The thought had no sooner passed through his mind when he heard a terrific roar come from his right. He tucked the book between his left elbow and ribcage, then armed himself with his sword. Cautiously, he approached the corner, hearing the sounds of a scuffle. His heart thrummed alongside the sound of hisses, snarls, and growls. Kane rounded the hall to the left and his eyes widened with disbelief.

Where he thought he would see the necromancers fending off a foe, he witnessed them attacking one another.

"What are you doing!" Kane yelled, the threat of the invisible beast forgotten. The two stopped immediately, their silvery, feline heads hung in shame. Still in shock, Kane continued with his interrogation, "I thought necromancers were peaceful, evolved beings? What could you possibly be fighting over?"

Both melted into their true forms, heads still bowed in shame. After a moment, Mezza answered, "Sorcia."

"Sorcia?" Kane sputtered, his brow creased. "I don't understand."

"We both...love her," Slater admitted, his galactic eyes spinning with angst.

Kane sighed. He understood what it was to love a woman so fiercely that it defies reason. A vision of Fate rolled before his eyes and how he'd felt when she ran away. Nothing could keep him from finding her, not his responsibilities, not his pride, not even Ever.

"I understand your predicament," he said, though he really hadn't considered this dilemma previously. It made sense that they would be divided when it came to Sorcia as there were two of them and only one of her. It was bound to become an issue.

But now was not the time.

Kane rolled his eyes, shaking his head. "Let's just get this book to the garden. We can discuss this later." He turned and started leading them back.

Heads lowered, they obeyed. The darkened hallways didn't seem as treacherous as they did on the way to the library. Kane felt a weight lift from his shoulders as they made the last turn towards the entrance of the garden. Perhaps the beast was truly gone; and they could leave the confines of their temporary home, start to bury their loved ones, give them a proper good-bye and begin to rebuild.

Suddenly a loud boom exploded in his ears, bringing Kane to his knees. The pressure inside the hallway squeezed him as though in a vice. Behind him, the necromancers had fallen to the floor unconscious. The book dropped from Kane's grasp as darkness fell over his eyes like a veil. His last thoughts were of Ever and Fate—and how he might never see them again.

Malus

A winding, snaking sensation crawled through her, feeling both sharp and slithery at the same time. It was like a vine of lovely yet deadly roses, the thorns pricking her insides. Malus tossed and turned in her sleep, the dark feeling writhing within. Her dream had her held tight by huge invisible hands, the right hand wrapped around her shoulders, the left about her hips and thighs. They rotated her in opposing directions, the top twisting away from the bottom. Then, after her shrieks of pain, the hands would bring her body back to center, and begin bending her abnormally in the contrasting position.

She could not see the owner of the hands, only that they were enormous and pale with a hint of translucency. They were relentless as Malus's spine bent beyond its capability, relinquishing loudly snapping and cracking as it broke with every unnatural turn. Her screams went unheard as she endured the torture...

"My queen," a panicked, insistent voice sounded in her head. "Wake up!"

Her consciousness rose to the surface, groping amidst the thick darkness, as if her lungs were desperate for air. She searched for herself, willing her eyes—Ever's eyes—to open. Finally, her soul saw the light and swam to the surface.

Myth

Malus sat up in her bed, perspiration dripping from her face, soaking her linens and comforter. Her sight, still blurry, fought to see clearly. What had happened? What manner of nightmare had overtaken her?

"My lady?" Maxim queried, his glowing white gaze fixed on her with concern. "You were screaming. I came as fast as I could but...I could not help you," he said, handing her a glass of water.

She took it from him, gulping it greedily. It wet her parched tongue, dribbling down the sides of her mouth and onto her heaving chest. There didn't seem to be enough air in the room to calm her panic.

After several moments, she felt composed enough to stand and put her robe on. Drawing it closed, Malus finally began to feel a bit more like herself.

Maxim, sensing she was better, descended the raised bed's staircase, bowing before he took his leave. He turned to her before exiting, stating, "Please call me if you need anything, my queen."

Malus nodded, holding the back of her vanity chair for support. She'd never experienced such terror, or such profound realism inside a dream before. Never the fool, she suspected her granddaughter's body as the culprit. It was rejecting the foreign soul inside of it, treating it as though it were a parasite, an illness from which it could rid itself.

When she was inside Sybil, she had anticipated it might happen but was surprised when it didn't. The oracle's body willingly, easily, adapted to having Malus's soul harbored within. Once Malus thought about it, it made sense. The oracle was a shade, a human made soulless by means of damnation, so it was simply a vessel, a home awaiting a new essence.

In contrast, Ever's body still had her soul intact, a powerful sphere of pure love and innocence—and it was trying to push Malus's soul out.

Malus looked into the mirror, seeing herself inside the girl's sapphire stare. There was only one way she could fix this. Only one way she could claim this body as her own.

She'd have to exorcise Ever's soul.

Fate closed her eyes, summoning the memories of the necromancers to the forefront of her mind. She could feel the silver blood stir within her, blending with her own as it filled her with the essence of a thousand necromancer souls. They whispered all around her, leading her through the last stretch of the labyrinth. While she couldn't picture what lay at the end, the entrance to the Guf, she simply allowed them to take over her thoughts and guide her to her soul.

As she walked forward, a soft, bell-like sound rang in her ears. Just as she rounded the last corner lay a sight she could not have imagined.

"The Guf," she uttered, her eyes filling with tears. She could not have invented something so beautiful, so perfect, so...*heavenly.*

The light she'd seen from afar, the white illumination that pierced the blackened clouds of Dark World, shone only a few steps away from her. It wasn't just a light, it was the doorway to the Guf. The entrance didn't appear solid, they wavered like a white and gold prism made of crystal. Fate could see thousands, millions, of souls floating just beyond, trailing streams of blue behind them as they seemed to gleefully, effortlessly, glide through the air.

There was a staircase leading up to the transparent doorway with seven steps, tentatively, she took a step up. Her stomach twisted as she awaited the arrival of the last test. The creature that had mimicked her had told her there would be one more test.

Only one before you has passed...

The creature's last message sent a shiver up Fate's spine. Only one other had made it through? That seemed impossible. How many had tried to win their souls back? What challenge could be harder than what she'd already faced? What could be worse than fighting Behemoth? Or a being that looks exactly like you but embodies pure evil? She thought back to all the monsters she'd endured since arriving in Dark World, all the creatures she'd fought successfully. What was one more? What could the Guf or the maze offer that was any worse than what she'd already encountered?

Fate knew, from Kraton, that she'd have to convince her soul to come back into her body, and that likely wasn't going to be easy. It looked rather peaceful in the Guf. If she were a soul, she probably wouldn't want to go back inside a heavy, pain-ridden meat suit either.

She glanced around, still nothing jumped out at her, so that was encouraging. She ventured another step, then another, until she stood before the mighty door. There were no door handles to speak of, so she was uncertain as to how they opened.

Touch it, the necromancers whispered in her ear.

After drawing in a shaky breath, Fate brought her hands up and pressed them against the glowing, ivory glass. A soft vibration tickled her palms, sending a gentle hum up her arms. Her instinct was to pull away, worried that it was a trick, but something inside her wanted to be near it, like a moth drawn to the flicker of a warm, golden flame. She closed her eyes, allowing herself to be pulled forward, taken in by the lullaby of song emanating from the Guf, the warm, infinite affection wrapping its arms around her, the tender sway of unseen hands as they rocked her like a newborn babe, swaddled in bliss and everlasting love.

She wanted to stay for all eternity. Everything outside, her life, her death, her friends and family, all faded like a dream that disintegrated upon awakening. She was in Heaven. She was home.

She never wanted to go back…ever.

Vale

Vincent forced himself to stay awake, his eyes dry and heavy as he pretended to sleep on the bunk above his sister. He took slow, steady breaths, feigning a solid slumber as he awaited her move to leave. It was nearly midnight by the time she decided it was safe to sneak out. Long, silvery fingers of moonlight stretched across the aged floorboards, embracing Sybil in an ethereal glow as she took careful steps towards the door and quickly slipped through.

Already dressed, Vincent threw off his covers the moment he heard the front door click shut. He swiftly donned his coat and boots, then followed his sister out into the night.

Packed snow crunched beneath his boots, the chilled night air brushing against his skin. It was colder this night than the one previous, when he'd followed Sybil to the bridge and overheard her plans to meet Blake. He shook his head, uncertain as to whom he was more annoyed with: his sister or his would-be best friend. Why did they go sneaking around behind his back? Why not come right out, be honest, and proclaim their intentions?

He sighed. Perhaps he wouldn't have accepted it that way either. It was strange but Vincent was— reluctant as he was to admit it—jealous of their relationship. He wasn't sure he liked the idea of sharing his newfound friend with his sister. It was silly, he admitted, that he wanted to keep Blake from seeing Sybil. After all, if Vincent had met a girl and fell head over heels for her, he wouldn't give a hoot if Sybil disagreed with it.

But something about this tryst didn't feel right. It wasn't their age, as Sybil was sixteen and Blake a few years older. It wasn't that Vincent thought Blake wouldn't treat her right, although he really didn't know the fellow well enough to stake a bet on the matter.

No, something else was niggling at him, stirring his instincts. Something just didn't sit right with him.

The midnight sky loomed like a dark curtain overhead, the stars nearly drowned out by the shine of the Harvest moon. Round and glaring, the celestial sphere burned a hole through the blackness, a ghostly silver halo hugging its edges tight. Vincent tried his best to follow Sybil's footsteps in the snow, but since he'd followed her the previous night, many a creature had plodded its own course through the forest, leaving Vincent to guess that she'd head straight for the bridge where they'd met up the night before.

It wasn't long before he came upon the bridge, its rounded shadow set against a backdrop of illuminated, leafless poplars. Vincent paused, straining his senses to locate his sister or Blake. The wind sat eerily still, bringing neither voices nor the groan of tree limbs. Where had they gone?

Annoyed, Vincent climbed the embankment and stepped onto the bridge. The road on either side was barren of fresh footprints, showing only the marks of many horses and their wheeled cargo. He closed his eyes, trying to think where they'd go.

Then he heard a scream.

It was faint, but he'd heard it carried upon the slightest breeze from the east. His heart pounded against his ribcage with the fury of a wild, caged animal as he ran across the bridge and into the thick of the woods beyond it. All he could think about was getting to Sybil, saving her from whatever evils might be holding her. A sick sensation curdled inside his stomach. Why did he suspect Blake of foul play? The guy had been nothing but kind, what with offering to teach Vincent to read. That sort of thing took time, effort, but there was always something else, an underlying evil lurking behind the stranger's smile.

Vincent thought back as he ran through the shin-deep snows, considering what he really knew of the person called Blake Dean. He knew he was a drifter, a traveller of many lands. He'd seen the way he looked at the ever-growing list of female admirers in town. He'd seen something in his eyes, something dark, something...

Another scream. This one muffled, pained, and cut short.

Panic pushed him faster! Harder! He had to get to her!

Finally, Vincent entered into a clearing, fully illuminated by the blaze of the Harvest Moon. In the center of it, a shadowy form stood over a strange marking upon the ground. Vincent approached the figure, fear thrust aside by shock and confusion.

Beside the black emblem lay Sybil's clothing, jacket, and boots—but Sybil was nowhere to be seen. Upon closer inspection, Vincent could distinguish a misshapen pool of deep red in the center of what looked like a star.

Vincent stormed up to the shadowed person, knowing instinctively it was Blake, and took him by the collar with both hands. "Where is she!" he shouted, his voice trembling as he shook Blake. "What did you do to her!"

Blake only smiled. Darkness playing about his face as he finally replied, "She belongs to Malus now."

"Who?" Vincent couldn't steady his quavering voice. "Who's Malus?"

Blake laughed at him, a twinkle of insanity afire in his eyes. "The new Devil, of course."

Despite his fury with Blake, and the sickness roiling inside his stomach, Vincent fell to his knees and tunnelled through the snow as though Sybil lay just beneath the surface. "Where? Where is her...body?" he whispered, almost to himself as he clawed at the frozen dirt beneath the bloodstained snow. He knew she must be dead as he couldn't feel her presence anymore. It was like she just didn't exist anymore.

"Where is she? What did you do to her!" Vincent screamed as he jumped up and took a swing at Blake, hitting him in the jaw and knocking him to the ground. He couldn't stop himself; the anger raged throughout him as he punched Blake over and over, spittle flying from his mouth as he screamed alongside every strike, "Where! Where is she!"

Amid all of this, Blake laughed. Finally, too tired to continue, Vincent rolled off into the snow and lay there, looking up at the sentient stars, wondering why they did nothing to help his sister, or him, or anyone.

They were witness to many a heinous event, yet never intervened, never saved a soul.

Both of them just laid there, their breath rising into the cold of night, until Blake spoke suddenly, "I can show you where I sent her."

Vincent felt exhausted, dead inside, while hot tears rolled from his eyes. "You can?" he asked.

Blake nodded. "Meet me here in one year. Then you will see your sister again. Tell *no one*."

A million questions bombarded Vincent's thoughts, but instead of asking any of them, he agreed, and then summoned the will to live three hundred and seventy-five days of agony.

Rory

A daunting path lay before him, narrow and cling-ing to the sheer face of an obsidian mountain. Some-thing below called to him, like a whisper without words. A knowing.

Below was nothing but a thick, silver miasma, veil-ing whatever lay beneath. He started his descent, hour after hour, holding tight to nothing but the faith that he was supposed to find something below. Halfway through his plight, he came across an oddity in the middle of the tiny road leading downward. It was a miniature, stone gargoyle; its eyes were frozen wide in fright. He stared at it, wondering what last sights it had seen that had induced such intense horror.

He shook his head. What was he thinking? This was nothing but a chunk of rock, shaped by an artist's hands into that of a mythological creature. Yet, it looked so real. So detailed, as though it had truly been a living, breathing creature. Then why had it turned to stone? And why was it up there, trapped on the side of a cliff? His foot ached to kick it over the side. It was in his way, after all.

But something stopped him.

Rory sighed, compelled by the unknown to do something completely out of character. He reached down, took hold of the small figurine, tucked it under his arm and continued navigating down the harrow-ing track.

A layer of grey cloud shielded the ground. At the base of the mountain, Rory took slow and careful steps as he maneuvered the last of the narrow pathway. He didn't know why he felt so compelled to go this way, all he knew is it felt right, like something he was searching for would be revealed here. Was Malus here? His heart fluttered with the thought. After all his loyalty upon the Surface, would he finally be rewarded with an appropriate afterlife? Clutching the statue like a teddy bear, Rory gazed upon his hands, arms, and abdomen, the scores of dark lines tangling like the web of a poisonous spider. He wondered again, as the hunger flashed inside, if this was his penance, his punishment for all the lives he'd stolen in the name of Malus. He wondered if all who were sent to this world, including those he'd damned, transformed into flesh-lusting monsters—or was it just those who'd done as they were asked by their goddess.

A twinge of sadness arose in him. He'd only wanted immortality, only desired powers beyond that of a mere, pathetic human. He had been human once, an average nobody that blended in with those around him. Then he'd become one of the brotherhood. He'd had to change his name over the century of his life so as to hide from those who might discover his secrets. He'd given himself names such as Blake, Josh, and Rory; though he'd kept his real name a secret, a memory he'd no longer wanted to hold. There was nothing special about that boy, nothing worth remembering as he recalled with the venom of bitterness climbing into his throat.

That boy had been nothing, if not pathetic. He allowed people to hurt him, cried himself to sleep at

Myth

night after his father's drunken rage bruised more than just his childhood ego. That boy died one night, after finding his brother's secret in the barn: the scroll with golden writing. And once he discovered what it said, what he had to do to win Malus's favor, he didn't stop until the night Scarlet's friend, and brother put an end to his reign.

Rory pushed aside his dark nostalgia and inhaled deeply before he descended beneath the shroud and into the unknown. Once the clouds cleared, he surveyed his surroundings. A maze loomed before him, comprised of intertwined rocky spikes, like a forest of icicles. Just ahead, though, was a large opening; the beginning of the labyrinth. Excitement filled him.

This could prove to be fun.

He looked down at his new friend, wishing for a moment that he was real and not made of stone. If only he had someone to join him on this lonely journey.

Hesitantly, he set the baby gargoyle down gently, off to the side as he presumed it would be safer hidden amid the shadows. Then with a longing glance, he walked away.

He took several steps towards the threshold, wondering if there was something he wasn't seeing. In a life as long as his, he'd learned never to trust anything, or anyone, at face value. Cautiously, he stepped through the doorway, intending to take the straight path rather than the others to his left and right.

Upon his next step, however, the ground began to shake and tremble ever so slightly beneath his feet. Startled, he looked for something to climb up on or anything to grab on to. He tried to scream but thick, cool dirt filled his mouth, stifling his last pleas for help. From the darkness, the little gargoyle's eyes watched with its stony, terrified stare as the ground opened up beneath Rory and swallowed him.

Rory tried to claw his way out, but the soil sealed him in before he had a chance. His last thought before he was pulled further into darkness was of his hundreds of victims, and if this was how they'd felt after he'd damned them to Hell.

Fate's entire body vibrated as though every cell was alight with golden rays channeled directly from the sun. Her insides hummed and sang with a melody so beautiful it could not be heard with mortal ears. The atmosphere was thick and warm and carried within it a mist tinged pink and gold, embracing her as she walked through the bliss. It was a like garden without any flowers or trees, but the presence of something alive and compassionate stood nearby, whispering devoted thoughts into her ears and caressing her with love. Every so often, a soul would drift by; pause with interest, acknowledging her presence, then move on as gentle as a butterfly carried upon a breeze.

Her skin tingled all over, the only reminder that she still inhabited a corporeal body. With fleeting envy, she wished she were like the other souls inside the Guf, free and unhampered by the restrictions of the flesh.

Ahead, Fate could distinguish what appeared to be a set of thrones. The closer she got, the more she could see elaborate etchings upon nearly translucent crystal chairs. She walked towards them, curious as to who they might belong to. Did they belong to yet another god within the Underworld? Or was she in the presence of something far more benevolent?

Danielle Q. Lee

Behind her, a soul passed by, traces of sapphire trailing long behind it like a ribbon of blue fire. This soul was different from all the others; it pulled at her core, willed her to follow it.

"That's her...that's my soul!" Fate thought excitedly, recognizing the essence of herself as it bobbed and swam through the pearlescent air. She followed her soul cautiously, as not to frighten it away. Something told her it wasn't going to be easy to coax something so free back inside an old jail. Part of her didn't even want to retrieve it; it felt a sacrilege to imprison something so beautiful.

Fate paused suddenly, feeling watched by unseen eyes. Though she didn't feel alarmed or in danger, she knew there was something or someone, examining her and her movements. Her soul wandered away, hiding behind a group of other souls as if it had sensed the long arms of captivity reaching for it.

Strangely unbothered by the presence observing her, Fate merely glanced all around, endeavouring to find her mysterious admirer. To her right a figure approached from the pinkish fogs blurring her vision. Fate narrowed her eyes, trying to make out the features. As the form got closer, she could see that it was a being made purely of light with no distinguishing structures, like eyes, a nose, or a mouth, just a silhouette like something born of the sun.

"Fate," it said with a lyrical voice. *"We are so pleased you have come."*

"We?" Fate uttered, awestruck.

"We are many living in one," it replied. *"Please, come."* The being led her to the twin thrones and, taking seat in one, offered the other to Fate.

Surprised, Fate sat slowly on the other crystal throne. Clearing her throat, she began to speak, "Thank you. I'm here to…"

"*Obtain your soul,*" the being of light finished her sentence. "*That may not be an easy task,*" it concluded.

"What do I need to do?" Fate inquired, still uncertain as to whether or not she should continue on her quest to steal back her soul. This place was truly Heaven, to rip her essence from it would surely be unfair. She herself was still in the process of coming to terms with the fact that she couldn't stay in this wonderful place. Despite her longing to stay she realized that Kane and Ever still needed her—Dark World needed her; and she was required to help open the Crystal Pyramid, without her, this world would die.

"*You must do now what you could not.*" The being tilted its glowing head in what Fate felt was an endearment of sympathy.

Confused, Fate frowned, asking, "Do what? What do you mean?"

Immediately following her question, the room began to spin so fast that she couldn't make out anything in her surroundings, only that it got darker and colder. She just knew, instinctively, that she was no longer inside the Guf, and a brief wave of sadness eclipsed her. In the next instant, she found herself upon the ground, the scent of wet grass and soil filling her nostrils. A cool wind nipped at her cheeks, sending shivers rippling over her body. A spotlight of silver illumination shone down from overhead, painting every blade of grass with light. She looked around dazedly, wondering why this place looked so familiar. That's when she noticed the stars and the moon. Tears filled her eyes as she took in the enormity of it all, the openness. She inhaled, taking in the sensation of freedom. Without Dark World's ceiling of rock glaring down upon her, it was like seeing the sky for the first time. A smile crept across her lips.

She was home.

A chilled gust of wind whipped at her just then, blowing strands of her hair across her face—and that's when she noticed the color.

"It's brown," she whispered, grasping a chunk of her hair within her hands and examining it closely. "My hair…it's brown again." She looked down at the clothes she was wearing: a short red skirt and black knee-high boots. She gasped as she took in the scene.

She was surrounded by trees.

There was a black pentagram tattooed on the grass.

A knife.

Her heart picked up pace, mind racing.

"This can't be happening…" she whispered as a winged shadow took flight from a nearby poplar, fluttering off into the darkness.

Before she could analyze anything further, she heard a moan escape from her left. Alarmed, she spun about, seeing a shadow rise to standing, holding his head in his hands.

As the light of the moon struck his face, Fate felt her knees grow weak with fear.

Her throat tightened in terror as she uttered, *"Rory?"*

Voices.

Whispers.

Darkness.

Kane willed his senses to focus, summoned his consciousness to the surface, fighting through the murky depths of oblivion to return to himself.

What had happened? Where was he?

"Kane?" a soft voice drifted through his awakening mind. "Kane, it's alright. You're back in the garden," It said, the voice reminiscent of Elder Ozen.

"Ozen?" Kane forced his mouth to reply, his tongue feeling as though it was made of stone. "What happened?" Slowly, Kane wrenched his eyelids open, a glare of white light shone overhead. Encircled round him were many of his friends: Ozen, Deme, even Syphon.

"The beast, it attacked you," Ozen explained. "It's a wonder you survived!"

Memories rose to the surface then, followed by concern. "Mezza? Slater?" he inquired hurriedly.

"They are fine," Ozen answered. "Let's get you up now."

Several helping hands took him by the arms and gently set him upright. His head swam and eyes blurred. Whatever that creature was that was stalking the halls of Legion could offer one heck of beating. He nodded his thanks to Syphon and Deme, after which they took their leave to allow Kane time to recover and speak with Ozen.

Suddenly recalling his mission to retrieve the book from the library to help the banshee princess, he asked, "The book? Sorcia?"

Ozen only smiled, replying, "Come, see for yourself."

Intrigued, Kane followed the elder on unsteady legs to the back of the garden. Upon parting the jade fronds acting as a veil, Kane's eyes widened.

"What…" he uttered, unsure if what he was seeing was supposed to be good or not.

Sorcia lay upon her back, her skin jellylike in texture, oozing and running with some kind of clear, viscous liquid. Kane suppressed a disgusted look. The once beautiful banshee had been reduced to a gelatinous blob.

But Ozen only grinned at the confused prince, which seemed a very odd reaction indeed, all things considering. Kane gave him an inquisitive stare, wondering if the old demon had lost what remained of his ancient mind.

Finally, holding up the *Encyclopedia of the Races*, Ozen explained, "Princess Sorcia appears to be in a sort of…*quickening.*"

Kane shook his head, offering the elder a bewildered expression. "Meaning?"

The elder frowned, apparently searching for the right words. "She's changing. Transforming, if you will."

Kane glanced over at the large globule that used to be a beautiful princess. Though wary of the answer, he asked, "What will she be?"

"According to the book," Ozen tapped the cover of the encyclopedia with the talon on his pointer finger, "She's undergoing a birthing process of sorts. The book referred to it as *mitosis*. The metamorphosis of daughter cells, really amazing, simply fascinating..." he rambled on.

Frustration building, Kane narrowed his gaze at his mentor. "Please, explain in simple terms."

The corners of Elder Ozen's lips lifted. "She's giving birth by splitting into two." Kane scrunched up his face, picturing Sorcia in two halves. Ozen elaborated, "There will be two of her, identical twins. Apparently," he chuckled, "banshees have the most remarkable reproductive system. Of course, we never knew of this, given we were not privy to knowledge of this race over the last few centuries. Of course, I'd have looked it up in the library had I known..."

Kane looked at the banshee, or what remained of her, with wonder. She was reproducing by splitting into two. Part of him was shocked, but it made perfect sense. When they'd come upon the banshee palace, he was surprised at how incredibly similar all of the female banshees were to one another. Then a thought struck him.

"How then, I wonder, did the banshee king come about?" he pondered aloud.

"Ahh, there is something about that in here." Ozen flipped the book open, perusing a few pages before announcing, "Aha! Here it is! *Whence the female banshee population becomes of suitable size,*" he read, "*a spontaneous mutation of the gender will occur, providing the race with a leader. This leader, a male, will not have reproductive abilities, but rather offer the race an inborn heir, relieving the females of the burden of choosing amidst their own, thus preventing disparity amongst the sisters."*

Kane raised his brows. "I wonder how many ban-shees need to be...born," he used the word tentatively, "in order to trigger the birth of the king?"

"I do not know," Ozen replied, obviously spell-bound with the entire process as he scanned Sorcia with interested eyes. "It is not without peril, howev-er." He tapped a long fingernail onto a page, offering a wary stare over his glasses. "She may not survive it at all."

From the corner of his eye, Kane noticed Mezza and Slater eavesdropping on the conversation, their faces bursting with a mixture of excitement and concern.

Kane smiled to himself as he left the makeshift critical care unit. Two Sorcias. Fixed that problem.

Now for the other one.

His entire being cringed with what he was about to do; but he owed it to his people, to Dark World and to his father.

Kane climbed up onto a large stone in the center of the garden and gazed down upon the survivors. His heart swelled with a mixture of pride and regret. While his people had done well without him, tackled the tragedy at hand with remarkable skill and bravery, he felt, and he knew with all his being, that he owed them so much more than he'd given them.

"Please," he started, raising his voice but smiling as he motioned for them to gather round. "I need a word with you."

His heart thrummed nervously in his chest as he readied himself for the worst. What if they didn't agree? What if it was the wrong choice? He steeled himself, knowing it was the right answer—it had to be.

Kane inhaled, then began. "I know these past few days have been extremely trying. I want you to know just how proud I am of your hard work and dedication to your brother and sister demons. I hope you know," he said, lowering his gaze, "that I wish I had been amongst you during your darkest hour. For that, I apologize." A low murmur spread through the crowd, but he continued, "I do however, have a plan...one that I hope you will embrace, as I feel it is the right choice."

Hundreds of eyes were locked on him, waiting, wondering. Did they still have enough faith in him? Would they concede to his idea?

"Queen Malus is dead, this I'm sure you've heard," he spoke solemnly. "Which leaves this world without a leader. As my father's son, rightful heir of Dark World, I..." Kane paused, "I hereby claim my birthright, and with your blessing, I offer myself to you as the Devil of Dark World."

Eerie silence smothered the room followed by hissing whispers. Did they not want him? Had they lost all faith in him?

Kane frowned, glancing about, looking for Elder Ozen. Instead, he met with Syphon's stare.

Syphon cleared his throat. "Sire, we thought you'd heard, that is, we thought you knew."

Kane stepped down from the makeshift podium. "Knew what?"

Ozen burst through the crowd then, making his way to Kane, his expression grave. "Prince, I'm so sorry. With all this...all the mess, we didn't think..." his voice trailed off.

Adrenalin surged through his system. What did they know that he didn't. "Please," he asked, forcing control. "Tell me."

"Sire," Ozen replied, tears welling in his eyes. "The queen is not dead."

Shock raced through his body, sending prickles over his skin. "Not dead?" He shook his head. "I watched her die. She is dead, I swear to you."

Ozen tried to explain, but only managed to sputter a few words before covering his mouth and turning away.

Syphon stepped in. "Sire, there is word from our spies in the Blood Palace...the queen lives."

"But how?" Kane asked, confused. "I saw her body, I saw her remains..."

The elder responded quickly, cutting the prince off in mid-sentence, "She lives on another body."

Kane shook his head, hoping it wasn't true. "W-whose?"

Syphon paused before answering, his eyes raised upwards in palpable torment, "Ever's, your highness."

Vale

The night had come. The night he'd waited an entire year to endure in order to see Sybil again. Blake had disappeared after Vincent had found him in the clearing, Sybil's clothes scattered beside a pentagram drawn in black, her body nowhere in sight. The year had been agony, his silence eating him inside out like a plague. His parents had been destroyed by their only daughter's disappearance. It broke Vincent's heart that he could not tell them what little he did know. He knew if he did, he was certain that Blake would break his promise and not show Vincent what he did to Sybil.

Blake had described the ceremony, which could only be done by the light of a Harvest Moon. In his grief, Vincent believed him, begging him to do to him what had been done to Sybil.

Blake promised he'd return on the agreed evening and perform the ritual on Vincent.

He made good on his dark promise.

Now, in the shadow of the void, Vale felt the sting of tears behind his eyes. If he had known exactly what Blake was going to do, where he was sending him—he would not have gone through with it.

Even for Sybil.

He'd stabbed Vincent in the heart, left him to drown in a tomb of wet soil as he sank into a dark unknown.

And that was the best part.

When Vale awoke from his human nightmare almost a century ago, he realized very quickly he'd made a grave error.

The heat licked at the boy's skin like the tongue of a great beast sizing him up for dinner. He couldn't focus on the world around him yet, his newborn eyes blurred as though they were not his own. This body felt wrong somehow, it was cold despite the searing heat surrounding him. He held his head in his hands, willing his thoughts to clear, trying in vain to remember what happened before this.

He could not.

The only memories he possessed at present was that of being born in the center of a black flower. He didn't know his name. He didn't recognize his own body. He only knew, deep inside, that he'd lived before this, owned a different body, a different mind.

"Achete mion!" a voice yelled from behind him, instinctive fear rose quickly inside of him and he cowered before even knowing who was there.

Rough hands took hold of him on either side, forcing him to stand upon his unstable feet. He summoned the courage to look at his captors, shocked by their appearance. Both had hair as white as snow with glowing eyes to match. While they had human attributes, they were most certainly not human. They appeared to be soldiers of some kind, as their garb indicated rank and both were armed with swords. They spoke in a foreign tongue, with words he could not comprehend nor had ever heard previously, he was sure. Despite his lack of memory, he felt a knowing inside of him, like his soul was whispering to him in a voice too quiet to hear.

"*Demach sul docha,*" one of the fiends said to the other, and they laughed as they dragged him to a nearby carriage, drawn by a hellish creature that looked like an enormous, hairless dog.

Thrown into the back of the cart, a steel door slammed, locking him in. He slunk into a corner and drew his knees to his chest. Whatever this place was, he sensed it was dangerous and unfriendly.

After a long, bumpy ride, they appeared to have arrived at their destination. He pressed his face to the window with bars, watching with wild, frightened eyes as he was being taken over a bridge and through a set of huge, golden gates. This was some kind of castle. He glanced back before they closed the big doors, seeing it had a moat that looked to be made of blood.

A shiver of cold fear raced over his naked skin. Where was he? Where were they taking him?

After a short ride, the conveyance stopped and the two soldiers hauled him out of the back, dragging him towards a large, stone building. Moans and screams echoed all around him, the scent of death and decay stinging his nostrils and filling his lungs.

He looked upward, taking in what appeared to be an enormous stone castle wall. Before he could examine any further, he was thrust into a small room to his right. Yet another white-haired being dressed him with a thin and dirty tunic, stained red with what he assumed was the blood of the previous owner. Then, with rough hands, the two soldiers escorted him through a series of winding tunnels, each darker and damper than the last. Dim torches lit their way as they descended into the bowels of the castle; the light seemed almost unable to penetrate the thick of the shadows. The echo of torturous screams were louder here, entering his ears and then seeping into his soul.

"*Melach no satcha*," the guard to his right said as he opened a cell door and unceremoniously tossed him inside. They laughed as they walked away, leaving him in nearly pitch blackness.

What was this place? Who was he? What had happened to bring him here?

And most of all—what was to happen to him?

Hot tears rolled from his eyes, fear owning every cell in his body. He shivered as he pressed his back to the wall and shrunk to the floor, sobbing quietly.

"*Donta seela may*," a gentle voice whispered in the darkness. The boy heard shuffling amid the shadows to his right. Instinct told him to be wary, but something in the voice calmed him, told him it would be alright.

Suddenly he felt a hand upon his head, he tried to move away but was frozen to the spot by some sort of paralysis.

"*Querasrias leacha dela mea*," the voice uttered and a spark of bright blue ignited atop the boy's head. "There, is that better?"

Confused, the boy replied slowly, "Yes, you are speaking my words now."

The owner of the voice chuckled softly, "No, now you are speaking mine. You can now speak *Attra*, Dark World's native tongue." An illumination grew then, muted amber hues lit up the dungeon walls.

Myth

Across from him was an elderly being, his skin colored pure silver. He was smiling at the boy.

"I...don't understand," the boy said. "Who are you? Where am I?"

The silver man nodded. "Yes, I suppose you have many questions." He paused, gathering his thoughts. "I am Vrill. I'm a necromancer."

The boy frowned, confused. "What's a necromancer?"

Vrill only smiled. "We'll get to that later. First things first, you need a name. How about...Vale? It means dark wanderer in my language."

"Vale?" the boy said, tasting the word on his own lips, then relinquished a smile. "I like it."

The necromancer then sat, arranging himself comfortably. "Well, then, let's get you acquainted with Dark World, shall we?"

For the next few hours, Vrill explained what had happened to Vale, where he was, and mostly, what was to happen to him. He explained that Vale was now a shade, an undead being whose soul had been stolen from him, and was now damned to a magical, yet vicious, underworld.

Vale shook his head, trying to comprehend. "So, this Queen Malus, she's going to test me to see how obedient I'm am? And if I fail?"

"You will be put to death," Vrill replied grimly.

Vale lowered his gaze, trying to wrap his head around this uncertain future. If he passed, he would be a slave to the Devil. If he failed, he'd face death. "What other option do I have?" he asked sadly.

Vrill's star-like eyes spun with a new light. "You can come with me."

They spent the next few hours discussing escape routes and strategies. By the end, Vale felt confident that he and his new friend could manage it.

"Now," Vrill began, his voice quiet as they awaited the guard to bring Vale to his examination. "There's one more thing I should tell you."

Vale narrowed his eyes, heart picking up pace. "What's that?"

"All shades have a magical talent," Vrill stated as though it was every day that one learned they were an undead creature with supernatural powers.

"Oh?" Vale was suddenly excited. "What's mine?"

Vrill shook his head. "It's impossible to know until you do it, but if you focus, you might be able to access it. It could be a gift that is very helpful to our cause. Try closing your eyes and breathing slowly, like meditation."

Vale obliged, breathing deeply until he felt a shift in his environment. Almost immediately, there was a new sensation surrounding him. A cool breeze wafted by his face and he opened his eyes. Shocked, he realized he was no longer inside the jail cell, but just outside of it.

"What happened? What did I just do?" Vale exclaimed, examining his hands as though they held the answer. He couldn't believe it. It was like he had turned into a ghost and simply walked through the solid door. He grinned, thinking for the first time that he might actually like something about this weird and wild world.

"Vale!" a hasty whisper came from behind the cell door, snapping Vale from his shock. "Unlock the door!"

Doing as he was told, Vale fumbled with the door. It was void of any real lock mechanism, and he found that it was merely held shut with a latch that could not be reached from the inside. Lifting it, he let Vrill out and they then began the arduous task of manoeuvring through the labyrinth of tunnels.

"This way," Vrill's quieted voice guided him through the darkened passage. It was strangely lacking in shade guards. Vale kept waiting for them to jump out at him from every corner. Then from what seemed like directly overhead, he heard what sounded like thousands of voices shouting and cheering.

"What's that?" Vale inquired, keeping his voice low.

"The testing arena." Vrill sounded grim. "If the one being tested fails, they are to fight the queen's pets."

"Pets?" Vale swallowed hard.

"You don't want to know," Vrill said honestly. "Let's keep going."

They wound their way for what felt like miles, all the while expecting to run into one of the queen's guard. Finally, ahead, a reddish light glowed bright, edging the exit in a blood-red hue.

"There it is," Vrill said. "The way out."

Vale's undead heart beat hard against his ribcage. He was so close to being free, to starting a new life of mystery and magic.

He was almost excited.

They moved cautiously towards the exit, ever careful of any movement or noise. Vale licked his lips, his tongue dry and sticky inside his mouth. His stomach wrenched with nerves, his thoughts tied in knots. He didn't want this to be yet another end. While he couldn't remember much of the life previous to this, he desperately wanted to live this one. He knew he had a purpose, something very important he had to do before his time here was over.

Sister, a quiet voice whispered inside of him, like a buried thought that had clawed its way out of a deep, dark tomb.

Before he had time to contemplate it, however, a cluster of shadows crossed before the threshold to freedom.

Their luck had run out.

Stillness.

Even the wind seemed to hold its breath as the scene unfolded before it. The moon gazed down onto the clearing, its silvery tendrils of illumination reaching for them within the pitch of night. It was just the two of them again — Scarlet and Rory.

Amid the quiet, even the tiniest breaths of wind rattled the parched leaves surrounding them, like whispers all around.

Rory stood, facing his prey, his eyes wrought with bewilderment. "I'm back," he uttered, almost unaware Scarlet stood before him.

Scarlet narrowed her gaze. "You're not real," she said aloud, though it was mostly for her own benefit. "This is just another test."

"Test?" he asked, seeming to be in a world all his own as he turned his chin up to the dark sky and drew in a deep breath as though tasting the Surface air for the first time.

Scarlet eyed him suspiciously, uncertain if this was yet another trick conjured by the guardians of the Guf. Was he just another figment? A ruse in order to teach her a lesson? Any moment now, he was going to morph into some horrific monster and try to kill her. It wouldn't surprise her.

She cast her gaze over the enclosed meadow. The trees appeared genuine. The sky above her, vast and yawning, hardly seemed fake. Bringing her hands up, she examined them, turning them over to see the palms and then the tops again. She smiled. The lamia was gone. The shade was gone. She was human again. Had she already passed the test? Was the nightmare over?

Or was it all for show? She'd seen and experienced the magic, both evil and good, of Dark World. This could just be an enchantment, created to give her an opportunity to relive the worst moment of her human life.

Scarlet looked at Rory, who like her, appeared to be mesmerized. "Are we really here?" he smiled. "Are we really back?"

Scarlet shrugged an answer at him, wondering what had transpired since she'd last seen him. Had he murdered more girls, damned them to the dark underworld? Fed their souls to the queen? Trepidation never left her as she continued to monitor his every move, readying herself for whatever he might do. He was evil. A killer. He'd left her for dead, bleeding and damned to Hell.

That horrible night surfaced in her mind; and how he'd used her affection for him to trick her, leading her to the clearing with the promise of stargazing. She recalled the fear she'd felt when she saw his friends in the clearing, knowing immediately that something terrible was amiss. How they'd chased her down, ripped off her clothing, and shackled her to the ground within the pentagram. Then, callously, he'd stabbed her, puncturing her heart, delivering her into the arms of evil.

She'd lost everything. Her family. Her future. Her soul.

Fury curled inside of her, tightening in her core, heating her blood. She glowered at him, wanting him to know what he did, to feel her pain.

She looked around, taking in the replica of the last moments of her existence as Scarlet.

The pentagram.

The knife.

It lay there, taunting her, begging her to pick it up and do to him what he'd done to her. He deserved it, after all. An eye for eye, as they say.

She took step forward, her hands shaking with anger more than fear. She could do this; after all she'd killed before as a shade. What would be the difference? It was payback? What was the worst that could happen? She would go back to Hell?

Scarlet almost laughed out loud as she inched ever nearer to the blade. It seemed to sing as it glowed in the silvery light of the moon. It was so close, right there, near enough to bend down and grab.

Her eyes rose to Rory, ready to see his evil blood drip from his body. There he was, her killer, standing before her looking just like the boy she'd had a crush on not so long ago. His wavy brown hair, so perfect and touchable; his steely blue eyes glinting with the full moon. He was right there, ripe for her wrath.

Scarlet stopped cold, something was different about him. The air of smug confidence he'd always worn like a shield had dimmed. He seemed damaged, weary, and...*changed.*

She watched him as he took in his surroundings, examining the markings on the grass and the knife with brooding eyes. Scarlet could almost see his thoughts rolling around in his head, then he looked at her with an expression she'd never seen on him before.

Remorse.

"Scarlet," he began, lowering his stare. "I...I'm so sorry."

A breath caught in her throat. Was this real? Was he truly Rory? Did he feel badly for what he'd done to her?

"I...don't know what to say," she admitted, truly shocked. Waves of mixed emotions rolled through her: hatred, pity, fear. How could she forgive him after everything he'd done to her and everything that had happened? How could she turn a blind eye to the things he had done? The things he'd forced to her live through? She fought with the emotions clashing within, wrath and sympathy trying to dwell in a space where only one could live. She thought of her parents, her brother, Greg, and Shelby; what they'd lost.

Scarlet closed her eyes, hot tears building. How dare he apologize? How dare he think mere words could make it all okay? To forgive him would be to admit there was still some sliver of good in all that happened.

What good had come from her misery?

Kane, a voice whispered from out of nowhere.

Her heart ached, torn by conflicting emotions. If not for Rory, she would never have met Kane. Nor Vale, Aura, Vrill, and Ick. She wouldn't have learned what she could become, how powerful a being she could be. Despite the delivery, Rory had given her a gift. A precious one.

"I know it's impossible to ask for you to forgive me," he said, looking boyish as he ran his hand through his hair. "But, I just really want you to know how sorry I am. I know I don't deserve your forgiveness, but for what it's worth, I'm sorry."

Scarlet was surprised to find that she'd smiled at him before saying, "I guess, sometimes, the worst endings pave the way for the best beginnings."

"Can we...just go home now?" he wondered with frown, searching the darkness as though it had the answers. Suddenly, he turned as though compelled, walking to the edge of the clearing. As he neared the wall of trees dividing the meadow from the outside world, a dome of light erected around them, sealing them in.

"Apparently not," Scarlet replied, noticing how the hairs on her arms were rising. The air had changed. Something was wrong.

Rory turned to her. "Do you feel that?"

She nodded, fear rising into her throat. She knew it was too easy. She knew it wasn't over.

Dark World wasn't finished with them yet.

The pain in Kane's heart transcended all wounds he'd ever known. His horned head lay heavy in his hands, woe consuming his every thought and action. The world moved more slowly around him, thicker, without any lightness to it.

His daughter, his Ever, was prisoner to his mother. The Devil owned his little girl.

Ozen stood nearby, his helpless energy drifting in his adopted son's direction. With what little awareness Kane had, he noted the presence of those who truly cared: Deme, Ozen, and even Syphon paid his respects by standing close by.

What was he to do? How could he get his daughter back? Could he? Once taken hold of by a demonic presence, a being rarely, if ever, received the gift of freedom again. For all he understood of possession, his daughter was gone. Dead.

The only way that he knew to get her back was for Malus to relinquish control. She'd have to leave her granddaughter's body willingly—which he sincerely believed would only happen when Hell froze over.

And what of Fate? She must have been there when all this transpired? Was she okay?

I shouldn't have left them, he thought, his soul aching. He felt weary then, thinking of all the people who had depended on him and that he'd let down: Ever,

Fate, the demons of Legion. How could one being rule all? How had his father done it?

Finally, after several moments of quiet contemplation, Kane asked, "What happened in Necrosia? Do we know anything?"

Ozen shook his head. "The message was vague, at best," he said. "It only spoke of Ever's...condition. We have such limitations at the moment." His eyes filled with guilt in his attempt to explain.

Kane nodded in understanding. The world was such a mess, it would be imprudent of him to ask any more of his people than they'd already done.

"If there's anything I can do," Ozen offered quietly, worry pulling at his furry, grey brows.

Kane shook his head. "No, there's nothing we can do."

"Sir." One of the demon nurses approached them, her face knitted in concern. "It's time."

Adrenalin surged through Kane's body, blessing him with the will to rise and walk swiftly toward the back of the garden. He hadn't yet re-evaluated his next moves, but regardless, he still had to keep alive the hope that he could save Dark World. Even so, without Ever in his own world, he wasn't even sure he wanted the rest of it.

Kane burst through a veil of trailing vines, anxious to ensure the survival of his one and only banshee. Would she endure this? Would they indeed be granted the gift of two? The beginnings of a race renewed?

He looked down at the once beautiful banshee, her stunning physique replaced by clear gelatinous goo. Where her locks of fiery red had once graced her strong and bronzed shoulders, were now strands of withered string, most of it on the floor beside the cot. Her lovely face, with skin the texture of silk, was contorted and divided right down the center. A blackened gap ran from the top of her head to the end of her torso, pulsating and tearing wider with every moment that passed.

Suppressing a gag, Kane watched with a mixture of fascination and abhorrence as the jellylike blob that was once Sorcia began twitching and quivering. Something was happening. Was it the end or the beginning of something new?

Frankly, at this point he just wanted it over with. It was rather disgusting.

All eyes watched with rapt revulsion as the cocoon began to split into two. Thick mucus ran onto the floor on both sides of the cot, oozing and dripping like clear, dense slime.

Then something interesting happened. Kane watched as the gel transformed from clear to milky, making it impossible to see the contents inside. Was this normal? Was it supposed to happen this way?

Everyone in the room held their breath, suspended anxiety hovered like a pulsing cloud. What was happening?

After several moments, Kane worried it was over, that the banshee had not survived the mitosis. It was, after all, a very brutal and obviously intense process, like nothing any of them had ever witnessed.

His brow wrinkled as he watched for any change, any movement, then turned to Ozen, asking, "Is it over? Is she…"

Before he could finish his sentence, the entire globule gave one last belching sound before it exploded, releasing its contents all over the room—and all over everyone.

Some of the female demons shrieked and left quickly to clean themselves of the gooey abomination that was covering them from head to toe. Kane, while thoroughly disgusted, smirked as he remembered Fate's experience with the birth of Ick and his exploding shell of goo.

Once the initial shock had worn off, and Kane wiped a bit of the stickiness from his face, he looked to the bed where the blob had been. And there, lying like newborn babies, were two perfect versions of Sorcia. Her long red hair, curly and cascading, had returned. Soft, perfect skin. Strong, lean body. Only now, there were two where there had been one.

"Well," Ozen said, finally breaking the shocked silence within the room as he removed the slime-covered glasses from his face and cleaned the lenses with his sleeve. "That was...interesting."

"Certainly was," Kane agreed, taking a step towards the banshees that were asleep in one another's arms like loving siblings. He reached for a blanket and covered them up, a smile curling on his lips. Strangely, he felt like a new father again.

Emotion welled up within as he recalled the news he'd recently received. His Ever. His sweet girl.

Nothing, he thought as a dark and powerful heat rose inside of him. *Nothing will stop me from getting her back. Nothing.*

Six exorcists filed into the main hall, shrouded in ebony cloaks, hoods shielding their faces. They chanted as they shuffled towards the altar, their voices low and eerie within the darkened chamber. The muted lights of a thousand candles flickered about the room, ghostly shadows creeping across the walls.

Malus's naked form rested upon the podium, atop a velvet blanket of crimson. She was beautiful to behold with milky skin exuding an unearthly glow. She lay as though sleeping, white wings spilled over the sides, draping long to the floors. A giant pentagram blazed golden, etched in the marble beneath her.

Maxim stood guard at her head, eyes wary of the upcoming ritual. He looked to the exorcists, wondering what horrors rested beneath their drooping cowls. He'd heard of these creatures before, of their powers over life and death, their reputation renowned in dealings with all things deceased. He eyed his sleeping queen as unease began churning within, this was beyond his comfort. He understood that Malus desired to remove Ever's soul from within the body, but the risks were too great. If they failed, Malus could be lost forever.

But if they succeeded, Malus would be unstoppable once the Crystal Pyramid was relit.

The part of him that loved the queen hoped the exorcists would do their job well, prodding the princess's soul from her body, freeing Malus to live fully again, unleashing her from her temporary prison.

But there was another side to Maxim, a quieted, submissive alter ego that prayed for something else. It was something he, after a hundred years as a shade, could not still within. Something foreign. Something warm.

Something *human*.

The six cloaked figures took their stances around the altar, their monotonous chanting escalating, reverberating about the dark room. Maxim winced at the black magic they were conjuring, the air thick and charged with evil energy.

Then, without warning, they stopped their infernal song, silence owning the air. Maxim watched with perverse wonder as each of the exorcists reached their hands to their heads, moving to remove the hoods from their faces.

As they drew the black material away and the horror of their faces were exposed, Maxim fell to his knees, biting his knuckle as he suppressed the scream rising into his throat.

Vale

Vale's heart thrummed inside his ribcage, fear radiating throughout his body. They'd been caught trying to escape, he and the strange silver man. Five white-haired guards with eerie glowing eyes stood between them and their freedom. With weapons drawn, they snarled with their sharp white teeth exposed as they moved ever closer to the fugitives.

Vrill turned his head sharply, extending his hand towards the newborn shade. "Take us out of here!"

Vale looked at him with horror in his eyes. "I can't! I...don't know how!"

The silver man smiled gently and whispered, "You are so much more than you think you are. Take my hand."

Vale complied, the guards rushing them now as if sensing something was amiss.

"Close your eyes," Vrill's voice soothed, the world moved beneath Vale's feet, shifting like sand. The sounds of the guards yelling ebbed away, the coolness of the underground jail altering to heat upon his skin.

Slowly, after a few minutes, realizing he hadn't been killed by the guards, Vale opened his eyes. "Where are we?" he asked, narrowing his eyes at the bright red glow surrounding him. He scanned his environment, left then right; but there was nothing to be seen. Miles upon miles of nothing.

"We are in the Never," Vrill said. "A world between worlds."

Vale frowned. "How?"

The silver man shrugged. "Your ability is instinctual, knowing it must keep you from harm. I suppose," he explained with a pensive expression, "it brought you, us, to the place it deemed safest."

Vrill's voice echoed through his thoughts, the necromancer's wisdom carrying over the winds of time.

In the darkness of the void, Vale smiled. He knew where he was now, or rather, where he wasn't.

But most importantly, he knew how to get back.

The shield surrounded them like a huge half bubble, wavering with blue and white lights. It would almost be pretty, if it weren't keeping them captive within the area that Scarlet had been killed.

"What's going on?" Rory asked, his voice faltering. Scarlet had to admit it gave her dark satisfaction to see him unnerved.

She shook her head in response, watching every angle for a possible attack. Rory took a step closer to the bubble that imprisoned them and raised his palms to touch it. As though mesmerized, he slid his hands over it. It mimicked his movements, an ethereal hand mirroring his own gestures. Scarlet watched him with quiet curiosity. Was this really the monstrous boy that murdered her? Was this truly the guy who had damned her to the Underworld? Plunged a knife into her chest?

He reminded her of a small boy, fascinated with a new, amazing toy. Suddenly the air around her changed, grew thick with electricity. Rory must have felt it, too, for he turned to her, eyes round with trepidation.

"What's happening?" he asked, moving closer to her side.

"I don't know, but be ready. Expect the worst," Scarlet replied, eyes scanning every corner of their strange cell.

Myth

The hairs on her neck stood up as though there were a thousand unseen eyes watching her from afar. She felt as though she were inside some kind of snow globe, waiting to be shaken up and observed while a storm of snowflakes swirled around her.

Then, a disembodied voice sounded, *"Only one may pass!"* It boomed, resonating off the transparent walls, causing the ground to rumble beneath them.

"Only one may pass? What does that mean?" Rory turned to her, panicked, his arms wrapped round his torso.

Scarlet only shook her head, though she was sure she knew what the voice wanted. Question was— should she tell Rory or just do what she knew she had to do to survive?

The world swirled around him as though it was floating in thick, dark liquid. Grief had settled upon his soul, hatred had torn his heart into so many pieces there was no way to find them all and put them back together.

Kane sat upon a seat of stone, his head heavy in his hands. If Ever had been taken by Malus, stolen from the city of Necrosia, what then had happened to Fate? He had left his daughter in her hands. Had Malus, in her secretive state as Sybil, betrayed Fate and left her to die? Where was she?

He'd lost everything.

Fate.

Ever.

There's no way to get her back.

Tears built behind his blue eyes, knowing that the only way to get his daughter back would be to have his mother willingly leave her host—and that would never happen. She had the most powerful body she could have hoped for. There was no one stronger to tempt her into leaving Ever's body, was there?

"Sire," a quiet voice drew him from his sorrow and he brought his eyes up, meeting Deme's concerned gaze. She cleared her throat before continuing, "I know you are in mourning right now, but I need to ask...that is, the others and I, we're wondering about the mission. The scrolls and the gathering of the races. What is it you have planned?"

Kane sighed. He'd completely forgotten about the quest to save Dark World, though now he wasn't sure he cared what happened to it. His world had been destroyed. Why save the outside world when the one within no longer existed? How was he to complete all the tasks that needed to be done? Besides, he was only one demon, there was no way for him to gather the scrolls and unite the races now within the short time that it needed to be done. As leader, though, it was his duty, his obligation. Wasn't it?

"Sire, if I may," Deme said, taking a seat beside him. "I have an idea, if you wish to hear it."

Interest awakened him and he nodded at her. "Of course, please tell me," his low voice rumbled, though weakened.

She exhaled, then said, "I feel it's time we take action. We must retrieve the scrolls and races now, before it's too late."

Kane shrugged. "How?"

"I say we split up," she offered with a smile. "Go in several groups and then meet up at the Crystal Pyramid when the tasks are complete."

Kane raised his brows in surprise. His people were stepping up even after all they'd been through, and all they'd lost. His heart swelled a little, just enough to find hope in a hopeless situation.

"You'd...help me?" he asked her, a smile forming on his lips.

"Of course!" She grinned. "You know what's wrong with you, Sire?"

He paused, shrugging. "No, tell me."

"You keep trying to be the hero all by yourself! A real leader doesn't rule everyone, bearing the burden of all the woes alone; he builds a whole world of heroes, so everyone is a leader." She patted him on the shoulder, standing. "So quit your damn wallowing and let's win this world back!"

He gaped at her a moment, eyes wide, then smiled. "Thank you," he said. "I needed that."

"Okay," Deme began. "Here's what I figure; you go to Myth, get the scrolls from her. I'll go to the wraiths and Sorcia..." she paused, biting her lip. "Both Sorcias, and the necromancers, can go to the reapers. Then we'll all meet back at the pyramid in a couple of days."

Kane took it all in, nodding. "There's only one problem."

"What?" Deme frowned, contemplating.

"We need Fate. She's the key to all of this," he explained, then cast his gaze downward. "And we don't know if she's dead or alive."

"She's alive," a familiar voice said from behind them. "I can feel it."

"Vale!" Kane stood up, a surge of relief racing throughout him. "Where have you been?"

The shade rolled his eyes, running a hand through his scruffy silver hair. "It's a long story."

Reapers, Maxim thought, unable to tear his eyes from the faces of horror. Shredded skin and muscle clung to their ashen bones, tendons running the length of their necks, the rest of their body blessedly still covered by the long black robes. It was no wonder their kind stayed hidden in the far reaches of Dark World. They were walking nightmares.

The six exorcists each carried with them a different charm of sorts, enchanted items for the exorcism. One held an upside down cross, another sprinkled unholy water upon Malus's inert body by swinging a rounded, violet vial that hung at the bottom of a golden chain. Three of them held gemstones that appeared to be emerald, sapphire, and ruby, each emitting an unearthly glow. The last exorcist, apparently the leader as he stood in the center of the pentagram, held an item that Maxim did not recognize. Gripped in his skeletal hand was something knife-like, it appeared to have five blades radiating from the hilt like the rays of the sun, its razor-sharp points glinting amid the candlelit chamber. A seed of worry burrowed itself inside him, wondering what that item might be used for.

He observed the six as they swayed, chanting over his queen with words he did not comprehend. Malus, peaceful upon a stone pedestal, seemed completely unaware of their presence.

Perhaps an enchantment was placed on her, he considered. The shade wondered what the outcome could be. Would Ever's soul be cast aside, sent back to the Guf where it had been born, or would the princess be a prisoner in yet another form? Destroyed and her soul torn apart by black magic?

Maxim shuddered at the possibilities, wishing there was another way. He adored his queen, but the fragile sliver of humanity that resided within him screamed its displeasure. This was wrong, and he knew it.

No matter how long he spent in the underworld, the centuries of service he provided to his devilish queen, he could not deny his humble beginnings. He had been one of the original humans damned to Dark World, turned into a shade by Malus after the successful assassination of Lucifer. He had been there at the end of an era, witness to the birth of a new, darker age.

He had seen the Devil die.

He knew the plan. They'd gone over it a hundred times, and he himself had replayed it over inside his own mind countlessly. They all had their orders, their place to be when the trumpets sounded.

The war had begun.

No longer would the humans tolerate their enslavement by the demons. No longer would they be the weakest race in Dark World. Maxim had once been part of a mighty empire, a warrior within the grand city of Atlantis. He'd fought and won wars. He'd stood upon the sands of cities fallen at his feet. He'd been a hero on the Surface, a god among men.

Myth

Then the Great Quake happened. Truth be told, there was far more than one earthquake that destroyed an entire civilization, but one in particular had devoured them whole. Thousands of citizens disappeared from the Surface, hundreds upon hundreds of collected magical creatures: sphinxes, unicorns, phoenix, and more. The earth beneath Atlantis opened up like a mighty maw, taking an entire island into its mouth, and swallowed them whole. Down they fell into what felt like forever. The lucky ones died — the rest survived to live in a nightmare.

Despite the love Dark World had for its great Devil, Lucifer, he was not kind to all. Whether he despised the humans or honestly believed they were lesser than he, his disregard for them was clear. In the end, Maxim felt they had no choice but to rebel, to rise up and take back their dignity. For too long the humans had been slaves to the demons and treated with less respect than any other race. Less than animals, truth be told. They mined ore for the demons, cooked their meals and bowed before their hooves.

Until Malus offered them a way out.

It had happened so long ago, but to Maxim, it was as clear as though it had happened yesterday.

She'd sent a message to the humans via their thoughts, as to keep the secret safe. Upon creating an enchanted whisper, Malus appealed to all the humans entombed within Dark World.

All those who wish to be free, her sweet voice carried through their minds as though drifting on a wind, *send your souls to me upon the day the trumpets sound.*

Alongside the whisper, images of what they would become were born inside their minds. Powerful, magical, stronger than any creature in Dark World: shades.

Drunk on the notion of their future selves, every human in Dark World, those that had fallen from the graces of Atlantis, kept silent and bided their time until the dark realm sang, announcing the start of the Uprising.

Many months passed, several worried the moment would not come, that Malus would not keep her word. Then, one day, a noise sounded in their ears, a noise heard only by them. One by one, they stood, their arms opened wide, chests exploding as their spherical blue souls raced towards their new master.

They'd only learned later that Malus had not been awarded the souls as she'd thought; although they'd returned to the Guf, the humans were given their gift regardless. They'd become the most powerful beings in the realm.

And Maxim was awarded the greatest task of all: to kill the King.

As Lucifer's personal slave, Maxim was rarely away from his side. He tended to his master's every need, every whim and fancy. Despite his feigned loyalty to his king, he craved freedom so much more.

Malus had remained close to Maxim, whispering her magical words in his ear, soothing and coaxing him. He'd have done anything for her.

And he did.

Rory turned to her, his eyes filled with fear. "What do they want?"

Scarlet sighed, her lone instincts guiding her, the necromancer blood seemingly gone. "They—the Guf—wants us to...fight until there's only one of us left."

"One of us has to die to win?" His brows pulled together in distress, though she was certain she saw a hint of his old, evil charm fire behind his blue eyes. It was too much temptation for him, too easy for him to fall back on his old ways, not understanding that it was a test, and that to win, he'd have to change.

His gaze fell upon the knife lying so still amid the pentagram. Scarlet's heart picked up pace. This is what the test was for, to see how they'd react given the exact scenario as before. But it had to be done differently. She had to do it right.

She had to kill Rory this time, instead of him killing her.

As if driven by her shade instinct, Scarlet lunged for the knife. Rory, standing within a few feet of the blade, anticipated her move and kicked it out of her reach.

"Wait!" he pleaded. "Let's figure this out first!"

She paused in shock. She'd assumed his natural instinct, his killer instinct, would possess him before rationality could. Sighing, she stood. "What do we do then?"

His eyes searched the perimeter as though it might give him the answers he sought. "What if..." his voice trailed off. Scarlet watched him carefully, his gaze landing on the scroll. "What if I go back."

"Back?" she narrowed her eyes at him. "Back to Dark World?"

Rory nodded. "I'd rather go there and be undead than die forever here and now." He gave her a crooked smile, uncertainty coloring his ocean-blue eyes.

Momentarily taken aback, Scarlet considered his proposal. Maybe the Guf didn't want them to fight after all. Maybe they just wanted Rory to experience what his victims had felt.

Or maybe they wanted Scarlet to be in his shoes for a change, witness to the horrors, yet removed from it herself. "I don't know," she admitted. "I don't think I can..." The thought of killing him the way she'd been killed made her stomach queasy. But if she did this, maybe she could see her family again. Live out her life the way she'd intended before the nightmare began. She could get married, have children, travel the world.

"There's no other way," he said, shrugging. "One of us has to die, right? I don't want to go back, but I don't want to die a mortal death up here either. At least, not right now," he added sheepishly. "I'd like a chance to redeem myself for what I've done. Maybe, I don't know, maybe I could do some good instead of bad." His expression burned with agony, regret, and sorrow.

"What would you do differently?" she wondered.

He exhaled. "I'd live, just live, instead of running from my own death. It was the only reason I did what I did, to live forever. Now I know I don't need to live forever, I just need to live better than I was, live like tomorrow is my last day. And I want to be in love, just once real love. You know, during all that time I had here, I never once let myself love anyone." He turned away from her, tears building in his eyes.

Suddenly Scarlet knew what had to be done.

"Rory." She stared up at him. "You can stay here. I'll go back."

He shook his head. "No, I killed you once. I don't want to do it again."

"You have to," she stated calmly, knowing that she was right.

"Why?"

She drew a shaky breath, her vision of running to her parents and Shelby with open arms vanishing into smoke like paper alight with fire. "Because my life — and my love — is down there." Scarlet looked sightlessly into the surrounding woods, saying goodbye to her human life forever, then said, "Rory, this time I give you permission to kill me."

Maxim

The trumpets sounded inside his head like the roar of a thousand lions.

It was time.

He knew what his job was. It was the most important one.

Kill King Lucifer.

Malus had chosen him above all her minions, entrusting him with the most sacred of quests. If he failed, all would be lost.

Until now, the plan appeared flawless. But now, suddenly faced with a new body, a shade body, Maxim wasn't so certain. He felt so different, physically strong, yet emotionally and mentally weak without his soul. It was like being reborn with wings and only moments later thrown from the nest, expected to know how to fly.

Maxim filled his new, undead lungs, feeling the emptiness inside. He reminded himself that he'd wanted this, he'd begged for this. Malus had rewarded him this gift of immortality, this new magical life.

He just hadn't expected to feel so different, so foreign and so removed from his recent humanity.

Hidden inside King Lucifer's chambers, he waited. He'd taken his station behind a dark curtain in the king's bedroom shortly after the king had left with the young prince to inspect one of the bloodstone mines.

But Maxim knew this was the first place the king would come once he realized the war had begun. He would want to check on the safety of his Bible. He eyed the ancient book, splayed open upon its enchanted pedestal. No one dared go near it except Lucifer; no one would survive if they did.

Maxim had been his faithful servant for decades, since Atlantis had first fallen into Dark World. Lucifer trusted him like no other.

Outside Maxim heard the chaos ensue as every human in the palace turned into silver-haired savages. Malus had explained to him once, after taking him to her chambers, how the humans would change—how he would change.

"You will become more powerful than the demons," she purred, her lily-white fingers trailing across his unclothed chest. "You will be one of a new race, created by me." She grinned up at him, curled around him with her naked body.

He'd loved her upon sight, fell for her grace and beauty, her long albino body, silky white hair, and eyes the shade of sapphire. After they'd become secret lovers, meeting in her private bed chamber long after the king had succumbed to slumber, Maxim had learned of her malevolent plans.

To overthrow the Devil.

At first it seemed easy, she'd made it sound exciting, rewarding, and fun. Drunk on her exquisiteness and her passion, Maxim hung on her every word.

But now, hidden in his master's bedroom, the Devil's bedroom, Maxim wasn't so certain. To kill the most powerful monster in the underworld seemed a feat he was not worthy to perform, even if Malus had promised he'd be even stronger than the ancient demon king.

Through strands of silver hair falling over his shoulder, his eyes glowing and focused as they penetrated the darkness with unbridled power coursing through his veins, he gained an ounce of confidence. Perhaps he'd succeed, then he and Malus could be together, ruling Dark World as one.

He crouched in the dark, clutching a curved blade in each hand—and waited.

Kane

A team of warriors gathered near a massive, newly-built cage for the ever-growing family of phoenix birds. Since Fate had visited, over a dozen babies had been born and were already hands taller than the average demon.

The pixie population was doing well, too. Far too well, it would seem, as everyone swatted and swished their hands about their faces in order to deter the little brats from biting.

"Alright," Kane said, eyes fierce with determination. If he had any hope in defeating his mother and getting Ever back, he'd need all the power he could muster. The only way that could happen, was if the Crystal Pyramid was relit, feeding him with pure, raw, undefeatable magic. "Here's the plan." His soldiers grouped around their leader. "Vale, you find Fate and bring her to the Crystal Pyramid. Deme, you go to the wraiths. Sorcia…Sorcias…," he corrected himself; "you take Mezza and Slater and go to the reapers."

"What about me?" Elder Syphon asked, raising his chin proudly.

"I'd like you to stay behind with the survivors and see that the injured are cared for. Once all of this is over with and we know the outside world is safe, we will re-establish Legion at another location."

Syphon bowed his head, a glint of happiness in his eyes that Kane had put him in charge of the people.

All of them nodded their heads in agreement. "And you?" Vale asked.

Kane looked at the shade. "I'm going to Exile Island to get the scrolls from Myth."

"But how will you carry them without a shade's help?" Vale asked. One false touch and Kane would age one thousand years in less than a breath.

Elder Ozen stepped forward upon Vale's comment, handing three small bejewelled chests over to Kane. "I had Elder Ozen create enchanted boxes to hold them," he explained.

"We'll meet at the Crystal Pyramid in one week's time," Kane stated as he handed an enchanted box to both Deme and Sorcia, keeping one for him.

A murmur began amongst them; their wary eyes made him pause. "What is it?" he asked with a frown.

Vale cleared his voice. "I'm not sure any of us can make it to our destinations and back in such a short time." He shrugged.

Kane smiled, turning towards the flock of adult phoenix in their cage. "Whoever needs a mount may use one of the birds. Elder Ozen is creating an enchanted saddle specifically for riding them, as to be able to steer and not get burned. Any other questions?"

"Aren't you, ahem, afraid of flying?" Deme said, stifling a grin.

Kane smirked back. "On the wings on another, yes," he answered. "I have another ride, thank you very much." He turned his gaze towards the Night Mare, excitement and anxiety melding together in his stomach. He didn't know if they'd all succeed, and at that moment, the future didn't seem to matter. What mattered was that they had chosen to help him. They wanted him as their leader.

Their Devil.

"So, how are we going to get out of here?" Deme asked, raising a brow as she examined the confines of the garden. "That *thing* could still be in the palace."

Kane smiled as he recalled Ever and Arcanum's escape from Legion, saving him before Ba'al's blood rain could envelop him. "There's a secret exit," he said with a wink, turning his gaze up towards the shining crystal sphere that lit the garden.

"Secret exit?" Deme reiterated, intrigued, following his line of sight.

"I found it by accident one day while...well," he admitted, his face infusing with crimson. "Let's just say I missed flying and I was trying to see what my wings would do despite the shackles."

Deme stifled a smile. "So, how do we get out?"

Kane walked over to an ivy-laden wall, pushed aside the foliage, exposing a hidden lever. Upon pulling it down, the crystal dome overhead began to open, folding back into itself as it revealed the darkened skies of the realm. Fresh, heated air moved in, embracing them as though they were long lost family.

"Of course, we'll have to fly out," Kane said as he glanced around at the expressions of wonderment. He didn't have to tell anyone twice. They all sprang towards their flying mounts with a zest he hadn't seen in decades.

The Night Mare, subdued by his newly crafted, enchanted saddle, was now being hoisted up through the open skylight via four large phoenix.

Just as Kane was readying himself to exit the garden, he saw a ball of orange light fly through the opening and descend to his location.

"Spark!" he uttered in astonishment, a mixture of happiness and worry overwhelming him. To see the phoenix could mean either good or bad news. Did this mean Fate was alright? Or was she hurt and needing help?

Kane then noticed a piece of parchment wedged between the bird's beak. Upon taking it from him, Spark then flapped unevenly to the phoenix cage and entered it, exhaustion overwhelming him.

With nerves writhing in his stomach, Kane turned the letter over in his hand. His name was on the front, written in Ever's hand. Tears welled in his eyes as he broke open the embossed seal.

As he read the words, the last words his daughter had written before she was possessed by the queen, his cerulean eyes widened.

"It...can't be," he uttered, falling to one knee. "It's not true!"

"Kill you?" Rory stammered, his expression pained as he eyed the long, silver blade glinting in the grass.

Scarlet nodded. "It's the only way." She paused, gathering courage as her heart raced and limbs trembled with fear. How she wanted to stay on the Surface, even for a while. To see her parents again, and Shelby and Greg. It didn't seem fair that she'd come so close to holding them again, only to have the moment slip through her fingers.

But Kane needed her. Dark World needed her. Despite where she'd begun her life, death needed her more.

Before she could change her mind, Scarlet laid herself down in the middle of the pentagram and closed her eyes. "Just do it quickly, okay?" Tears worked their way out of the corners of her sealed lids.

Rory sighed. "Are you sure?" he asked as he bent down to pick up the weapon. "There's no other way?"

Scarlet shook her head, knowing this was right. Knowing this was the only way to remedy the situation. This was what her soul wanted, proof that she'd grown, changed since last she was faced with the notion of death. She was putting others ahead of her. Putting their needs before her own desires. If this didn't prove her worth to her soul, what would?

Danielle Q. Lee

Rory began speaking, recalling from memory the words he'd recited so many times before, silver moonlight poured over him as would a spotlight. His voice was weak, sad, torn; shaking as he uttered the same words he'd said the last time he killed her.

"Hear us Queen of the Dark," he said with far less enthusiasm than the first time he'd uttered the incantation. "We give you this soul in exchange for power and eternal life." He paused, inhaling and exhaling, then said, "Before I say the last words, I just…" Scarlet opened her eyes to meet his. "I…thank you. For giving me a second chance. Even when I didn't deserve it."

She nodded, smiling as she shut her eyes once more. Then he continued, a rogue tear rolling down his cheek as he finished the spell, raising the knife over her body. "Take this child into your bosom of evil, feast upon her spirit. Grant us immortality."

Scarlet braced herself, remembering the pain and suffering that was coming at any moment. The blade would plunge into her chest, piercing her heart, then the ground would open up and swallow her whole. She'd sink down, down, down through the layers of the earth, changing, mutating, dying before arriving into the belly of the world.

Dark World.

She waited, but the pain never came. Opening her eyes a crack, she expected to see Rory standing over her, knife coming down.

But he wasn't there.

He was gone.

She was back in the Guf, surrounded by beings of light!

"W-what happened?" she asked, standing as she took stock of herself. The black markings on her hands, on her arms, had vanished. The lamia curse was gone. The beast inside was no longer. They had cured her.

"*You passed the test,*" they said inside her thoughts.

"Where's Rory?" She looked around, wondering if he'd been real at all.

"*He has been sent back to complete a mission,*" they whispered.

"A mission? What kind of mission?" Fate wondered.

"*As penance for his sins, he's chosen to seek out Malus's many minions, those that sacrifice the innocent and damn them to Dark World — and stop them.*"

"Stop them?" Fate repeated quietly, though she was sure what they knew what they meant. Rory had returned as a hunter; but this time it was for the good guys.

Before she had a chance to ask any more questions, a brilliant ball of blue light hovered towards her, bobbing like a miniature moon, though close enough to touch.

It was her soul.

Gently, softly, lovingly, it glided closer, and closer still, until it came in contact with her chest. Blue fire burned around the sphere, its brilliance overwhelming her eyes. Suddenly it pushed itself inside, over her heart, her body igniting with a power she could even comprehend.

Scarlet's memories, feelings and thoughts, rushed into her head, flashing past her eyes like lightning. As the two became one, Scarlet and Fate, the human and the shade, her body changed once more. She became the first shade with a complete soul. She became a new being.

She had evolved.

A new race was born.

Part III

The Devil's Exorcism

Dearest Daddy,

Please don't be sad. I've known my destiny for a long while. Do not blame Fate, nor anyone else you left to protect me as they could not have known. I've felt my grandmother's presence around me for some time, her energy darkening the auras of those unaware. I could not tell you this — among other things.

But there is something imperative you must know, despite my promise to keep it secret. I never told you I could speak with animals, that I heard their thoughts and they could hear mine. All my life, locked away within Legion, I made friends with the beasts of the garden.

Especially Arcanum.

Father, please understand it was not my secret to tell, but circumstances have altered our destinies and sacrifices must be made.

Arcanum holds grandfather's soul. He is, for all intents, King Lucifer. He possessed the dragon at the time of his assassination, though he was unable to communicate with you or anyone until I was born and realized I could hear him.

He asked me not to tell you, for reasons of his own.

I must go now, they are coming. I know you will find a way to save me.

I love you,
Ever

Their wings beat in unison as father and son took flight into a crimson sky. Light from the Crystal Pyramid was waning, mirroring the setting sun on the Surface. Lush, green foliage rushed by beneath them, a magical jungle in a darkened land. If not for the pyramid, and the reaching rays of the Surface sun, such pleasures could not exist.

Lucifer's heart pulsed with pain, he hated what he would soon have to do to save his kingdom, but Malus had driven him to do the unthinkable. Any day now, any moment, an evil plot was to be unleashed, a conspiracy so devilish it rivalled all others.

The problem was, Lucifer didn't know exactly what that plan might entail. He'd heard from his spies that a war was brewing, a rebellion of sorts, led by none other than his own wife. Unfortunately, the details were sketchy at best. He didn't know a key aspect: who was she conspiring with?

He had many enemies with whom she could have joined forces with. Dark World was littered with the falls of his iron fist, any number of races, or a combination of species, could want him dead.

If only he knew who she'd sided with, he could better prepare for the challenges that lay ahead. As it was, he'd readied himself for the worst. Over the centuries of marriage to Malus, he'd gradually seen past the mask of beauty she'd worn, revealing a monster greater than any he'd witnessed before. She was the epitome of evil, the face of malice, and would stop at nothing to gain power over Dark World. He learned she was a sorceress, a rare breed of demon naturally gifted in the black arts. She'd cast spells upon herself, ones that kept her from harm. Ones that kept her from dying. While all demons lived a near eternal life in Dark World, thanks to the Crystal Pyramid, they were still capable of being fatally injured.

Malus, it would seem, had found ways around being harmed. Utilizing the Crystal Pyramid's powers, she'd enchanted her body, charmed it in such a way as to elude receiving injury from others. If anyone attacked Malus, that individual would die or be injured the way in which they'd tried to harm her. It was truly an ingenious curse, but it made her a very dangerous adversary.

He learned, too, that she had other nefarious plans. One in particular that he could not allow to happen: to take over the Surface. He had to admit it was an ambitious scheme, but one wrought with peril and certain failure. The Surface was not what it once was; occupied by frail, weak humans that cowered before anything they deemed greater than themselves.

They'd grown.

Changed.

Evolved.

They were dangerous, cunning and deceitful. But most of all, they'd learned the art of destruction. They had guns, bombs, and methods of torture Lucifer himself wouldn't use on another living being. Even the Devil had his boundaries.

Myth

He knew he had to stop Malus, but unfortunately she had discovered a few of his secrets as well. Over the centuries of their marriage, she'd learned the one thing Lucifer had so carefully held close: he was dying.

He was a fallen angel, felled from the realm of Heaven. He wasn't like the demons born unto Dark World; he was part of another world, another kingdom that beheld the light above all other sources of power. For a time, the Crystal Pyramid kept him well, kept him nourished; but as centuries passed, he grew weaker, fragile — mortal.

When Malus discovered this, it wasn't long before Lucifer began hearing the murmurings of mutiny. He knew then something was amiss, and that he'd have to stop it. He'd have to stop her.

His plan to intercept Malus was almost complete. He had no choice but to implement it, despite what it would do to Dark World and each and every one of its residents.

He had to close the rift to the Surface, which in turn would leave the Crystal Pyramid orphaned of the light that nourished his world. All the plants would die, for certain, and many of the creatures that depended on the light would perish. But he felt he was left with no choice.

It would leave his world and his people vulnerable, weakened, with minimal magic, and, worst of all, mortal. But that was necessary to stop Malus. It was the only way she could be killed — permanently.

To do this he'd have to make many sacrifices. Ones that were irreparable.

He glanced at his young son, so innocent, so kind. Pride filled his chest. He knew that someday Kane would discover the secret, put together the clues to heal Dark World and overtake his mother.

"Father, look!"

Lucifer stopped in mid-air, his attention drawn to his palace in the distance, black smoke rising from the city's center. Below, racing over the Crimson Desert were thousands upon thousands of humans, their appearances altered dramatically. Their hair had turned pure silver, eyes white with glowing rage — and powers. Magical powers that they did not — could not — harbor. Some fired sparks of red lightning from their bare hands, others conjured fire from their eyes. Demons, Lucifer's people, fell dead from just one hit; their magic was no match for the creatures. Almost all suffered the worst fate: their souls torn from their bodies, devoured by the newborn beasts.

Lucifer turned to Kane. "Son, listen to me." His eyes watered with emotion, knowing this could be the last time he saw his son. "Go to the caves in the Blood Mountains, hide there until Elder Ozen arrives," he explained quickly, hoping Ozen was alive and able to meet up with the boy as planned. He'd known this day was imminent, he'd already secured Kane's future as best he could.

"What about you?" Kane asked, his lower lip trembling.

Lucifer forced a smile alongside the lie. "I'll be there soon. Now go!"

The Devil watched as his only son flew away to safety before he plummeted into the chaos below. He landed in the center of the courtyard where the Sacred

Elm, an ancient, enchanted tree that had stood for thousands of years, was alight with fire, its branches now black and twisted as its essence turned to ash.

Without delay, avoiding as many of the white-haired humans as he could, he made his way to his chambers. There, hidden amongst the pages of the Devil's Bible, he'd placed the key to Malus's unravelling.

He forced his attention away from the mass of slaughtered demons at his feet. Angry tears built behind his eyes. His people. His world. All of it was gone.

He had to do the one thing that would save the ones who lived.

Finally reaching his chambers, he charged across the room and placed his hand upon the enchanted glass dome that protected the book of black magic. The separation disintegrated into thin air, allowing the book's master access. Lucifer turned the pages quickly, knowing there was no time to spare. Hidden amongst the leaves, kept separate as not to touch one another, Lucifer removed each page carefully, rolled them up, and then tucked each into an enchanted silk sleeve. The scrolls glowed with lavender incandescence, magic literally dripping from each.

Just as he'd safely stored the last of them, he heard the slightest noise from behind him. He spun about and met eyes with one of the new humans. The creature glared at him, sword poised and aimed to strike. Lucifer froze, he had to get to the pyramid. He had to close the fissure to the Surface.

"King Lucifer," the creature spat. "How nice to find you here."

"Maxim?" Lucifer's brow furled as he recognized his once faithful servant.

Maxim nodded, relinquishing an evil laugh. "My how the tables have turned."

"But why? How? What are you?" the old king sputtered, clutching the sheathed scrolls closer to his chest. He suppressed the fury curdling in his core, quelling the desire to tear this insolent slave's throat open—for now.

"So many questions." Maxim sneered, taking a brazen step closer to the king, the point of his sword aimed at his heart. "We are shades! The New World Order," he proclaimed, black lips curling into a smug smile.

Lucifer glared, it all made sense now. The humans wanted freedom and Malus gave it to them, and to her they gave their undying loyalty. Power and evil had coalesced to create a new race of super beings. Stronger than demons.

Maxim brought the blade to Lucifer's throat, saying, "Bow before me, slave."

Lucifer had had enough. He dropped the scrolls to the floor as he emitted a low, baritone growl from his throat, bringing his hands together to summon his dark weapon.

"Ego sum legio," he whispered, calling to the elements, the powers that obeyed him. "Ego sum legio."

A flicker of fear crossed Maxim's eyes and he took a step back. Lucifer had so rarely used his powers, the shade most likely had never seen what the demon king could do.

He was about to find out.

Lucifer narrowed his gaze at the frightened shade, calling to the powers that heeded him. He rose to his full height, towering over the silver-haired human as his blood-red wings expanded to their full width. Shiny, black horns, curved as would the rack of a bull, drew to a tapered point atop his head. Eyes black as midnight pulsed with supernatural poison.

The orb within the devil's palms twisted and writhed as though a dozen ebony asps fought to be the first to strike. Crimson lightning snarled and crackled round the anomaly, building, churning with the darkest power.

Something took over, something else. Whatever beast Lucifer hid below the surface of his hot, red skin was released; charging forth as though imprisoned for a century.

Maxim turned to run, dropping his sword as he raced for the door to the chamber. Just as he managed to fling the door wide open, Lucifer released his weapon. A sphere of evil energy raced towards the human abomination, inches from striking him dead — only someone else blocked its attack.

Lucifer's power stopped mid-air and began racing back towards its master. The enchanted orb, his own power, betrayed him as it struck him in the chest, exploding as would a volcano. Knocked to the floor, his right wing torn and nearly ripped from his back, he roared from the pain and rage of being bested.

He blinked, sensing a presence in the room. He didn't have to see her to know she was there.

"Malus," he sputtered, the taste of his own blood slid across his tongue.

"Darling," she purred as she swept into the room, a dozen shades on her heels. "We've been waiting for you." Malus's ice-blue eyes, the very eyes Lucifer had once gazed upon with love in his heart, stared down at him with a cold, calculating glare.

Lucifer tried to push himself up to sitting, hot blood streaming from his head and chest. His right wing burned like it was on fire, the thin membrane torn and shredded, rendered flightless. His own weapon had been used against him, rebounded from Malus's powerful spell. He'd meant it for Maxim, but Malus intervened at just the right moment.

And now he, the Devil, was dying.

"Darling," she began, feigning an expression of concern. "You've gone and hurt yourself." A ghost of a smirk grazed her dark red lips. "Here, let my servants assist you."

The shades drew to a close around him, jerking him to his hooves with rough hands.

"What is the meaning of all this?" he spat angrily, though weaker than he'd hoped.

Malus smiled sweetly before answering, "The time has come, I'm afraid, to replace the old with the new." Her eyes moved over the aged king with a touch of disgust. "You simply can't rule Dark World anymore, it deserves, shall we say, better."

The shades on either side of him held his arms with a grip so strong he could hardly fathom it. What had these humans, these once meek and weak creatures, become? Dark magic emanated from them. Magic he'd never felt before despite his thousands of years of existence.

"What do you want?" Lucifer growled.

Myth

She laughed darkly, though it came out light and melodic, like the ringing of silver bells. Even the air itself seemed to shudder alongside her malevolent mirth. "What do I want?" she mocked. "What I've always wanted…" She leaned over him, her thin, perfect brows pulling together in a sinister glower as she whispered, "Power."

"And what of Dark World? What will become of it?" Lucifer asked, stalling as he weighed his options. He had to break free of their hold, gather the scrolls and get them to the pyramid. It was his only hope.

It was Dark World's last chance.

She shrugged and rolled her eyes as though she thought him utterly pathetic. She turned to leave the room, then stopped mid-stride, and without looking back, without an ounce of care or remorse, said, "Kill him."

The shades smiled and started to close in on him, stalking him like prey. He knew they would succeed in finishing him off.

Thankfully, he had one deep, dark secret Malus had never discovered.

He calmed himself, slowing his heartbeat, taking long, deep breaths. He reached back, back through the eras, through the ages for a light he barely recalled. It hurt to gaze upon the stars of his past, to open a door to another life he'd rendered dead and buried. Old wounds still bled there, still carved scars upon his heart, his soul. It was the one thing his father had let him keep, as a reminder of what he'd given up, what he'd lost.

Lucifer summoned the power he'd put to sleep centuries ago, let fall dormant as it was too strong to release, too unpredictable within a world built upon dark arts. Under his breath, he whispered an incantation, a prayer, calling to the energy that lay inert inside his core.

Malus stopped at the doorway and spun about. "What are you doing? What are you whispering?" She commanded, her blue eyes wary as she took a step back. Lucifer had to suppress a smirk, she thought she knew everything there was to know about him, but she'd forgotten one thing—he used to be someone else.

Something else.

The magic grew, reviving itself, nourishing as though it had been deprived of water for centuries. It was almost painful as the light propagated, pulsing, writhing, twisting as it recalled its true form.

Fear colored Malus's eyes as she watched with horror as Lucifer's chest emanated with an unearthly radiance—a heavenly glow.

"My lady, perhaps we should go?" Maxim's voice quavered at the sight of the devil's transformation.

Lucifer felt his chest crack open, pure, white light pouring forth. The shades behind Malus turned about and ran from the room, leaving Malus and Maxim to gape at the morphing being before them.

The room throbbed, a deep, resonating whir permeating the air. At its peak, Lucifer fell to his knees, overcome with warring energies: good versus evil. He had not been this creature for eons, had not been part of that realm in what the world knows as forever.

Malus and Maxim turned and rushed from the room, sensing they would not survive the outcome. The last sight Lucifer saw of his conspiring wife was that of her taking hold of Maxim, batting her wings, and lifting him to safety in the atmosphere.

Lucifer growled and shouted as the light exploded from his body, ripping the room and everything within a hundred yard radius to shreds.

The aftermath was gruesome, dead shades and demons alike obliterated and left in pieces within the castle. Lucifer loathed that he'd had to utilize the power of last resort.

His body badly wounded, but again in his demon form, Lucifer forced himself to standing. He gathered the scrolls (that were blissfully indestructible) and wandered through the wreckage until he came upon the stables. Thankfully, his weapon had not reached that far and the dragon was still well. Climbing upon the beast, he set him in the direction of the Crystal Pyramid and then closed his eyes for the rest of the journey, praying he'd stay alive long enough to complete his mission.

She had to be stopped.

He only hoped it was enough.

The tip of the Crystal Pyramid glinted and gleamed like a captured star, shimmering alongside a loyal ray of sun trickling down from the Surface. The narrow crevasse that stretched all the way from Dark World, through the miles of mantle, and up to the land with an open sky, allowed but a strip of yellow sunlight through. It had always amazed Lucifer how such a small sliver of light could fuel an entire realm.

He'd been to the Surface numerous times, though not as often as his wife. Thankfully he'd learned of her impending treachery before it had transpired, giving him time to bait her in his trap. Sometime before she'd unleashed her evil plot, Lucifer noticed that one of the pages from his bible had gone missing. Suspecting his wife, he had her chambers searched one evening when he knew she was away, attending a party in a nearby city.

As suspected, she indeed had his missing page. Instead of confronting her or taking it back, he and Ozen constructed an enchantment upon the page, one that would be crucial to his plan. The scroll would be the key to opening the fissure once Kane discovered how to relight the pyramid, bringing all the scrolls together again.

The stolen scroll was bewitched with a prophecy. With the devil's blood, charmed invisible to all eyes but his own, Lucifer wrote:

> *I call to the powers of light and dark,*
> *Find the diamond among the stone.*
> *Seek out the soul so pure of heart,*
> *The one to open the door.*
> *For they are the key,*
> *The power,*
> *The savior of the world of dark.*

Then they'd placed the scroll back in her room—and waited. Lucifer, having traced the power several weeks later, was shocked to learn that Malus had taken the scroll to the Surface. It further convinced him that her evil plot would soon be unveiled.

The dragon's wings beat with hypnotic rhythm, Lucifer's weary eyes begging to be shut, but he knew the moment he closed them—it would be the last. He had to keep going, just a little longer—for Dark World. For Kane. It was to be his final battle, his last honor.

The closer they got to the mammoth quartz prism, the more Lucifer realized he was doing the right thing. This thing, this monument, gave Malus her powers that made it impossible to kill her, impossible to destroy a monster so potent that no one, not even him, could stop her.

The dragon landed at the base of the pyramid, his breath jagged and heavy; he'd not flown for quite a time as he was held captive within the palace walls. It was for his own safety, but there was no way to explain that to him.

Lucifer fell from the dragon's back, sensing he had little time left. He staggered to a doorway known only to few as it was hidden by a charm, and placed his hand upon it. The glass shimmered once, then vanished, leaving a hollow place—a door into the heart of the pyramid.

He cringed as he realized that only hours before he had lied to his son, telling him he'd never seen the inside of the pyramid. It was a necessary untruth, no one in Dark World could see the into the heart of the structure—not until it could be used for peace. For a time when all the races worked together as one.

Once inside, the king set to work; even as the blood leached from his broken body and trailed crimson smatterings behind him. Painted upon the floor, engraved in black, was an enormous pentagram. Quickly, he placed the scrolls on the pentagram's points, one for each, and performed a secret ceremony, uttered words never heard by demon ears. Upon his dark summons, the great rocks atop the pyramid shifted, the landmasses slid towards one another, closing and sealing out the sun.

The pyramid dimmed, ushered into darkness; its power gone. Lucifer felt the effects immediately, what was left of his dying body had grown cold.

He staggered to the door, sealed it, and then drawing on what little strength he had left, climbed atop the beast.

"*Home,*" he whispered. "*Take me home.*"

Ozen

The cave was cold, echoing with the quiet sobs of a broken-hearted, terrified young demon. Ozen patted his back, comforting him as best he could. The sounds of death, of brutal massacres, drifted in from the outside. They were safe — for now. High up, hidden deep in the bowels of Blood Mountain, Ozen and the boy waited until the monsters left. How long it would take, he could not know.

"W-why is this happening?" Young Prince Kane inquired through tears. "Where is my father?"

Ozen sighed, sensing that all was not well. But he could not bring himself to tell the boy of his fears. "He is out there, fighting for us, for Dark World." He offered a sad smile.

"Will he be okay?" Kane's bright blue eyes penetrated the darkness, pleading with the elder.

"I do not know," Ozen replied truthfully, realizing it would do the boy more harm to lie, and then later be confronted with the truth. Ozen didn't know the outcome, whether the king would survive or not. He only knew what his heart and soul hoped for, that his oldest and dearest friend would stand before them again — but deep down he already knew the truth, he just couldn't bring himself to admit it.

"How long do we have to stay here?" Kane asked.

"As long as we need to," Ozen said, standing as he retrieved some food from his pack and held it out to

Kane. He and Lucifer had planned for this day, knowing it was inevitable.

"Are we safe here?" Kane took the proffered nourishment from the elder.

"Yes, we are." Of that he was certain. He'd spent many an hour concocting enchantments with which to seal the mouth of the cave. Above all, he had to protect the future king of Dark World. It was Lucifer's only request—that his son be kept safe.

Hours passed in the darkness, leading into what felt like days. Minute after minute, Ozen worried over the outcome of this war. What would remain of his world? Who would be left among his allies—and of his foes?

After several days, Ozen dared to take a peek outside the cave, wondering if it was safe enough to travel to the palace. He hadn't planned beyond that. Where they'd go next. How they'd get there. At the moment, he could only consider the present.

An eerie hush owned the lands; all evidence of war seemed to have receded into the reddish sands. The blood dried and the bodies decayed. From his vantage atop the mountainside, Ozen scanned the desert, hoping, praying—waiting.

Soon, he felt it was time to go. Their food supply had depleted drastically and both he and Kane had begun to wither, their health declining.

Taking hold of the boy-king's hand, Ozen led him out of the cave, down the mountain, and onto the path towards home.

Ozen felt the sting of tears in his eyes as he laid sight on the palace for the first time since the Uprising.

Much of it had been destroyed, left to litter the crimson sands as mere rubble. A once powerful and proud fortress had been reduced to nothing but dust. A stifled sob drew him from his sorrow, realizing that Kane, too, had lost everything and everyone, and was just now bearing witness to it.

"Come now," Ozen said, sighing as he took the child by the hand. "We must be grateful for what we have, not for what we have lost." They were hard words to say, laced with bitterness and remorse, but needed none-the-less. He couldn't have the boy wallowing; he needed to find strength where there was none.

This was the way of the demon.

"Why is it so dark?" Kane asked quietly, his cerulean eyes scanning the skies with worry.

Ozen suspected that Lucifer had made good on his promise, the dwindling of his own magic was proof enough. Lucifer had extinguished the Crystal Pyramid's light, silencing a world of its immortality and enchantment.

He suppressed a sigh, knowing it was necessary. Knowing why it had to be.

As they neared the heart of the palace, the bodies of the dead became more and more prevalent, any that were intact had had their souls stolen from their bodies, chest cavities torn open, their insides exposed by a perfect, round hole. The stench of decay hung in the air whilst delighted scavengers chewed and gnawed on what remained of the dead.

The further they walked amid the devastation, the more Ozen realized he had no idea where he was going or what he was looking for. Where were they to go now? In what kingdom was Kane to reign if no kingdom remained?

Then hope germinated inside his chest, blooming like the last bud before winter. Ahead, part of the castle remained, standing proud and strong and white before the dark horizon. He knew that this portion of the castle was forged of the thickest marble, it was where the king would take shelter if ever there was an attack.

If the king was alive, this was where he would be.

Ozen hurried towards the remains, his heart fluttering with a mixture of fear and anticipation. Kane close on his heels. He realized too late that he should have encouraged the boy to stay away; at least until he could assess the situation.

There, in the corner of the room, between the enormous forepaws of a large, coppery dragon, was what remained of King Lucifer. Ozen gasped when he saw his old friend, chest torn open, empty of its soul, barren of his essence. The fiends, the white-haired humans that feasted upon souls, had stolen it. Though he had to admit, the hole in which the soul had been so forcefully taken appeared far less perfect somehow, it was ripped and shredded compared to the others he'd seen outside, marked by long, thick lacerations.

Kane cried out, running to his father's side. Ozen's heart broke, a pain like he'd never felt before radiated throughout his ribcage.

Those monsters, he thought as his soul cracked. *Whatever will we do now?*

Ozen approached what remained of his friend, placing an arm around Kane's heaving shoulders. The boy was inconsolable.

Myth

Amid their mourning, the dragon suddenly growled. Surprised that he hadn't even considered the beast's presence, Ozen stood, ready to take a step back. But before he could, the dragon lifted up his right paw — the claws oddly stained with copious amounts of dried blood — a small pouch dangling from it.

Cautiously, Ozen removed the bag, eyeing the dragon with curiosity, wondering just how clever he really was.

Attached to the outside of the pouch was a letter, written in Lucifer's hand:

Ozen,

I know there is much to explain, but alas I have run out time. I pray that the dragon, whom I've named Arcanum, has found you alive and well. I've tied a pouch to Arcanum's paw, its contents deadly to the touch; cursing whomever dare to age one thousand years in the blink of an eye. Please see that one scroll is delivered to each race, alongside the warning of their dark enchantment.

Someday, my old friend, this will make sense. Trust in me as I trust in you.

Tell my son, my dearest Kane, that I love him and will always be with him.

Lucifer

Inside the warm, cocoon-like confines of the Guf, Fate awoke. Gauzy golden air hung suspended around her, reminding her of what it must be like to be in Heaven.

Perhaps the Guf is Heaven, she pondered with a soft smile.

Her new friends, the beings of light that dwelled within the Guf, responded to her thoughts, *"No, this is not Heaven. It is a world between worlds, an illuminated dimension amidst space and time."*

Fate shrugged. She didn't understand what they meant, but she was too happy to care. She had her soul back. She was well again, no shade curse, no lamia monster forcing her to eat flesh.

She'd been reborn into a new version of herself, a better, stronger form of what she once was. Her new body hummed with thrills of electricity. Her hair had, once again, turned soft silver, but her eyes were no longer alight with white fire. They were her own, Scarlet's eyes of ocean blue, but rimmed with a pewter glow. Her naked body was cleansed of the lamia curse, skin pale white and perfect. She felt herself again, but now filled with the deep simmering of a power she could not name.

What was she now? Not quite human, yet not quite shade; she didn't know what to call herself anymore. The beings of light radiated as though observing their first newborn child. As though sensing her internal deliberation, they spoke through telepathy, *"You are the Nameless. The Unique. You have no need for a name."*

"W-what do I call myself then?" she wondered as two new light beings entered and helped dress her in a skin-tight uniform made from sheer black netting, only the necessities shaded darker.

The Guf beings shone brighter before answering, *"What do you wish your name to be?"*

She paused. She was no longer completely Scarlet, of that she was certain. But was she still Fate? What was a name anyways? Simply a word to distinguish oneself from others. Perhaps she was a feeling instead. An emotion that could not simply be made lesser by a label.

Or maybe she was the power that pulsed inside. The soul that she was and always had been. She realized in that moment that she did not hold the power within, but it held her. She wasn't the body, she was the eternal, the vehicle for something far greater than herself.

In that moment both Scarlet and Fate died, yet also joined together as one. Her family on the Surface would always remember her as Scarlet, Kane would always call her Fate, but in her mind, she had been reborn of the ashes of humanity and Hell.

A phoenix.

She was the Nameless.

The only one of her kind.

A constellation forged of flesh and magic.

A myth.

Kane

Kane held Ever's letter between his fingers like a parched leaf that might shatter into a million fragments if he dared grip it too tightly, his eyes perusing the delicate cursive script over and over, word by word, disbelief and unshed tears blurring his vision.

All this time, he thought, *my father was before me, in my midst, and I couldn't see it!* Images of the copper dragon moulded in his mind: formidable body with long, leathery wings and amber eyes that gleamed with unspoken wisdom. For over a century, the beast had held his father's soul, cradled it inside like a fragile egg unable to hatch. In a way it made perfect sense, though Kane still found it impossible to grasp. He felt strangely betrayed, led astray from the truth. Why hadn't Ever told him this before? Why hadn't his father allowed her to enlighten his only son?

Kane willed himself to believe in his father's cryptic reasoning, as confusing as it was at the present. He must have had sound motive, why else would he have left his son an orphan, his realm without a king?

"Sir?" Deme's voice broke through his despondency. "We need to leave soon."

Kane nodded, gently folding Ever's letter and sealing it inside the envelope it arrived in. Deme was right, they still had work to do. He needed time to consider this, time to sift through the shattered remnants of his life. But first he required one thing to allow his mind to rest at ease.

"Chiara, Glax," he called two of his demon warriors to his side. "I would like you to retrieve Arcanum from the city of Necrosia and bring him to the Crystal Pyramid."

The two guards nodded before turning to leave, though a hint of puzzlement lay within their eyes.

"Ready?" Deme inquired, sidling next to him.

He shrugged, giving her a smile. "Do I have a choice?"

Kane watched as his warriors took to the sky, their forms disappearing into the horizon. All on mounts of fire, the phoenix birds carried their precious cargo with pride. All but Mezza and Slater, who had changed into two enormous silver eagles and each carrying a banshee, had chosen to fly upon a phoenix. Even Vale, though nervous, allowed himself to be swept up into the atmosphere by a fiery bird. Kane watched all of them as long as he could, wishing them well and a speedy return. His heart ached as he considered the possibility of their quest turning out badly.

It occurred to him then that he hadn't told Vale the news of his sister. In all the commotion, Kane had completely forgotten it. Perhaps it was for the better, it would only add to his worry. Vale had offered to find Fate, claiming that he felt she was safe, that he'd sensed her presence. With all his heart, Kane sincerely hoped his trust in the rogue shade was not foolish.

The Night Mare whinnied as Kane neared, shaking his mane in obvious protest of his new saddle. He eyed the demon prince with a wild, red eye as he pawed at the red sands of the Crimson Desert, forming rusty, diaphanous billows to drift between them.

"Calm down, boy," Kane spoke softly, reaching a hand to the black stallion's neck. "I need your help." He stroked the immense beast's shining, ebony coat.

The Night Mare seemed to understand and calmed down, allowing Kane to lift himself into the enchanted saddle. The flames upon the horse's back subsided as not to burn the prince, though the great horse snorted his displeasure.

Kane turned his eyes into the distance, the reddish glare from the slow simmer of the volcanic range staring back. He had a long way to go to reach the Black Ocean, though crossing it to get to Exile Island was going to be the difficult part. He'd chosen to go it alone; lending what remained of the demon warriors to Deme and Sorcia. Vale also wished to travel unaccompanied in his quest to find Fate.

It was, Kane felt, his destiny to ride solitary. Selfishly perhaps, he desired to be secluded with his thoughts. Between learning his father's soul inhabited a dragon and his daughter's body was possessed by his mother, his mind was cluttered and confused. How was he to right the many wrongs in his life? How was he to help his family reunite?

A geyser fired in the distance, heralding the coming night. He had to embark on this new quest.

He had to end what his father had begun so many centuries before.

It was time.

Deme

Deme's amber eyes narrowed in attempts to seal out the blistering winds assaulting her at breakneck speeds. Her phoenix, which she'd named Lumina, flew with grace and astonishing speed amidst the varying lengths of spiky columns that made up the ceiling of rock. She leaned forward on the saddle, increasing the aerodynamics of the fiery bird. The faster she dealt with this matter, the better. It was against her better judgment to accept the mission to the wraith village, Cryptica, but she felt she had no choice in the matter. Kane needed her help—he rarely asked for it, let alone accepted it when offered.

Memories flooded back as she thought about the last time she'd been to the wraith village. Wounded by sphinxes and barely aware, the wraiths had healed her. While she was grateful at the time, she'd been left unaware of the drama unfolding outside. Kane was fighting the wraiths to free Fate.

Deme's teeth grit together, fury building in her core. After all they'd endured, after all the death they'd seen at the hands of the shades, how could Kane protect her? Fight for her?

How could he love her?

Bitterness colored her heart black as she thought of the two together. *He was supposed to choose me,* she thought, emotion climbing into her throat as she recalled the first moments she'd realized Kane had fallen for the shade. It seemed sick, twisted, and wrong on so many levels. How could he choose a mate from another species? And a shade! They were the enemy!

Then Deme smiled wide, smugly. *I wonder how she liked her potion?*

It was the perfect solution. The perfect ruse. The old potion master was blind, he hadn't even seen Deme add just a drop of the Night Mare's blood to the vial. She knew what it would do to Fate, she just wished she could have been there to witness her anguish as the affliction spread through her veins. She'd seen the lamia before, out in the desert while tracking a pack of blood wolves. They were inhuman creatures with veins of black trailing over their body like a poisoned spider's web. Vicious, soulless creatures, yet oddly intelligent, they seemed to think still despite their insatiable, ravenous hunger. They could hunt, strategize even, though she didn't know how considering they appeared to be completely savage. They were a mystery to most inhabitants of Dark World, a new and terrifying predator that seemed to have appeared from nowhere after Malus took over the realm.

It was merely good fortune, one afternoon, that she'd eavesdropped on a conversation between Elder Ozen and another member of the council discussing the new and horrifying creatures. Elder Ozen admitted that he'd been experimenting with the blood of the mysterious Night Mare, and had discovered to his shock that it transformed any being injected with it into a remorseless, flesh eating monster. The lamia.

The hard part was getting the blood. The enormous horse did not give it up easily. Deme had had to sedate the beast first, firing several tranquilizing darts into his hide before he fell.

Then, after covering her tracks so no one had known she had been there, she slipped into Elder Goretus's room and added a drop—or two—to the elixir she knew was being made for the shade in order to help cease her lust for souls.

Deme hated betraying Ever, the one who'd inadvertently told Deme of the secret potion Elder Goretus was making for Fate. It had been an innocent slip really, the princess didn't even realize she'd said it until she'd whispered afterward, "Don't tell anyone, okay? Especially my father."

The red demon closed her eyes, thinking of Ever. Of Kane. She thought she'd be chosen to replace Seren. There were so many times Kane seemed to share her romantic feelings. So many times Deme wished it were true.

Apparently not. She curled her talons into her palm. *He chose a shade instead.*

"Cryptica," one of the demon warriors called out, pointing to the village in the distance.

A flurry of nerves filled Deme's stomach as she doubted the wraiths would welcome them after what happened with Kane. If he hadn't cared so much for the shade, if he hadn't interrupted the fight between her and the wraiths, none of this would be a problem. Not that the demons and wraiths had been particularly friendly over the centuries, but they certainly didn't have the animosity they had now.

Lumina swept down towards the village entrance, her wings of fire trailing black smoke as she dived. The city was nestled inside the center of an enchanted storm, an impenetrable barricade around them. If they so desired to allow the demons passage into their city, and if anything went wrong, Deme and her party or warriors would be unable to leave.

They landed their mounts before the front entryway that way she and Kane had entered the last time they came. Deme didn't recall much about her previous visit, though, as she'd been semi-conscious much of the time.

She wondered how she should get the wraiths' attention. Feeling the eyes of her comrades upon her, she took in a deep breath and called loudly, "Wraiths of Cryptica, it is I, Deme of Legion. I ask you to allow us entry, I have important matters to discuss."

Her muted voice barely sounded over the turbulent vortex twisting before her, and for several minutes, nothing happened. She was certain they could not hear her, but just as she opened her mouth to call out again, the winds parted to reveal a dark hallway.

Swallowing hard, she led the others into the tunnel—the door sealing behind them. Whispers sounded all around them, ghostly voices hissing, breathing, murmuring. Deme's shoulders tensed as she peered through the dimness of the tunnel. The diaphanous forms floating amid the winds all around her were never there long enough for her eyes to focus upon. Every few moments, one of her warriors would whimper or gasp, the limitations of their courage challenged and worn thin. For better or worse, Deme had been unconscious when Kane carried her through the tunnel the first time. Part of her was grateful to have escaped the terror of the tunnel, but the another part of her was now extremely worried regarding what to expect when they emerged from the passage.

If they emerged.

Then, after what felt like forever, the winds of the tornado suddenly parted before her with the graceful likeness of pewter swags. Deme walked through despite the nagging awareness that if the wraiths decided she and her small group of warriors were enemies, they'd never be able to leave Cryptica — alive, anyways. Her breath caught in her throat, she took the last few steps into the wraith city, the hurricane closing behind her.

They were officially trapped.

Deme and the five warriors stood in the eye of the storm, a raging cyclone rising high into the atmosphere above their heads. On the ground, dozens of wraiths encircled them, hovering, their hot red eyes watching the newcomers raptly beneath dark, semi-transparent hoods. One stood out amongst the others as he was perched upon a throne of gleaming obsidian.

"Why have you come?" the seated wraith inquired, his baritone voice firm but curious.

Deme cleared her voice. She was uncomfortable with all eyes on her, seemingly waiting for a damn good reason for her presence. She silently cursed Kane and his petty squabble with the wraiths. There were times, like now, when she questioned his leadership abilities. She realized that much of the turmoil within Dark World wasn't Kane's fault: he was but a mere victim of his parents' poor decisions. While she'd adored King Lucifer as a child, she could now see how his actions had affected her and the people she cared about. She'd watched her own parents die, watched them wither away inside the darkened mines as they excavated bloodstone for Malus.

The wraiths eyed her with hateful suspicion, deeming her dangerous and unworthy despite not knowing her and her painful past. She fought the urge to reach for her blade, to slice every one of the haters into pieces. What did they know? Who were they to judge her?

Then she remembered her quest. Her promise to Kane. She was nothing if she could not keep her word. Kane depended on her. Dark World depended on her.

Still she struggled with the task, the weight of responsibility. For a split second, she empathized with Kane's plight. None of what happened over the last few centuries was his fault, his mess. Yet he forged ahead, plowing through the rubble, heading into every storm with conviction and valour. She understood him more than he realized — and she cared for him more than he knew. She'd just never been able to tell him. There were so many times when she almost uttered the words, almost allowed the emotions to cross the distance between them. How she'd wanted to.

When Seren died, Kane was inconsolable. His only reason for living was Ever. Little else pulled him from his sorrow. Deme wanted so badly to be there for him, to be the shoulder he could lean on. But he wouldn't even consider it. Why, Deme couldn't say. His devotion to Seren ran deep, fathomless. He could not see beyond the mourning, could not see Deme through the veil of pain.

There were so many moments in which she thought he felt the same for her, but over time she realized it was just wishful thinking. He would never get over Seren, centuries passed and still he harbored a deep, pining love for his dead wife.

Until Fate, that is.

Deme's teeth ground together as she thought of the shade. Why her? Why had he chosen her as his savior, his reason to breathe again? Had he not loathed the shades as she did? They were the reason his father died, his wife, and countless other demons and creatures. How had that changed because of one shade?

She knew she had to let it go. Besides, if she was lucky, the potion she'd tampered with had altered Fate into something far worse than the monster she already was. Perhaps then Kane would be a little more hesitant to love her if she was incapable of controlling her murderous lust, her desire for flesh and blood.

Deme pulled in a centering breath, readying to speak. This was more difficult for her than a battle with a pride of sphinxes. She was a tracker, a hunter, that was her playground. This stuff, these political matters, felt foreign to her. The words slid slowly over her dry tongue, her hands balled into fists as she willed herself to speak on behalf of Kane.

Finally, she said, "We humbly ask your assistance in a dire matter."

If the wraith indeed had brows beneath his cowl, they'd certainly have raised in quiet surprise. "Continue," he urged, leaning forward in his seat.

"Yes," Deme said, taking in a deep breath. "We ask for a volunteer to join us on our mission, to become one of five in a circle to reignite the Crystal Pyramid, hence opening the fissure to the Surface." She hoped it was enough to sway them. She hoped her words reached beyond the animosity.

The wraith leader appeared to mull this over before asking, "And to whom do you pledge allegiance to, my dear?"

"Allegiance?" Deme's brow furrowed, confused. She hadn't expected this to have anything to do with her own, personal convictions. Why would it matter? This was about Dark World, was it not?

The leader stood, hovering a few inches above the ground. He then drifted closer to her. "Yes, to whom do you kneel before…Queen Malus or Prince Kane?"

Her heart picked up tempo inside her chest. She knew her answer, that was for certain, but would it seal her and her band of demon warriors' fate if she spoke it aloud? She knew Kane had created a deadly rift between himself and the wraiths upon their last visit.

Fate. Deme seethed inside as she thought of the reason why Kane had all but declared war against the phantoms. *This was all* her *fault*.

Deme fought the urge to lower her eyes alongside her answer, anticipating a negative response. "I serve Prince Kane," she answered honestly, then added, "but I kneel before no one."

The wraith leader visibly started, then approached the steadfast demon tracker. "I believe, then, that we can strike an accord."

Ochre eyes wide, Deme stumbled over her words, "I beg your pardon, sir."

The leader's blazing eyes glowed brighter with what Deme assumed was amusement. "We will comply with your request," he said, waving his hand to his right, beckoning one of his followers forward. "This is Xi, he will be our contribution to your undertaking."

Deme was dumbstruck, speechless. Then she found her voice. "T—thank you!"

The wraith leader bowed, responding, "Even though we are at odds with Prince Kane, it is your unwavering faith in yourself we reward. Be well, demon."

Stunned but grateful, Deme and her group bowed once then moved to leave. The silvery drapes of the tornado opened once more and she led her men outside the village.

As she climbed onto Lumina, she glanced back at the wraith that had now joined their party. Seated atop a phoenix, behind another warrior, she stifled a grin. She'd done it, and without incident. Yet something inside, her demon instincts, warned that it had been too easy. They agreed too readily.

"Let's go," she stated as Lumina began flapping her fiery wings.

"Where to?" the demon warrior, Eges, inquired.

A new tightness formed inside her chest as she answered, "The Crystal Pyramid."

Vale

Vale's instincts drew him east. Something inside told him, though he had no idea why, that Fate was there, somewhere. Ever since they, Fate, Sybil, and Vale, had resurrected Kane from the brink of death, he'd felt strangely linked to both Fate and his sister. Lately, though, he'd sensed a great unease with both. With Sybil, he felt cold and confused. Fate's energy, however, was a pendulum of emotion; from exhilarated to frightened, but there was something else there, something he couldn't name. Something powerful and different.

He held tight to the reigns of the phoenix as it flew overtop the darkened landscape. From above, the Crimson Desert appeared tranquil, a sense of peace occupying the lands. He knew better though; Dark World was never quiet, never without upheaval and danger.

At least his latest dark adventure, escaping the void, went better than the first time he'd tried to get out.

The first time he was in the void, he was with Vrill. They'd just escaped from the Blood Palace by means of Vale's newfound wisping ability, only to find themselves imprisoned in an unseen sphere between realms.

"Where are we?" Vale asked, his voice echoing amid the eerie stillness. The air didn't move in this place, as if they were inside a vacuum.

"The Never," Vrill replied, a tremor of unease betraying his attempt at sounding Zen. "A world between worlds."

"Okay," Vale replied. "How do we get back?"

Vrill sighed, his star-spun eyes glittering amidst the dark backdrop. "I've known only one that entered—and was able to escape without dire consequence."

Prickles of anxiety stung Vale's pale skin. "What? Who?"

The necromancer smiled sincerely, then answered, "Your sister."

"Sybil!" Vale nearly shouted. "You know her? Where is she?"

Vrill shrugged. "This I do not know, but since you know her best…"

"Wait," Vale said, narrowing his gaze. "How do you know of my sister?"

The elder being sighed, then answered, "There are forces in Dark World that see all, know all. Beings that whisper to those they see fit to voice their secrets. I am such a creature, privy to that in which my Goddess speaks."

"Where is my sister now?"

Vrill closed his eyes, concentrating. "She is in hiding," he said. "She runs from the Devil. That is all that I know."

"But she was here? In The Never?" Vale felt as though he was grasping for anything, any knowledge of his lost sister.

The silver man nodded.

"How did she get out?"

Vrill said nothing, but pointed to speck of bright light shining in the distance. Like a star, it flickered and winked, but as they neared it, it grew bigger—and eventually had a shape. It was a being, a being of light. Vale failed to see how this could be warranted as dangerous, but was hesitant nonetheless.

As it approached, both had to shield their eyes from the brilliant radiance that emanated from the figure. Vale's heart thrummed with trepidation. What would happen when they reached it? What trial would they face?

Would they survive?

Vale willed his shaking legs forward. Despite having endured a painful and traumatic death on the Surface, he feared for his new, undead life. He was here for Sybil. He'd died for her, to help her. If his journey ended here, he would die a failure.

Suddenly Vale heard a voice inside his head, so unlike his own internal voice. It whispered so softly it was almost imperceptible.

"*Choose*," it said as unbidden images formed inside Vale's thoughts. "*Choose your opponent.*" The pictures of four hideous creatures flashed before his eyes. One being as tall as a skyscraper, furious and red with devil-like horns upon his head, crimson rains pouring from his fingertips.

"*Ba'al*," the voice uttered an introduction. The water elemental. A beast that could control the storms, rage amid the skies and send down poisonous wrath from the clouds.

The second being was that of air, a barely visible form that could manipulate the winds to slice like that of a sword. The vision of a lithe, curvaceous female sylph with long silver hair entered his thoughts, her hands manifesting gale force winds and deadly tornados with a mere flick of her wrist.

The voice said a name alongside the image, "*Vesper.*"

The next picture confused Vale. It was that of a small boy, a coy, mischievous smirk on his lips. Behind him, mountains rocked, throwing vast stones and boulders about as though they were merely pebbles. He sounded a small giggle and the soils behind him split into two, devastating an entire plain of the Crimson Desert.

"*Seth,*" the voice whispered and Vale shuddered, surmising the child's appearance was simply a ruse, wherein he was far more deadly than he looked.

"*Seere.*"

The last adversary was that of fire. Blaze and brimstone tore through his thoughts, the figure of a temptress emerging from amid the flames. Her hip-length red hair rippled as though ignited, eyes black as night, matching her lips. Her skin was that of obsidian, gleaming and of the purest ebony.

Vale shivered at the sight of her, from both fear and desire. It amazed him how something so beautiful could be so lethal.

"*Choose,*" the voice said as the images of the elemental demons faded away, replaced by the calm emanating from the being of light.

Danielle Q. Lee

Vale looked to Vrill, who stood in quiet observation with his hands tucked into the arms of his cloak, awaiting the shade's choice.

"I don't know which to choose," he admitted, butterflies taking flight inside his abdomen. They all appeared to be formidable foes; each would clearly kill Vale with little effort. How was he to defeat even one of them?

He shook his head, sighing. All he'd wanted was to help his sister, to save her. Now it appeared as though he was the one needing saving. His first choice was Seth, the earth elemental, likely because he looked the least intimidating; which is exactly why Vale wouldn't choose him, it was obviously a trick. Ba'al, the conjurer of red rain, scared him the most. He appeared ruthless and impossible to outrun.

That left Vesper and Seere. He had to admit, he was leaning towards Seere, but mostly because he was eager to meet her in person. She was really quite beautiful, despite the fact she'd likely roast him alive.

"Have you chosen?" Vrill inquired, a hint of angst hiding behind his galactic eyes.

Vale inhaled, then said, "Yes, I believe so."

"Which opponent do you choose?" Vrill asked.

As if on cue, a raging bonfire erupted before them, the figure of a beautiful, flaming woman stepping out from it.

"*Her,*" Vale replied with a glint of mischief in his smile. "Seere."

Vrill's silver eyes widened, in either lust or fear, Vale couldn't tell. "H-how do you propose we win against her?"

"We? Oh no, you just sit back and wait, okay?" The shade rubbed his hands together with feigned confidence. "I can't die twice in one week, can I?" he asked rhetorically, hoping he wasn't tempting fate.

Although the fire elemental was truly a stunning creature, Vale was not swayed enough by desire to forgo the fact that she was deadly. He knew even before he'd chosen her that he couldn't win against her power — this was to be a game of wits.

Vrill watched intently from the safety of the shadows, his swirling eyes locked on the two opponents. Who would strike first?

Her body rippled with flames, pouring over her curves like lava sliding down the side of a mountain. The black marble floor beneath her melted with her every step, burning into it the impression of her bare feet. Thin wafts of smoke curled around her, veiling her in a wreath of steam.

Without thinking, intoxicated by her presence, Vale moved a step closer.

He instantly regretted it.

She hissed, dark eyes narrowing as two long whips of fire manifested from her palms, snapping and lashing at him. The two crops of flame reached for him, over and over, missing him by mere inches. He rolled out of the way twice before vanishing into a wisp, reappearing on the other side of the shady room.

This caught her attention. Her eyes scanned him up and down with evident curiosity. Apparently she'd never seen that trick before.

Even better, it appeared she was impressed by it.

Vale took a tentative step closer to the flickering beauty, her obsidian eyes measuring him carefully, her full, luscious lips curling with a ghost of a smile. He mustn't underestimate her. She was an immortal, alive far longer than any creature he'd ever known.

Therefore, she wasn't going to fall for his charms easily.

"Good day," Vale began, bowing as he offered her a smile. "Nice day for a barbeque, wouldn't you say?"

Seere's face broke into a full grin, nodding in reply.

"I don't suppose there's anyway you'll allow my friend and me safe passage out of this place and back into Dark World?"

She frowned, shaking her head.

"Hmm," he replied. "I thought not. Might I ask if you know my sister, Sybil. I'm told she has been here, and made through unscathed. Could you enlighten me?"

At this, Seere turned from him, once again shaking her head in response.

Vale paused, wondering, then asked, "Do you not speak, my lovely lady?"

Her smile faltered as she shook her head, eyes wary of him now.

Vale considered this a moment. "Hmm, that is tragic, for I'm certain you have a beautiful voice."

The elemental's eyes read like a book: dark, brooding—sad. Vale watched her with empathy, thinking how awful it would be to live through the eons without being able express oneself except through violence.

"Please excuse me a moment," Vale said and walked to Vrill. "You are a very powerful sorcerer," he began, "Is there not a way to give the lady what she needs? An enchantment, perhaps?"

Vrill considered this, stroking his chin with his long silver fingers. Finally he nodded, replying, "Yes, for a price, yes."

"A price?" Vale was uneasy with this.

"All spells come with a price, something the user must sacrifice," the necromancer explained.

Vale exhaled, looking at the fire elemental as she paced impatiently, tiny spheres of fire building within her palms, readying herself for a fight.

"Anything, I'll sacrifice anything, let's just do it," Vale said with a forced grin. Inside though, he was quavering. He really knew nothing of this world. Nothing of the dangers and what making sacrifices really meant. But they had to get out of this place, he had no choice.

Vrill's forehead creased. "Are you certain? You will not know the sacrifice until afterwards."

Vale sucked in a breath. "Let's do it."

"Very well," the necromancer said with wary sigh. "Repeat after me. *Centhura au larqura.*"

"*Centhura au larqura,*" Vale mimicked slowly, keeping an eye on Seere as she scowled at them with uncertainty. The fires in her palms growing larger and hotter. He knew they had little time before she lost patience.

"*Mia centara du mesira.*"

"*Mia centara du...mesira,*" Vale said, stumbling over the exotic words.

"Kee satano me arestia!" Vrill's voice rose in accentuation.

Feeling mildly silly, Vale complied. *"Kee satano me arestia!"*

Once the words were spoken, a bright light appeared upon Seere's throat. She was afraid at first, clutching her neck with both hands. Vale worried that something had gone wrong, that he'd said some other spell and now she would roast him like a Thanksgiving turkey.

After a moment, she removed her hands from her throat, and the light was gone. Vale watched her with Vrill right beside him, wringing his hands. Suddenly, she parted her perfect lips and whispered, "Thank you."

Her voice was as melodic and sweet as Vale thought it would be. "You're very welcome."

She gazed at the two with warmth in her eyes as she said, "I've not been allowed to speak for many centuries."

"Allowed?" Vale's brow creased. It had not occurred to him that she'd once been able to speak. "Who prevented you?"

Seere's sight dropped to the floor. "My master."

Vale took a tentative step towards her, asking, "Who is your master?"

Her eyes filled with tears that evaporated with a sizzle the moment they attempted to roll over her blazing skin.

For a moment, he was uncertain she was going to answer, but then she whispered, *"Malus."*

Kane

The Night Mare's hooves pounded like a heartbeat upon the sands, even and steady, nostrils flaring with fierce determination. Heat waves from the beast's flaming mane streamed backward, the coppery tendrils flickering like a miniature bonfire in front of Kane's face. Powerful, sleek muscles rippled beneath the stallion's black velvet hide, showing no signs of lethargy due to his recent, long-term incarceration. Exhilaration filled Kane's chest as hot, tormented winds exhaled all around him. He'd never ridden a horse before, yet he found it profoundly natural. Like something he'd been born to do, but hadn't yet discovered.

After several hours of hard running, the massive horse finally slowed to a trot. Until then, Kane had started to wonder if the mysterious creature would ever tire, or if he was going to run all the way across the desert without stopping.

Long in the distance, Kane could distinguish the dark, inky edge of the Black Ocean. He'd seen it once before, when he was very young. His father had taken him on a tour of the realm, showing him the high-lights—and lowlights—of every corner. They'd avoided a few areas, for sure, like the notoriously reclusive land of the reapers. Restricted by a fence made of melded animal flesh, barbed and enchanted with an evil curse, the hostile tribe made it abundantly clear that they did not wish to be disturbed. The demon prince felt a wave of guilt wash over him as he imagined Sorcia leading her posse into the territory of the reapers. He worried what kind of reception they would receive—and whether or not they would survive it.

Whatever happened in the past, to create such animosity between the reapers and the rest of Dark World, Kane did not know, nor would his father elaborate when asked.

Kane pulled in a deep breath, the air tasting of hot ash and lingering decay. Dark World had been so different back then, before the abandonment of the light from the Crystal Pyramid. How he ached for his home to return to the glory it had once been. If only his father hadn't...

He stopped himself from dwelling once again on the past. Things had changed now that he knew his father still lived, in some form or another.

There had to have been a reason why he did it, Kane pondered as he thought of his father's actions so long ago. Why did he use the pages of the Devil's Bible to render this world obsolete? And how was he to obtain the last scroll from the Surface? He cursed his father for making this task so difficult for him.

He shook his head, ridding himself of doubt for his father. There had to be a reason. He had to trust him. He had to.

The Night Mare snorted suddenly, paused his steps and rearing his head as though something had startled him.

"What is it?" Kane inquired, his voice hushed as his cerulean eyes scoured the landscape which presented him with little more than stark red sands. Despite the quietude, the Night Mare still pranced with uncertainty, not wanting to go on.

Dismounting, Kane took the horse by the reins and patted his thick neck, still eyeing the desert raptly. One never took Dark World's silence for granted; in fact, it usually meant something evil was amiss. He took a few tentative steps forward, the stallion following slowly, reluctantly, behind him. The air seemed to have stilled, as if holding its breath in fearful anticipation.

Kane's insides stirred with heightened apprehension, his pointed ears perked, eyes narrowed in suspicion. He reached to his back, drawing his black diamond sword slowly, readying it. The Night Mare grunted, his flaming hairs rippling wildly as though tethered to the beat of his racing heart.

Kane stopped in his tracks, and waited.

All was still.

Quiet.

Then the Night Mare screamed, and all went dark.

Candlelight flickered against the crimson walls, manifesting shadows that shivered and shook as though their sightless eyes could not fathom the horrors happening before them.

Fear crept into Maxim's heart as he watched the reapers sway and chant over his queen, her chest rising and falling rapidly as if Ever's soul fought to break free from her prison. As the dark song rose to the rafters, malevolent words melding into invisible enchantments, Maxim fought against the urge to cover his ears. The way the room rumbled with magic, he felt if his own soul still inhabited his undead body; it too was be struggling to burst through his chest. Soon the cacophony elevated to a deafening crescendo, bringing Maxim to his knees as his queen's red lips parted and relinquished a blood-curdling scream, followed by a blinding flash of lavender light.

Then, silence.

Shaking, Maxim opened his eyes and focused on the altar. Malus was still, eyes closed, her naked body glistening with beads of sweat. The six reapers stood in a tight circle, clasping something inside their hands. Maxim rose, taking a few steps forward.

Held within their skeletal palms was a perfect blue sphere, spinning slowly and crackling with white lightning. He'd seen many a soul in his lifetime as a shade, devoured too many to count, yet this was truly the most beautiful, the most pure, he'd ever witnessed.

The soul stirred as though it felt his presence, as if concerned he might consume it, but strangely, the thought never crossed his mind. This soul was different. Good. Kind.

It was the demon princess.

Ever.

Despite his shade nature, he was concerned with what they were going to do to the princess's soul. The lead reaper removed his hold on the soul, stepping away to retrieve something from behind him. Upon his return to the circle, he held an ornately carved box. Black with swirling gold markings, the box pulsed with a dark and evil energy. Slowly, carefully, he opened the lid and moved towards Ever's soul, as though to capture her unawares. He moved slowly and steadily closer, and closer still, until he snapped the lid shut suddenly, causing Maxim to jump.

The reaper then sealed the box with a black lock, glowing violet. Finally, after placing the box on a nearby table, the six reapers pulled their dark cowls over their heads, veiling their faces of horror, and walked out of the room without looking back.

Maxim turned his blazing white gaze to the mystical black box on the table, certain he could hear Ever's kind, sweet soul screaming from within.

Fate

Her new body was calm, surreal, so unlike her human self. Her mortal body had been so worrisome, filled with doubt, regret, love, and hate. Always hot and cold, never perfect. Her human mind had been a constant whir of emotion, thoughts, and angst.

Likewise with her shade body, its ravenous hunger seemed never appeased. The dark cloud of hatred she'd felt from everyone in Dark World incessantly haunted her, the constant fear of the distrust and judgment of her race.

Frankly, she wasn't altogether unhappy they were gone. Of course she'd always be herself, her soul hadn't changed, just the vehicle that carried her around had evolved.

This body was just right. Though it held the usual human attributes, and in the same light as she was when she was Scarlet; there was an inherent difference, an essence she could not name.

A knowing.

A *gnosis*.

For instance, she knew things she could not know, things she'd never been told but was now privy to. It was more than the necromancer telepathic link. It was more than being psychic. It was…a presence. Like something inside whispered clandestine knowledge, secrets of the universe.

Myth

Part of her wondered if she truly still belonged in the underworld, yet the Surface didn't feel right either. She knew, deep down, that there were other places she could go. But would she? Could she leave Kane?

"It's time to go," the beings of light said softly, gently. *"You know what you must do."*

She nodded. "I do."

She turned to leave the Guf, part of her longing to stay, the other half ready to face her destiny.

As she stepped over the threshold of light, the doors to the Guf closing behind her, she felt more alone than she ever had in her life. Yet, she knew what she carried within; the light would never leave her now. Her soul was her own again. Forever.

Dark World looked so different to her now, no longer did it own a gloomy, oppressive ambiance. It didn't carry with it the weight of the Surface, burdened like a mule with the world on its back. She saw it reborn, as if her new eyes could penetrate the layers of pain and suffering the realm had seen for so many centuries.

She'd decided, for lack of a better name, to continue to call herself Fate. The name didn't matter as much as the essence. Whatever it was called, it was beautiful. She was beautiful.

Fate wandered down the path the beings of light had sent her. The narrow road twisted, meandering left and right, looking vaguely familiar until she found what she was looking for.

As she approached the area in which she'd last seen her friends, she gasped. "Ick?"

She knelt down, taking the shattered pieces of stone into her hands. Her brows pulled together as she examined the fragments. Who would have done this? Why?

Her new, inherited knowledge had told her how to transform her little friends from their prison of stone, how to bring them back to life. She'd left Ick and his friends here in the middle of the labyrinth not long ago. And now it was too late.

Now, the statues were rubble. Broken by unknown hands. Tears welled in Fate's blue eyes; she'd never see her little friend again. She shouldn't have left him here, but how was she to know something would come along and destroy what remained of him. For a brief moment she felt betrayed by her new, inherent knowledge. Why couldn't she see her friends' demise? Why didn't she feel some shard of pain rip through her when they met their fate? She realized she couldn't be completely all-knowing, omniscient and sage in all things, but this seemed particularly harsh. The cruelties of this world seemed to follow her no matter where she went. Was there no kindness amid the darkness? No mercy?

She drew a meditative breath, standing and forcing herself to carry on. The beings of light had promised her safe passage through the labyrinth so she might find her furry friends. Her heart broke as she walked away from the tiny graveyard of stone, but she had to find her way back to Kane.

It was time to do what she was reborn in this world to do.

Sorcia's lavender eyes scoured the darkening scenery. She'd never experienced such tormented skies, such shadowed lands. The closer they got to the reapers' den, the Nether Caves, the worse the atmosphere surrounding them became. A wall of gray fog loomed, hovering just above the reddened sands, yet reaching all the way to the fanged ceiling overhead. The further they walked, the thicker the strange miasma became.

Sorcia's new sister, whom they'd named Calyx, said in a hushed tone, "I don't like this place." Mezza wrapped a silver arm around her shivering shoulders, pulling her closer.

"I agree," Sorcia replied, her body tense with anticipation. She knew without a doubt that she had to do this, it was part of her destiny. Since the moment Kane entered the gates of the banshee city, she'd known she was meant to help him save Dark World. She'd always known, of course, that her fate was entangled with some mysterious future quest, but it had surprised her just how it had unfolded. She had not foreseen the devastation of her race, the loss of her king and sisters. It was an indescribable pain she wasn't sure she'd live through.

Thankfully though, her kind replicated quickly. She cringed inwardly, disturbed that the other races now knew of their secret reproduction process.

Termed *panmesia*, it was a sacred ritual in their culture, one they'd cherished and had kept to themselves for many a century. She shook her head, it no longer mattered. Her family was dead, gone forever. It was up to her and Calyx now to rebuild their kind. It was a painful process though, one in which not all survived. Sorcia prayed that she and Calyx could endure at least one more replication each, or all could be lost.

Slater's muscular arm brushed against hers and Sorcia moved closer to his side, feeling his warm aura surround her. His presence was immense, yet comforting. She was glad Mezza and Calyx had taken to one another. Before she'd given birth to her sister, she was worried about having to choose between the once peaceful brothers. She'd sensed animosity between the two of them since they'd all met, wondering how she'd ever be able to choose one over the other, inevitably leaving one with a broken heart. It took her aback, however, when she'd come to the conclusion that both of the necromancers appeared smitten with her. It was flattering, to say the least. She'd never known of courtships or attractions as their king was the only male within their species. And he was their father figure, their caretaker, one with whom none of her sisters ever had any kind of relationship with. To do so would have been considered perverse.

Her duty was her life before Kane and the necromancers showed up on their doorstep, she hadn't considered another life beyond that. Banshees, though taught to use their beauty as a weapon against enemies, were not allowed to leave the city or seek out another existence.

Considering all she'd experienced since, she thought it a sad way to live. Despite the banshee memories embedded inside every new daughter, Sorcia thought it best to begin anew, to allow her offspring the choice of adventure, to give them opportunities beyond the walls of their heritage.

"Stop," whispered Slater suddenly, his star-like eyes scanning the perimeter suspiciously.

"What is it?" she asked, though she'd begun to sense unseen eyes upon them as well.

The fog thickened then, clouding their vision in all directions. Sorcia squinted but could barely see own hands as she reached for Slater's arm.

Slater's deep voice broke through the veil, "Stay close."

The mist was cool and damp, licking at her bare skin, leaving tiny beads of moisture upon her face and chest. She sensed something moving around her. Every few moments a shadow drifted past. Then another…and another. They were all around them.

They were surrounded.

Sorcia's chest tightened as she forced herself to be brave. "Who's there?" she called out, her voice echoing through the white smoke.

Silence.

Deafening silence.

Just when she was about to ask again, she felt something brush against her arm, a figure draped in a long black cloak answered with a whisper in her ear, "*Death.*"

Sorcia gasped, having heard the lore surrounding the reapers' touch. It had been said that just one touch could kill. She rubbed her arm where she'd felt the contact, noting that she felt nothing amiss. Behind her, somewhere in the fog, Calyx whimpered in fear.

I shouldn't have brought her, Sorcia thought then, guilt washing over her. Her new, little sister was still a baby, a newborn in a dark and threatening world. She was too vulnerable, too susceptible to the evil lurking around every corner, and Sorcia had brought her to the darkest part of the realm, where most travellers did not return.

The shadowy figures neared again, their cloaked bodies drifting closer and closer. Slater tensed against her grip, obviously readying himself for a fight. Sorcia, too, was leaning toward that innate, primal part of herself. Whatever these creatures were, they were going to learn that banshees didn't go down without one hell of a fight.

Reluctantly, she let go of Slater and drew her dual, curved blades from her belt. If there was one thing she felt confident in, it was her combat abilities. Banshees began training the moment they arrived into the world; it was a necessity, but also an inborn need, a desire to protect oneself and her people. Sorcia regretted that Calyx had been born at such an inopportune time, her training postponed, but because of the genetic passing on of information between the sisters, she hoped her sister would have retained enough knowledge so she could assist her if the time arose.

That time had come.

To her left, a shadowy figure charged her, disrupting the thick gauze of smoke all around her.

"Look out!" Slater yelled, taking Sorcia by the waist and manoeuvering both their bodies from harm's way. The reaper missed them by mere inches. From somewhere in the mist, Calyx screamed.

"We have to get out of here," Sorcia said. "*Now!*"

Slater complied, shifting into a large, silver lion. He nuzzled her leg, urging her to climb on.

"Calyx!" she called out, praying her sister could hear her. "Where are you?"

There was no response.

Sorcia felt the sting of tears creep into her eyes. She had failed the mission and lost her sister.

And now they were running for their lives from the keepers of death.

Six or more shadows surrounded her now, the sensation of pressure mounted upon her body. They hissed as they drew ever closer, their arms raised, skeletal fingers reaching for her. Slater bared his massive teeth at them, his snarl echoing through the thick fog. He pressed his feline torso against her, nearly knocking her over as he swiped at the phantoms in the mist.

Sorcia's mind raced, there had to be something she could do, something she could say to stop them.

Finally she found her voice, "Reapers, I am here in place of Prince Kane," she began, noting they'd immediately stopped their approach. "We are on a quest to save Dark World, but we need the scroll that was given to you, and a volunteer."

The silence was deafening as they appeared to consider her words. Their answer came as a united hiss, "*Why?*"

She responded quickly, "Prince Kane needs to relight the pyramid, to return the magic to Dark World."

Beneath their cowls she was certain she could sense them smile. Again, they replied with a cohesive whisper, "*And the fissure, the passage to the Surface, will it open?*"

She nodded, a shudder running down her spine as she weighed their words. *Why would they care about that?*

"Come," they said, burying their fleshless hands into the arms of their black cloaks. All around them, the miasma lifted, revealing the lands once more.

Sorcia glanced around, her lavender eyes searching for Calyx and Mezza. She breathed a sigh of relief when she saw her sister in the arms of the silver being, striding towards them.

Ahead, the six reapers walked in a line towards a tall, dark fence that seemed to stretch for miles in each direction.

"What do we do?" Mezza asked as Calyx lay whimpering in his arms like a fragile babe.

"You are to stay here with her—Slater and I are going inside," she said determinedly.

Upon shifting back into a necromancer, Slater eyed her with a mixture of admiration and uncertainty.

Mezza frowned, his allegiance palpable. "Are you sure?"

She nodded. "I have no choice in the matter," she stated firmly, then ordered, "If we do not return by nightfall...I want you to leave us, take Calyx and return to Kane. Tell him of our failure."

Mezza hesitated, then nodded, sadness glazing over his stare.

The necromancer brothers then looked into one another's eyes, obviously speaking in thought. Likely saying their farewells, just in case. After a moment, they separated and Slater rejoined Sorcia before the reaper barrier.

The band of reapers stood perfectly still in front of a fence that, as Sorcia neared, appeared to be comprised of fused body parts. While this stirred nettles of fear inside, what she saw next would haunt her dreams for years to come.

The fence was *alive*.

Body parts writhed; decapitated heads keened and cried out for help. Bloody stumps and oozing limbs, bodiless faces and wriggling torsos; the massacre that made up the Wailing Wall was truly the portal to Hell. Whatever the Surface imagined this evil world was — this was it.

Sorcia and Slater stood several feet from the reapers and their wall of horror, awaiting the next move.

"Where's the door?" Sorcia whispered to Slater.

He shrugged, his widened eyes obviously as disturbed as she was.

Then the reapers raised their hooded faces to the living fence and uttered a hushed enchantment. Suddenly the mesh of dismembered body parts released their hold upon one another, pulling apart in order to form a doorway.

Sorcia exhaled sharply, disgusted and trembling with fear. If they went in there, they may never come out again. Worse, they could end up a part of the body wall.

Closing her eyes and holding the hilt of the curved blades tucked into her belt, she and Slater moved forward. Upon the last step into the reaper village, the arms and legs sealed themselves behind her with a squishing and slithering sound.

"Where are they taking us?" she whispered to Slater, knowing he was likely as clueless as she but needed someone or something to soothe her terror.

He took her hand into his, squeezing it gently. "Perhaps they are taking us to their leader, maybe they are complying with our demands."

Prickles of unease raced over her skin as dozens of cloaked reapers watched them pass through the city. Above, like a hive riddled with dark holes, were hundreds, possibly thousands, of cave openings. Each appeared to house at least one, if not several, reapers.

Sorcia shuddered, burying her face into Slater's thick, silver arm; all the unseen eyes upon them, hidden within the shadowy cowls. They watched, observed, judged. Sorcia could feel their glares crawling over her skin like the reedy legs of a million spiders. Fleetingly, she wondered what these beings looked like without their long, black garb; then she reconsidered, praying she'd never be shown. She just wanted this over with, to get the scroll and a volunteer and get far away from this place.

The original six reapers they'd met outside the wall finally stopped before a large cave mouth, one so dark that no light could seemingly penetrate its fathoms. Two of the reapers flanked the entrance, then waved a skeletal hand as to invite them in.

Sorcia's heart thrummed inside her chest, wanting nothing more than to run away. She searched her soul for courage, for the bravery that her father and sisters had once taught her, willing it, summoning it forward.

Slater seemed to pause before moving forward, glancing down at her with kind eyes. "I will protect you with my life," he said, giving her the last bit of nerve she needed to go on.

She nodded, forcing a smile. "Let's go," she said.

The darkness swallowed them whole as they disappeared into the cave, a horde of reapers gazing curiously after them. Inside the cave reeked of death and decay, of things rotting and recently deceased. Sorcia had heard rumors of these beings, that they were cannibals and fiends, dining on anything flesh, living or dead. She shivered uncontrollably as a cold draft slid over her skin, the sense of ghosts all around her.

Finally, as they moved through the shadows, a golden light illumed in the distance. Lit candles wavered amid the gloom, dancing to a silent song as they cast spectral forms upon the dark, jagged walls.

As they came closer to the light, Sorcia could distinguish a figure seated in a large chair made of bones. He was yet another reaper, but he wore a cloak the shade of dull silver.

"He must be the leader," she whispered to Slater, still clutching firmly to his arm.

The reaper sat perfectly still upon his throne, hands tucked into the sleeves of his robe. On either side of him were tall, muscular guards, their heads shrouded in black masks; wearing only metallic, gold kilts and wielding long double-edged sword staffs. Behind the throne, the wall appeared to have thousands of carved eyes, their lids closed.

"Come closer," the reaper hissed as he lifted a boney finger, beckoning them.

The two took several hesitant steps closer as Sorcia summoned the courage to speak. "Greetings," she began, her voice shaky. "I am here in place of Prince Kane. He intends to relight the Crystal Pyramid but needs the enchanted scroll and a volunteer from each race to complete the ritual. Can we count on you for your support?" She exhaled shakily though pleased with herself.

The reaper appeared to mull this over, his unseen eyes drinking her in from beneath his hood. After several moments, he replied, "And what would we receive in return?"

Sorcia's blood froze. She had not considered they might request payment. "W-what do you want?"

She sensed him smile, as though he'd been awaiting this moment for centuries. "I will comply with your request," he said, adding, "provided my race is granted full access to the Surface."

Slater squeezed her hand so slightly it was nearly imperceptible. Should she grant them their wish despite her lack of authority? What if Kane were to disagree? But more importantly — what did they want with the Surface?

She tried to think like Kane, what would he say? What would he do?

He would do anything to save Dark World, she realized. *I'm going to have to lie.*

Sorcia lifted her chin determinedly, stating, "You may have your request, so long as we receive the scroll and a volunteer."

"On your word?" the reaper queried, toying with her.

She sighed, a flurry of mixed emotions stormed inside her. "On my word as Princess Sorcia, you will have your access to the Surface." *As for how long, I cannot say,* she added silently.

Upon her words, the wall behind the reaper seemed to come alive, the thousands of carved eye lids suddenly fluttering open, watching her with wide interest.

"Excellent," the reaper's words were frighteningly cheerful as the wall of eyes behind him parted, revealing a hidden room. The reaper then stood, waggling a skeletal finger at them, beckoning them to follow.

Her heart tight in her chest, Sorcia trailed after the reaper leader, praying she'd made the right decision. She couldn't wait to get the scroll, leave this horrible place, and return to the Crystal Pyramid so she could put this nightmare behind her.

Malus

The queen's eyes fluttered open, her sight blurry and weak. She reached out with her thin, ivory fingers, knowing Maxim would be near. "W-what happened?"

Maxim's hand enveloped hers. "It was successful, my lady. The princess is gone from your body," he explained, though his voice suggested he was withholding something.

"What is it, Maxim? Tell me."

He sighed, then said, "Let us wait until you are stronger."

Though weak, she growled a response, "Tell me!"

"We have word that Kane is on his way to meet with Myth, one of our Shadow Rangers has been following him," he said quietly.

Malus forced herself up to a sitting, her head spinning and stomach churning. "Why? Why is he going there?"

Again Maxim hesitated as he draped a long crimson robe over her shoulders, which she then wrapped around her chilled, naked body.

"Maxim," Malus warned.

The shade lowered his gaze to the floor. "Apparently Myth has a number of the pages of the Bible; Kane has gone to retrieve them."

The queen frowned. "Myth had them?" Her blood boiled, giving her renewed life as she rose, using

Maxim's shoulder to leverage herself to standing. "All this time?"

"Apparently so, my lady."

"Then, if I'm correct, he will be heading for the Crystal Pyramid next." A smile crossed her lips.

Maxim's brows pulled together. "What does he mean to do there?"

Malus crossed the room, her full strength returning to her as she eyed herself in a gilded mirror hanging upon the wall. "He means to open the crevasse," she explained, an evil grin pulling at her lips. "He means to relight the pyramid...and give me back my full power."

"Why would he do that?" Maxim looked confused.

She laughed loudly, answering, "Because he doesn't know it will." Then she ordered, "Ready my carriage."

Maxim swiftly left the room.

Malus moved towards the mirror. She caressed her skin. Her hair. Her face. It was all hers now, the body held just one soul — *hers*. Malus eyed the black box that held her granddaughter's soul, the softest of heartbeats sounding from within. The box would hold her; keep her safe until Malus could decide what to do with her.

Perhaps I'll give it to my son, she mused. *As a gift from his dear, sweet mother.*

She smiled wickedly as she imagined the look on Kane's face when she presented what remained of his daughter to him. How she loved that expression, that soul-crushing, heart-breaking moment when she obliterated someone's reason for living.

She came by it honestly; she was, after all, a demon. Hate was love for her, the two emotions entangled, writhing together in some morbid, exotic dance. Her heart carried little in the ways of sentiment. In fact, growing up, she often wondered if she even had a heart. It was as though she'd been born without one. Even as a small demon child, her own mother watched her daughter with a wary eye, questioning, waiting, sensing something was so very wrong with her only daughter.

Her father applauded her though, claiming his daughter was strong, resilient to the weaknesses that plagued Dark World. It was her nature, was it not? To be evil? Why should she deny her inheritance, her inborn malevolence?

Of course, she'd tried to love. To care. But it simply was not there. Even for her only son, there was nothing, no love, no desperate sentimental fall for something she'd created with her own body.

She sneered at herself in the mirror. No, she didn't have any of it. Sympathy, compassion, care for anyone but herself.

"Pathetic," she whispered as she thought of Lucifer and his soft heart. He'd loved. He'd loved so deeply it was unbecoming of a demonic being. How could he call himself the Prince of Darkness? The Devil of Dark World? How was it possible that the Dark Lord himself had — *feelings*?

Lore from the Surface had painted him in the darkest of hues, a monster, a powerful, ruthless creature spawned of hatred, sin, and above all, evil. What room could he have in his heart for love and empathy when his soul was supposed to be black?

She shook her head, disgusted by the notion that she'd had to marry the very person she loathed the most. It all worked out though, her plan to take over Dark World came to fruition.

Her face darkened then, thinking of how she'd not yet succeeded in overtaking the Surface. She wanted to rule all beings, not just the ones in Dark World.

Why should she suffer the darkness, trapped in a world beneath the feet of mortals? Why should she not reside topside, where the sun could kiss her face, adore her, worship her as she should be?

It will be done.

She would claim the Surface as her own — soon. And with her son's help, no less.

She turned her head as Maxim entered the room. "We are ready, my lady,"

"And my pets?"

He nodded with a barely veiled wince.

She smiled.

Very soon.

Vale

The phoenix carrying Vale navigated the balmy atmosphere like an angel on fire, graceful and blazing, darting and diving. He was profoundly indebted to the demons for crafting the enchanted saddle, he winced as he considered the consequences if it were to fail him.

Dark World lay spread out before him, seeming so peaceful from heights that veiled its true demeanor. How different this world was from his own, he marveled at how it could still amaze him after all these years; both the beauty and the brutality. On one hand, the underworld was a land lush with magic and mysticism, how the Surface would gasp if it were to lay sight to its wonders. But the dark side of reality was merciless, a bitter mistress to that of evil. She gave far less than she took.

Vale's eyes narrowed as the memory of escaping The Never drifted through his thoughts. How naïve he'd been back then, how easily he'd accepted the sacrifices he did not realize he'd made. While Seere had graciously allowed them to leave the void, he didn't learn until later what he'd surrendered as a price for using magic to give the elemental back her voice.

His price, he discovered too late, was Sybil.

He wouldn't be allowed to find her for at least one hundred years. Even then, he was told afterwards, he might never find her at all. It was a blow he hadn't been prepared to hear. He'd died for her, descended into Hell for her — and then lost her all over again.

Vrill did his best to console the heartbroken shade, bringing him back to Necrosia and treating him as a son. The necromancer lovingly trained the wayward boy-turned-monster, never once allowing him to take the blame for his foolish gamble. Vrill had warned him, after all. He had told him the price for using magic could be steep. Had he only known just how steep, he might not have chosen the path he did.

Though it took him a while to realize exactly where he was the second time he was trapped in The Never, Seere was pleasantly lenient, allowing him passage with a lesser penalty. He smiled at the thought, relishing in the idea that the attractive elemental was sweet on him. He blushed as he reminded himself of Aura. She wouldn't need to worry anyways; he was devoted to her and only her.

His immense luck surprised him though. Vale sincerely doubted anyone else had made it out of The Never without great harm, if at all. Vrill had said that Sybil was able to escape, though he had no idea how. Other than that, most creatures were left there to rot in their own misery forever, unless the elementals took pity on them — but according to Vrill, they took pity on no one. Vale was a rare, if singular, exception.

He drew in a breath of hot, ash-laden air, happy that the nightmare of finding his sister was over. She was safe now, free from the torment of facing damnation alone. Vale took comfort in the fact that she was safe inside the walls of Necrosia.

Or was she? Again that feeling ate at his conscience, as though she wasn't alright. That she was again pursued by darkness, by evil forces. He pushed the thought away, not trusting his intuition. He couldn't allow himself to think that way, not right now. For if he ever lost her again, he didn't know what he would do.

He wouldn't let himself worry over it now; he had a job to do — he had to find Fate. She was crucial to the lighting ceremony, though he had no idea why. What purpose did she serve in the ritual? How was it that a human from the Surface held the key to opening the fissure and reigniting the pyramid?

Vale shrugged, he guessed he had to find her first, then all his questions would be answered.

His infrared eyes scoured the sands below, instinct guiding him. He felt a pull within, a small source of gravity that lured him to Fate's location. All he knew was he had to trust it.

Ahead he saw the outline of a very large maze beneath a white fog.

"The Guf," he whispered to himself, somehow knowing the name of something he'd never seen before. How this information was being given to him, he had no idea. He just knew it was important to listen to it.

The phoenix descended, circling and circling until she finally reached the red sands and landed as gracefully as she flew.

Fate must be nearby, Vale thought as the new force inside of him thrummed louder.

He gazed about himself, taking in the oddness of his surroundings. He'd heard things, rumors, about the Guf. That it was the gateway into the light realm: Heaven. Legends told of Lucifer's fall from grace, and how he'd come through the doorway into Dark World through the Guf. Upon his arrival, he found a world without reason, without a leader. Claiming it as his own, he asked the elementals to create an army, a legion, of creatures like himself.

They complied, and demons were born.

Vrill had told Vale the many tales of Dark World's humble beginnings, though Vale had always sensed the old necromancer had not told all. He'd held back some of the darkest lore, the deepest of secrets — secrets like who Myth really was and why she was so important to this world.

As he dismounted his fiery mount, Vale narrowed his sight, looking for anything that would lead him to Fate. He took several steps forward, sands crunching beneath his feet. Before him lay a canyon of unfathomable depth and width, stalagmites peeking out from amid a thick, hazy mist. He considered his options as he felt Fate was down there, in the maze somewhere. Should he fly down upon the phoenix? It seemed the more logical route, but was there anywhere safe to land? Without being able to see the ground, they were flying blind.

With a sigh, he realized there was just one alternative — and considering he'd never tried anything like it before — he just hoped he'd live through it.

Pulling in a deep breath, Vale closed his eyes and *saw* himself at the base of the mountain. It was how he wisped, envisioning himself in that place, then arriving there. The problem was, with these types of wisps, if he couldn't see his destination clearly from where he stood, he wasn't sure where he'd end up.

He forced himself to trust the powers, they'd rarely steered him wrong (save for the times he'd ended up in The Never). A soft breeze kissed his face as he traveled between the spaces, his body evaporating into smoke. He often wondered what happened to him as he journeyed. Though fleeting, he seemed to disappear into thin air, his corporeal body disintegrating, then reappearing in the next space. Did he become a ghost whilst in transition? A formless spirit?

He'd often wondered these things, wishing he was wiser in the ways of science when he was on the Surface. Perhaps now, a century later, doctors up there would have the means to study him, interpret his power and find out why it works.

With his eyes still closed tight, he willed them open; unsure if he wanted to see where he'd landed. Relief flooded through him as he opened his eyes and viewed his new environment.

He'd made it unscathed, a thick layer of fog now drifted over his head, a forest of dark pillars surrounding him. A great doorway loomed to his right and he sensed that he needed to go that direction. Fate was very close by, her frequency thrummed wildly inside him.

Vale crossed the threshold to the maze, hoping he wouldn't have to go far to find her, thus likely getting lost in the process.

As he took a few steps forward, his foot bumped into something solid. Looking down, he saw the remnants of what appeared to be a small statue. A gargoyle.

He bent down to inspect it, wondering why it was there. But as he reached out to touch a piece, he heard footsteps come up from behind.

"Don't touch him!" a voice shrieked.

Vale stood, hands in the air as he backed away from the shattered figurine. "Sorry, my bad," Vale offered peacefully.

"Vale?"

He spun about, coming face to face with Fate — sort of. "W-what happened to you?" he sputtered as he inspected his friend, now sporting bright blue eyes.

She smiled at him, then cast a wistful glance to the broken gargoyle upon the ground. "It's a long story," she confessed. "I'll tell you on the way."

"The way?"

"To the Crystal Pyramid," she explained with a wink. "It's almost time."

His head spun with confusion. "Time? For what?"

Fate linked her arm in his, nodding to indicate she was ready to wisp up the side of the mountain, saying excitedly, "You'll see."

Sybil

The cell stank of putridity and rot beyond anything her senses had ever endured. The scratching of small, carnivorous beasts emanating from between the walls tested the limits of her courage. She could never lie down, never rest her eyes, even for a moment, because she knew they were waiting for an opportunity to catch her unawares, waiting to eat her alive.

But was she truly alive? She felt the hollow of her chest, the place where her heart lay orphaned without her soul. The place where she felt she used to reside. Her human life had been full, wonderful, if not perfect. Despite her brother's reservations about Pa, she loved everything about her family, her Surface life — until Blake Dean stole it all away from her.

She'd had glorious plans for her life. Pious, she had plotted out a lifeline filled with a devotion to God. When she was a young child, she'd steal away to the orphanage nearby, a convent that took in wayward children. It filled her with such bliss to see the nuns tend to the lost boys and girls, filling their dead eyes with newfound gladness, and all seemingly through prayer, songs, and a kind hand. How Sybil had wished she could do that, offer herself to a higher purpose.

But she'd made a mistake, an awful mistake. She'd trusted when she should have run.

Myth

Now, all she had was the consequences to contend with.

It seemed horribly, unbelievably, unfair. But she'd come to terms with that long ago. She knew she had a higher purpose, and her test was to discover that she could do that from anywhere — even in Hell.

Screams echoed from every direction, prisoners crying out in fear, desperation, or insanity. She'd seen things in this place that she wished she could erase from her memories, heard things that froze what little remained of her soul. Inmates tearing their own eyes out, clawing at their faces as their minds spiralled into madness.

Malus kept all of them in the dark, the barest of lights filtering in from cracks in the stones. No windows, no bars — no doors. Once the prisoner was thrown in, the walls magically sealed themselves shut. Apparently there'd been escapes when they had doors and windows.

She didn't have long, she felt, before the grips of insanity took hold of her as well. Shades didn't do well in captivity, especially without food or souls to consume. It wouldn't be long before she became like the others, mad for nourishment, crazy with lust for souls.

But she was happy the end was near. She couldn't endure this world any longer — even with Vale. This place, this hell, was more than she could bear. The worst thing, however, was learning that her only brother, her beloved Vincent, had followed her into the pits of the darkened world.

Though weak from malnutrition, she called to her innate shade powers to locate her brother. She blocked his intuition, not wanting him to feel her suffering. The less he knew the better.

She smiled in the darkness, her plan coming to light. It would all be over soon, for her and for every-one she cared about. The nightmare would end—and she could go where she belonged.

Closing her eyes, she summoned all the power she had left. She had to help, had to do one last act of kindness. It was, after all, what she'd promised the elementals she'd do when the time came—sacrifice herself for the good of Dark World. It was how she managed to escape The Never: an ancient promise of sacrifice to save the world.

For what better way to serve the Heavens than to spite the Devil?

Shelby

Inside her dream, a beautiful, yet tormented creature with long silver hair and glowing white eyes came to her. She was sad, caged in what looked to be a lightless tomb. Shelby, in a dreamlike state, walked towards the girl, helped her beaten, weary body to a stand.

"Who are you?" Shelby asked of the girl.

The girl smiled weakly, as if her life force was fading before Shelby's eyes. "I am called the Oracle."

"The Oracle?" Shelby frowned. "Why are you here?"

"There isn't time to explain—do you still have the scroll?" she asked hastily, glancing about herself as though the dark corners hid spies.

Shelby thought a moment, unsure as to what the girl meant, then replied, "The old page with gold writing? Rory's ritual paper? Yes, I still have it."

The white-haired girl exhaled with relief, then said, "I need you to take it to the clearing; The Devil's Gate. There, I need you to bury it in the middle of the field."

"Bury it?" Shelby shook her head, suddenly lucid, realizing this was not a dream at all.

The girl nodded, her knees giving out beneath her. "I don't have…much time left. Please, help me."

Shelby felt a wave of sympathy and panic rush through her. "I will. I will help you."

"You must...say these words...*sopheara sanctumis,*" she whispered, her glowing eyes fading, closing.

"*Sopheara sanctumis,*" Shelby repeated, engraving it into her memory as she watched helplessly as the girl collapsed to the floor.

Then she smiled as she curled into a ball, her life force fading. "Thank you, Shelby. Thank you."

Shelby knelt down beside the girl, stroking her hair. "I will do what you ask, but...why me?"

Her last words came out a whisper, barely audible, but Shelby gasped when she heard them, yanking her out of the dream. She sat straight up in her bed, hair wet with perspiration, shivering uncontrollably as she recalled the last words the girl had uttered, "*Scarlet needs you.*"

Shelby threw back the covers with force and jumped out of bed. Keeping the light off, she dressed quickly, throwing on whatever she could find amidst the collective piles of laundry littered upon the floor. After tucking her cell phone into the pocket of her pink hoodie, she opened her closet door and reached for a strategically placed box. Behind the box she'd stashed the scroll, alongside some love (or lewd, depending on your idea of romance) letters from Greg that she didn't want her parents finding.

The curled paged gleamed in the darkness; the narrow shafts of moonlight streaming into her room seemed drawn to the parchment. Golden letters swirled and danced around the page, the strange and foreign words intoxicating, hypnotizing.

The image of the white-haired girl swam to the surface of her thoughts. Who was she? How did she know Scarlet? The questions plagued her, churned inside her like a quickening storm. Suddenly Shelby snapped out of her trance, sensing urgency. She had to do this—now.

"I have to tell Greg," she whispered, careful not to alert her parents as she opened her bedroom window and scurried down the white, plastic lattice. She ran across the road, texting Greg's phone as her feet carried her to the familiar white house only a block away.

"Please be awake," she said aloud, hoping Greg hadn't yet fallen asleep, despite the late hour.

Once she reached his house, she glanced up to his window, noticing it was already open. A pang of sadness struck her heart as she looked over at Scarlet's darkened bedroom window, a place with so many good memories, so many good times. Tears burned behind her eyes, how she wished she could have her best friend back. How she wished things were different.

"Hey," Greg's voice emanated from above. "What's going on?"

She spoke quietly, but clearly. "Come down, I'll explain later."

Shrugging as he rubbed his tired eyes, he moved away from the window and reappeared several minutes later from around the side of his house.

It took some convincing, as Greg thought she was crazy to go tramping around the forest in the middle of the night to bury some murderer's scroll because a dream girl told her to, but Greg was rarely one to pass up an adventure.

"I'll go get a shovel," he said with a sigh of submission.

Shelby clutched the paper tightly as she settled into the passenger side of Greg's car, her mind a whir of thoughts and emotions.

Scarlet needs you.

The oracle's words played themselves over and over, whispering obsessively in her ears.

If Scarlet needs me...she must still be alive, Shelby thought, her heart skipping a beat. She gazed outside the car window, darkness blanketing the prairies as they headed out to the place where Rory had almost killed them. Where he'd killed Scarlet.

Shelby forced herself to relive the nightmare, to really see and hear all that transpired that night. She'd stabbed Rory in the center of the pentagram, seen his bleeding body, then, when her back was turned — he was gone. Where could he have gone? Mortally wounded, in the middle of nowhere?

Down, she realized, her blood like ice in her veins. *He went down, into the ground.*

It was the only explanation. Why else would all of these victims, Rory's victims, have gone missing without a trace? But *where* did they go? Hell? Shelby shivered, pulling her sweater tighter around herself.

Finally Greg pulled over to the side of the road, alongside the place where'd they'd had their harrowing incident with Rory.

"You sure you want to do this?" he asked, his boyish face curious, concerned.

She nodded, clutching the parchment to her chest as they left the car and headed out into the dark.

The cool night air exhaled around her, blowing her hair from her face like the breath of a lover. Moonlight cascaded over the forest, painting the leaves pewter, shimmering. Eerie cracks and groans sounded all around them; unseen eyes of nocturnal creatures watching their every step.

After what felt like forever, they came upon the clearing in the forest. Shelby stopped, surveying the landscape. Though dark, the full moon lit up the meadow like a floodlight on a stage.

Greg sidled up beside her, his warmth giving her courage, strength. What would happen? Was all this crazy? Was it just a dream?

She walked to the center of the enclosure, the faded, black markings of the pentagram still etched in the grass. Taking in a deep breath, Shelby pointed to the center of the emblem. Shovel in hand, Greg dutifully began digging.

After he'd dug a little more that foot deep and a foot wide, Shelby took the paper and placed it inside the hole.

"Okay," she said quietly. "Cover it up."

He complied.

Once he finished, Shelby let the enchanted words told to her by the oracle slide over her lips. "*Sopheara sanctumis.*"

Several quiet moments went by before Greg whispered, "Did it work?"

Shelby shrugged. "I have no idea."

Greg grinned, his teeth gleaming in the dark. "Let's dig it up and see."

Curious herself, she knelt before the tiny heap of dirt, soil loose and loamy as she pushed it aside.

She dug and dug—and found nothing.

"It's gone!" she exclaimed, rising as she wiped her hands on her pants.

"Can't be," Greg uttered, taking his own turn to search the hole, then said disbelievingly, "It is gone."

Shelby beamed, she'd done it, she'd helped Scarlet!

"Now what?" Greg asked, resting his chin on the handle of the spade.

"Now," Shelby said with a twinkle in her eye, "we wait."

Kane

Darkness blanketed his eyes like a shroud, his surroundings unfamiliar, cold and dank. The taste of copper coated his tongue, his own blood he surmised as his head thudded with the pulse of a fresh wound. A fetid stench overwhelmed his nostrils as he attempted to bring himself to standing. He was, however, denied as a set of shackles clanked and pulled at his wrists, another pair latched around his ankles. Where was he? Who had the power to bring him down, render him unconscious, and without him even seeing the perpetrator?

This situation did not bode well for completing his quest. How was he to obtain the scrolls now? He didn't even know where he was.

"The Night Mare!" he hissed aloud, voice echoing off the rocky prison walls. Where was the stallion?

He groaned as he slumped against the wall behind him, head heavy in his hands. All was lost now. There was no way he could save Dark World trapped within an unknown hell.

"Hungry?" a quiet, gravelly female voice, inquired from somewhere amid the gloom. As his eyes adjusted, he could see a tiny shaft of illumination piercing the shadows from above.

"Who's there?" Kane demanded as he peered into the near lightless world surrounding him.

Danielle Q. Lee

The voice cackled softly followed by the sound of a tin plate being pushed towards him along the stony floor. "Eat."

"What is it?" Kane asked warily, distrustfully.

The voice scoffed in offence. "Does it matter?"

Yes, Kane thought to himself considering the smell and obvious filth of the place. Despite his better judgement, but not wanting to appear rude, he reached out, feeling around for the proffered sustenance. Upon locating the plate, he pulled it closer and lifted it to his face. He inhaled, trying to get a sense of what it was by smell.

It didn't smell bad; it reminded him of an apple or peach.

"Eat it," the voice ordered.

Kane sighed, both from exasperation and worry. He didn't want to offend this being; it could be his only way to learn of where he was and — more importantly — how to get out.

He picked up the food with his fingers, it was round, firm, and not at all slimy (as was his primary concern). With trepidation, he brought the mystery food to his lips, opened his mouth, and took a bite.

Surprise overwhelmed him as he savored it, crisp and juicy; it was a burst of lovely flavor and texture.

"What was that?" he asked, licking his lips, wishing there was more.

"Dragon fruit," the voice in the dark replied.

Feeling an iota of trust germinating, Kane asked, "What is this place?"

"Exile Island."

It was said so plainly, so nonchalantly, that Kane almost believed for a instant that he wasn't doomed.

Everyone in Dark World knew that Exile Island was a death sentence. He pondered a moment at how he'd naively thought he was going to simply waltz in, find the most elusive being in the Underworld, and then leave again.

No one left Exile Island — ever.

"How did I get here?" he asked, holding his aching head.

"The Fourth Horseman found you, I imagine," she replied.

Kane frowned. "The Fourth Horseman?"

"Yes, the guardian of Exile Island."

Kane suddenly felt weary, aged beyond his already compiled years of immortality.

"Who are you?" Kane inquired, eyes narrowing as he scanned the shadows for her.

"Someone long since forgotten," she replied hauntingly. "And you? Who might you be?"

He debated whether or not to reveal himself to the unseen woman, but ultimately decided that truth was the better option. Perhaps he'd need her help. "Prince Kane, son of Lucifer," he said humbly.

He sensed her amusement in the darkness. "And what brings you here?"

Again, Kane wondered whether or not he should divulge everything, but again, his paranoia quickly subsided. There was something about this being that drew forth his trust. "I am here to speak with Myth; to ask her for the scrolls she guards, so that I may reignite the Crystal Pyramid."

Silence ensued as she appeared to mull this over, then asked, "Why do you wish to light the pyramid?"

Kane replied, "To save Dark World. It is dying and the only way to save it is to bring back the light."

"Is it?" she offered.

His heart skipped a beat. "Is it what?"

"Is it the only way to save Dark World?"

He paused, searching his thoughts. Who was this? What did they know that he did not?

"Who are you?" he demanded a little more force-fully.

"A friend," the voice said, though it had softened, turned melodic.

Kane froze, he knew who this was. "Myth?"

"I have many names," she replied. "Many faces, many forms…but yes, I have been known as Myth."

As the last words left her lips, the shackles upon Kane's wrists and ankles opened and fell with a clatter near his hooves. Before him, a great light grew: white, pure, and incandescent. It seemed too bright for his eyes to behold, yet it did not harm his sight. He stood in wonderment as the form took shape, its wings spreading wide.

She was an angel.

Speechless, Kane fell to one knee, bowing before the glorious creature before him. His mind reached in a hundred different directions, trying to explain this anomaly, this level of beauty, of power. He'd as-sumed, because she was the creator, the goddess and soul of the necromancers, that she'd resemble them in some way, be the source of their appearance. But he was wrong; she looked unlike anything he'd ever seen before.

"Forgive me, my lady, I had no idea it was you," he spoke reverently, unsure as to why she'd first presented herself as an old crone.

She giggled softly. "Rise my prince," she stated. "I had to disguise myself in order to learn your purpose for coming to me."

He complied, standing. "I understand," he said. "I-I thought you were a prisoner here?" Kane gazed about, now standing in a room without walls, and somehow, without floors.

She nodded. "I am, though of my own accord."

He frowned.

"I choose to be here," she explained. "To watch my children from afar."

"The necromancers?" Kane wondered.

"All of you are my children." She smiled. "What is it you seek, my son?" she asked with a voice like a thousand bells ringing, though he had a sneaking suspicion she was all-knowing and already knew what he wanted.

Her aura was so bright he desired to shield his eyes. Like that of the sun, she radiated warmth, heat akin to the beams he'd heard that the great star emitted. A small ache pulsed within as he recalled his father's description of the Surface. Kane felt so close to that dream now, so near achieving his dream of witnessing the Surface's sky.

Finally, he answered, "I seek the scrolls, left in your care by Vrill."

She contemplated this, then asked, "Why?"

"I wish to save Dark World by relighting the Crystal Pyramid," he explained.

"Why?" she asked again like an inquisitive child never satiated by any answer given.

He paused a moment, truly wondering why he wished to save his world. What answer would suffice? He did not want to save Dark World the way it was, war-torn and ruled by a greedy, self-fulfilling queen. He did not want to save a world filled with racism, hatred, and darkness.

Kane's mind searched for the right answer. Why was he doing this?

Finally he knew.

"Love," he replied as Fate's face etched itself into his mind. "I want to save this world for love."

Behind the light, Myth smiled. "That," she began, "is a wonderful reason to save this world."

In a blinding flash of light, three scrolls manifested before him, each tightly bound in a lavender satchel.

Knowing they were safe to touch as they were covered, Kane reached for them, taking them into his care. Suddenly he was aware he'd forgotten something.

"The last scroll," he said. "It is supposedly on the Surface. How am I to retrieve it?"

She smiled knowingly. "Have faith, it will all come together as it meant to be."

"My horse, if you please," Kane said. "My Night Mare, where is he?"

The angel paused momentarily before answering, "Horse? I'm afraid the Fourth Horseman found you alone."

A sick sensation rolled through Kane's abdomen. Where had the Night Mare gone? And if Myth was as omniscient as the necromancers claimed, why didn't she know?

It was then that her illumination flickered, dimmed, reminding Kane that she was ill—dying.

Kane frowned, muttering as a sense of defeat washed over him, "How will I get back to the pyramid in time?"

"I can help you with that," Myth whispered softly.

"Wait!" he yelled as the floor gave way beneath him, her light fading from view. "Go where! What's happening!"

As Kane fell into a void, a blackness that seemed like forever, he heard Myth whisper to his thoughts.

"Bring the light to Dark World, my prince, save this world. Save us. Save her."

"Save her? Who?" his mind said back. *"Save who?"*

"She must see the light." The angel said weakly.

"She?" his mind shouted. *"Who are you talking about? Myth!"*

Myth whispered sadly, *"My baby."*

Part IV

The End

The wings of the phoenix flickered like a bonfire, trailing long lines of smoke behind her and Vale as they sailed over the unsettled sands of the Crimson Desert. Blustering volcanoes spewed angrily, garnet tributaries of searing lava gliding down the worn, smoothed mountainsides. The dangling fangs over-head, the barrier between Fate and the Surface, snarled unwelcomingly, as though to warn her to stay away.

So much had changed in her life, and in her death. She was no longer the same young, naïve and foolish girl that lived breath to breath. No more did she yearn for love that wasn't returned, for consent from others, for a life not her own.

She was something else now. Something other than human, other than a fiend. She was somewhere in between, somewhere in the space amongst the living and the dead—something otherworldly. What, though, she didn't know. Was she more human than monster now? Or the other way around? Other than psychic intuition, she didn't know what powers she had left, if any. If she had no powers, no magical abilities or weapons, did that make her more human? She didn't know what lay ahead, where she belonged.

Fate smiled as she thought of Kane, of his shy smile, his brooding inner turmoil, his kind heart. How she loved him, his essence, his soul. She realized in that moment that she didn't care where she was, or what, as long as she was with him.

During the short flight, Vale had filled her in on the quests Kane had bestowed on himself, Vale, Deme, and a banshee named Sorcia. Fate was pleased that Kane had taken hold of the situation, delegating tasks to make the entire plan run more efficiently. It was the true mark of a king to be able to relinquish control, to offer trust in others.

"There it is," Vale's voice was reverent as he pointed to the dark pyramid in the distance. She marveled at its magnificence, even in its muted state. She could imagine the beauty it once beheld, when the sun's rays reached down from the heavens, through the fracture in the earth, and set fire to its walls. The light, the resplendence, would have reached every corner of the darkened world, reached every set of eyes and shone into every heart.

Fate held tighter to Vale's torso as the great flaming bird dipped lower, circling the ground as they neared the monument. Fate wondered what they'd find inside, what magic had lain hidden for centuries, concealed from prying eyes. Even her new intuitive insights couldn't penetrate beyond the clandestine layers of ancient time. They could, however, allow her to see through the eyes of those she cared for. It allowed her to feel energies, to sense auras.

She concentrated on Kane, focusing on his essence. He was somewhere strange, foreign to him, but very close by. He was unhurt but confused. She saw him rise, bringing himself to a stand, the scrolls safely in his possession. Fate pulled her sights back, envisioning him where he stood, then smiled.

"Kane's at the pyramid already," she shouted to Vale over the rush of winds flying past them.

"He is? Can you see him?" Vale squinted into the distance, narrowing his vision at the pyramid.

She laughed. "Yes, but not like that."

He frowned, shrugging as the phoenix drew ever closer to their destination. "And Sorcia? Deme? Can you see them? Have they got the volunteers and the reapers' scroll?"

Fate concentrated, then replied, "They will arrive shortly; they have succeeded."

Then something dark churned inside her, a familiar presence nearby, an evil she knew too well.

Malus.

The queen was on her way to the pyramid too.

Energies flowed in from all around her, unknown energies, good and evil. All were called, drawn to the historic event about to transpire. The demons of Legion traveled from the west, the wraiths from the east. Even the reapers and necromancers in the north abandoned their homes to witness the birth of the new sun. Everyone wanted this, wanted to see the Crystal Pyramid relit, wanted the fissure to the Surface opened—but all for different reasons. Some innocent. Some nefarious.

Warring auras, red, blue, white, and black, thousands of them, came from all directions. Fate's heart hurt, realizing this was the beginning of something, perhaps the end. She could not foresee the outcome. Could not tell who would win—and who would lose.

"There he is," Vale said, pointing to Kane's form in the distance.

As they drew nearer, Fate was overwhelmed by the size of the Crystal Pyramid. Even from a distance it appeared massive but up close, it occupied the space of an entire city on the Surface. The city she'd lived in on the Surface, Edmonton, was home to almost a million people – the Crystal Pyramid was even larger than that.

It was immense.

The phoenix swooped once before landing gracefully on her feet. Fate was on the ground even before the bird had time to tuck her fiery wings to her sides. Then she was running, harder than she ever had before, towards Kane. Arms open wide, her long silvery hair streaming behind her, she ran like nothing else in the world mattered. And at that moment, nothing mattered but him. Getting to him. Holding him.

Kane's blazing blue eyes lit up when he saw her, though there was a hint of confusion behind them as he took in her new appearance. Opening his arms, he fell to his knees as she approached him, awaiting her touch.

Finally, after what felt like forever away from him, she fell into his strong, black arms, swimming in his embrace as though she'd been lost for years.

Kane held her close, smelled her hair, kissed her forehead, her cheeks, her lips, whispering, "Let's *never* be apart again, shall we?"

"Never," she said through tears of joy. "Never again."

After several moments, he pulled away, taking her petite face into his massive hands. He stroked her jaw with his thumb as he looked into her eyes, her *new*, blue eyes. "What happened to you? You're different. Your eyes…"

He hadn't known of her plight with the lamia, the poisonous monster that crawled through her veins, plagued her every waking moment, threatening her life and her soul. She wondered if she should even tell him everything, but decided that now was not the time. He would need all his focus on the battle to come.

"I'm not a shade anymore. But I'll tell you all about it…some other time," she said as she wrapped a gentle hand around Kane's neck, savoring his hot skin beneath her palm, drawing his lips to meet hers.

His mouth found hers hungrily. Over and over again he kissed her, as though he had an insatiable, unquenchable thirst and she was the last drop of water. Kane's large hands searched her body, sliding over every curve, every contour, talons dragging lightly over her soft, snowy skin. Her nails dug into his back, hands running throughout his long, navy hair. A moan escaped her lips as he caressed her, kissed her, gently nibbled on her ear…

"*So*," a sardonic voice came from behind them. "As much fun as it looks like you're having, we do have a world to save, do we not?"

Fate giggled, turning to Vale with feigned annoyance. "Do you mind?"

Color rose into Kane's cheeks as he stood, helping Fate to her feet. He cleared his voice, trying to summon some sort of dignity before his peer.

"Right," he said as he took Fate by the hand before turning and marching towards the pyramid.

Myth

"How did you get here so fast?" Fate asked, sensing his journey to Myth was not as he'd planned.

He raised a dark brow at her. "How did you know I went there?"

"Vale filled me in." She smiled.

"Ah," he said. "Well, to be honest, I don't know how I got here. She...Myth...had a hand in it, I'm sure. All I know is that one minute I was on Exile Island talking to Myth, then I was falling into an abyss, Myth whispering to me to save her baby—and then I woke up here." He shook his head as though he couldn't comprehend it.

"Her baby?" Fate looked at him confusedly. "What does that mean?"

He shrugged.

They stood before the pyramid, taking in its immensity. Its glassy walls shimmered as it reflected the muted reddish hues of the distant but active volcanic range.

"Where's the door?" Vale asked, his brow furrowed as he scanned the long wall of the large tetrahedron.

"Very good question," Kane replied, bringing his hand up to the glass. He started to slide his hand over the cool crystal wall, its power hypnotizing him but was halted when he heard a familiar voice call out from behind him.

"*Stop!*" it said. "We have to wait for everyone to arrive."

Ozen limped towards Kane, what remained of Legion's demons following behind him.

"Elder Ozen!" Kane smiled at his old master. "You're all here!" Fate watched his face beam with pride as his family of demons encircled him. They were visibly exhausted, worn from a long journey across the desert, shackles weighing heavily upon their imprisoned wings. Many carried stretchers, carting the wounded with them. It appeared that no one had been left behind.

From the opposing direction, Deme and her band of demon warriors, plus one wraith, landed and then descended from their winged mounts, walking up to the reunion.

"What's going on here?" Deme asked with a smile, her eyes moving between Kane and Ozen. But when she noticed Fate amidst the crowd, a flicker of shock registered in her stare. "Fate, how nice to see you again," she said coolly, glancing casually at Fate's recently cured hands and neck as though surprised to see them uninfected.

In that moment, whether it was her new intuition or simply Deme's glare, Fate knew who had poisoned her. "Deme," she replied, forcing a thin smile. She tried to remain Zen, calm and focused, just as the beings of light in the Guf had taught her. It was tough though, when all she wanted to do at the moment was kick Deme square in the throat for all the suffering she'd had to endure, not to mention losing Ick and his friends in the process.

Kane, still overwhelmed, asked Ozen, "Why have you come? Were you attacked by the invisible threat again?" Alarm rang in his deep blue eyes.

Ozen shook his head. "No, but the palace was no longer suitable, right Syphon?" The elder turned to face the demon commander as he emerged from the crowd.

"Correct," Syphon stated officially, nodding at Kane. "Structural damage to the kingdom, combined with the weight of the Crimson Desert above, was causing it to collapse in on itself. We had to evacuate early."

"You did well." Kane gave them both a nod of approval and gratification though a shadow of unease flickered behind his eyes. Fate felt his angst, where would the demons live now?

"And," Ozen interjected, "you asked for this before you left." He handed Kane a large magenta vial, its contents swirling black and red as though he'd trapped a storm in a bottle.

Kane grinned. "Thank you, I hope we won't need this...but it will come in handy if we do."

"What is it?" Fate asked, mesmerized by the charmed flask.

Kane brought his finger to his lips, winking. "It's a secret."

Sorcia arrived just then, her diverse group riding upon the backs of two winged, silver lions. Once she, Calyx, and the reaper had dismounted, the metallic-skinned brothers morphed back into their original forms. They approached Kane, and Sorcia handed over the reapers' scroll, safely contained within one of Ozen's enchanted boxes.

"Thank you, Princess Sorcia." Kane bowed in gratitude.

"What about the last scroll?" Vale asked. "The one from the Surface?"

Kane shrugged. "When I asked Myth the same question, she simply told me to 'have faith'. I suppose we have no choice in the matter." He then moved closer to the pyramid; the crowd around him quiet with anticipation. "Now, how does this thing open?"

He touched the glimmering wall with his palm and a pleasant frequency rang out, like the soft, airy hum of a tuning fork. Immediately a doorway appeared, a portion of the wall seemingly melted away, vanishing like a transparent curtain merely pulled aside.

Fate's heart beat excitedly inside her chest as she, Kane, Deme, and Ozen walked across the threshold. It was pitch black inside, no light to be seen anywhere. Her eyes fought to adjust, to locate any source of illumination, but there was none to be found. The air smelled old and stale, not surprising as the monument had been sealed off for nearly three centuries. The floor was solid beneath her feet, like marble or stone.

Amid the darkness, she heard Kane whisper, "*Lumis.*" Immediately a ball of orange light ignited inside his palm and the entirety of the pyramid glowed as the crystal walls reflected the illumination into every dark corner.

Fate gasped as she looked around. It was huge inside; she could hardly see the base of every wall. Like the ocean's horizon looming into forever, it was a vast, empty space—except for the enormous pentagram glowing gold upon the floor.

Kane frowned. "What do we do now?"

Upon his words, a vision manifested before Fate's eyes. Every race stood on a point of the pentagram, each reading from their scroll. She turned to Kane, explaining, "I think you're supposed to stand on the points and read the words on the pages."

Myth

"But we can't touch them," Deme pointed out with a touch of acid in her tone. "The pages are cursed."

Somehow Fate just knew the answer. "Not in here, something about this place will protect you."

Deme scoffed, crossing her arms over her chest. "Prove it."

Fate reached for Kane's satchel, but he stopped her. "No! What if you're wrong? You're not a shade anymore." His eyes pleaded with her to reconsider.

She took in a deep breath. "It's true I'm not a shade, but I have a feeling about this. Trust me, okay?" she said, hoping her smile didn't falter. Her human side begged her not to touch them; she was no longer protected from the king's curse. Only shades could touch the scrolls and be safe. If she was wrong, she'd age one thousand years in the blink of an eye.

"*Trust*," she whispered to herself, closing her eyes as she reached into Kane's pack and pulled out one of the sheathed scrolls. Slowly, carefully, she opened the lavender pouch that protected the parchment, revealing a rolled document encircled with a scarlet bow. The aged page gleamed eerily against the amber light within Kane's palm. Still holding onto the bottom of the scroll with the last of the silky covering, she pulled in a deep breath, praying she was right.

Everyone around her stared, wide-eyed and in awe as she reached out with her bare hand, taking the scroll into her palm. Fate winced, anticipating the worst as her skin met with the cool, ivory paper.

After a moment, when nothing happened, everyone released the breath they'd been holding.

"Okay," she said, unraveling the scroll. "Your turn."

They all looked less than convinced, despite her brave performance. One by one though, each of them pulled out a scroll and opened it up, marvelling afterward that they hadn't been transformed into a shrivelled shell of themselves.

"Call Sorcia and the others, let's get this done," Kane ordered, taking hold of his own scroll.

Once they'd all arrived, Fate explained, "Each of you must read from your race's designated scroll. The words must be said in unison."

On each point of the star stood one member from each of Dark World's races. Sorcia for the banshees, Kane for the demons, Xi for the wraiths, Slater for the necromancers, and an unnamed reaper. They unfurled their scrolls simultaneously, preparing to utter the words Lucifer had hidden from the world so very long ago.

Fate waited off to the side, nerves churning in her stomach. What would happen? She was both thrilled and terrified. If all went well, the crevasse to the Surface would open and sunlight would pour down like smelted gold, landing upon the point of the pyramid and transcending throughout the realm.

With the fissure opened, she might be able to see her family again, as well as Shelby. Excitement rushed through her, and she hoped they would hurry up.

Within moments, they all began to read. Their voices echoed in harmony, reverberating off the reddish crystal walls of the pyramid. Their eerie chant swirled around Fate as she waited for the world to change.

And then they were done. Silence owned the air around her.

Nothing had happened.

Frowning, Kane asked. "Did we do something wrong?"

Fate bit her lip. She'd explained what she'd seen, hadn't she. She closed her eyes, willing the vision forward. In it, she could see the races surrounding her, reading from their open scrolls. What was she missing? What hadn't she done right?

Then she realized what it was she'd missed.

Herself.

She was in the center of the pentagram in her vision, the others reading all around her. Excitedly, she began to explain when there came a thunderous crash from outside the pyramid, screaming and chaos ensuing.

"What's going on out there?" Kane shouted as he ran towards the exit.

Each of them dropped their scroll to the floor and ran out the doors to see what had happened.

As Fate exited the pyramid, it was immediately clear. Before her was an entire army of shades and various dark creatures. Amongst them, two enormous wild hellcats pulled a chariot of gold. Seated upon the carriage was the reincarnation of Malus through Ever.

She must have blocked me from sensing her arrival, Fate thought, her eyes narrowing in suspicion, both worried and annoyed that Malus still harbored great power despite the lack of light from the pyramid. A thread of worry wound its way through her body as she considered just how strong the demon queen would be when the monument was rekindled. The king had deactivated the pyramid for a reason, was it because of Malus? Had he known something about her and the pyramid's power that they did not?

"Ever?" Kane spoke, his voice tight.

Fate watched the color drain from Kane's face as he looked at his daughter's form bewitched by another. Though she appeared just like Ever, walked, talked, and moved like his daughter, she was not. A blood red ring encircled the blue of her eyes, indicating the evil soul residing inside. Her face was hardened; her stare cruel, hateful, and calculating.

Malus laughed, her malevolence resonating. "No, my *son*," she spat sadistically, "I'm not your wretched daughter."

Kane's rage boiled over, taking a few steps towards the queen with clenched fists. "Get out of her!" Kane then closed his eyes and took in a breath, centering himself. "Get out of my daughter," he repeated, dangerously calm.

Malus giggled. "Sorry," she said as she reached down to the seat of her golden chariot, retrieving something, then raised a black box over her head. "Ever isn't in this body anymore."

Kane gasped, staring aghast at the dark container. "You...*monster!*"

He lunged for his mother, Fate and Vale took hold of his arms, restraining him.

"You'll never win that way," Fate whispered in his ear, recalling her fight with the being that mimicked her, learning that anger and force would not triumph. "Your time will come, my love."

"Please, continue what you started." Malus sneered, Ever's beautiful face contorting evilly as she glanced over at the open doorway to the Crystal

Pyramid. "I'm *ever* so excited to witness the relighting of the great pyramid."

Fate pulled Kane aside. "Something doesn't feel right about this," she whispered. "Your father did this for a reason. He shut it off to stop her, I just know it."

Kane went very still as he contemplated this. "You're right," he agreed. "We need to find out why."

He turned around, searching for someone in the crowd. Finally he found Ozen and, taking Fate by the hand, manoeuvred through the people.

"Ozen, did my father ever tell you of his plans to close the fissure?"

The elder demon appeared flustered, and replied guiltily, "Yes, he did."

Kane brightened. "Why? Why did he do it?"

"He only said that he...he had to stop Malus," he stammered. "That her power was too great with the light."

Kane turned to Fate, a dark realization settling in his stare. "We can't do it. We can't relight the pyramid or she'll be too powerful."

"But Dark World will die if we don't," Fate said quietly, hoping the panic in her voice wouldn't be overheard by the crowd. "What are we going to do?"

"I'm *waiting*," Malus called out with a melodic lilt to her voice, her arms crossed over her chest, lengthy fingernails tapping impatiently.

"Stall her," Kane hissed then vanished into the throng of demons.

Fate gaped after him, wondering what on earth she could do to keep the Devil occupied.

Swallowing hard, Fate moved slowly towards the demon queen. Her eyes drifted to the dark box seated beside her on the carriage. A surge of anger gave her courage to ask, "What did you do to Ever?"

Malus sneered. "I had her exorcized; there simply wasn't enough room for the both of us in here." She turned her attention to her long, white nails, feigning boredom.

"At the very least," Fate commented with a glare, "you could give him back his daughter's soul."

Malus let out a short laugh. "I could, but I'm not going to." She smiled at her, then her expression turned serious, looking at Fate as though for the first time. "What happened to you? You're not a shade anymore."

"No, I'm not," Fate replied with a smirk.

Suddenly Fate heard a noise behind the queen; a familiar animal sound. The queen smiled evilly, noticing.

"What is that?" Fate asked, concerned.

"Oh," Malus said coyly. "Just a new pet I acquired."

Fate's left hand suddenly warmed, her ring finger burned as though on fire. She looked down — the soul crystal was glowing. Gasping, she watched as Malus's shade guards brought forth an enormous black cage. Inside was the Night Mare, whinnying and snorting, flames of anger and fear pouring from his immense body.

The words Kane had said, the legend he told her the moment he'd given her the ring, drifted across her thoughts: "*So the angel used her magic to create a mate, only he was made of dark magic, and she, light magic — then the curse was manifested. She got to see him just once before he was transformed into a beast and hidden away from her.*

These crystals, he pointed to the ring he'd just put on her finger, *"are said to be the angel's tears, pieces of her lonely soul, searching for him. When one finds him, the curse will be broken and they can finally be together. But it's just another of Dark World's myths, no one knows if it's really true…"*

"Let him go," Fate demanded as the queen's minions poked the horse with the tips of their swords, enraging the beast.

The queen rolled her eyes and waved her guards back, they obeyed, disappearing behind the chariot with the Night Mare. *"Never,"* she whispered with a smile.

Fate's soul powered up inside, almost as though it had had enough of the queen and decided to take matters into its own hands. Without thinking it through, Fate took a few steps towards the carriage before springing effortlessly into the air and landing on the bow of the chariot in a cat-like, crouched position. She stared the startled queen in the face before slapping her hard across the cheek.

Mayhem erupted as the shade soldiers surged towards her, Fate quickly grabbed Ever's soul and sprang backwards off the carriage and into the swelling crowd of demons that were now forming a protective line between Fate and the queen's army.

Malus held her reddened face a moment, her shock soon melting into calm, cool malevolence. The crowd quieted, petrified. Malus then ordered quietly, "Bring me my pets."

Fate watched in horror as dozens upon dozens of shade soldiers emerged from the thick of the ranks, each holding onto a short, chain-link leash. At the end of each chain was a *lamia*, masked and maddened with starvation. The shade soldiers barely held on as the flesh-craving monsters shrieked furiously, desperate to be free, to attack, to eat whatever — and whoever — stood in their way.

Malus smirked evilly as she gave her soldiers a nod.

Then they unleashed the monsters.

Each of the lamia paused for a split second, marveling in their newfound freedom — then turned and tore apart the shade that had held onto their leash, stuffing chunks of flesh voraciously into their mouths.

This gave Fate only seconds to spare.

"Run!" Fate screamed to the demons, to the people, to anyone who would listen. She herself turned and sprinted towards the pyramid. Behind her were the sounds of frenzied growls, terrified screams and the shredding and ripping of skin.

"Get inside the pyramid!" she shouted, leading the swarm of horrified onlookers through the doorway.

"That went well, don't you think?" Vale said as he appeared out of thin air, ushering the crowd inside with a calm wave of his hand.

She gave him a quick glare, then ordered, "Get everyone inside, then barricade the door." She turned to face the onslaught of lamia. "I'll slow them down."

"Gotcha," she heard Vale remark as she ran back out towards the slaughter. "It was nice knowing you."

Fate had no idea how she was going to fight the lamia, since obtaining her soul she honestly hadn't considered the fact that she no longer owned any special powers other than what she'd already discovered. She knew she had developed intuitive abilities and, obviously, physical strengths, but as for weapons, she was at a loss.

But she had to try.

The lamia had already moved on from the shades and had now taken down several innocent demons, the remnants of their torn wings, disembodied limbs, and sprays of blood lay strewn upon the sands of the desert. She scanned the carnage, horrified.

"*What have I done?*" she whispered, wishing she knew what to do next.

Kane was suddenly beside her. "What did you do?" Shock registered on his dark face as he instinctively reached back for his sword. "I only asked you to stall her, not declare war!"

"I'm sorry," she said, slightly annoyed. "I didn't know she brought these…these *things*." She looked to the six lamia now stalking them from a few feet away.

Behind them, the last of the demons had reached the safety of the pyramid—but now Kane and Fate had almost all the lamia surrounding them.

There were at least twenty.

From her perch in the carriage, Malus watched with perverse amusement.

"Call them off, Mother," Kane said her, keeping his eyes on the creatures.

"Alas, I cannot," Malus shouted back. "Not until they've eaten their fill." She laughed.

"What are we going to do?" Fate whispered. She knew intimately the cravings of the lamia, the wild, unrelenting lust for flesh. There was no stopping them.

Before Kane could answer though, a deep, resonating hum shook the floors of the earth, like thunder rumbling under the soils.

The lamia whimpered, uncertainty scarring their eerie, blood-red stares. Slowly, one by one, they backed away as the ground grew more and more unstable.

"What's happening?" Fate shouted, taking hold of Kane's arm as they turned and ran towards the pyramid.

"Remember that little bottle Ozen gave me?" He smiled coyly.

"Yeah," she replied, her eyes wide.

Kane looked around as though searching. *"They're coming."*

"Who?"

He didn't answer her, but Fate heard an angry voice screeching and she looked back at Malus. Chaos ensued amid her army as they, too, moved away from the epicenter of the earthquake.

The ground gave one final shake then heaved as two large chunks of earth split apart, revealing a gaping hole in the sands. Fate watched, fascinated as a thick, dark mist began twisting and rising from within the crater. It poured out and upwards like an upside down waterfall. The black miasma reached high into the sky, nearing the ceiling of rock overhead, before it arched amid the atmosphere and came plunging downward, smashing into the Crimson Desert.

Fate jumped back as it exploded into a million little pieces, scattered like chunks of obsidian. She barely had a chance to glance questioningly at Kane, a cocky smile upon his face, before the black pieces began to twitch. All around them, the fragments moved, writhed—then grew.

Before long, each piece had taken the black and ghostly silhouette of a demon.

"It's...a demon army," Fate uttered, bewildered.

"A *shadow* demon army," Kane confirmed with a proud smile.

"What is the meaning of this!" Malus's voice sounded over the throng of black phantoms now guarding the perimeter of the pyramid.

"Kill them!" Malus shrieked to her lamia, now advancing the front line of shadow demons.

Silently, the entire fleet manifested long, pointed staffs at their sides, then charged the lamia, destroying them within seconds.

"Wow!" Fate grinned. "Bet she didn't see that coming."

Kane raised his eyes to watch his mother's upset, but frowned just as fast. She wasn't fuming anymore, she was waving her arms in the air, chanting, casting—calling.

Fate followed his line of sight. "What's wrong?"

In the distance, a dark shadow festered like a storm. "It's the one thing my army can't fight...*Ba'al*. Get inside, quickly!" He took her by the arm and they moved into the safety of the pyramid. The moment they were inside, Kane slid his palm over the crystal wall, sealing it shut and locking them in.

"Hello again," Vale said to them as he strolled over, leaning casually against the wall of the pyramid with his arms folded over his chest. "I don't suppose you two have any bright ideas on how we're going to survive this?"

Kane shot him a dirty look.

"What are we going to do?" Fate glanced around the inside of the pyramid. They were safe, for now, but still trapped. No one could survive Ba'al's blood rains.

Kane frowned. "I don't understand why Ba'al heeds her command," he muttered. "The elementals were loyal to my father, not her. The shadow army can defeat anything — except the elementals. She must have known that," Kane growled through sharp, gritted teeth.

"Ba'al?" Vale questioned with wide eyes. "Your army can't stop him? Or the other elementals?" His white eyes narrowed pensively. Then, without another word, he vanished into a wisp of dark smoke.

"Coward," Kane said with a shake of his head.

Fate rubbed his arm, mostly to soothe herself. What could they do? They were prisoners inside the monument. The only thing they could do was stand around, starve and…

"We should open the crevasse!" she exclaimed suddenly.

"We can't," he said, wild-eyed. "She'll become too powerful. What if we can't defeat her?"

She took his face in her hands and stared deep into his eyes. "You forget, don't you?"

"What?" he asked with sad eyes.

Fate smiled. "You'll get *your* powers back too."

A spark ignited in his eyes.

"All of you will." She panned her gaze over the crowd of demons.

Myth

He gave her a long look, one mixed with love and fear. Finally he nodded. "We have no other choice — let's open it."

Fate stood in the center of the pentagram, the lash of Ba'al's blood rains pelting the outside of the pyramid. While they were safe for the moment, it was only a matter of time before Malus's army or the other elementals would break through the weak enchanted barrier that Ozen had erected before the door. The elder was the first to admit that he was not nearly as strong magically as the Devil or her minions.

All around Fate, the races held tight to their scrolls, uttering the words that would hopefully reignite the pyramid. Doubt grew within Fate, however. Without the scroll on the Surface, she was unsure that the ritual would work.

The words, the ancient poetry, blended together as they rose and rang throughout the pyramid. Legion's demons watched in silent awe, waiting for the great monument to come to life.

Amid the chanting, Fate could hear Kane's strong, deep voice speaking the words of the demons' scroll:

I am legend,
I am lore,
I am the essence of nightmares,
The dawn of fear,
A fallen angel,
A winged beast,
Spawn from the seeds of evil and black magic,
I am Lucifer,
Lord of the Dark.

Danielle Q. Lee

To his left, Sorcia's melodic voice uttered her families' inherited verse:

A secret underworld,
Alive beneath the feet of man,
To rise,
To ascend,
The races must blend,
Must blur the lines of disparity,
Must come together,
With the pages united,
Dark World will be enlightened,
Darkness will meet the Light

The reaper hissed his with a creepy voice that made Fate shudder:

And the cursed will become cured,
Born free of the dark.
With the undoing of the dark one,
What once was lost,
Taken,
Will be returned.
The doors of Heaven will open,
Returning the essence,
Merging once more,
The souls reborn.

Then the wraith's words resonated:

A legend,
A fantasy,
A lore,

Myth

Asleep,
She waits to be awakened,
A song of Four,
She waits to hear,
The legend,
The fantasy,
Myth.

And lastly, Slater's beautiful voice echoed above them all:

There can be only one,
Upon the throne of blood,
A ruler among fiends,
A leader over beasts,
Old will expire,
New will succeed,
But only one is meant to be,
Meant to reign,
Meant to rule,
The Devil's Heir.

Over and over, the various races united, repeating their inherited song, given to them so long ago by a king desperate to save his world. Tears welled in her eyes as she absorbed the ironic beauty of the moment. These races were brought together, despite adversity, despite their inborn differences and learned hatred for one another. They'd overcome their fears and distrust for their fellow citizens of Dark World and were brought together to save their world.

Perhaps this was what King Lucifer had desired all along? Or was this simply an unexpected gift that had sidled itself next to need?

Fate considered the disparity among the races on the Surface. How would they react if their world was suddenly threatened and the only way to save it was to work together?

Sadly, she was less than hopeful.

The Surface had been tested many a time over the course of the ages, failing time and time again to come together and protect humanity. They'd been lucky, though, that their existence hadn't depended on releasing their fears and hate and working as one to save the planet—yet.

The spoken words swirled about the pentagram, danced, flowed all around her. For a moment, she worried that once again, nothing would happen. That all this was for naught, but then she saw a tiny spark. Just one miniscule fragment of light, like the twinkle of a star, catch at the top of the pyramid.

Her face upturned, she watched, and waited.

Suddenly something was falling; something had passed through the glass, magically, and was descending. Opening her hands, a weathered and torn ivory scroll fluttered like a white butterfly, down, down, and into her expectant hands.

She held it a moment, bewildered by disbelief.

It was the lost scroll.

Everyone stood in stunned silence as she unfurled it, swirling, golden letters waltzing across the page.

Fate cleared her voice, then spoke the words:

And from out of the ashes comes the soul,

Myth

The healer, the ruler,
The One.
Who will bring the world together,
United,
Free,
A new world,
A new land,
A world once dark,
Now made light.

The moment the last word escaped her lips, a great cacophony of bells rang out inside the pyramid. The earth shook violently beneath their feet, lightning and thunder played like gunfire outside, winds beating upon the glass.

"The elementals," Kane shouted to Fate above the noise. "They've all been summoned!"

"Not all of them," a voice said from behind them.

Kane and Fate spun around to find Vale behind them. "Where did you go?"

He just smiled. "To meet with a friend."

Fate frowned, but just as she was about to ask him to clarify when she could see through the now transparent glass of the pyramid, a great chunk of earth overhead cracked into two and slowly pulled apart from one another.

All faces were lifted skyward, watching in awe as the crevasse formed and was reborn into the light.

Then all was silent as the movement stopped, the world seemingly paused as it awaited a miracle.

It felt like forever, like a minute trapped on a clock—then the first rays of light struck the pyramid. The panes surrounding them exploded into a rainbow of illumination, so bright it stung their eyes at first. Golden beams stretched across the lands like long, reaching fingers, caressing the darkness, loving the landscape. The mountains suddenly shone, gleaming and bouncing the sunlight off of them, as though sharing it with the world.

The volcanic range fired fresh lava into the atmosphere, as though cheering and blasting red fireworks into the skies. Creatures crawled out from their dark prisons, wincing confusedly at the strange benevolence spreading over the lands.

All around her, the demons rose, stood taller, glowed with a new power. Their auras altered, their wounds healed — their souls shone as though they wore a new armor outside their skin.

Beside her, Kane closed his eyes, groaning as the light touched him, nourished him, fed him as though he'd been without food for a hundred years.

Finally, there was silence.

And peace.

"Let's go outside," Kane said quietly, taking Fate gently by the arm.

"Are you sure?" she asked, alarmed. "Malus, Ba'al — they're still out there."

"I have the feeling there's been a few changes." He smiled gently.

She agreed that the energies outside had changed, but she wasn't sure it was all for the better.

The air outside the pyramid was warm, dense, tropical; instead of blistering and ash-filled. Darkness had lifted, the oppressive veil that had for so long weighed heavily upon Dark World's shoulders had vanished, leaving behind an essence of lightness.

Kane stood beside Fate, his eyes closed, his chest rising and falling as he drew in deep, tranquil breaths. He no longer had to depend on bloodstone to feed his soul. Magic rippled off him, though Fate sensed he was not yet completely healed. Something else was still needed, and she was sure she knew what it was. The shackles on his wings still held him back. They were enchanted, not only to prevent the demons from flying, but from harnessing their true powers. They were still prisoners of the queen.

Fate glanced around, wondering where Ba'al had gone, and the other elementals that had flexed their furor only moments before the pyramid was rekindled. Kane's conjured shadow army still stood despite Ba'al's attack, forming a fence between them and the queen's army. They were safe — for now.

Then Fate looked for Malus.

The chariot in which she'd ridden in upon was empty. Her army restless, lost without their queen to guide them.

"Where is she?" Fate asked quietly, keeping her voice low as not to break the serene ambiance.

Kane shrugged, his forehead creasing, worry rising. "She couldn't have gone far."

Suddenly Fate sensed a multitude of energies arriving; she turned towards the source and saw an army of silver beings, necromancers, marching peacefully across the sands. She smiled, feeling their joy, but something was still amiss. They were still ailing, as though the light had done nothing for their goddess.

She looked for Slater and Mezza amid the crowd. "Slater," she said once she'd found him. "Why are your people still unwell? Is Myth not cured now that the pyramid is relit?"

His star-like eyes fell dark, and he shook his head. "Nothing in this world can heal her now," he explained, his sad eyes staring at something just behind her.

"What do you mean?" Fate asked, alarmed as she followed his gaze.

There was Malus, atop a great boulder, cackling as she held something dark within her grasp. Fate moved closer, walking as though in a dream turned nightmare.

Surrounded by a mixed crowd of her minions and opposing demons and necromancers, all stood in shock by what she held in her hands.

It was the head of the Night Mare.

Fate's insides twisted, the air becoming thick and unbreathable. She turned away from the sight of it. The queen had planned this, had waited until the perfect moment to slay Myth's darker half. She must have known, must have realized that once the light was reborn, that she could rid herself of the angel of Dark World once and for all.

She held onto Slater for support. They were lost now, despite all they'd done to save the world.

"W-what does this mean?" Fate asked, her voice thick with emotion.

Slater shook his head. "It means...we don't have long. Even if she were to return to her rightful realm, Myth cannot live now that her other half is dead."

Myth

The necromancers, thousands of them, began to mourn; relinquishing a soft, sad song from their silver lips. Fate was shocked that, after all the queen had done, they were still peaceful. A lesser race would have attacked the queen, charged her and torn her to pieces for her evil deeds. Not only for killing Vrill, but for sealing them to a doomed fate.

Suddenly Kane was beside her, his face a mixture of horror and sadness as he took in the scene.

"So her minions found him, stole him from me outside Exile Island. How could she?" he uttered, shaking his head in disbelief.

Fate couldn't answer him. His mother had done so much evil, done irreparable damage to an already ravaged world. What were they to do now?

But, little did they know, Malus was just getting started.

Atop the boulder, she smirked, waving the stallion's limp head as she shouted, "Your goddess is dying, soon to be dead. You know as well as I do that we cannot live without her spark within us..."

Fate frowned. Where was she going with this? Wouldn't she die as well if Myth died?

Malus threw the head to the ground, it landed with a piteous thud upon the sands, still and lifeless, his wondrous flame extinguished.

Then the queen folded her fingers together and said, "But there is another way..."

"Another way?" Kane questioned quietly beside Fate.

Malus continued. "You can live on, you can endure. You can have your immortality, your powers, and your lives..."

Every ear listened in dark anticipation. What could she mean?

The queen paused for effect, then said, "If you surrender your souls to me, I will grant you life. I will give you back your world. I will hand you your immortality. You need only to make me your one, true Devil, and I will repay you with the world. Raise your hands; show me you will join me. Live! Live forever with me!" She shouted and then smiled, sweetly and convincingly.

"How?" Fate whispered to Kane. "She tried this before, with the shades, the souls all returned to Guf. They didn't go to her."

Kane's brow furrowed. "I don't know, but she's up to something."

Unreadable murmuring consumed the crowd, and before long hundreds upon hundreds of hands began to rise all around them.

"No!" Kane shouted suddenly. "Stop! You can't believe her, she's lying!"

The queen laughed at him. "Am I?"

Fate spoke up, "You tried to claim the shade's souls and it didn't work! Everyone will become monsters and…"

Suddenly she realized why Malus wanted everyone to relinquish their souls to her. It had nothing to do with owning their essence, and everything to do with controlling the people of Dark World.

Beings without souls are easier to control, she thought as she gazed around at the thousands of shade soldiers that blindly followed their queen's every command. Save for a precious few, like herself and Vale, almost every human she'd received from the Surface, having been transformed into a soulless fiend, obeyed her without question.

She shared this revelation with Kane, his eyes flaring with anger and dark realization.

"But if Myth dies, we die," he said, confused as he tried to sort out the queen's plot. "How can she get around that fact?"

Fate considered this. "She must know something we don't, but what?"

Kane shook his head.

As the masses shuffled like cattle towards their newly accepted queen, several dozens of wraiths arrived, taking their position behind Malus.

It would seem that, once again, Kane was gravely outnumbered.

"What does she know that we do not?" Fate rehashed the notion over and over in her mind. "She must know that either Myth will not die or..." She stopped suddenly.

"What?" Kane asked, his blue eyes turning to her.

"Her baby," Fate whispered. "When I first saw you today, you said she told you to save her baby."

Realization dawned in his eyes. "Yes! But who? And where is this baby?" he stammered excitedly.

Just then Vale appeared before them in a wisp of swirling black, a concerned expression upon his face as he scoured the large crowd of necromancers, asking, "Has anyone seen Aura?"

Aura

The warm hands of the newborn sun stretched long, golden fingers over the red sands of the Crimson Desert, penetrating every shadow, illuminating every darkness. Tiny seeds, long since dormant beneath the soils, began to twitch within the saturation of the light, wriggling and writhing, thrusting their way towards the sun, willing themselves to live again.

Animals and beasts squinted at the brilliance, their eyes unused to such a thing. A cool breeze whipped up a tiny cloud of sand, carrying it several miles before depositing it gently upon a pile of opal rocks.

Amid a seemingly unimportant cluster of white stones, surrounded by erected monuments made of opalescence, a soul's eyes fluttered, stirring from its sleep. Nestled deep, safe, inside a cocoon made of white marble, the soul awoke.

As her soul stirred, her creator—her mother—died, far away on Exile Island, her essence weakening until the effervescent spark was distinguished and she began her long ascent towards home.

Then the shell around the new soul began to crack.

It was slight at first, a hairline fracture crackling over the stone, building slowly, crawling throughout the thick rock like a vein filling with blood. Then, the tiny fissure spread, like a web it reached out, gaining strength, momentum.

Myth

Finally, as the alien rays of light cast fully over the pearlescent shell, the cocoon exploded in a cascade of white.

And a new Myth was born.

"Have you seen Aura?" Vale asked, panic rising in his eyes as he scanned the necromancer crowd, asking anyone who would listen. "Or my sister?"

Fate followed Vale through the throng, searching every pair of eyes for either Aura or Sybil. She couldn't sense their presence anywhere. After a few moments, she turned back and located Kane.

"We can't find Aura or Sybil," she stated, her voice laced with worry, especially for sweet, little Aura. She was a relative newcomer to Dark World, having fought off several other zombie contenders for a chance to live again, not as a human, but as a necromancer. Fate had developed a considerable soft spot for the spunky girl.

Kane's eyes darkened. He knew something.

"What?" Fate inquired, alarmed. "What do you know?"

"I don't know what has become of Aura, but Sybil…" his voice trailed off.

"Please tell me," Fate pleaded.

"I didn't want to tell you, or Vale for that matter, until the relighting was complete, but I suppose I have no choice now." He looked at the ground. "Sybil was possessed by my mother after we won the battle against her at the necromancer palace," he explained, though Fate felt he was holding back.

"And?" she urged him.

Myth

"And while under the influence of Malus...Sybil killed Vrill." He winced aside the confession.

Fate's eyes widened, her heart plunging into despair. Vrill? Dead? How could that be? He was the kindest, sweetest...who could ever harm him? "Oh no," Fate finally managed to speak, then glanced out over the crowd, searching for Vale. "This will destroy him."

Kane sighed again. "That's not all."

Fate swung her head around to face him, uncertain she could handle any more bad news. She braced herself.

"Malus, according to our sources, has Sybil imprisoned, and..." he paused, "she is not known to show mercy to prisoners. I wouldn't be surprised if the oracle was already dead." He gave her a solemn stare.

"How am I going to tell Vale this," Fate said, tears forming in her now-blue eyes. "He'll be devastated. She was the reason he came to this place, he died for her."

"I confess, that is why I haven't told him yet," Kane replied, his face awash with guilt.

"Come on." Fate took him by the arm. "Let's go break the bad news to him."

They started to make their way through the crowd, but were suddenly stopped in their tracks by a horrific noise sounding through the air. Kane and Fate spun about, trying to locate the source.

Overhead, a large shadow loomed, circling. Its enormous wings flapped slow and methodical as it seemed to search for a place to land.

"Arcanum," Kane whispered reverently beside her, his eyes locked onto the coppery dragon soaring aloft.

As he landed, quite gracefully for such a large, old beast, the crowd of necromancers parted, giving him room.

"What is this?" Malus shouted over the throng of those inching towards her, readying to surrender their souls to her. "Why is this aged monster here?"

Was it Fate's imagination or did Malus's eyes betray her? Was she fearful of the dragon?

"I need to talk to you, quickly," Kane said, taking her by the arm and leading her towards Arcanum.

"O-okay," Fate replied, confused.

She watched as Kane searched for something in his pack—then he produced Ever's letter.

Fate gasped. "Ever's note! It got to you!" She was pleased with Spark's success in delivering the note. "What did it say?"

He smiled, a twinkle of something she couldn't decipher warming his eyes. "It explains," he started, "that Ever had a secret ability to converse with animals."

They continued to walk towards the dragon as Kane explained.

"It would seem," he lowered his voice, drawing closer to her ear, "that my father did not die at the hands of a shade."

Fate felt her eyes widening. "Are you serious?"

"He faked his death," Kane said excitedly. "He transferred his soul into Arcanum."

"Secret," Fate considered as she recalled Ever telling her so long ago that the dragon's name meant *secret* and that the king had named him upon his death bed.

Kane nodded, then slowly left Fate's side, approaching the dragon. Arcanum bowed his head, his rich, golden eyes focused on Kane, a wisdom shining beneath. He tucked his coppery wings to his side, lowering his large body before Kane. She could hear the demon prince as he regarded his father for the first time in three hundred years:

"Father," Kane whispered, running a dark hand over the dragon's snout. "How I wish you were here in demon form, to counsel me, to guide me through this storm." His voice was thick with emotion as he spoke. Nearby, Malus had begun speaking in tongues, the souls of dozens, hundreds, seeped from their bodies as they began to transform into shades.

They didn't have long before the majority of Dark World would voluntarily become monsters. Monsters controlled by Malus.

Kane continued. "I need to know what to do," he said. "I need your help. How do I stop her?"

Arcanum, the king, watched his son with saddened eyes, his ancient voice muted. Sadness overwhelmed Fate as she watched the scene unfold. How she wished there was someone who could help them speak to one another. Someone like Ever.

Just beyond the safety of the phalanx of shadow demons, Fate watched the gathering chaos by Malus's chariot, hundreds had been turned now; demons and wraiths turned to shades, the lust for souls growing behind their now searing, white eyes.

The war was brewing.

Soon everyone on her side was changed. An army of fiends faced them.

"What are we going to do?" Fate asked, nerves churning in her stomach as she scanned the thousands now on Malus's side, and merely hundreds on theirs.

He gritted his teeth as he turned from Arcanum. "We fight; we give it all we have. There's no other choice."

Then Malus, atop her chariot, called out, "Now that my children are ready, I have a little present for you!"

"Oh god, now what?" Fate muttered as Vale suddenly appeared beside her, weary and obviously unsuccessful at finding neither Aura nor Sybil.

Fate was just about to console Vale, and tell him what had happened to his sister, when Malus raised her arms into the air and uttered an enchantment. At first there was quiet, a hush that rolled over the crowd like a dark blanket. Everyone watched, waited.

Soon, the ground beneath them began to quiver, the air around them picked up and storms gathered overhead.

She'd summoned the elementals again. This time, she'd called to three of them. Ba'al roared overhead, his devilish face peering out from roiling black and crimson clouds. He bared sharp teeth as he hurled lightning bolt after lightning bolt at Fate, Kane, and all their followers. Everyone scattered, running to safety.

It was then that Vesper arrived, the water elemental, seeping through cracks in the earth, her lithe, silver-blue body glistening like she'd just stepped out of a lake. She smiled as she took aim with her long fingers and churned out ocean-like waves, drowning anyone in their path.

Then a crack ran between them, throwing Kane and Fate into differing directions. The earth split into two large chunks, rising as would a newborn mountain range.

What remained of Kane's army, a handful of demons and a crowd of necromancers in mourning for their goddess, fell to the ground, broken and battered. Deme and the banshee princess stood diligent, their swords raised as the elementals drew near, Slater and Mezza at their sides. The necromancer brothers appeared weak, their metallic skin dull and peeling.

"What's the matter with them!" Kane shouted as he tried to bring himself to a stand. "Why don't they fight!"

"They need a leader," Fate called back. "They need *you!*"

Kane took a moment to look around, assessing. Finally he stood, his black diamond sword in hand, and marched towards his mother. Deme and Syphon moved follow him, but Kane halted them by raising his hand, indicating he needed to do this alone.

He stepped through the barrier of his shadow army, then said firmly, "Mother, stop this."

Malus laughed. "Or what?" she mocked.

"This needs to end," he pleaded valiantly, his shadow army stepping closer to Kane as her ravenous shades eyed him hungrily.

"Oh, it will," Malus said, contorting Ever's once loving face into an evil sneer. "Kill him," she ordered with a mere flick of her wrist and the entirety of the crowd surged forward, all targeting Kane.

Danielle Q. Lee

"No!" Fate screamed as the queen's army of monsters lunged for the demon prince. Merely inches from him, Kane took one step back and sounded the call for his shadow demons to attack. The dark phantoms plunged ahead, fearless, soundless, as they took down the first row of shades—but many got past them. Kane's eyes widened as he realized the barrier had been breached and the shade army was advancing on him. He turned to run, but was taken down by over a dozen shades who instantly fought over who was going to rid the prince of his soul.

Fate panicked, wishing she knew what to do. Without her shade powers, she felt helpless. She suddenly felt foolish for getting her soul back; she'd given up her abilities in the process. She was just a human now. She was nothing.

Powerless.

Inside though, she heard the stirrings of a long forgotten voice. *"You cannot find magic; you are made of magic..."*

"Vrill," she whispered, eyes stinging with tears. "Oh Vrill, I don't know where it is anymore. I don't know how to find it!"

Silence.

Who was she now? What was she? The beings of the Guf didn't even know what to name her. She was nothing without a name.

Nothing.

She ran towards the mob attacking Kane, unable to see him beneath the pile. Then the shades stood up, confusion crossing their faces.

Kane was gone.

He'd vanished from beneath them.

"Where is he?!" Fate shouted. "What have you done with him?"

She scanned the crowds, searching every face, every shadow. Where was he?

Deme and Syphon emerged from behind her with a small army of demons warriors, their weapons in hand, ready to fight. They charged the incoming shades, their blades slicing and swinging with graceful strokes.

Several lethargic necromancers, who seemed unable to transform into beasts, attempted to assist only to be cut down in moments. Fate glanced around to see who was left. Sorcia and Calyx were guiding those who could not fight back into the pyramid where Ozen was erecting yet another enchantment in order to keep the fiends from entering.

On Malus's side, the stakes were getting even higher. While half of her army attacked Kane's followers, thousands were lining up beneath the fissure. Hundreds of wraiths and reapers in the lead.

How are they going to get up there? Fate thought, a sick sensation winding through her system. Her question was quickly answered as the sound of beating wings resonated through the air. She looked to the covered sky, blackened in the distance by a dark swarm.

Cold fear crawled over her skin as she realized what they were.

Bats.

Thousands of them. All big enough to carry two, maybe three, passengers.

"They're heading to the Surface," she whispered, her blood running cold as she thought of thousands of shades devouring the souls of her family, friends—the world.

Malus, amid all this, was simply laughing, smiling at the devastation she'd created, loving the chaotic destruction. There were hundreds of fiends between Fate and the queen, but fury fueled her, overwhelming the fear she felt inside.

She had to end this.

She had to kill the queen.

Fate looked at her hands, willing the magic forth. It was still there, somewhere, she just had to find it. She closed her eyes, summoning the power that lay dormant just beneath the surface of her soul, calling to it, hoping for it to come.

She felt a well inside, deep and dark, foreboding as her psyche searched the darkness. It had to be there. Somewhere.

Fate turned her palms upward, closed her eyes and calmed herself. She had to trust it was there.

Trust.

A wave of power bubbled up from deep within, silver and blue light charged over her open hands. Lightning crackled and danced before her, surging from her, powering up.

The magic found its way to the surface, and Fate opened her eyes—and targeted the queen. This was going to end, and she was going to be the one to do it.

It wasn't what she'd hoped though, the power was small, weak compared to what she could do before, but it would have to do.

Fate let go of the energy, aiming it at Malus who stood up in her chariot of gold, eyes alight with malevolence. The power found its mark, sparking and exploding in a brilliant, white splendor as it struck the queen head on—but something was wrong. The power, Fate's own creation, suddenly turned around after touching the queen, searching its way back to her.

In the blink of an eye, Fate was blown backwards, her own magic used against her.

Darkness, confusion, pain. What had happened?

Rough hands helped her to a stand, then someone said, "I think we now know why Lucifer turned off the pyramid." It was Deme, Ozen pacing worriedly beside her.

"W-what?" Fate uttered, unable to comprehend as Sorcia and the necromancers joined them.

Ozen piped up, "It would seem," he started, stuttering, "that the queen has a very powerful rebound spell upon her."

"Rebound?" Fate said, holding her woozy head.

"Yes," the elder confirmed. "Anything we try to do to her will simply be returned to the attacker. Quite ingenious really," he muttered.

"Are you okay?" Sorcia asked, her eyes filled with concern.

Before she could find the answer, Vale was suddenly beside her. He was giddy, edgy as he took her by the arm. "Come with me," he said firmly.

Still reeling, Fate gave him a confused look. "Why?"

"I have to tell you…" he started, then his eyes widened with shock at something behind her.

She followed his agonized stare, and her jaw dropped.

It was Sybil, her broken, battered body tied to a wooden cross, blood dripping from gaping wounds. Her head bobbed as Malus's minions carried her through the crowd, several lamia lapping at the crimson liquid trickling over her bare toes.

"Sybil!" Vale yelled, pushing his way through the crowd to get to her.

"Vale, stop!" Fate shouted, but it was too late, he'd wisped to his sister's side, determined to set her free.

He kicked at the lamia licking her blood, fighting off the queen's guards as they tried to get him away from his sister. Finally Fate reached the base of the tall podium upon which they were struggling to erect Sybil, marking her an example of what could happen should anyone not comply.

The guards struggled to keep hold of Vale as he wisped out of their grasp. Fate climbed atop the podium, unsure as to what she planned to do next, but had to help.

"No, no, no," Vale whispered as he finally got to Sybil's lifeless body and gently lifted her face up. There was no life left, no breath. She was gone. He cradled her youthful face, then brought his forehead to hers. Even the guards paused, allowing the shade his moment of grief.

Directly behind him, the queen's chariot pulled up. She was laughing smugly. "See what happens when one disobeys me?" she stated, narrowing her eyes and smirking.

Fate glared at the queen, then rubbed Vale's arm in attempts to console him. Time seemed to stop for just a moment as a brother shed tears for a sister he'd never see again.

Then, in a moment of fury, Vale spun about, taking Fate by the hand and wisping. Before she knew what was happening, Vale had wisped the two of them into the queen's chariot—and were now right in front of her.

"What is the meaning of this!" Malus shrieked.

Vale took hold of Malus's arm in one hand, Fate's wrist in the other—and vanished.

It was dark at first, the air unmoving, lifeless. There was no beginning, and no end. No walls. No floor. It just—was.

"Where am I?" Fate asked, reaching out in the gloom for someone, anyone. "Vale?" Suddenly her fingers touched something warm, smooth.

"No, it's Kane," he whispered, taking her by the hand and pulling her to his chest.

"Kane!" she cried, falling into his arms. "Where are we?"

He sighed, his large chest rising and falling beneath her cheek as she hugged him tighter. "Vale calls it The Never. A void between worlds. He wisped me here during the shade attack."

She then recalled their last moments before this place. "Malus! He grabbed Malus too!"

"I know," Kane replied. "That was the plan."

"Plan?"

Suddenly a bright light emerged in her peripheral; it brightened, growing larger as it drew closer. From amidst the shadows, a being stepped out, a radiant woman made of fire.

"I am Seere, guardian of The Never," she said, her black eyes watching them intently.

"What is this place?" Fate wondered.

Seere answered, "This is the home of the elementals, the place in which we dwell until we are summoned by the Devil."

Fate paused, remembering Ba'al and the others attack on them. "But...you work for the queen."

Seere nodded. "We did, but no longer."

Fate frowned. "Why?"

"Kane has told us of King Lucifer, that he is very much alive inside the dragon. We no longer have to serve Malus."

"Where is Vale? And Malus, for that matter?" Fate asked, worried for her friend.

"Vale is safe," she replied, offering nothing further. "And the queen is now a prisoner of The Never."

"A prisoner?" Fate's heart skipped a beat, hardly able to come to terms with the notion. Was it really over? The nightmare, was it done?

Kane turned to her, explaining, "No one can leave The Never, it has no doorways. Only Seere and the other elementals know how to get out of here."

Fate frowned, still not understanding.

He continued. "It was Vale's idea," he said with a sad smile. "He suggested we bring Malus here to...negotiate."

"Negotiate?" Fate inquired.

"Yes," Kane replied. "She cannot leave this place unless she complies with our terms."

Excitement rose inside Fate, and she allowed herself to believe that this war really was nearing its end. "What are your terms?" she asked eagerly.

He nodded to the right, answering, "Let's go lay them out for her right now, shall we?"

Malus stood in the center of the void, a circular force field of fire erected around her. It dawned on Fate just then that the elementals were stronger than even she was, far more powerful. They'd only done as she commanded because they are loyal to the Devil.

"Vale!" Fate called out, seeing him standing off to the side, beside Seere. He looked up, slowly, almost sadly.

"Mother," Kane started, taking slow, casual steps around the ring of fire, hands behind his back. "How nice to see you like this." He grinned.

"Let me out! Now!" she glared at Seere. "I shall have more than your voice for this insolence! Do you not recall the last time you disobeyed me?" The queen warned.

Seere raised her chin in defiance. "You are no longer my master."

"What do you mean?" Malus huffed. "Of course I am, I am the Devil!"

"No, Mother," Kane interjected. "You are not." He paused for effect, then added, "Father is still alive."

Malus's eyes widened in horror. "W-what? That's impossible, I saw his body. He was dead!"

"No," Kane explained. "He possessed the dragon before he died. He's very much alive."

"That's a lie!" Malus seethed, though her eyes told a different story. Being inside Ever, sharing her soul, her memories, somewhere deep inside she must have known. That was why she had such fear of the dragon when he arrived. Finally, as though reality had set in, Malus asked, "What do you want?"

"Two things," Kane said. "One, remove the shackles from the demons. And two—leave Ever's body."

Danielle Q. Lee

The queen's eyes were alight with hatred as she listened to the terms. Anyone could see that these were the hardest things for her to abide by, but eventually, she whispered, her voice low and broken, *"Privus liberum."*

The words rang in Fate's ears, summoning a memory from when she'd first arrived at the necromancer palace. The ghosts in the stairwell, the ones that reached for her from the walls, those were the words they'd whispered to her. And in her dreams, they'd found her there too. There were beings trying to help her, to help all of them.

Within seconds after the queen spoke, there was a loud clank from behind Kane. The metallic shackles lay in a heap upon the floor.

His wings were free.

The demons were finally free.

"And the other," Kane reminded his mother as Vale stepped out the darkness with the black box imprisoning Ever's soul in his hands.

The queen resisted. "Where will I go? I have no body to possess!" Her venomous eyes searched each of them as though she was considering a replacement.

Kane shrugged. "That's not our problem. You can either stay here forever or live as a bodiless soul. It's your choice."

Malus threw her arms over her chest and pouted.

The moments ticked by until finally the queen, in a flurried motion, waved her arms in the air and said a few words of enchantment. Within seconds, her chest began to pulsate and finally a sphere of bright white drifted from her. Ever's body slumped to the floor, lifeless.

Myth

It's rather beautiful for such an ugly soul, Fate thought triumphantly as she watched Malus's incorporeal form bounce restlessly about the room, then vanish into the darkness of the void.

Vale knelt down, placing the black box on the floor and opening the lid. Ever's soul gleamed, shone like spun silver, threads of blue and white light wound around it. It shimmered as it rose into the air, leaving a trail of effervescent beams behind it.

Slowly, gracefully, Ever travelled the short distance to her body, then ever so gently entered it. Everyone held their breath as they awaited her awakening.

Finally, her blue eyes opened, rousing as though she'd simply taken a long, rejuvenating nap.

"Daddy?" she said, rubbing her eyes and smiling.

Kane fell to his knees, sweeping her up into his arms, holding her, rocking her as tears streamed down his cheeks. "Baby," was all he said.

He gathered her up, carrying her like a princess and approached Seere. "Thank you so much for everything," he said, his eyes shone with sincerity.

The elemental nodded. Vale stood beside her, his gaze downturned.

"Vale? What's wrong?" Fate asked, then remembered that he'd just lost his sister all over again, this time forever.

"Come," Kane said quietly. "We should go."

A tunnel opened up behind the fire elemental and she moved her hand as to usher them through—but Vale didn't budge.

"Vale?" Panic rose inside Fate.

He took her hand in his, whispering, "Just go, I'll be fine."

"What do you mean?" she nearly shouted. "Why aren't you coming?"

Seere suddenly repositioned herself between the two of them, forcing Fate into the tunnel and preventing Vale from going with her. The vortex pulled at her, sucking her in.

"Vale!" she screamed as she was swept away like an ocean tide stealing her into greater waters, her voice fading away.

"Why?" Fate asked the moment they had returned to Dark World. "Why is Vale staying there?" Her eyes were wild as she approached Kane.

Kane set Ever down gently, allowing her to stabilize herself before letting her stand on her own. He turned to Fate. "He chose to stay, for us," he explained quietly. "The Never requires a sacrifice in place of a battle. Vale offered to stay with Seere if she let us pass."

Pain surged inside Fate's chest. "He sacrificed himself? So we could come home?"

Kane nodded, sadness in his stare. "It's not forever though," he added with a small, hopeful smile. "Just...a very long time."

"How long?" She eyed him with a frown.

He cleared his throat. "A century."

Fate gasped. "A century!"

Kane reached out for her, taking her into his arms. "He will be returned to us, someday."

Then Kane's eyes were drawn to something behind Fate, she turned around to see the remains of

Sybil being respectfully removed from the wooden cross.

He walked over to her body just as his demons had placed her gently on the ground.

"Sybil," he said, mixed emotions crossing his stare.

Fate nodded, bowing her head in reverence.

Silence owned the air a moment before Kane spoke, "At least Seren can now be at peace."

Fate had forgotten that Sybil was the shade that stole Seren's soul, and now that the oracle was dead Seren's soul would be free. She could leave the poltergeists and return to the Guf.

"Kane!" Deme ran up to him, out of breath, her eyes filled with angst. "The reapers and wraiths, they're gone!"

"Where? What do you mean?"

The demon tracker sputtered, "To the Surface!"

Kane considered this a moment, then glanced around himself, noticing the multitude of broken shackles scattered about the red sands. Then he flapped his large, black wings, taking him effortlessly into the air as if it hadn't been three centuries since last he tasted the freedom of flight.

Calmly, the dark prince stated, "Let's go."

The Crystal Pyramid gleamed silver, spreading shining tendrils of pewter across Dark World.

"Moonlight," Fate whispered as Kane took her into his arms and lifted into the skies.

"Take hold of anyone needing a ride to the Surface," Kane ordered his army. "We'll need all the help we can get."

Fate looked around herself, noting that the necromancers were too ill to fight. They lay about the sands, their metallic skin peeling, their star-like eyes dimming. Mezza and Slater's once strong, formidable forms seemed wizened and lesser by comparison.

They're dying, Fate thought sadly. *Why? Why hadn't they been healed when the light came down?*

Deme took Sorcia into her arms while Syphon grabbed Calyx. Ever and Ozen stayed behind to help any wounded, and to do what they could for the necromancers.

A few hundred demons took to the air, a mere handful by contrast to the thousands of reapers and wraiths that now dominated the Surface. Fate wondered how they could possibly force the dark masses underground once more. What could they want with the Surface? Like Malus, did they also want to rule the humans? Without their queen, their leader, they ran amuck, no rules, no limits.

How were they going to stop them?

Myth

The long teeth of the canopy neared, the gaping mouth of the fissure yawning, awaiting them as though they were a morsel of food to be eaten. Fate closed her eyes as they breached the threshold, heat from the earth breathing down upon them.

Kane held her tight, his warm, comforting arms embracing her. She opened her eyes, glancing around. Hundreds of wings beat around her like a heartbeat, the sound of the demons' freedom sounding, echoing off the stone walls.

As they neared the Surface, threads of silvery light trickled through the opening, like dark waters rippling amid the shine of the moon. She wondered what awaited them.

Defeat? Death?

Or something else.

Kane sped up as they reached the breaking point. She looked to his face, it was beaming with eagerness.

The hole above them grew as they drew closer and closer. The hum of wings increasing as the army of demons pushed themselves harder, faster. None of them, she surmised, had seen the likes of the sun, nor the moon and stars. None had known the glory of a spring breeze kissing their face, or the cool splash of the ocean waters lapping at their toes.

What things she'd taken for granted. What marvels and beauties she'd ignored simply because they were a constant for her eyes to feast upon. Until Dark World, she hadn't known what she'd lost, what she thought she'd never see again.

Until now.

They broke through the invisible barrier between dark and light, the night sky alive all around them. A cool breath of wind licked her skin, tousled her hair with gentle fingers. She turned her face to Kane; he pulled the air deep into his lungs, filling his chest with the life of the night.

He landed gently, his dark hooves buried by long blades of grass painted silver by the gaze of the moon. Breath after breath, he stood in silence, taking in the immensity of the moment. The stars blinked back at him as though they too were as surprised to see him as he was of them. The great metallic disc, encompassed by the thick blackness of space, regarded the demon like the eye of God.

"It's...beautiful," he whispered as if fearful the world around him was sleeping and he'd awaken it, ending the dream too soon.

Fate smiled, drawing in a soft breath of her own.

She was home.

The rest of the demons arrived, releasing their passengers safely on solid ground. All stood in quiet reverence, marveling at a beauty their eyes had never beheld.

As much as she hated to break the spell of the moment, Fate asked, "Where are they?"

In an instant, Kane recalled his mission, his brows furrowing as he scanned the dark woods. "I don't know, be on your guard."

Everyone took a defensive stand, arming themselves as they scanned the perimeter.

"Where could they have gone?" Fate's heart pounded as she considered the worst possible scenario. "What if they've already reached the city?"

"No," Kane said. "I sense them out there, I know they're here."

Suddenly a scream pierced the dark of night and the sound of rustling leaves and brush shattered the quietude. A girl, followed by a tall man, came rushing out of the copse of trees and into the open meadow.

They stopped dead in their tracks when they caught sight of the demons standing in their midst. Screaming again, the girl turned to run away.

"Wait!" Fate shouted. "Come back! We won't hurt you!"

They stopped, turning around with caution.

Moonlight streamed onto their frightened faces, eyes widened in terror.

Then Fate realized she knew their faces.

"Shelby? Greg?" she said, her voice trembling.

"S-Scarlet?" Shelby's eyebrows pulled together, peering through the shadows in disbelief.

"Scarlet!" Greg shouted, breaking into a run, Shelby close behind.

Scarlet's brother scooped her into his arms, taking them both to their knees as they held each other as tightly as possible. Shelby arrived and wrapped her arms around both of them.

"Oh my god, oh my god," Greg whispered, cradling his sister in his arms. "You're alive." He shuddered around a sob.

Shelby wept, stroking Fate's head. Between tears, Shelby looked at her, her expression suddenly perplexed. "What the hell happened to your hair? I mean, I like it, but…whoa."

Fate laughed through tears. "Oh, I missed you so much!"

Suddenly Kane was beside them, his sword raised in a protective stance, eyes locked on the bushes behind them.

Shelby and Greg turned their eyes to him with a mixture of horror and amazement.

"What. The. Hell?" Greg uttered.

"Sorry to ruin the reunion," Kane said in a low tone. "But we have company…*a lot* of company."

Fate scanned the wall of the forest, thousands of glowing, red eyes glaring back at her.

"Find a safe place," Kane ordered.

"Stay with me," Fate said, taking Greg and Shelby by her side and moving into the center of the meadow, the demons forming a circle around them as they attempted to ward off the predators stalking them from all angles.

At first no one moved. A stalemate. The wraiths and reapers stood in the shadows, hidden by the dark of night. The demons, their bodies gleaming silver by moonlight, eyes shining like cats, waited.

Then, as silent as they'd arrived, the reapers and wraiths closed in. The demons, however, sounded their attack with a loud, guttural growl as their bodies lurched forward.

Amid the demon army, Sorcia and Calyx suddenly paused in a combat pose, back to back, their curved swords poised and ready. Both opened their mouths at the same time and released the loudest shriek Fate had ever heard. A tremor of energy rippled over the crowd, skipped over the demons, and struck the first wave of enemies, taking them down and knocking them out cold.

"Cool!" Greg whispered, his eyes alight with excitement.

Then came the chaos. From their phantom fingertips, the wraiths fired off sparks of red lightning. The demons used their swords to deflect the energy, striking a few of the incoming reapers in the process.

The reapers fell easily, but got right back up again, as though the weapons had no permanent effect on them. Still moving forward, they neared the circle of demons.

"Don't let them touch you!" Deme screamed as she speared a wraith in the throat with a long, sharp staff.

All around her demons fell, overwhelmed by the onslaught of foes.

"There's just too many," Fate said. "I have to help. You guys stay here."

She moved to leave, but Shelby grabbed her hand. "Be careful."

Fate nodded, then tried to find Kane. She scanned the throng, the sound of swords and fireworks exploded all around her. Every so often, the banshees would expel a deafening scream and a bunch of bodies would fall to the ground.

To her left she spotted Kane fighting off three wraiths at once, his black blade swinging, cutting the air, slicing the ghostly beings. But they couldn't be destroyed that way; the sword only slowed them down.

From out of the dark of the woods, a lone reaper crept, making his way towards Kane. Fate watched in anguish as it appeared he would be ambushed.

"Kane! Look out!" she yelled, but her voice was lost amidst the cacophony of war.

Deme heard her though and turned her sights onto the lone reaper. She ran towards Kane, blocking him as the reaper raised his finger to touch Kane on the cheek.

He touched Deme instead.

Kane spun about, his face registering what happened as he stabbed the reaper in the stomach and then fell to Deme's side, holding her head as she began to die.

Fate ran closer, watching as Deme's body started to wither, her red flesh disintegrating as though being eaten by unseen insects.

"Kane," Deme whispered, blood leaving her body from the many holes in her skin and leaking onto the grass beneath.

"I'm here," he said, his agony palpable.

Deme forced a pained smile. "I...I loved you, you know," she uttered, fading.

Kane winced as chunks of flesh fell off her, the white of her bones gleaming with the moonlight. "I know."

With her last breath, she uttered, "Tell Fate...*sorry*."

And she died in his arms. Fate stood by, horrified, lost. Kane fought back tears as he set her gently down, standing.

Before Fate could console him, however, Deme's bony arm reached for him, her skeleton coming to life.

She'd become a reaper.

"Run!" he shouted at Fate and she returned to protect Shelby and Greg.

With sorrow in his eyes, Kane turned his blade onto Deme, her transformation nearly complete and drove it into her ribcage.

The remains of Deme shuddered once before falling to the earth and remained there, unmoving.

Kane had little time to mourn as a dozen wraiths emerged from the woods and attacked him. He swung his sword bravely, blindly sometimes, just to keep them at bay.

But there were simply too many. The reapers and wraiths just kept coming, advancing from out of the darkness. The bodies of dead demons started to add up.

Tears built in Fate's eyes, what could she do?

The moonlight poured down on her like silver water, filling her with light, filling her with power.

She had to do something.

To her left, a reaper glided towards her, his evil eyes gleaming as he neared. She called to her powers, knowing they were there but unsure as to how to summon them. Fate raised her fingers to the reaper, thin sparks igniting at her fingertips, a far cry from the power she used to have when she was a shade. The thin line of electricity shot out and hit the reaper in the face. He staggered, but was not deterred.

"Kick his ass!" Shelby yelled from behind her.

The reaper suddenly stopped — and turned his attention to Shelby and Greg.

Shelby shrieked as the creature began moving towards them.

Fate gasped. "Don't you touch them!" Anger surged inside her, her soul lit with rage, love, hate, and power. Suddenly, whatever had held her back snapped in two and energy like she'd never known rose to the surface.

Fate's eyes stormed, the blue swirling silver and black as she ran towards the reaper. She pulled the power from her core, willed it, bent it to her command.

The magic wasn't on the outside of her—it came from *within*. She didn't need her hands to kill; she just had to *look* at him.

The reaper stopped, bringing his skeletal hands to his head as he screamed in agony. Both the demons and their current combatants stopped to watch as the reaper suddenly burst into an inferno of silver flames, disintegrating to ash within seconds.

Fate, as though in a meditative trance, turned to face the swarm of wraiths and reapers charging them from the treeline. She walked calmly towards them, the demons breaking the circle and moving aside for her to pass.

The wraiths and reapers glanced at one another as the girl with white hair and metallic eyes walked towards them. Most didn't have time to put their hands up in surrender before she melted them in the blink of an eye. Hundreds fell, left as a pile of dust upon the twinkling grasses.

Just then a fluttering sound drifted up from the crevasse, growing louder and louder, as though the sound of a million butterflies flapping their wings. All heads turned towards the fissure, wondering who—or what—was coming.

Was it more wraiths? More reapers?

Concern clustered in Fate's chest as she and all the others awaited the arrival of whatever army was clawing their way up the hole from Dark World.

As the sound grew louder, everyone covered their ears and began to back away. Even with her new-found powers, Fate was uncertain that she'd be able to take on any more than she already had.

Kane and Fate stood closer to one another, Greg and Shelby hugged each other, overwhelmed with — well, everything!

Suddenly the mouth of the crevasse exploded with light and thousands of winged beings littered the open air.

One of the beings floated towards Kane and Fate.

Fate smiled, recognizing her friend. "Aura!" She spread her arms and hugged the spunky necromancer, who seemed to have an all new, preternatural glow about her.

"Sorry I'm late," Aura said, her voice melodic.

All around them necromancers, revived and alive, with silver wings mounted upon their backs, rounded up the rogue wraiths and reapers, marching them back towards the crevice.

Once gathered, Aura hovered above them and pointed to the hole in the ground, her voice booming as she ordered, "*Go home!*"

Surprisingly they obeyed, all of them mounting their bats and retreating to the underworld with their tails between their legs.

Fate marvelled at the necromancers, their light returned, their zest reignited.

"What happened while we were gone?" Fate asked of Aura.

The necromancer shrugged shyly, answering, "I just had a nap and then woke up with Myth's powers. Somebody's going to have to fill *me* in on everything!"

"Myth's powers?" Kane's eyes dawned with realization. "Her *baby*! Of course! She wouldn't leave her necromancers to die, she transferred her powers."

After the wraiths and reapers had descended, the demons and necromancers dove into the fissure and the now empty field loomed all around them.

Kane and Fate stood side by side, breathing a sigh of relief.

It was over.

"Okay, Sticks," Greg said, referring to the teasing childhood name he'd bestowed on her, hugging her. "That was awesome."

Fate laughed. "Thanks."

"I can't wait to get you home! Your parents are going to be…" Shelby started, then stopped when she saw Fate's face.

"Shelby," Fate said softly. "I'm not coming home."

Her friend's face fell, and Greg asked, "Why not?"

Fate sighed. "I don't belong here anymore, my home is with him." And she locked arms with Kane.

Both Greg and Shelby looked shocked, but after a few moments, Shelby asked, "Will you be able to visit?"

Fate looked to Kane and he smiled. "Of course she will."

Fate

It took a few months to sort everything out. In the end, Kane agreed that the pyramid would be a wonderful place for the demons to begin anew. They began to build homes inside immediately, welcoming the necromancers and any other race that wished to coexist peacefully. The reapers and wraiths declined, of course, returning to their sides of Dark World to lick their wounds quietly.

The citizens who had recently been turned into shades by Malus's manipulation were awarded their souls once more, with implicit instructions to never adhere to a mad-demon's word ever again. Many traitors, however, like Maxim and several hundreds of loyal Malus followers, were imprisoned and awaited trials. Elder Syphon, promoted to Captain, was put in charge of the new army and patrolling system.

The banshees ended up being Ozen's first patients in his new infirmary, as they were due to replicate any day. Slater and Mezza, like anxious fathers-to-be, stood happily and dutifully by their sides.

Aura attempted to negotiate with Seere, to release Vale from his imprisonment in The Never, but the fire elemental would not comply. Devastated, Aura entered The Never with the intention of fighting Seere for Vale's freedom, but upon entry, she discovered that they were gone. Aura returned from The Never broken-hearted. Vale's and Seere's whereabouts are still unknown.

Kane, curious as to who or what was responsible for attacking Legion, as well as levelling the banshee village, discovered that Ba'al and Seth, the air and earth elementals, had taken it upon themselves to try and prevent the opening of the crevasse. Apparently they felt it imperative that the pyramid was not relit, hence preventing the restoration of Malus's powers. While Kane could understand their motive, he held a trial in which the two elementals were found guilty of mass murder and sentenced to one thousand years on Exile Island.

Now that Ever was back, Kane and Arcanum were able to communicate, and they agreed that Kane should reside over Dark World until Lucifer could find a proper body in which to possess and then resume his rule as the Devil. Time was of the essence; however, as Arcanum's aging dragon body was failing quickly. Kane, wishing Deme were still alive as she was the best out of all his trackers, sent demon scouts to every corner of Dark World in search of a suitable host that could hold such a powerful soul. According to Elder Ozen, though, the host had to be an exceptionally large, magical creature, for no other could withstand the unique and enormous power of Lucifer's soul.

After a thorough sweep of the Surface to ensure no reapers or wraiths had escaped detection, Ozen erected a special spell over the crevasse, which meant no unauthorized trips to Surface.

Fate sat in the sands, watching the Crystal Pyramid mirror the setting sun on the Surface. The glow of the distant crystalline mountains shifted with the lights; orange, red, and muted yellows, echoing the changing moods radiating from the place she used to call home.

Home, she thought. *Is it a place? A feeling?* Or was it, as she suspected, thinking of Kane, a person?

She wrapped her arms around her legs, resting her chin on her knees, thinking of all the memories she'd made. Some as Scarlet, some as Fate. She wondered if the two would ever merge, creating one being from the many. Who was she beneath the name? Beyond the body?

She smiled. She knew who she was.

And it didn't have a name.

"Ready?" her favorite voice asked, walking up behind her.

"Yup," she said, rising and brushing off the sand.

"You're sure about this?" Kane's eyes flickered with a touch of fear.

Fate shrugged. "It has to be done."

The large demon sighed. "Okay, let's go meet your parents."

She linked her arm with his. "It'll be okay, Shelby and Greg warned them."

"Oh good," he said dryly, not looking any more at ease.

Fate giggled, linking her arm with his.

Just then Kane and Fate were attacked by unseen forces, their legs held tight, tripping them.

Spitting out a mouthful of sand, Fate turned herself over quickly, just in time to see about twenty furry balls of fluff turn from invisible to visible.

"Ick?" asked a familiar, growly voice.

Danielle Q. Lee

"Ick!" Fate cried, grabbing hold of the little, downy-white body and bringing it to her chest. "I thought you were dead!" Her intuition spoke suddenly, showing her an image of a shield. The stone the gargoyles had erected around themselves had simply been protective armor.

He frowned, giving her a look like she was crazy. He shook his head, then pointed back at his ever-growing brood. "Ick," he said with a matter-of-fact smirk.

She glanced behind him, grinning as she recognized all his friends from before — including Nibbles who was chewing his nails anxiously — and many, many more, though considerably smaller than Ick but eyeing her with very familiar bright, green eyes.

"Are these," Fate wondered, "your...children?"

Ick grinned, his sharp teeth gleaming with pride.

Fate just shook her head, smiling, then turned to Kane. "I think this makes us grandparents."

Kane laughed, pulling Fate close to his chest and giving his wings a flap, raising them gracefully into the air, kissing her as they drifted alongside a breeze. He touched her face lovingly, whispering, "Let me get through meeting your parents, then we'll discuss children."

She blushed. "We can have children?" she said, then added, "What race would they be?"

He smiled kindly. "Does it matter?"

She shook her head, then kissed him on the lips.

Fate took one last look at the pyramid as they entered the doorway to the Surface, amazed at how her life had changed through death. She couldn't help but wonder what adventures she'd have now, but with him by her side, she couldn't wait to find out.

Epilogue

Deep within a pit in a long-forgotten palace, a little girl cursed a lamia sits upon a mountain of bones. Living on insects, and unfortunate rodents that make their way to her hole, she waits.

The silver skins had gone, left her behind, left her to die.

Her soulless body aches for flesh, screams for blood, rages for the moment when she is free, free to kill, free to eat like the monster she is. Her black eyes search the fathomless pitch, hoping, praying for salvation.

Then, in her eternal darkness, she sees a light, dancing at the top of her prison. It circles overhead, drifts downwards, illuminating the abyss like an angel without wings.

It draws closer, as though examining her, watching, studying.

The little girl, her hunger temporarily at bay, reaches out to the floating star, mesmerized. As her little fingers touch the orb, toying with it innocently, the sphere suddenly surges forward, pouring itself down the child's throat, igniting inside her chest.

The child struggles, choking, clutching her at her neck, falling to her knees.

Then she is calm.

She opens her eyes, the black of her eyes now rimmed crimson.

Myth

She stands, no longer a child.

No longer a just a lamia.

Yet still a monster.

With her new body, Malus takes in her surroundings — and smiles.

www.ingramcontent.com/pod-product-compliance
Lightning Source LLC
Chambersburg PA
CBHW072020020726
47501CB00006B/1876